HEAVEN REDISCOVERED

By *Marinella Monk, M.D.*

An eternal love story

HEAVEN REDISCOVERED

by Marinella Monk, M.D.

First edition paperback

Copyright 2017 by Marinella Monk, M.D.

All rights reserved. This book or parts of it may not be reproduced in any form, copied, transmitted, or stored by any means – electronic, photocopy, recording, mechanical or retrieval systems – without prior written authorization of Marinella Monk, M.D. or as provided by United States of America copyright law.

This novel is a work of fiction. Any names, characters, places, businesses or organizations, any places or events, are either the product of the author's imagination or are used fictitiously.

ISBN: 978-1542929912

Dr. Marinella Monk also wrote two inspirational books, YOU ARE NOT ALONE and GENTLE THERAPY.

All these books are available worldwide through www.Amazon.com, e-book format, and in most bookstores.

ACKNOWLEDGEMENT

This book is a love story. It is one more tale, adding to so many, about the ideal and eternal love.

All facts and characters presented in this book are entirely imaginary and any incidental resemblance is not intended. Although we always find inspiration from our own experiences and refer to places or events that are part of what we know, this is not a personal tale.

If the reader finds that some details might be reminding of someone familiar, it is only a part of what makes us all humans, with our multiple common denominators.

Isabelle and Gérard are the ideal of any man and woman, yet to be born, therefore, their characters, as any wishful contemplation, are not referring to anyone that I know.

And no, this story is not about myself, and any situation that can associate Isabelle with me remains beyond reality, (and please, do not hold it against me).

This book is intended to inspire and bring hope to my readers, as I truly believe there is a better place for all of us, within ourselves and in the universe, here on Earth and in the heavens, where love has no barriers.

My very special thanks go to my wonderful husband for understanding me and supporting me in fulfilling my dreams.

This book would not have seen the light without your help, and it is for you, Robert, the best of myself, my love.

Heaven Rediscovered

PROLOGUE

Chi-Chi, the baby mocking bird, was enjoying her new place, thriving and learning how to fly. This morning was the first time I carried her improvised cage to the large, screened, back porch. She already trusted me, and I could hold her in my hand. At times, she would climb on one of my fingers and stay there while I was feeding her. After having her only for a day, she learned how to open her beak as soon as I was close by. With this new soft pleasure of temporarily fostering her until she would be strong enough to fly on her own, I always had food and water close by, ready to care for this demanding new addition to our household pets.

Chi-Chi was brought to us by our nine-year-old cat, Prissy, who found her in the woods next door. We already noticed a couple of mocking birds making a lot of noise, proudly letting everyone know that they were new parents. We were very impressed by their devotion and means of constantly warning cats and other animals to stay away from their chicks, while making frequent rounds with food to the nest. I was only vaguely aware that they were nestled close to the ground, and so their chicks were very vulnerable to all kind of predators, which explained their constant and distraught sounds.

The first time Prissy showed up with the tiny bird in her mouth I panicked, and happy that no harm was done to the little creature, I went further into the brush and gently placed her down, under the frantic watch of her parents. Later, close to the evening hours, as I was looking out the window I saw Prissy outside again, busy and proud, trying to show me her "new baby". She was hovering over the baby bird as she would have done with her own kitten, which she never had, since she was already "fixed" and the gift of motherhood had been taken away from her before we adopted her.

Prissy's antics made me think she would continue to bring home the frail chick she had found on the ground. We had to make a quick decision, and Chi-Chi, chirpily called after the sounds she was constantly making, was placed temporarily in a cat carrier we used when bringing the pets to our vet. I thought that some diluted cat food would provide her with the proteins needed for her nourishment, and a dropper would help give her some water. We started feeding her every few hours and this quickly became a pleasant routine. Duke, our sweet little dog, followed us everywhere with great interest, looking lovingly at this little bird with his kind blue eyes.

BOOK ONE

It all started with this little mocking bird. After her, came her parents and the other chicks that had fallen from nearby trees. As I looked around, I was so happy that we had decided to enlarge the screened porch even more.

After a while, Minot, the feral cat, came in as well, getting along perfectly with the newly formed community of domesticated and wild members. The weather remained beautiful, with a perfect blue sky and the ideal temperature for outdoor enjoyment for us all

Later, another happy event made me almost think that any miracle could happen: Jewel came back home! Jewel was Purr-Purr's beautiful sister that we had adopted when they were only five weeks old as Prissy's surrogate babies. For over four years we followed these two sisters growing, playing and sleeping inseparably, becoming these amazing creatures who filled our days with laughter and delight.

While Purr-Purr was a playful and mischievous kitty, Jewel was exactly what her name suggests: she was a beautiful, longhaired cat, almost like a precious piece of jewelry that adorned anyone with her presence. For she knew how to play her charms and acted as if no one could ever resist her.

After a little over four happy years, Jewel disappeared. No flyers, phone calls, visits to all kinds of animal shelters, online posters and messages could bring her home. Every time someone called about the ad we had posted, we would rush out praying, crying with hope and no embarrassment, driving to places we could never imagined we would ever go. When we were coming home empty handed we were devastated, but somehow, we never lost hope that one day she would find her way back home.

And now I could not hide my joy at having her back. I was ecstatic, I was dancing and telling her how much I loved her and missed her, and how happy I was to see her again. We were all celebrating, being silly, playing, and kissing her.

Slowly, more cats, along with lost and abandoned dogs, started coming to this place I began calling my Sanctuary. A few squirrels joined, then possums, ducks, more birds, and even a little pig.

Now, sitting on a comfortable long chair, I realized that the weather was still good. Not good, great. This must be the reason I felt so wonderful, happy, and relaxed. Again, looking around, I acknowledged my satisfaction at having the porch area enlarged; it now reached some half an acre, and was rapidly filling with new residents.

I reflected on how beautiful all this was. The house was telling of our dreams and memories where we invested so much of our time and efforts and was coming along as an ideal place for perfect happiness. And with my heart filled with delight, I turned my head in all directions to admire the blue water of the sound, knowing that every morning was celebrated with the glorious rays cast by the sun rising, while in the evenings the most dramatic sunsets created a different show around the house. Further down, discretely concealed by the thick foliage of the old trees, was a park with alleys leading to small fountains and statuaries, even a hidden gazebo, while a dock reached far over the water to the boat hauled safely under the boathouse.

As my eyes continued to make this gentle tour of the place, I noticed that the grass was thicker and had given the lawn a greener shade than ever. The roses had never displayed such brilliant colors and balmy fragrances.

Before long I realized as more animals were coming to the Sanctuary, that they were all having something wrong with them, some injuries or abuse happened to them. I noticed with great relief that they were quickly healed, and I was so happy to be able to care for them, although I never needed to do much for them. Just a simple surgical kit, a few bandages, good natural food, and fresh water from the source, all worked wonders for my new friends' recovery. Shortly after, these sweet creatures found again the desire to play, take a nap under the palm trees, or relax in the shade of blooming shrubs. I also noticed that with each one of my unusual patient's "consultation", my prayers were every time answered. I did not know much about caring for animals, but I could use my formal medical education, as I found out that calling upon my angels for assistance always helped.

Another fact that made it all so pleasant was that I had time to care for my little tenants and time to slow down. I felt rested, learned again how to unwind reading, playing or listening to music. There was enough time for adding to my collection of recipes, cooking and baking, giving a bath to my zoological family, and even to take a stroll on the beach.

Mainly, I was happy thinking back on my decision to give more time to my Sanctuary, and away from my busy medical profession.

-//-

Things were changing in the United States; the medical profession that was once respected, coveted by younger generations, and in most cases rewarded by a comfortable social status, was now seen by doctors as a nightmare of bureaucratic tangle. We, doctors, were witnessing more and more the dangerous down slop taken by money making, profit-oriented insurance companies, controlling the medical decisions of practitioners and constantly trying to increase their profit. And these companies had all the power: they employed top lobbyists and high-paid lawyers, gaining strong influence over government decisions, in the name of "health care cost savings ".

Doctors knew that all this was a sad and disastrous joke; money was plenty but not fairly distributed to people who were paying heavier premiums, deductibles and co-pays every year, and getting ripped off with less services. Doctors and patients witnessed powerlessly how an increased fraction of the population had become stripped of proper health coverage.

The same applied to retirees left with even less choices, after seeing mandatory contributions taken from their paychecks towards Medicare for all their working years. They were now constrained to pay out of their pocket for medications and procedures, removed each month in higher number from the formularies. Older patients did not know how to navigate the new online system and robotic telephones, less accessible to them. During this time, doctors were too busy to fight the system, already swamped under paperwork and bureaucratic regulations that were continuously changing, while trying to find out what adequate medication was still covered by insurance, or getting a simple procedure paid for.

Cornered between the limited choices of essential care provided to their patients and risking increased liability, and authorities breathing down their neck looking for a reason to accuse someone of fraud or over prescribing pain medication, doctors were fed up of no longer being free to do what they were supposed to do: just practice medicine. It took just a generic piece of paper printed in thousands of copies saying that the services provided were not medically necessary to endanger the survival of any medical practice not receiving payments for treatments already provided.

I heard many of my fellow colleagues complain, repeating everyday how close they were to stopping practicing. It became a common conversation as to when one could retire or not, but all wished they could quit on the spot.

I was, myself, very disappointed to see such a poor health care system penetrating in this prosperous land of advanced technology so rich in brilliant medical researchers, not being able to offer the public the level of care other countries less well-off could offer. All this led me to think that I would remain in the medical profession I loved so much, as long as I could do it the way I thought was right and I could allow the time and the proper care I was trained for and for which I made an oath to honor, I would continue to be a physician.

Nevertheless, I was afraid that soon I would have to choose a different path, and subconsciously, I was already preparing myself to offer my services looking in new directions. And here was my Sanctuary, helping to make this transition and giving me another reason to continue my modest contribution to the noble profession of healing.

-//-

As Isabelle was sitting in the pew at church, she was captured by the music. It was a trilling ambience created by the joy exuding from the performance of this talented band. Everyone was under the spell of their tunes, as each musician took the lead and brought the instrumental dialog to an intense level of energy and virtuosity. They were "talking" to each other, they were competing in dexterity, while they were having a great deal of fun. They were playing their instruments with the pleasure children would have at a birthday party.

It was a simply decorated white church by the sea where people of all Christian faith went, attracted by the music and friendly acceptance of the nondenominational community. Worshipers represented a sample of this small, beach resort town where Isabelle and her husband, Gérard, liked to come. They had started living there more permanently several years ago, with the hope of building a new phase in their life where they might retire one day. Leaving behind the familiar places and their ties in the city they had known most of their lives, Gérard and Isabelle were delighted to settle for this family property, until then destined mostly for family vacations. People from all corners of the country found their way to this well-kept secret destination. Some of them, after traveling around the globe, cast their anchor here, bringing with them a wealth of experience and a large diversity of professional and cultural backgrounds, contributing to the attraction of the place, where there was always something exciting to do.

The church community was a warm and a genuinely caring assembly, and Isabelle and Gérard knew most of the attendees, well-established town people who were respected and involved in social and charitable local activities.

It was a beautiful day, and the light was filtering through the windows of the building, casting the soft colors of saints and angels from the stained windows into the church. As she completed a string of her usual prayers, Isabelle was transported by the deep feelings awakening inside her, and her thoughts started drifting away. Suddenly she had a clear view of her life, and Isabelle realized how everything came full circle, how perfect her life could be.

She realized that it was, indeed, the best time of her life, feeling in her heart grateful for the many blessings bequeathed to her. At 56, she was still a very attractive woman, having kept her youthful face and figure. Her skin in particular was the envy of many women, not marked by age lines thanks to a healthy way of living and food habits, and, as she was often saying, to her good genes.

She was a doctor associated with a reputable medical community, away from the nasty competitive tensions found in the large and impersonal university centers she had experienced in the past when living in metropolitan cities. Isabelle had the kind of practice she loved, was passionate about science and the latest medical discoveries, and remained genuinely dedicated to her patients. She worked as a pathologist at the local hospital while continuing to be part of several research committees, keeping however a small clinic for the follow up of some patients participating in clinical trials.

Gérard and Isabelle were fortunate enough to afford living in a house conforming to their dreams. Their beautiful southern French style home was built by

Gérard's parents, who when visiting the area had fallen in love with this lost paradise and found a large piece of land on the sound, perfect for family vacations. With time, additions and details were perfected, and this superb villa became able to cater to the increased needs of a larger family.

Memories were gathered by the generations to follow, the solid structure and well thought out design of the house accommodating several members comfortably so they could enjoy unforgettable times together. Slowly, the grounds started taking form, trees and shrubs following a park like pattern, with tropical and continental vegetation native to this part of Florida, which enjoyed a climate close to four-seasons. When Gérard and Isabelle started occupying the house as their main dwelling, they planted citrus and other kind of fruit trees, and began producing their own homegrown preserves or pressing fruit for their morning juice. The interior of the villa adopted some of their personal touches, defining their private quarters and work areas, along with designated suits reserved for the children and their families, when they visited.

The most beautiful beaches one could search for were a few minutes away, and they were comparing them many times with other faraway places, happy they did not to have to travel to exotic islands to find the white sugar sand beaches they had so close by.

Their children were married, with stable lives and careers, and the grandchildren were healthy and growing well.

Isabelle and Gérard had many wonderful friends and loved to entertain. They held receptions or small dinners at home every year. Although their house was not a "show house", every time they had visitors they realized how beautiful it was, containing many of the souvenirs they had accumulated over the years. It represented their own story with objects collected during travels around the world, and family pictures and artwork passed on by family artists. And the house was always filled with laughter startled by the playing of the many pets living happily in this loving home.

With these thoughts, sweet feelings and a great peace invaded Isabelle as she started to see a solution to her deepest sorrows.

-//-

Gérard and Isabelle met in Paris, France and married shortly afterwards. It was their fairytale, and it seemed the same for everyone asking about their first encounter. They lived in Paris, and then moved to Geneva and Montreux, Switzerland, and although those were some of the most expensive places in Western Europe, they attracted Isabelle. She liked the feeling of the classy security and the natural beauty of the French-speaking Swiss region, while Gérard saw in time his main office transferred to Geneva.

During their time in Switzerland, Isabelle broadened her medical education practicing in a clinic as part of an international establishment and she loved exchanging medical information with this cosmopolitan community, learning the cultural history of her colleagues. She was also fascinated by the diversity of this country where French, Italian, and German languages were spoken, to which was added English, thanks to the international affiliations they belonged to: the scientific field for her and diplomatic for Gérard. Over time, Isabelle discovered a passion for all that was Italian, from the Roman Empire to Italy's modern architecture, fashion, and cuisine.

Gérard took her to places they visited on their weekends or short vacations. This way, they walked for hours in the streets of Florence, scoured the Tuscan countryside, and absorbed the artwork and unique atmosphere of the scenery. They skied in the Alps and stayed in mountain chalets relaxing by the fireplace, a snow blanket covering houses, trees and streets around them and creating a soft, magical landscape.

They fell under the spell of romantic Venice during their honeymoon, and wandered hand in hand through the narrow alleys, went on gondola rides and fell asleep listening to the serenades from the gliding vessels under their windows. She drowned in the azure of his blue eyes, and he in her fairy-like blonde grace, getting lost in each other's arms.

After one escape to Venice, she found out she was expecting a baby, and nine months later they were blessed with a baby girl. They called her Marina, the princess of the sea, and she brightened their life, growing to be a beautiful and happy child, surrounded by her new family, her parents and Patrick, Gérard's older son from before his marriage to Isabelle.

After a few years, Gérard had to follow his career demands as a cultural attaché and return to the Washington DC area. This adjustment proved difficult; they were already busy building a family life and their new professional directions appeared to be very demanding on them both.

Isabelle, although well accepted by Gérard's parents, missed her family and their support, and was facing more efforts and new challenges to adapt to a new culture and new professional exigencies. She loved this vibrant and energetic country, and loved the self-confidence of its people, but she needed her family's complicity and their passionate discussions about art or philosophy, or their debates on ideas found in the latest books they'd read, as they used to do in the past.

She discovered fundamental differences in the way their respective families looked at life. Gérard's British and French remote origins linked him to a deep stability found in the southern American families. Its members were, driven and competitive, with strong family values. They appreciated a simple and honest life, but their self-assurance they exuded, seemed to suggest they had no worries in life. Gérard's calm and perfectly controlled manners made Isabelle consider him for a longtime as her 'wise-man'.

On her side was a family of intellectuals with high professional ambitions and expectations, made up of impractical and naïve individuals, art collectors who were financially broke, highly artistic and unrealistic dreamers. There was no feeling of stability in her family after her parents and grandparents had been thrown in all directions of Europe after World War II. Isabelle wondered on occasions if people in the United States could have any precise idea of the tragedy the war inflicted on the people in Europe.

From various social classes, ethnic origins, or religious extraction, they had practically all suffered devastating losses and incommensurable ruin of proprieties, while families were dismembered. Her family had scattered in all directions of the rose wind; many members disappeared in either gulags or German concentration camps, depending from which direction the occupant came. There was an underlining feeling of uncertainty and no hope of material stability, but there was a conviction that a strong education represented all the assets needed in life, which could be carried anywhere, and that no one could take away.

-//-

For many years after their arrival in Washington, DC, life continued at a frantic pace, keeping them busy between family and work. At times Gérard and Isabelle had the impression that they hardly could catch their breath.

Their children grew up, completed their education, and moved on with their own lives. Patrick, as he had decided at a young age, followed in his father's steps and became a very talented diplomat. His profession, much like the life he knew when growing up, carried him in many directions and countries. Patrick, happily married and becoming a parent himself, was learning the joys and worries of adulthood. Marina had showed a real inclination for music from the time she was only a few years old. She had a beautiful and powerful operatic voice and studied music, and when her voice stabilized in her late teens, she started taking belcanto lessons.

Marina earned a scholarship to attend Julliard School of Performing Arts in New York City, and showed real talent in this difficult and competitive field. She had an exceptional stage presence where she felt naturally at home, and against all obstacles one could foresee, she decided to pursue a career as an opera singer. She attended concerts and rehearsals, and, as her success increased, she felt happy with her life. She even married a rising star, a young musical director from Austria newly celebrated in New York. They traveled often together, Gunter casting her in his productions, and they managed a surprisingly stable family life. A little boy was born a couple of years after their marriage and they proved to be remarkably good parents.

After almost 20 years of marriage, Gérard and Isabelle finally felt free to settle to a place where they hoped to slow down, to have time for themselves, and for their hobbies. They needed to look at who they had become as they were advancing in age; they were not young adults anymore, but "adult-adults" as they jokingly said.

When they celebrated their 25th anniversary, Gérard invited Isabelle on a very romantic trip to Tahiti, staying in Bora Bora in a thatched bungalow at the end of a long dock advancing over the turquoise waters of the lagoon. It was one of these unique chances to reconnect in a place suspended in time and where they felt like children playing in the sun, with no obligations and no agenda. For once, Isabelle and Gérard could sleep late and let the sound of the waves and the whispering breeze cradle them like babies. In the morning, breakfast was served on their deck, and as they sipped their freshly squeezed tropical juice, they could see mesmerizing sea creatures through the glass floor.

They took horseback rides on the beach, swam with sharks, and had picnics on an isolated motu, one of the myriads of small sand banks, where they imagined playing Robinsons.

Other times, they mingled with the local population going to the markets where Gérard bought flamboyant bouquets of tropical flowers for Isabelle, and where she browsed small boutiques for beautiful mother-of-pearl jewelry. A few evenings they even ventured out to attend Polynesian dinners—interacting with locals was easy since they both spoke French, and letting their guards down, they joined the locals in their graceful and animated dances.

One day, Gérard took Isabelle to an island that cultivated pearls and chose a magnificent heart-shaped pearl for her that looked beautiful on her sun-golden skin. But the most touching moment was when they renewed their vows on a beach they had for them only with a Polynesian minister performing a simple traditional ceremony. The minister was very impressed by the loving glow that surrounded them; Gérard looked like a Greek god, and Isabelle reminded him of a Roman grace. Gérard could not take his eyes away from her and offered her an extravagant anniversary diamond ring, even though she was barefooted and wearing a simple but delicate cotton and lace dress, crowned by a traditional orchid wreath. They seemed to flow on the breeze above the sand and the waves washing on the beach.

Above all, the greatest feeling during these blessed moments was rediscovering the time when they first met. It was that overwhelming recognition of each other, as though their destiny was for them to live together forever. It was as profound as only soul mates can understand, as if they had at last arrived at the end of a long journey, after an endless longing to find the other.

Isabelle, spellbound and happy to surrender to her charming prince, let herself be swept away by this dizzying experience, erasing the distance that had grown between them over the years. Suddenly it became clear that they had been desperately searching for each other, across thousands of years and many lives, but also across this lifetime, when routines and difficulties had taken over, and when this one single being was peeled into two images and thrown in the hazard machine of destiny. She understood that the real reason for them coming back again was to try, one more time, to be together and put an end to this very long quest.

Returning home, Isabelle and Gérard stayed for a while under the blissful sensations experienced during their incomparable vacation, but slowly the humdrum of home life took over. The time spent in Tahiti became a special moment in their lives, almost like a dream, to remain enclosed in a treasure box and to be opened only on rare occasions over the years.

They were busy with their work and habits, and, with time, things started changing, and Isabelle noticed against her long denial, that something had gone terribly wrong.

-//-

Changes in Gérard's attitude started at first insidiously; nothing too serious, just a few papers neglected, some sarcastic remarks without any reason, then sleeping late and frankly not seeming to care. Stormy clouds gathered on the far horizon of their life, and a few thunderclaps were heard only from time to time. Isabelle was too busy with her work and too tired to give much attention to his behavior. One time, when Gérard went out slamming the door after she called him for dinner several times and he ignored her, she felt hurt and started wondering what could be the problem.

Then Gérard became moody and cranky with her most of the time, and he would rush out and take motorcycle rides late at night, impulsively and ignoring all danger. He continued the consulting work he had started since they moved to Florida and at age 62 he was still looking 45, as his mature years had been kind with him and made him more seductive as he aged. But he knew that Isabelle had the same advantage, gaining more knowledge and wisdom, and seemingly blessed with an almost miraculous ability to save her youthful looks. And while she was not jealous by nature, he was, and could not help but become suspicious of any special attention she received. From there, and since she was surrounded with people that admired and loved her sincerely, Gérard developed the habit of putting her down whenever she received compliments.

After a few months, their relationship deteriorated rapidly. Isabelle tried to have a heart to heart approach with her husband, but it only got worse. Now he was behaving like a spoiled child, and the work that he enjoyed doing in the past, administrating their properties and paying the bills, was now left unattended and additional fees were accumulating because of his negligence. When Isabelle offered to take care of the paperwork that required urgent attention, he refused flatly and furiously. But a few days later, when Isabelle entered his office, concerned and upset by the folders spread and left everywhere in disarray, he shouted "You have no idea how much I hate doing this", and asked her to leave the room as she was answering "then, let my do it." However, he stayed up late that night catching up on some important letters and bills, and went to sleep in one of the guest rooms.

This started a new phase in their life; him using one of the guest suits, and she in the master bedroom with the cats. The dog came at times to sleep with her and was the most confused, wanting them both, "mama", who always remembered to feed him with some of her fine dishes, and "papa", whom he worshiped.

Isabelle was very affected by this change, and laid awake most nights trying to understand and find a way to restore their relationship, and to return to the happy and loving ways they lived back in the not so distant past. Exhausted physically and drained emotionally, she cried herself to sleep every night. She consulted a marriage counselor, but Gérard would have nothing to do with it, and would not even consider it a possibility stating that, "I don't have any problem and there is nothing I can't take care of by myself," even though Isabelle said she needed an objective person to look into their differences.

As much as Isabelle suffered from watching powerlessly as their life crumbled, she thought it must be a late midlife crisis, and all would come back to normal. Putting his consulting contracts on hold, Gérard continued his long bike rides and fishing trips, not telling her where he was going. She tried to dismiss all this unusual behavior as childish and silly. She did not want to consider that he was having an affair, although the thought traversed her mind on some suspicious occasions.

A turn for the worst happened when they attended a professional dinner together, where Isabelle was holding a round table with other doctors. As part of a research program, she was presenting the latest results of their work using the newest applications of stem cells in spinal cord injury treatments. Gérard started interrupting her, was telling her to speak louder, and correcting her in front of the astonished audience. Then, the tension escaladed when he tried to serve as "interpreter" of what she was saying, making her feel like she was incapable of explaining her ideas, and basically treating her like an idiot in front of her colleagues.

This time she felt that the situation was more than she could tolerate, as she had always been a highly respected professional in this particular field of medicine, and this humiliation in front of her peers was more than she was willing to take. For the remainder of the evening she focused on the subject, trying to keep a good and polite face, but when they were finally alone in the car, she let go of her frustration that had accumulated for so long.

"Do not ever dare to humiliate me like this again, ever," she shouted, "this is something that I won't take from anybody!"

Gérard answered that he only wanted to prevent her from getting "embarrassed" by her "mistakes", but he could not specify which ones, then stated that he would no longer talk to her, and that he would not endure all her "crazy stuff." They remained silent and scornful, while he drove erratically, making her become truly scared.

After this incident, Isabelle asked herself if she could continue to stay in this marriage. She was exhausted by the stress, sleepless nights, work, and now by the realization of a total disconnect between the way Gérard and her judged and thought about situations. Was there a future for them? Could this situation ever return to the one they had enjoyed so much in the past, or at least improve a little?

Gradually estranged from each other and barely tolerating the other's presence, Isabelle hated to see that she grew resentful and accusatory of him destroying their happiness, their marriage, and their life.

Above all, it was hard not to have the courage or the desire to confide in someone else about their differences. Isabelle and Gérard kept a social façade and continued to go to some public events and visit with friends for dinner in town or at their place, though one could hardly imagine the turmoil tearing them apart inside. Children and other family members were far away, immersed in their own qualms, friends had their problems, and they, too, reached out to Gérard and Isabelle many times for advice.

Each one continued to further recoil into their secrecy, neither of them feeling right to burden any other person with their heavy issues. Mostly, they did not know what they really wanted. Gérard accused Isabelle of being mean and difficult, while she was going insane seeing him going through some weird "'andropause'" and becoming a total stranger.

-//-

Isabelle was trying to relax in the only way she knew, by playing the harp. She needed to regain some clarity as she was too hurt and confused, but she wanted to find a solution to their problems, or at least to search deeper inside and see which way she should go with her life.

As she played, her fingers started warming up finding the right strings. Trying to keep her mind on other things, she chose a very difficult classical piece by Salzedo, with variations in an ancient style, and she charged it with passion to tame the raging feelings storming inside her.

Calm came as she concentrated on her playing, sensing this old musical instrument responding to her touch and its vibrations diffusing all around her. She remembered again all the joy she always felt when the beautiful sounds carried her to a peaceful dreamland. The entire house had an exceptional acoustic, and music was now flowing everywhere, reaching each corner of the house and of her soul.

She kept playing when an idea came to her; why not go to Salzburg and spend a few days with Marina? Gunter, her husband, was directing Parsifal in Bayreuth at the Richard Wagner Festival, and although Gunter had a strong German musical education, this was a major step in his career and he needed all his concentration. Marina, on her side, needed to explore Salzburg for a series of recitals featuring opera music by Mozart, with the hope that one day she would be singing at the Mozart Festival. However, very attractive concerts were offered in this famous town all year long, and although Marina had a real inclination for the Italian opera, Mozart's music with its jovial and spectacular coloratura testing one's vocal artistry attracted her and made her develop her own German repertoire.

Isabelle, invigorated by the prospect of a well-needed change, realized that going away would give her a break during these morose times, and being far might help her to see clearer what were her intentions for the future. Once her decision was made, she picked up the phone and called Marina in New York. She was happy to find her at home and they both became quickly filled with excitement, thrilled to spend some happy mother-daughter times together in Austria. They arranged to meet in Vienna, and after a weekend of enjoying the Austrian capital, they would continue their trip together to Salzburg.

-//-

The night before flying to Vienna, Isabelle and Gérard had dinner to a local restaurant owned by friends. It was the best way to keep a light mood; the evening was pleasant, the weather mild, and the food excellent.

It was a French restaurant with outdoor tables amid fragrant shrubs, romantically lit by torches. They were warmly received by the owner, who was always happy to see them and stopped to chat with them in French. While their table was getting ready, they had cocktails by the bar where they ran into close friends as the place usually hosted a happy and animated gathering of their acquaintances.

They decided to sit at the table together and catch up on the latest events, making Isabelle happy for the diversion diffusing the tension before her departure. When their food arrived, the conversation turned to Isabelle's trip and everyone exchanged some souvenirs and gave her advice for her trip. Suddenly, Isabelle realized that this was the first time she was going on a holiday without Gérard, and was again reminded of how much their life had changed lately.

As the evening unfolded, they became quieter, listening to the soft music from a distant band, men sipping Cognac, and the ladies choosing between cappuccinos and herbal teas. Paul, who liked to do some soul searching, brought up the subject of satisfaction in this lifetime, questioning the others what would they like to be or do in their next one. Everyone became excited and a spirited conversation followed, each of them describing their imaginary future existence. Gérard made some jokes, jumping from the idea of being a gigolo, a rock star, or a geisha. Then he became more serious, and expressed some desire of being a researcher, either in genetics or astronomy.

At this point, they noticed that Isabelle had remained silent during the whole conversation, and turning towards her, they insisted on hearing her prospects for her next life. At first, she was not prepared to give such an unexpected and important answer, but after reflection, she arrived quickly at the conclusion that she did not have the slightest desire to experience another terrestrial existence.

"I think I am done, I won't come back again," she answered, "I don't think I could live in harsh and violent times like these one more time, it is too hard for me."

Gérard interjected that she was too negative, after which they took leave from their friends and went home as Isabelle had more preparations to make for her morning flight. During their drive home, Gérard spoke a few cynical words about her being depressed and spoiling everyone's mood. Isabelle could not suppress the thought that she had made a good decision to go away for a while.

-//-

After Isabelle's departure, Gérard enjoyed his freedom like a child on vacation. He behaved as if no one was there to watch him or to question his whereabouts. He took immense pleasure in waking up late and going to bed at any time of the day or the night. He indulged in junk food and too much drinking, never making the bed, indifferent to leaving the house unkempt. He even told the housekeeper to take leave, "I don't need anybody around", he explained.

He continued roaming the country roads on his motorcycle and he even made some acquaintances with some other bikers at bars on the sides of the road, drinking with them like a college student on a spring break. Occasionally, he would take his boat deep-sea fishing, frequently taking with him some of his newly made friends.

One night, after hosting a large gathering at his house, where everyone ate and drank without limits, the new "friends" trashed his beautiful home, devastated the wine pantry, and rendered Gérard heavily intoxicated. Sometime in the middle of the night, they decided for a motorcycle ride, however, Gérard decided to go alone on a deep-sea boat ride.

This turned out to be an unexpected experience and brutal wake up call for Gérard. Somewhere, distant from the shore and in complete solitude, when the first rays of the morning had diffused through the hazy mantel above the sea, Gérard emerged from his semiconscious state. As his mind was regaining clarity, surrounded by the immense isolation of the ocean, he suddenly realized the chaos he had created in his life.

Far away from the land, Gérard felt distanced from his own actions, like a stranger looking into his own reality. Gérard had a very hard time realizing that all this was not a figment of his own imagination, and what he saw terrified him. He shuddered at the vision of the events he had initiated lately.

He stayed for a long time immersed in an intense contemplation. After leading an exemplary life, cherishing the values passed on to him and complying with his duties, it appeared that his mind had wanted, for one time in his life, to explore the depths of darkness hiding in his own soul.

Slowly, this epiphany had brought to the surface his real essence, his profound and noble nature, that for a short instance he had denied himself. What Gérard experienced was like a quake that shook off and unloaded all his destructive deeds, guiding him towards the decision of turning his life around once and for all.

In the distance, a tiny line of land became visible and approaching the shore, Gérard remembered that he had avoided talking with Isabelle on the phone since her departure for Europe.

-//-

During this time, Isabelle was enjoying her special time with her daughter and little Benjamin. She started relaxing and giving in to the charming moments spent with her grandson, filling her spirits with the beauty of these famous European cities. However, certain places reminded her of the magic moments she had shared with Gérard, all unique times engraved forever in her heart, a heart that now was aching when comparing those souvenirs with the present reality of their relationship.

She would brush away those thoughts trying to be strong and offer pleasant company to her daughter and grandson, but in the solitude of her room at night, she tried to analyze what had gone wrong. She missed her husband badly, and came up with many scenarios of how to mend their union, sometimes feeling guilty for not understanding him.

Most evenings she fell asleep realizing that what she really wanted was to go back to the relations they had before, and right now she did not know if this would ever be possible again. She practically did not hear from him since she had left Florida and she did not want to imagine the reasons for it.

-//-

Gérard was sitting on the dock, deep in his thoughts, replaying in his mind many of the events that had brought him into this situation. He was depressed, scared for the first time as an adult, and very angry with himself. He had a hard time to even understand his own behavior, and finally admitted he had acted like a child, and hated to review in his mind some of the words he had said to Isabelle. Her answers were still resonating in his mind and pain and fear were tightening around his heart like an unforgiving knot.

He remembered waking up in one morning and feeling as though he wanted to be young and vibrant again, and to prove it to himself by going through the extremes of a reckless life he had never experienced in his youth. Now that he could have it all, why not dare and show to everybody that he could handle any challenge? He needed this reassurance that he still "had it." Even when he was charming some lady hanging out in a bar, he could not even remember her face or conversation, but rather what impression he had made upon her. He realized that it was all about himself and he knew it was a stupid act to impress; the old Narcissistic myth, the Don Juan who did not care about the women he seduced, only that no one could resist his appeal.

Well, he now had the confirmation of maintaining his powers with renewed sparks of his youth, but when viewed from another perspective he realized he had not proved anything that really was of value. He was still strong, young, and captivating, but he had a lot more going for him at this stage in his life. He had acquired so much more knowledge and experience, and above all, he was so blessed to share all of it with the woman of his dreams. And now, he was about to lose it all because of his selfish and irresponsible actions.

Gérard decided to start first by making order in this mess, keeping his mind busy while cleaning up the house. There was an urgent need to take care of his consulting business that he had neglected and had gotten alarmingly behind. He also needed to allow himself some time for reflection before making any decision. Very soon after he called Isabelle, in the beginning just to make small talk about the house and the pets, and then, that he was missing her. After a while, he told her he was sorry about his behavior and for being unkind to her.

The more he cleared his mind from the frenzy of roaming wildly across the countryside and found some needed rest, the more Gérard distanced himself from the misbehavior he had enjoyed just a few days ago. He became more reclusive, not answering the calls of his recent "friends", not even feeling like riding his motorcycle anymore. He needed for a little longer these quiet times of introspection, and deep in his thoughts, often sat on his dock, or was gently rocked by his boat tethered a few yards away. Gérard took real pleasure in these quiet times to redefine himself, find new directions in the quest for serenity and happiness, as he was reevaluating the bases of his marriage.

As peace gradually returned, he started to think of the past in the calm of the moonlight of an early summer night illuminating the sound. Admiring the lights faraway, memories as a child came back to him of times he enjoyed so much getting up early in the mornings to go fishing with his father on a lake or a pier at the beach. Sometimes he hardly could find any sleep, as he checked and rechecked in his mind all the preparations they had made. He would be afraid that he did not have the right lures, poles, or baits.

Then, once arrived on the pier, he had as usual, brought too much of everything.

However, tonight, lost in one of these meditative escapes, Gérard was feeling a calm he had not found in a long time. He realized his recent acting out had been to test his limits and the direction of his life. Within, he had been measuring the trajectory of his destiny, questioning his past and his future. He was gauging all his values, achievements, and position in society, while questioning future projects and his desires. He discovered that while he had reached other depths and heights in his life, he had not lost any of his energy and virility. He also realized that he now experienced a much better balance between youthful enthusiasm and an already established personal and familial situation. Gérard was becoming himself again. His main concern now was losing the most precious thing to him, Isabelle. He could not see or conceive a future without her. Not now that they had found each other, while so many people went through life never knowing what real love was.

Lately, he had started reading old novels and poetry from an old volume by Victor Hugo, remembering how eternal his writings were. Shortly after, Gérard tried writing some exquisite letters intended to his wife, with poetic verses included at times. These letters he thought he would never show to Isabelle, were free incursions into his own mind, helping him to see clearly and sort through his feelings without embarrassment. Like little elves gliding into his soul having fun and going everywhere without any rules, they uncovered corners of his mind, memories and suppressed longings he was not aware of.

And all that was good, for Gérard realized how much everything in his life, every little plan, memory, or desire was intertwined with the presence of his wife; there was no desire and no future without Isabelle being at the center of all. As the evening unfolded, he thought about her and he wrote, silently calling upon her, "You are my life, my love, and my treasured reason for everything I do. You are the kindest and the sweetest person I know. You took me as I am and made me whole."

He realized and repeated often that without her he was only a fraction of a person; they needed each other to be complete. Without any doubt in his mind, he made the resolution to do all he could to gain her back, and enjoy the rest of this life being aware they would share it with each other.

-//-

After over four wonderful weeks spent together, Isabelle made her farewells to Marina and little Benjamin, as her sabbatical could not be extended any further. This was the longest she had ever stayed away from her office, and she was already getting worried about everything she had left behind in Florida, her job, her home, and particularly, her husband.

During her return flight home, she had a short layover in New York City and was happy that she did not have to transfer from La Guardia to JFK to catch her connection. This allowed her time to spend two relaxing hours in the President's lounge prior to her connection for the three-and-a-half-hour trip back home to the Florida panhandle. However, she used this time to refresh, check her email on her iPad, and even answer some of her messages.

Her overnight flight was as tiresome as usual, since she never could really fall asleep on an airplane. She had only a fruit juice prior to landing and now she needed something to keep her alert, while enjoying the plush setting of the first-class lounge. The strong smell of freshly brewed coffee was calling and led her to the dining area. She found a small table a little away from the early morning crowd for her tray of coffee, croissants, and orange jelly.

She felt much better after her first cup of coffee, but she already missed the taste of the espresso and the croissants of Europe. It was a Friday morning, and with no plans to go back to work until the next Monday, Isabelle was pleased at the idea of using the weekend to take care of urgent paper work and get over her jetlag. Still, checking the time difference, she called her office in Florida as soon as it opened, and took care of some business. She was reassured that there were no emergencies, and relaxing a little, she chatted with her secretary about her trip.

After picking up a magazine, she went further to the back of the lounge and sat in a club chair. She thought that reading would keep her mind away from her imminent reunion with Gérard. She did not notice that a middle-aged man who was staring at her for a while, came and sat in the chair next to her.

"They don't know how to make a good strong coffee around here, in New York City."

Isabelle, lifting her eyes briefly from her lecture, nodded and smiled politely, then returned to her reading.

"I am coming from Paris and going home to Dallas, and I will be happy when I get there to grind myself some well grilled coffee beans, and make the best coffee you can get in all of Texas! But I always enjoy going to Paris; each time I discover some new amazing places. I've never been attracted by artwork before, and now, I've started collecting it!"

When Isabelle made a gesture to look at her watch, he got up and very gallantly apologized, "Pardon me, Madam, I got carried away and did not properly introduce myself. My name is Randy Goldwin, and I did not intend to impose, I was just happy to get closer to home and hear English spoken again."

She chuckled a little, since she still had not said a single word yet, but with her usual well-trained social manners, she extended her hand and said, "I am Dr. Isabelle Beaumont."

"A French name, is it?"

"Yes, I kept my maiden name for my professional life." With this said, she decided to return to her fictitious reading.

Mr. Goldwin was discreetly studying her, and suddenly he burst out, "Are you married?"

Startled, Isabelle raised her head from her magazine and looked at him, her eyes now wide open in surprise.

"I apologize again, a thousand times, as all this sounds so out of place, and it has never happened to me before. But it struck me from nowhere, and when I first saw you I said to myself that you are the kind of woman I would spend my life trying to make happy. And nothing would be too much for you to ask."

Isabelle was quite used to receiving compliments and never made a serious case of it; her elegant features and demeanor, and the special radiance surrounding her, were often reason for admiration or jealousy. But she spent her life trying to succeed and set her values on her achievements and not on her looks. So, not phased, she looked straight into his eyes and answered, "Yes, I am married. And very much so."

With this said, she stood up ready for her flight; she almost wanted to laugh, maybe because of the fatigue or the incongruity of the situation. She had received some unusual proposals in her life, more or less serious, but one in an airport lounge from a stranger topped them all. Anyway, it was a good distraction from the tension she had already started sensing at the approaching meeting with her husband.

Randy Goldwin quickly stood up, and making a bow said, "He is a very lucky man, ma'am, and I wish you great happiness."

Isabelle, with a whisper said, "Thank you" and left the lounge to reach her departure gate.

On the airplane, Isabelle donned her travel headphones and finally found the muted quiet she needed to think of her situation at home. She wondered how Gérard was doing, in what state of mind, and how she would react, according to a variety of scenarios. Above all, she wanted to find out what she really wanted in her future. A multitude of memories flooded her, from the past one more idyllic than the other, to the more recent ones, painful and confusing. She knew that what she longed for were the happy, enchanting moments from the past, but she was not sure whether all of this was still possible. It had been a while since she had concluded in her heart that she was not capable of continuing her life with Gérard as it had been lately.

The one thing she was sure of, however, was that she missed him terribly, and that she was committed to trying her best to restore their life together.

-//-

Going to the airport to meet Isabelle for her homecoming trip from Europe, Gérard was nervous. A lot more nervous than he would have liked to appear; one by one, he revised in his mind the preparations he had made for her return: the house was spotless, flower arrangements adorned many corners of the house, linens in the bedroom and bathrooms freshly changed, and all the bills paid. Most importantly, he had sold his bikes as a sign of turning the page connecting him with this recent and dissipated episode in his life.

He was looking young and handsome, neatly shaven and with a fresh haircut. Wearing tan linen slacks and a fine cotton dark shirt, after a few weeks of sobriety and rest, Gérard regained once more his stunning looks that could dispute the ones of any mature movie star.

He parked his car, and fetching the roses he had picked from the garden and arranged in a bouquet, he noticed that his hands were shaking. More than ever he wanted everything to be perfect, he wanted to regain her love and to return to the life they'd known before. After Isabelle had gotten some rest, Gérard had made plans to take her on a boat ride to a secret place and have a welcome dinner he ordered at a famous local restaurant owned by longtime friends.

Henry would prepare baskets for their picnic with their specialty of fresh caught grouper prepared in an almandine crust, crab claws Provençale, prawns with seaweeds, a tray of cheeses, and Isabelle's favorite dessert – sinful triple flourless chocolate cake. He also had a cooler with Perrier water, Sancerre wine for dinner, and a bottle of chilled Dom Perignon Champagne rosé 1996 for their dessert.

The airport arrival area was crowded with people of all ages waiting for friends and family coming for a short vacation or to return home. They were all excited for they anticipated having a good time in this vacation resort atmosphere. Isabelle's flight had been announced a while ago, and passengers began to trickle through the arrival gate with a wave of new energy when they reached the pack of people gathered close by to meet them. Gérard strained his neck trying to see past them and started to worry that she might have missed the flight.

When he finally saw her, he felt the same electric jolt he had felt the first time he ever saw her. Her quiet beauty, aristocratic stance, and her entire presence made her stand apart from the crowd. Many stood aside as she passed, wondering if she was someone they might know. Gérard was swept off his feet, and one more time, he fell in love with her.

He almost threw himself ahead, making a path through the crowd, and not being able to restrain his happiness at seeing her, scooped her off the floor into his arms. Isabelle, at first surprised and breathless, returned his embrace.

The very first words that came out his mouth were, "Will you marry me?"

She answered playfully and overwhelmed with joy, "I am already a married woman, monsieur!"

To which Gérard returned, "I meant, will you marry me again?" At that very precise moment, the memory of a similar proposal invaded them both, and holding each other, they went out the door, kissing and crying like they had at the time of their engagement. She held the bouquet of roses with one hand, and with her traveling tote secured on his shoulder, she could slip her other arm around his waist.

As they walked away from the entrance, she remembered, "Wait a minute, I need to get my luggage."

They started laughing like children, and went back inside the airport hall where her valises were already on the turning carrousel. While he was loading her luggage in the trunk of the car, she suppressed a smile at the thought of having two proposals in space of a few hours.

During the 40-minute drive back home, Gérard did his best to concentrate on the road ahead, feeding Isabelle with domestic news about the pets, the flowers, friends, and local events. Isabelle, while listening to him, was ecstatic at the change in Gérard, and at the same time, scared that this return to his real self was only an illusion and would not last. It is why, when he asked again, more collected this time, "I am serious, would you marry me again?", she switched to French, as they often did, "*Quelle bêtise as-tu fais encore?*" (what stupid thing did you do this time?)

"*Tu as raison, j'ai fais beaucoup de bêtises dans le passé, et je te demande pardon*" (true, I made many mistakes in the past and I demand forgiveness), and this is why I would like us to start all over again, to make it right again and forever."

-//-

When they arrived home the surprises continued. Isabelle discovered with renewed pleasure her beautiful home, all in order and boasting a festive ambience. She was welcomed with sloppy kisses by her bichon and the purring of the cats. She could barely walk for fear of stepping on their tails. After treats were distributed and luggage carried in the house, she was happy to breathe the familiar air of this elegant residence, and retreat into the calm of her master suite.

She took a long and warm shower, slipped into a fresh satin gown and sighed with satisfaction when she finally stretched out as far as she could in her king size bed. What a delight after a night spent in the airplane! In no time, she was deeply asleep, and when Gérard came to bring her a glass of fresh water, he could only give her a gentle kiss on her cheek. As he left to close the door, he turned to look at her, and one more time admired this tranquil sleeping beauty, stricken once more by the thought that this gorgeous person was his wife.

Gérard went to collect the dinner he ordered, readied the boat, and made sure that all the preparations for their picnic were fine. He was still shifting around some cushions, when Isabelle came down from the house. She knew about Gérard's plans to take her for a dinner on the boat and she was now wearing a sheer sarong of blend colors of blue, green, and turquoise over her bathing suit. A large straw hat covered her long blond hair and sunglasses protected her deep-sea green eyes; she had never got used to flip-flaps and her feet were protected from the wooden deck by pretty but comfortable green sandals.

When Gérard saw her arriving, his heart started racing again, full of hope of regaining her love. She smiled and looked rested, and soon after, they left the dock. They had a good hour before sunset, but Isabelle was starving as she had not had any lunch with the distraction made by the time change. Gérard had a conspiratorial look on his face, when she asked where they were going. "It is a surprise," was all he would give out. "More surprises," she thought, and leaning against the cushions, she abandoned herself to the gentle rocking of the waves.

They were silent for a long time, content with each other's presence without having to talk. Occasionally he would take a quick glance at her, and she would take her eyes from the horizon and meet his, happy to rediscover these tucked away sensations. He thought she was the best thing that had ever happened to him, and she was more at peace, enjoying his presence with renewed hope for their future together.

Instead of heading out to sea, Isabelle noticed that Gérard turn the boat to idle to enter a cove on the north side of the sound. The cove was small but hidden from the sound by a narrow entrance, and Isabelle discovered how beautiful this place was. The cove was a small lagoon with emerald waters, and trees grew close to the edge, combining native magnolias, pines, live oaks, and a few palm trees.

Gérard slowed the boat as it drew near a sandy beach, and turning off the engine, jumped into the shallow water, and then secured the boat to the closest dune. Suddenly they were in a silent oasis by themselves. Isabelle, taken aback by this unexpected discovery, asked Gérard how he knew about it.

"It is my secret little paradise I wanted to take you to," and continuing for himself, "and I hope with my life to win you back."

Isabelle did not want to disturb the plans Gérard had made for the evening, and not knowing what he had in mind, followed him for a while back and forth from the boat as he unloaded baskets, blankets, and towels, and placed them carefully on the sandy beach.

It had been a beautiful summer's day and now, late in the afternoon, the sky had changed from a bright blue to softer shades of pink, making the air vibrate in the subtle golden light. Gently, all became quieter and the two of them fell under the spell of this magic place. Sitting on the blanket, they took in their surroundings, looking at the mouth of the lagoon and beyond, where discreet lines of water mixed with the reflection of the main beach, and far out, the large ocean itself, barely seen between the trees. A light ocean mist was evaporating and created a veil as delicate as lace, slowly dimming from pink to orange, then to red and fuchsia.

Gérard moved closer to Isabelle and tenderly wrapped his arm around her, and after a moment of silence, told her he would get their dinner ready. All was quickly laid out on the blanket as it had been prepared in easy to use containers; only the wine and Champagne needed a little more attention, but Gérard took care of that too. He swiftly filled buckets with ice and secured them, digging them half way in the sand.

The flavors of the gourmet food revived their appetite and they savored the fish and salad, then took their time with the cheese assortment and wine. With renewed energy, Isabelle was very tempted to go into the water. She missed the warmth of this subtropical place, and floating in salty water was one of her greatest pleasures.

"Ready for a swim?" she asked.

In response, Gérard jumped up and ran the few yards to the shallow water. She tested the temperature, first dipping the tips of her toes in, and then, with a sigh of relief, she joined Gérard. She felt so relaxed, perhaps mellowed by a few sips of Sancerre or by the magic of this rare moment, and went naturally into his arms.

They floated together, holding each other, turning gently, and feeling as though they were the only people in the whole world.

A great peace and reassurance descended on them, as if they were aware one more time that they were made for each other and their union was sealed in Heaven to last forever. At this moment, they were falling in love for the thousandth time. Gérard marveled at her velvety skin, and gently sniffed her neck, inhaling the fresh smell of her hair mixed with salty water.

She started shivering, not sure if it was from the cool evening air or from the sensations sparked by his body against hers. She let him bring her back to the blanket, still holding her tight. When Gérard took her head in his hands and looked at her with loving eyes, they both got lost in the depth of their feelings. Then, ever so softly, Gérard approached his mouth and touched her lips tenderly, with infinite gentleness. Their passion grew and Isabelle remembered the feelings when they had kissed for the very first time, melting under the most delightful sensation he always generated in her. Then, they started to kiss with ardor, and reaching for each other, they enjoyed the feelings of their bodies being reunited in the most intense embrace. They traveled again unified, as the only children in a lost paradise, through this life and this galaxy, and perhaps through different times and different dimensions. It did not matter for they were one soul, eternal lovers, the only way it was supposed to be.

They fell asleep and made love again, and slept again, losing the perception of passing time. At certain moment, they were hungry again and laughed when they recalled the chocolate cake and the Champagne, and feasted on both with renewed joy.

Then slowly life manifested again with a few seagull cries at first cutting through the fading night, then birds awakening from the land with swallows, cardinals and mocking birds joining in. Dawn was only a timid transparence of the eastern sky, but there was excitement in the air welcoming the arrival of a new and glorious summer's day.

Gérard got up carefully so as not to disturb his sleeping muse and made sure she was wrapped up in a soft cover. He started bringing the remainder of the dinner onto the boat and after dragging the boat into the water and starting the engine, he took Isabelle onboard. Awakened by the movement around her, Isabelle started to marvel at the beauty of the dawn, and the two of them remained immersed in this mystical moment. The horizon became more luminous, the light evaporation above the water making everything look unreal, and the color of the sky and the sound changed constantly and quickly. Some dolphins came close and accompanied them in celebration of the rising sun, which suddenly appeared majestically, and all became alive.

They made it back to their dock and entered through the back porch where they were greeted by the household pets. They gave their pets food, then decided to have breakfast later, and were fast asleep in their bedroom. Isabelle, tired and very sleepy, remembered thinking she was the happiest woman in the world and that she just wanted to rest in bed for the entire weekend.

BOOK TWO

I slowly emerged from my sleep. I'd had a restful time of recuperation, was relaxed and happy, and finally could let go of all my worries. I had many dreams, some of them so vivid I longed to linger in them. I wanted to keep my eyes closed a little longer before returning to reality.

I even dreamed of Shou-Shou, our cat who had died two years before; Shou-Shou was so real in the dream and I was reminded of her tricks and presence, but her loud snoring is probably what woke me up. I tried however to prolong these sweet moments, remembering the tender and passionate weekend I had spent with Gérard and the thrill of our reconciliation. I knew that when I opened my eyes I would meet the deepest aqua blue eyes in the world and I would one more time dive into them and be lost again, and I would feel safe in his loving arms.

Slowly I turned toward his side and reached gently for him on his pillow. The void let me know he was not there. I finally opened my eyes, but I could not see him in the room when I was greeted by a brilliant morning sky. Light filtered into the room where the drapes were slightly parted. Music was playing softly in the house and I recognized "The Four Seasons" by Vivaldi.

Strangely, I was not hungry but the appealing smell of fresh coffee from downstairs tickled my nose, and now I even recognized the scent of croissants just taken out of the oven. However, something caught my attention. Turning to sit on the edge of the bed, my feet searched automatically for the slippers I usually kept close by, but to my big surprise, Shou-Shou was lying on them the way she always had. Getting old, she could not jump in the bed with us and she would make her own bed on my soft house shoes. She watched me with her beautiful blue eyes, looking comfortable and healthy, and her purring increased when, without any hesitancy, I bent over and patted her. I decided to try to understand later how she or her double were there; maybe Gérard was giving me another of his unexpected gifts.

At this moment completely awake, I ran under the shower, splashing in a hurry, donned a light linen summer dress, humming the song that rested with me from our night on the beach. It was an old-fashioned song chosen by Gérard, "The Ceremony", with George Jones and Tammy Wynette, but a song that expressed so well our deep commitment.

I felt so happy, invigorated, and young, I almost flew down the stairs to meet my husband. I found Gérard in the living room, but I stopped, startled to see him sitting in the couch, gazing into the void. I called him, and at that moment he buried his head in his hands, sobbing desperately. I could not understand what was happening, and I drew close to him thinking he had not seen me. Approaching the couch, I wrapped my arms around his back and rested my head against his neck.

As I did this, Gérard shivered and wept harder as he felt my presence, and at that time I noticed he was holding one of my blouses I wore to work, except it was all wrinkled and wet from his tears. I started talking to him, reassuring him that all would be all right, nothing would ever separate us. My pleas became more intense as his sorrows would not lessen and I became desperate to bring him comfort. I started talking to him as I was drying his tears with my kisses, holding and rocking him like a lost little child.

After a long while, realizing I was not giving him any solace, I went to my harp and started playing for him, as I had many times in the past. Even though I had not practiced in many weeks, my fingers moved flawlessly on the strings and I played one piece of music after another, choosing the ones Gérard loved the most. I had the impression he felt some consolation, and I kept playing for a while, encouraged by the effect the harp music was making on him.

When I finally stopped, he was asleep, as though he finally could relax enough to find some rest. I spent a long time watching him, admiring his handsome features, sending him all my loving feelings, speaking soft words of comfort and eternal love.

Letting him rest, I thought of my Sanctuary and my little friends needing my attention. I walked out, and once more I felt the joy brought by this place. It had grown quite a bit in size and the number of residents. Beautiful flowers and numerous fruit trees coexisted with the happy members of our little refuge.

I noticed how beautiful all was; the fragrant bushes were loaded with flowers and the healthy animals were playing and getting along so well together. The sky had a few puffs of nice clouds and birds were singing in a divine harmony.

After a long tour of my Sanctuary, I felt reassured that everybody was doing well, so I went back inside the house to check on Gérard. As I approached him, he started to wake up. Now sitting next to him, close enough to be more aware of how he was sensing this splendid day, our gorgeous home and expanding view all the way to the far end of the bay. I felt the sadness still within him, and I cuddled close, my head resting on his chest. Then, I looked in the direction he was looking.

What was that? It was so strange; it could not be the same thing we were looking at together! It was night and dark in the house and there was nothing shining beyond the living room windows. Then I noticed that the house was a mess, things dropped and not picked up, mail accumulated on a credenza, everything in disarray.

When Gérard got up and went outside to the back porch, my surprise grew even more. It was a lot smaller, as it had been before we started the Sanctuary, but the pool and the flowerbeds were unkempt and some of the dishes of the pets were dirty. And, where were all our new residents, all the rescued babies? I could see one of our dogs and two of the cats. They looked sad and lost like Gérard, and trailed close by him. He patted them absent mindedly as they rubbed against his legs. Duke walked on his hind legs, trying to reach him and give him kisses.

At this point, I asked Gérard what was happening, but his mind was far away, deep in his thoughts. He looked so miserable and obviously had not heard me. All this made me wonder what was wrong and I questioned my own sanity, especially after I noticed even more bizarre things. If I stayed close enough to Gérard and tried to see what he was seeing, I was overwhelmed by a depressing vision of desolation and abandon. However, when I just turned my head to better see all on my own, everything went back to normal and it was bright and beautiful.

By now, I was insisting to get an answer from Gérard and needing to obtain a reaction from him I became even more desperate. I started shouting to get his attention, but it was even more heartbreaking to realize he did not hear me. I tried to shake him out of this gloomy state, but he only shivered every time I touched him.

-//-

After a time that seemed hours, days, or weeks of attempts to get in touch with Gérard, I finally regained some control of myself and went back to my Sanctuary. For a long time, I walked around trying to distract my racing heart and my questioning mind by talking and caressing my animal friends and birds. I saw then that they surrounded me, showing me love, as if they tried to cheer me up. Feeling more at peace, I nevertheless decided to find clarity in this new situation. My mind and my heart were bursting with questions until I could no longer hold them silent, and I surprised myself by imploring aloud, "Oh, please God, tell me why Gérard can't hear me?"

At once, I had my answer. The Sanctuary became filled with the most magnificent glow, extending without limits and vibrating with the most superb colors. A marvelous presence of total love and understanding embraced me. Held in this cradle of unconditional love, I experienced with ecstasy what celestial splendor was, for I instantly recognized it.

"I am the Creator of all that is and I am your Father. You are with me now and Gérard cannot, yet, hear you, my child."

"You mean, I am not of this world anymore? You are saying I am ... dead?" I asked as my throat strangled with emotion.

"What world are you referring to? All worlds are here, together, present and alive. You must be referring to the earthly life. Yes, you are no longer on Earth, but you are very much alive; you are with me in the eternal life and with all creatures that finally come back to their original place."

Although everything made sense now, I was still in shock. I recognized the feeling of being back with The Creator, and I instantly knew that all was perfect, designed to find absolute order. Still, I did not understand all of it.

"But why now? Why did you decide to call me back when all was so good for me, and when finally Gérard and I had attained such an extraordinary harmony and a love to last for our terrestrial existence and beyond?"

With infinite gentleness I heard His response, "Isabelle, my child, I did not choose for you, YOU did. From the beginning, I granted mankind free will, and you are, as are all people, free to make your own choices."

At this point, I was not able to follow or to understand how such a choice could have been mine. I struggled to consider even the possibility of changing my decision, if it were possible.

"No Isabelle, your choice is final. You cannot, momentarily, go back to your earthly life," came the answer. And before I even asked, I heard, "But you can see why you decided to be here."

And then it all came back to me.

-//-

Suddenly I felt so good. All pain disappeared and I was flowing and dancing in space, in the light. I was free, and the brilliance of the most beautiful shimmers surrounded me as I flowed with the colors of the rainbow. With no difficulty, I gracefully made loops in the air, like a child playing with the discovery of the third dimension, laughing and turning effortlessly in all directions. After a while of enjoying my play, I realized I was slowly traveling through many places. Although galaxies passed beyond me one after another, I transitioned through these many worlds without any sense of speed or rushing of time.

Then things appeared to stabilize, the glowing light became more intense, and I started to feel the presence of many beings. In the beginning, there were only faded silhouettes, then, some came closer to identify themselves, and ...to welcome me. Great kindness and gentle words became clear and I began seeing angels opening a path to relatives and friends long parted from Earth. I was not surprised any longer, since I started to understand the reason for all of this. I was to be reunited with my passed family and I was happy to see them.

Some light beings coming closer made my heart rejoice as I recognized my mother. She was at the best of her youth and beauty, and expressed to me again her infinite love. Words were superfluous, since we could understand each other perfectly well through our feelings. Then many other relatives joined us. My father, grandparents and close or distant relatives, then friends, teachers, and every person that had ever influenced my time on Earth, came one by one to tell me that they were fine, happy and vibrant. They told me that they had not forgotten me, and most surprisingly, that they continued to expand their own interests and talents.

They were all young and beautiful beyond belief, and my astonishment increased even more when I ran into some of my patients. Some I had even forgotten, but suddenly all the memories came back as they thanked me for the time I cared for them. They made me see how I held them in my arms and loved them when they became frightened of passing into their new life. Although that seemed a natural thing for me to do at the time, now reunited, it all made sense, and gave

49

value to these incredible moments we had shared in the strongest, most compassionate kind of love.

Later, I found myself in an amazing garden when I realized that I was visiting some of my father's new artwork. At this moment, it became easier for me to understand that, he too, had started creating dazzling images of landscapes. Beyond these incredible images was the fact that they were real places suspended in what I already called Paradise. The petals of the flowers, and all the colors depicting objects in the pictures were made of solid precious stones, one more brilliant than another—huge emeralds, rubies, and diamonds of all shades were spread around— while the most extraordinary designs of the flowers and butterflies amazed me and left me in awe.

I laughed and embraced my father, telling him how happy I was to see him and how content I was to know that he produced such great artwork and continued to surround himself with beautiful creations.

The time to reacquaint with this new dimension could not be measured by any earthly clock. I went to all the places I had to visit, to acknowledge everyone and renew with them and their new interests. Then I was told that it was time to consider my own new direction.

I found myself in my Sanctuary, and although this was not the very first time I had visited it, I realized in a most natural way that here was where I felt the happiest to settle. For a while, I was given time and solitude to think and make my choices.

-//-

Isabelle was going back to work early Monday morning, following the enchanting weekend she spent with Gérard. She was still under the spell of their renewed love, felt rested and confident in a new era of happiness and success. She was humming the song Gérard had played for her on the beach last Friday night, 'The Ceremony'.

She was driving on a straight two-lane road, approaching the medical center where her office was located. A few cars were going in both directions at this early morning hour, and she was almost there - her office building was already visible. She was concentrating on the files she would review before anyone else arrived at work.

Larry and Josh were two college students taking a few days off to come to the beach and party hard before going back to their graduate school in Boston. With the weather turning cold soon in the north, they decided to make the most of their time in this beautiful resort area, snorkeling, surfing, and partying.

Their hotel was directly on the beach, and they first started drinking at the hotel bar, then at a nearby nightclub, and then directly on the beach. They felt responsible since they did not have to drive to get back to their hotel room, although they had more than their share of alcohol in their system.

Young, feeling bulletproof and invisible, they hooked up with some girls, ready to continue the party at another location. Their judgment, clouded by liquor, allowed them to agree to go along. They went to a club near the small town center, the hottest new bar around. With the night well advanced toward Monday morning, there were only a few cars on the road and only vacationers in the club.

When the bar closed at three in the morning, they were all excited and talking loudly with other young people they met, not ready yet to call it a night. Their company had grown by then to seven or eight and they decided to continue the party and the drinking back on the beach.

Three other young men came along. They were tough military guys appreciating some well-deserved R&R upon return from Afghanistan, where they had been deprived for months from any comfort or leisure. The two boys from Boston were unhappy to see that the two girls they had met at the beach now showed a lot of interest in the marines. Some words started to be exchanged, but the girls intervened, as the military guys had more interesting stories to tell, and the young women argued that this should be a good education for all of them.

Larry and Josh left the party at the beach and jumped in their car, half asleep, and half wanting to continue the night somewhere else. They were considering their options, and, as the sun had started rising, they noticed the girls leaving the beach and getting into the marines' Jeep. It took the military guys a little time until they could restart their vehicle, but finally they moved slowly toward the main road.

The curiosity of the young men from Boston was piqued by now, and they decided to follow them from a distance. The Jeep driven by the marines slowed at the approach to gas stations, but they were all closed. When they finally found one open, they stopped to fill their tank. The marines were aware of the two students from Boston on their trail and decided to have some fun and play one of the tricks learned during tactic training and used sometimes while in the war zone.

After making the fill of gas, the Jeep took a sharp turn in one of the side roads, and then stopped and hid behind a building.

The trick worked and the two college students soon showed up, zooming past in their massive Ranger truck. The marines let them pass, and then pulled behind them. From there, a chase started, at first for the fun of it, and then some obscenities were exchanged. Everyone wanted to have the last word and be the first in line. There weren't too many cars on the road yet, so the race continued, the students animated by the frustration of having the girls won over by the newcomers, and the marines playing the winners, wanting to teach the civilians a little humility lesson.

Gaining more speed, the marines were in front now, after passing each other several times. Pushing the engine to the maximum, the college students gunned the engine and went to the left into the incoming line, trying to pass the Jeep. When they saw Isabelle's car approaching, it was too late for them to pull back, now almost at the level of the car they tried to pass. It took only a second for the head-on collision to occur, but it seemed a lot longer when lived in slow motion by the students. Unfortunately, Isabelle did not have much time to see, nor to react, when the massive truck appeared from nowhere in front of her and hit her at high speed.

The crash made an enormous noise like an explosion blasting in the quiet morning. The marines' vehicle suffered only minor damage, while the students' ranger seemed untouched, but it was now lying almost on top of Isabelle's little two-seat BMW. The young men that raced just a few instants before, along with the two women, came out quickly from both cars, brutally awakened and terrified by the sudden accident.

The girls were crying and screaming hysterically, the college students acted like zombies stricken by the enormity of what had just occurred, and the marines rapidly went to find out how to extract the unfortunate passenger from under the truck. Soon they realized that they were in proximity of a hospital and some of the doctors and morning shift nurses' cars were stopped by the roadblock created by the accident.

Dr. Angel Mendoza, neurosurgeon and friend of the Forrest's, came out of his car, concerned about the person trapped under the truck. He was not able to see much of the car, nor the driver, but as soon as an ambulance was there and a fire truck showed up, the rescue drill was on the way.

-//-

Gérard was sitting alone in a pew in the small chapel of the hospital, praying. He was in a state of total shock, holding the blue cotton dress Isabelle was wearing at the time of the accident. This was all he had obtained from the emergency room; a simple but elegant dress now in pieces and soaked in blood, ripped by the metal that had gone through her body, and cut off by the ER nurses to free her body to the doctors' care.

He was aware that she was in surgery and three of the best trauma doctors were trying to save her. Many of the hospital staff knew Isabelle and admired her and they considered her and her husband, Gérard Forrest, as friends. There was a neurosurgeon, Doctor Mendoza, who was at the site of the accident, then an orthopedic trauma surgeon, and finally a cardio thoracic specialist, since Isabelle was already identified not only with head injuries, but also with a crushed thoracic cage and massive lungs and other internal organs damage.

The hematology department was preparing to collect more blood units, as the ones in reserve were almost all gone. Isabelle had a rare blood type, AB+, and Gérard was already prepared to give his blood, being a blood type O- and, therefore, a universal donor.

In total agony, Gérard prayed desperately, the only thing he could do, refusing to think that his wife could not be saved. He implored and begged God, repeating that he and Isabelle were made to be together forever and that God would not allow, in His greatness, for them to be separated. He even attached more hope saying that the doctor's name operating now and trying to save Isabelle, was Angel.

Many hours went by, when dreadful torturing times were alternating with high hopes. Like a pendulum, Gérard's feelings oscillated from conviction that his wife was strong and healthy, to complete despair; from assurance that she was in the most expert hands, to the excruciating worry of losing her. He was in an altered state, where time was at a standstill and no other feelings could fill the emptiness except that Isabelle would be fine, and that all would return to the way things were before.

During this time, the team of surgeons and nurses were trying their best to attend to Isabelle's injuries. There was a massive internal bleed, and three units of blood were already transfused to avoid cardiac failure and brain deprivation from the lack of oxygen supply. An endotracheal tube was already in place pumping enriched air into her lungs trying to keep them inflated, while chest tubes were placed to drain the blood that was quickly accumulating where the lung tissue had already collapsed.

They found that the sternum and many ribs in the central area of the chest had been crushed, creating large bruises to the pericardium that in turn started filling up with blood, which enveloping the heart was now constricting the pumping chambers. There were quickly more tubes placed to empty the pericardial fluid, while the initial skull x-rays taken on arrival, showed the left occipital area sunken and compressing the back of the brain, the brainstem, and the emerging spinal cord.

Dr. Angel Mendoza had already made a Burr hole to decrease the intracranial pressure and was gently removing the broken pieces of skull. The on-call anesthesiologist made attempts to give the smallest possible anesthetic amount intended to avoid depressing the brain function even more, and followed frantically the vital signs displayed by the monitors.

Doctors, nurses, and technicians were all working with concentration and precision, after the initial horror of seeing one of their most beloved staff members brought to their own ER. A medical evacuation helicopter was on standby to transport the wounded doctor to a larger trauma center as soon as she was stabilized enough to sustain the flight. They all fought to save Isabelle, and they all prayed.

It was getting late into lunch hours, and many friends of the Forrests had learned about the accident and were coming to the hospital. The lobby was filling with people and many of the hospital staff themselves stopped by periodically to gather more news, all wishing they could do something to help.

Gérard barely noticed Paul coming into the chapel bringing with him a large cup of coffee, and nodded automatically at his greetings and words of encouragement. Letting out a sigh, he sat back on the chair and accepted to drink some coffee.

At long last, the door of the operating area opened and Dr. Mendoza appeared. Looking for Gérard, he made his way through the crowd asking for Mr. Forrest, and he was shown the direction of the chapel.

The doctor entered slowly and quietly closed the door behind him. Gérard bounded to his feet and with great expectation looked at him, then stopped at the sad expression he saw on Angel's face.

Dr. Mendoza could only whisper, "I am so sorry, Gérard, so very sorry". It took him a few seconds to grasp the sense of these words, but they seemed to last for hours, then Dr. Mendoza, Angel, the family friend, caught Gérard in his arms as he passed out.

-//-

As Isabelle sat in the Sanctuary. She felt this was a temporary place where she was being left alone to contemplate her last decision: going back to her earthy life or staying in Heaven. One by one, important moments in her life passed before her eyes; happy and important moments, or just small details of situations she had forgotten. In awe, she remembered the time of her arrival on Earth, when her mother and father tenderly saw her for the first time.

Then she saw herself as a baby, a toddler, at kindergarten, and eventually graduating from high school. She was amazed she could read her own thoughts as she was presented with these images and to see how much she could understand of reality, even though just a baby, hearing and being entirely part of situations as they were shown to her now.

She could see her older brother, when they were playing together, their rooms and their birthday parties. She saw herself growing into this remarkable person and choosing science over relying on her looks in life. She felt again her thirst for knowledge, and her passion to expand her views of the world. Ultimately, she remembered her commitment to contribute in her modest way to the good of mankind.

So many happy times appeared in front of her; unique moments when she met Gérard, them falling in love, and the ecstasy of their wedding when they felt like they were walking on clouds. Then she cried again with joy at the birth of her daughter, Marina, this time not feeling any pain, but only the bliss of becoming a mother. She could better appreciate now the frenetic activities of her busy young parent life as a spectator only, and laughed and cried at the sight of the children's games, visits to the doctor's office, or holidays with the family. Isabelle was pleased to see that their couple overcame all the difficulties and sadness life presented them with, in situations that at the time, appeared insurmountable.

Then, it was shown the episode when, in a discussion with friends not so long back, she expressed the desire never to come back to life on Earth. This time, the words she spoke then resonated in a more profound way, as a choice made for the future, as a statement that would decide what would happen when the time of reckoning came.

However, very quickly the scenery changed, and Isabelle was now presented with the vision of herself in the future, back on Earth. And what she saw filled her with the worst fright she ever experienced. She was in a light coma state for months now, and somehow, she was aware that this situation was to remain unchanged for as long as she lived.

For many more years to come, she would slowly deteriorate, become more emaciated, contractures would deform her body and limbs, and tubes everywhere would maintain her in an artificial state of life. Isabelle could see through her body now and all her knowledge as a doctor permitted her to evaluate the extent of the damage done to her body: her brain had sustained injuries to the areas controlling her vision; she was completely blind, but most importantly her brainstem was irreversibly destroyed.

She was not able to breathe on her own, as the automatic control center of the brainstem along with the first segments of the cord were severed, and there was no motor function of any kind in her body from the base of her neck and below. The respiratory muscles, diaphragm, lungs, arms, and legs could not respond to basic movements or activities. She could only move her eyes but she could not see, she could open her mouth but she had lost her ability to talk or to react. And above all, Isabelle had strangely kept the sense of being alive but unable to communicate any of her thoughts, feelings, or the intense pain that was constantly torturing her body.

The shock of this atrocious vision was so unexpected and so intense, that it made Isabelle shiver with horror, and without any hesitation she cried out and aloud her decision. She would not live in a vegetated state, with no purpose, no joy, only to prolong an agony for herself and for the ones she loved the most. In fact, she was more frightened to impose this horrible existence on her husband than on herself, feeling that she wanted to free him from her suffering and let him have a future, a new life of his own, and, by all means, to find love again.

While Isabelle was in between the two worlds, an excruciating pain ripped through her entire body and she screamed out her pain and her rejection of returning in a gigantic "Noooo..." Her scream traveled the space and time and reached the one shouted at the same time by Gérard at the same moment he received the news of his wife's death.

BOOK THREE

I settled in my Sanctuary, which became my chosen place in Heaven, and where I could dedicate myself to rescuing the wounded and abused creatures of all kinds as they came back home. It was natural to find a place that fitted the description of a newfound paradise, where the beauty, the peace, and the satisfaction in my work provided me with a blissful new existence.

It must have been quite some time that I was there, although I did not feel or could not estimate the passing of time. All this concept of time appeared to me now without importance, since I was here to stay for eternity. This made me feel entirely content. I did not need anything to be different, although all that I could want appeared instantaneously before me, or I could appear in a place with the speed of my thoughts only. I discovered I never felt hunger or thirst, although I could enjoy a special dish or a meal if I had the impulse to prepare it or feel the pleasure of it, and all was easy and fun to obtain. The same way I never felt sad or lonely, for I remained in a state of pure satisfaction, elated to have no time or place barriers, be with loved ones when I felt the desire, or get no intrusion if I needed time for myself. All pain of the body or struggle of the heart disappeared.

All was, or I better say is, perfect here, with the décor that could take the most incredible aspects of the imagination with forms, colors, and textures I never saw before on Earth. My feelings could trigger the space surrounding me to produce sounds of voices or of musical instruments playing symphonies or songs I remembered sometimes in my dreams. I particularly enjoyed being entirely liberated from gravity, able to flow in all directions I wanted, up and down, or glide if I did not want to walk. I felt like I could dance or sing anything I wanted, and felt like "the happiest person in Heaven."

The most astonishing thing I found from the beginning was that just upon arriving here, one received an enormous amount of knowledge. Suddenly everything made sense, we feel like recognizing a place we just left, and the way the Universe functions is as natural as is the Creation itself. What we still needed to learn, surprisingly, was the very reason we were on Earth, the reason certain things happened, and why injustice and cruelty were possible there.

We needed to better understand who we were as soul travelers, what our own divine essence was, and what we were supposed to accomplish and learn during our journeys through terrestrial lives. During this process, we sorted out our relationships and, with newly discovered patience, we tried to understand how the reactions of others had affected our past lives. We also reconnected with those we had known during other existences, and were instantly aware of who they were and the way we were related to them.

Another celestial gift we were granted is the ability to get close to the ones we had left behind at any time; we could pray for them and send them our love, even to protect them with warnings or divine inspirations. Yet, we could not, as we were already aware from the beginning, change their destiny, or make a choice for them.

-//-

In my travels back to Earth, I attended my own funeral, and it was a strange feeling to see my loved ones' sorrow and anguish, when at the same time I wanted them to know that I was happy and at peace. Touched by their testimony of love, my desire was for them to be happy, to enjoy every bit of the holiness given throughout this existence. I continued to feel this close connection and supreme and eternal love towards my husband, as I was aware that we would be united again for we were meant to be together forever.

I saw Gérard during the burial preparations moving in a trance, despair and misery written on his face and in his actions. He was doing his best to honor the memory of his wife and, in spite of all this tragedy, trying to comfort the children and relatives. And everyone was making efforts to help him through his enormous grief.

I was there, with him when alone at night, he sank into his misery, not wanting anyone around, and not responding to phone calls or any kind of messages.

And I would continue to be there as long as he needed me.

-//-

Gérard had the hardest time facing these events, all happening so fast and throwing him off balance without time to recover. He had the impression of falling and being knocked out again, before he could get back on his feet. Friends' and family's attention helped and he appreciated them with the practical issues that required immediate attention. But he was in agony when confronted with decisions for the choice of funeral home, memorial service, or signing and registering the death certificate. At times, in spite of his best efforts, he felt as he could not deal with any of that. Somehow, he found the strength to manage it all, as he was too proud to show how desperate he felt inside.

Family members came to town and Gérard made arrangements for their stays. Somewhat, this helped him keep his mind occupied. Flowers arrived by small vans from the local florists, who were busier than they had been in a long time. Everyone wanted to express their regret, as the whole small community mourned. Close and distant family members, colleagues, friends, patients, and simple acquaintances flocked to the funeral parlor long before the announced viewing time.

One of the most difficult moments for Gérard was when he had to bring some clothes for Isabelle to wear in the coffin. Marina had already arrived, accompanied by Gunter and little Benjamin, and Gérard asked her to help with this wrenching task. Stricken with grief, they both browsed Isabelle's dressing room, crying without retention in the intimacy of her personal objects, still feeling her presence, smelling her perfumes and touching her dresses, all bringing back so many sweet memories. Finally, they settled for the simple and beautiful light cotton and lace dress she wore on the beach in Bora Bora when Gérard and Isabelle renewed their vows.

From there, everything was like a bad dream for them. The viewing displayed an Isabelle that was calm and at peace, her porcelain complexion now turned into alabaster. Everyone admired for one last time her beautiful face and hands. But what very few knew, was that the mortician did a great job reassembling as best he could all the parts of her body which was torn to pieces, all hidden beneath her pretty dress.

Gérard was shaken by Marina's resemblance to her mother; she was still tall and regal in her demeanor, but she had lost so much weight and looked tiny, confused, and crushed with sorrow. Their minister delivered an emotional service and eulogy. Although sad, they did their best to celebrate Isabelle's joy of life. However, the hardest time for Gérard was when, at last, the coffin closed over Isabelle's body and she was slowly lowered to her final resting place. He remembered her telling him that when she died what she feared the most was to be left alone under the ground in the dark. He stayed a very long time by the grave site, talking to her and telling her that she would always be with him, and that he took her in his heart and he would keep her there, forever safe.

Friends came, and gently, respectful of his suffering, finally managed to bring him home, where many participated in creating a wonderful reception in memory of their beloved friend. Everyone tried to change the mood by telling true stories of happy and even hilarious times they had spent with Isabelle. Finally, Marina softly walked Gérard to his bedroom, and after she made sure he was ready for some rest, closed the door quietly, but stayed close by and checked on him from time to time. When the guests left, the family members retired to their rooms exhausted and in need of some sleep. Gérard did not know how long he slept, but when he woke up he had to attend to other daily routines or obligations, which kept him distracted only a few moments at a time.

Then the time came when Marina and her husband, along with Patrick and his family, were called back to their careers and obligations, and they had to leave. They were still very worried about Gérard and left with promises he would answer to their phone calls and messages through Skype.

For a long time, Gérard faced the sudden quiet of the house, wandering from room to room, from back to front of the property, followed by their cats and Duke, their dog, who understood that their master needed time to heal. Little by little, Gérard had to go back to a semblance of regular life, and slowly, absent-mindedly, he settled into simple but necessary routines.

-//-

I found out that my Sanctuary was as large as I intended it to be, as I could carry it with me wherever I was going and wanted my chosen heaven to follow. I marveled endlessly at how perfect everything was, although new friends were coming constantly and most of them needed care. Most recovered quickly and were soon young and beautiful again, enjoying an idyllic eternal life, where love and happiness was the rule, and where all got along completely. With ease, I could help them regain great health in no time, and added more and more companions to my Sanctuary.

Indeed, my heart was rejoicing at the sight of wild animals like lions and tigers playing delicately and making new friends with antelopes and does. They did not have to chase or hunt for food, since all was displayed at the single thought or need. And no one was hungry, only the newly arrived kept some of the cravings from physical deprivation, after having suffered from all kind of afflictions while on Earth. But soon, given attention, plenty of food, and unlimited love, they were replenished and felt completely satisfied.

I also encountered the most beautiful birds, butterflies of incredible designs or colors flying close by, and marine life that I found mysterious and fascinating. The music of the birds was mixed with that of the wind flowing in the branches, and chimes of all kinds made their own symphonies. I admired a constant display of flowers and trees, brushes and green lawns, mountains and rivers, cascades and beaches, and the most spectacular galaxies that drew a gigantic aurora borealis of color in the sky I never even knew existed. Everywhere colors seemed brighter and had a life of their own. However, I could name any animal, plant, or constellation, and I instantly and wholly knew how they were created, their purpose or their mode of function.

Another important thing that I learned was the way I could relate with other persons. My parents were young and caring, always available, and we had the most loving relationship, continuing the connections the way we had always wished to maintain on Earth. We knew that we had all eternity to see each other, so we did not have to constantly be together. To the contrary, they encouraged me to go on and learn and enjoy my new "freedom." Thus, I learned about my former lives and how much we all stayed connected in one way or the other. Along the way, I learned how and why some people were so important in a given life, and why they touched or marked mine during that particular existence.

Upon my arrival in Heaven, I slowly met guides and teachers that could have been angels or initiated spirits evolved enough to be part of the higher wisdom. I had many questions about the reasons for injustice, cruelty, disease, and unhappiness, and while many were answered, I realized how much more I still had to learn from them. Somewhere, deep in my soul, I found some answers, as though they were always there. All was tightly linked with the reason for us being on Earth, the reason that we solely made the choice of why and how we were to accomplish what was the purpose of that particular life. Ultimately, that purpose was to evolve, to achieve perfection on having to overcome the limitation of a physical dimension of a low energy such as the constraints of a terrestrial life; it is to be as perfect as the soul that has been given to us as a birth present. And, if need is, to come back again and again, to repair the mistakes or the mal-doing, until the body is completely liberated and united with the soul.

I also learned that the evolution could continue towards higher and higher levels, to as many dimensions that coexisted, and room is given to anyone to experience them and to reach superior levels of understanding, then choose to stay at the energy level one feels comfortable with. All was open and acceptable, with the Creator embracing everyone, with no person considered superior to another.

In fact, Heaven is in many ways a celebration of attaining a perfect state of happiness, knowledge, and purity, for the diversity of God's creation is infinite. Here I had the confirmation that there was a creation and an infinitely loving Father, our Creator, who accepted our differences because He created them. He is also infinitely above the small and limited vision of our egotistic impositions of how we see Him, how we name Him, or even how we celebrate Him. And seeing Him laugh at our childish arguments made me laugh with Him, realizing what a waste of time and anguish we inflict on each other, when all was so simple.

It all comes down to what we have already heard back on Earth: just show love. When one comes back for another life on Earth, that person is a little part of what He wants us to re-establish during our earthly existence: all to learn that harmony and love must prevail over hatred, harm, revenge, and ego. For humans, the thing to learn during the trials of a new life is of how to turn hurt done to you and the desire to pay it back, into a way to get along and find serenity.

Only pardon would stop the violence and suffering and allow time for healing. Then mankind could discover the bliss of living in harmony, better knowing, appreciating, and helping each other.

-//-

Gérard made all efforts to go on with his life. With the help of attentive friends and loving contact with his children, who, although far away, called frequently to check on him, he managed to carry on one day, one night at a time.

There were days when he fell into total despair, walking through the house, touching Isabelle's harp or desk or burying his head in her clothes in an attempt to revive memories of her. Oh, how much he wanted to hold her tight in his arms, never let her go, to protect her and make sure she stayed alive, always by his side.

He was also going through rage spells of wanting revenge for what was done to her, for having her taken away from him and from their life together. He could not forgive the reckless behavior of the youths that had led to this stupid and meaningless accident that had deprived him forever of the love of his life. Gérard was consumed by thoughts of making sure that the drivers of the two cars be punished, as they deserved.

Meanwhile, he was a ghost in his own house, disregarding the usual times of eating or sleeping, did not feel cold or warm weather, and became ill and shivered with fever without treating it. He lost so much weight, hardly had any clothes that fit him, and depression took hold of him. Little by little, Gérard started giving up. He did not return phone calls anymore, when friends invited him he would promise to get together, but he rarely showed up.

After a while, neglect became visible and the bills were unpaid, the house and the garden were unkempt. Fortunately, Marina started to suspect that all was not going well and came to Florida to care for her father. In fact, she, herself, did not have time to grieve; her family and professional obligations had swallowed her as soon as she arrived in New York. Together, they comforted each other, and finally some order returned in the household. Marina left only after she was reassured that her father was on the way to recovery, and she gave herself a little time to somewhat accept her mother's passing. However, she also had a family, many years of happiness ahead of her to share with loved ones, and she was young and resilient.

After Marina went back to New York, Gérard managed for a while to accept his new existence. He remained sad and isolated, but was more angry and indifferent. However, he experienced periods of neglect and self-destruction, and finally let his health deteriorate, allowed his anger to explode, and his misery take over him completely.

-//-

My sanctuary was my rediscovered Heaven. It was the way I imagined my Heaven, even more perfect and more beautiful than I could expect, making me immensely happy. Everyone else had 'their Heaven', fashioned according to each one's idea of how their perfect place in the afterlife should be.

We all could go and visit each other and stay as long as we desired. We also could change at any time our picture of our Heaven and our talents and the occupations we wanted to pursue.

More importantly, we could co-exist in our Heaven with any other place on Earth or any other corner of the Universe. This way, I chose to place my Heaven where Gérard lived. Our existences were superimposed, and mixed together. There was no time, only different dimensions, but they were contained in the same space, blending together. Mine was luminous, expanding to the infinity of the blue sky, while his was restricted and dark. I saw him and answered him when he talked to me, his sadness affected me and I constantly sent him waves of loving energy when he did not take care of himself, because my desire was for him to be happy. I wanted him to remember the times we were happy together, for this was the reason we were united in this lifetime. I tried to tell him when I saw him crying that this was not the way I wished him to think of me.

I also knew that I would stay here as long as he needed me. My Heaven and his Hell would remain intertwined, as my Heaven was there to lessen his Hell, my Rediscovered Heaven.

BOOK FOUR

Gérard and Isabelle met in Europe and married shortly after they met in Paris, France. Their love seemed like a fairytale right out of a children's book to anyone who asked how they first met.

Isabelle stood apart from other children of her generation because of her intense focus on everything that was cultural and scientific. She concentrated on building a career based only on her intellectual abilities.

She remained unaware of the effect she made every time she entered a place, thanks to her grace and beauty, although her friends were always surprised and puzzled by her kind and unassuming manners when they approached her. Since she was very young, Isabelle knew what she wanted, was determined and organized, taking complete control of her pastime. She selected precisely what concerts she wanted to attend, what exhibit was the latest of interest at the museums, and her playground was The Louvre, Grand and Petit Palais, Comédie Française, and The Opéra House, where she went frequently. When she was a little girl she liked going either to the concerts held at Salle Playel, or to some other concert hall or church, where she would quietly wait by the entrance. Most of the controllers, who knew her by name, would usually let her "sneak" in just before the concert was to start, leading her inside with an amused nod and pat on the shoulder.

Isabelle had remained all these years, since her childhood until her mid-twenties, an unusual person, gifted and beautiful, distant and reserved, considered almost untouchable by the young men. Most of them admired her, but they were intimidated and felt awkward in her presence. Although Isabelle was almost hypersensitive and capable of profound feelings for others, she kept herself private, instinctively trying to protect herself from getting hurt.

Women's emancipation in France was achieved slowly but surely over the centuries. Practically all kings had steady and powerful mistresses, initially sought after for their great beauty and youth, who were often kept at court for their exquisite manners and supreme "savoir faire", but also because their understanding in the finesse of political strategies of their time. During the time of Louis XIV, Louis XV, and other kings, the expression implying that behind every great man was a great woman, "cherchez la femme" (look for the woman), was the rule.

Exceptional women like Madame de Pompadour, friend of Voltaire and patron of the arts, to whom has also been given the surname *reignette*, little queen, remained at the court of France until her death. She acted behind the scenes and continued to be highly appreciated by Louis XV for her grace, wisdom, and consumed perception of international intrigues.

Diane de Poitiers was at first part of the court of Francis I, and later became a lifelong companion of his son, Henry II, although she was 20 years older. Women like Diane were highly educated, not only capable of reading in Latin and Greek, but they were essential to court life with their knowledge of languages, music, dancing, and the art of conversation, and they were often skillful at hunting. Diane de Poitiers remained beautiful into her 50's and her name was often associated with the Roman goddess of the moon. Because of her political shrewdness and her sharp intellect, Diane was closely involved in the court decisions, and King Henry II charged her to write many of the official letters, some jointly signed as "HenriDiane". Because her influence was so far reaching, it was said that even Pope Paul III presented her with a necklace of pearls, a gift of considerable value for the time.

Women have always been part of the public life of the French people; they came down into the streets along with the men during the French Revolution, they claimed their own gender recognition and identity as a person. Assuming a professional career, French women continued to remain attractive and refined in the way they dressed, coifed, or accessorized. They introduced refineries such as everyday use of perfumes, and pushed the fashion to the level of international corporations.

It is understood that a young man or a young woman that belonged to the bourgeoisie, the French middle class, were expected to have a profession, and to continue their education, be it technical or academic. Along with her physical appearance, a French woman had the privilege or obligation, passed on by social traditions, to remain seductive while also being expected to be an excellent mother, a partner and a mistress to her husband. Social manners, sometimes regarded by foreigners as a little bit snobbish, were, in reality, expressed in a very natural way of customary living, bringing the French etiquette as the standard of diplomatic interactions.

Raised in a traditional Parisian family, Isabelle had known as a child, then as a young woman, a more conservative kind of life than one would expect. Becoming a young adult and financially independent, she could have taken her own flat in town, but she continued to occupy her place in her parents' old, but spacious apartment in St. Germain de Prés. This situation accommodated Isabelle as well, particularly in the first years of medical school, when the academic classes were held in the big amphitheater of one of the oldest universities in Rue des Saints Pères, close to her parents' apartment. This never surprised anybody, as most young people stayed with their parents until they got married or had to move away for work.

Paris being a city of many universities, it facilitates the access to college education to high school graduates, thus young people found that staying home with their parents made their attendance easier and more affordable. It is why, in the western European culture, little is known of college drinking or hazing, and, while the university system is based on academic achievements with affordable tuitions, in exchange there is a strong competition to succeed, leaving little time or interest for too much partying.

Due to her training years in the scientific field, Isabelle had an unforgiving schedule, and her total attention and dedication were part of the success in her studies. At times, she had to spend many nights away from home during her calls in the hospitals as an intern, and later as a full staff medical doctor.

By 26, after obtaining a doctorate degree in biology and genetics at the University of Sorbonne and then graduating from the Marie and Pierre Curie University of Medicine in Paris. Isabelle was working in neurophysiological research programs. She was considered to have a promising future, both as a clinician and researcher in the field of repairing neurological injuries of the brain and spinal cord. During her studies, Isabelle displayed exceptional aptitudes of concentration and ability to absorb tremendous amounts of information.

Because of her absolute commitment to her studies, she completed her academic requirements much earlier than usual and graduated ahead of her class. Her passion for science and new discoveries in the functioning and healing of the human body, kept her from the usual distractions of friends of same age. Complying with the requirements of her profession, she would go without taking time off for vacations, weekends, or even holidays, but this represented little sacrifice compared to her desire to expand her knowledge.

However, during all these years Isabelle did realize how much she needed the protection of her family. Her highly educated and financially restricted parents, were appreciated by a small elite of famous artists. She grew up with her older brother, Eric, whom she adored. The Beaumonts belonged to an old family with origins that came from across Europe, and included anything from landlords to trade merchants along the Meuse, Rhine and Danube, to impoverished nobles still living their dreams lost in their artwork, like her parents who had adopted a more bohemian lifestyle.

This made for an unusual combination of recognized and celebrated artists in high levels of society, who mingled with philosophers, writers, academicians and scientists. This way, the "Montmartre spirit" of starving artists coming from all over the world taking their chance, was kept alive. Ardent followers gathered in some of the Parisian salons and debated passionately on a variety of subjects.

Their family diversity made the relations amongst some of them quite strenuous. After the devastation of

World War II inflicted on Europe, some family members found themselves thrown into either German or Russian concentration camps, as they got caught in opposite sides of the war, and alas, many of them disappeared. Few survived such a tragedy, and Isabelle's family was a small island left, setting up camp during and after the war in the southwest of France and northern Italy. The grandparents died when they went to save some merchandise they had stored in outposts along the Danube estuary entering the Black Sea, killed by Russians who came as "liberators" of Eastern Europe.

Isabelle was a lover of nature and enjoyed spending time at the family property in Rambouillet, but she did not feel like a spoiled, mid-upper class child. Her family could refer to memories of better glory, but their sense of tradition and their natural class prevented them from the need of displaying wealth in order to establish their origin or value. Isabelle could recall when she lived in the family castle in the south of France, lost long ago to pay the debts accumulated after World War II, when most of the family had disappeared or dispersed across Europe.

After that, her parents gave up legal actions in the European courts intended to regain the family's scattered possessions, and continued to live a more "artistique" life. Nonetheless, there were still plenty of mementoes and collectibles of family memories in the summerhouse in Rambouillet and in their apartment in Paris.

Isabelle had only two boyfriends before she met Gérard; during her junior and senior high school years, when she was also following the musical education at the Conservatory in Paris, a very special and tender friendship grew between her and a colleague who showed up at the same concerts she attended. Although Eduard was completely taken by Isabelle's remarkable beauty, he deeply admired her talent and fondness for music, and fell in love with her. Isabelle, however, considered Eduard just that, a very special friend, and their friendship was to remain this way their entire lives.

Later, Isabelle had a love affair with a doctor, a romance that developed over the long years of their medical studies. They shared for a long time a slowly growing complicity, and while it became an attraction for Isabelle, Pierre had felt a true passion for her all along. Establishing a solid foundation in her romantic relations, Isabelle needed to share also common interests.

With time, Pierre became more insecure in his abilities to maintain Isabelle's interest in him, since she was more interested in following her career and was driven to reach the goals she set ahead of her. When Pierre lost his confidence and became somewhat jealous, Isabelle broke up with him, tired of continuously trying to reassure him. They remained good friends, however, and at the time Isabelle met Gérard, romantic relationships had no appeal to her.

Now part of a research team at the Institute Pasteur, Isabelle was involved in a program that aimed to restore tissues using stem cells. She was also seeing patients at the institute's clinic and during hospital rounds, where she supervised the response of recipients to the new treatments. She loved interacting and closely following the results of these advanced methods, proven almost miraculous for the skin repair when used for burns or multiple trauma patients.

The restoration of the neurological tissues was in the early stages of development with a newly started program, making Isabelle most enthusiastic and passionate at the encouraging prospective of using a patient's own stem cells. Isabelle realized how much was to be done in the future for the repair of damaged organs and tissues, and, in particular, for the structures of the brain and the spinal cord. And this became an interest that would last her entire life.

-//-

It was a June day in Paris, one of those days when everyone wanted to be on the street, enjoying the beautiful scenery and its vibrant energy. Quite out of the ordinary, Isabelle felt that same impulse to leave behind the work at the laboratory and to go out and refresh her spirit. She had turned 27 years around Christmas and her life was almost entirely dedicated to her scientific profession, leaving little time for relaxation. She would find, however, leisure time for music and the rich cultural life around her, along with the moments spent with her family. From time to time, Isabelle would succumb to the need for a break and take a short trip to clear her mind and immerse herself in the beauty of many places available around Paris.

A weekend in Giverny would give her the pleasure of walking inside the actual gardens painted by Claude Monet, or feel the thrill and excitement of the light, waterfalls and music shows in the spectacular and immense gardens of the Versailles Palace. Once, just before competing for her Sorbonne specialty training, she left for Rome where she spent the weekend, and came back relaxed and rested to pass the merciless examinations with flying colors.

Isabelle, feeling this rare desire to listen to her impulses, checked her schedule and found that there was nothing she could not leave behind for a while. With a light heart matching her steps, she went out. She decided to visit the splendid exhibition of Velazquez that had recently opened at the Grand Palais, after a stop in the inner court of the Louvre.

Arriving in front of the glass pyramid in the Louvre courtyard, she wandered around like the many visitors, then stopped at one of the numerous stands. There, she bought a deliciously smelling *croque monsieur*, a combination made of toasted French bread and cheese, added a small bottle of Evian water, then directed her steps across the square towards the Gardens of Tuileries. Here, she sat on a bench close to the open-air museum made of statues by Rodin and facing the Arc de Triomphe du Carrousel, the beautiful stone arch topped by four horses and built as part of Napoleon's urban concept. As she had done many times in the past, she admired the endless beauty unfolding in front of her.

Looking past the Carrousel, her gaze embraced the expanding gardens with infinity pools, bordered by the artfully drawn geometry of the Jardin de Tuileries. Ending the Tuileries on each side and facing the Place de la Concorde, stood the two famous pavilions, Jeu de Paume and Orangerie, housing French impressionist artwork. Further along more gardens hosted the Grand and Petit Palais and Palais de la Découverte, and beyond was Place Clémenceau.

Her eyes followed this final dramatic progression, the splendor of the Avenue des Champs Élysées, culminating at the top with the grand Arc de Triomphe sitting in the middle of the Place de L'Étoile, the star square. Isabelle always loved this view, and although it would be hard to walk its entire distance, there was an enchantment for the eyes not only on a brilliant day like this one, but the magic took place on any other day, or when magnificently lit at night.

As she took small bites of her lunch, relaxing at the view of the majestic display in front of her, Isabelle could not help thinking of the words her brother Eric had said last night at the family dinner. "Isabelle, you need to laugh a little more, actually, you should laugh a lot; you are too serious."

Eric, four year her senior, had come home for dinner with his wife, Danielle, and their two children; two little angels Isabelle adored. She hurried back in time from her lab to shower and change, for she would not miss the joy she felt when her brother and his children were around. Marielle was five and Benjamin three, and there was always a competition between her and her parents for hugs and kisses, but the thrill of those moments was a great joy for all of them. Isabelle seemed to have an instinct for approaching children of all ages, as she did not need to make any particular effort to reach and capture those little ones' hearts, the way she did with her own parents and her brother from the moment she came into this world.

Growing up, Isabelle had never been aware of the striking and lasting impression she made upon people. Even now, walking through the crowd or sitting on the bench, people could not help but stare, stopping in their tracks at the sight of this ethereal beauty, surrounded by an aura of her own world. As she remembered the evening before, Isabelle smiled at the thought of the children chasing and following her everywhere, constantly asking questions. Marielle loved to imitate her, trying her clothes on or attempting to walk with her shoes, while Benjamin was totally in love with her, trailing behind Isabelle with adoring eyes and declaring with a cute lisp, "I will marry you next year."

-//-

Gérard Forrest belonged to a southern family that was well established and with deep roots in Virginia, USA. Two different branches of the family were at the origin of the Forrest family. The first was the Newton family who founded Jamestown, first capital of Virginia, and the second, the Comte de Rochambeau, the French protestant branch, who settled on the banks of the St. James River.

The French and British, who colonized the rich land of "The Old Dominion", the first establishment of British America, would inevitably intermarry. One of the descendants of Marie Fouchet and the Comte de Rochambeau married Robert Forrest, one of the relatives of the Newtons, and it was from this lineage that Gérard resulted.

The following generations were exposed to and deeply involved in the rich history and passionate creation of the Commonwealth of Virginia, a result of George Mason's Virginia Declaration of Rights and Thomas Jefferson's Declaration of Independence. Virginia was an instrumental part of the creation of the New World and of the United States of America, producing four out of its five first presidents.

As the independence and peace negotiations were held in Paris, the Forrests became part of a long tradition of diplomats and thanks to their origins, they were raised speaking English and French equally. At the time when the diplomatic language was French, before modern times, when the English language gained a lead internationally, their fluency in French became very valuable in establishing the first diplomatic alliances of the newly formed nation.

The Forrests were surely knowledgeable in politics but they tolerated relatives from opposite parties, and it was not unusual to see them challenging each other in critical political matters during family gatherings. All these debates helped them to sharpen their arguments as they could see the different perspectives when participating in diplomatic negotiations, and ultimately learn how to defend crucial positions without taking them personally.

Gérard went to George Mason University first, and then he completed his education at The University of Virginia with a degree in International Law, followed by E. Walsh School of Foreign Service at Georgetown University in Washington, DC. He also completed an Internship at the Paris School of International Affaires ('Sciences Po') in France.

During his years of training in Washington, DC, at Georgetown University, Gérard met Alicia, a young artist attending on and off some archeology and art classes. They ran into each other at the nearby cafés on the rare occasions when Gérard, at the end of the day, would meet some of his close friends. That gave him also the opportunity to stay in touch with some of his cousins who were enrolled in various academic areas, as most of them were preparing for diplomatic careers. Slowly, he became attracted to this unconventional, carefree girl, living a bohemian life, as many were during those last years of Vietnam War. It was a time when, across America, young generations were protesting the establishment, living a hippy-like, "make love not war" style of life.

They made an unusual couple, Gérard, a young athlete, the confident descendent of a traditional American family, and a free spirited young lady, wearing long flowery dresses, more concerned with attending antiwar marches than thinking of building her own career.

At first, Gérard introduced Alicia to his cousins in Georgetown, and then he took her to his home; he was still living in Washington, DC, in the family mansion. His parents, James Wallace and Laura Forrest, met Alicia during one of their vacations in the US, coming from Italy, where Gérard's father was ambassador. It was early fall of 1974 and Gerald Ford was just taking office after President Nixon's impeachment, and Gérard's father was reconfirmed as American ambassador to Italy. Jim and Laura were casual and cordial during their first family dinner with Gérard's new girlfriend, slightly amused, but tolerant. They felt it was better to let things take care of themselves and see where this relationship would go.

Alicia remained very much involved in her antiwar activities and joined the Student Liberation Movement formed in 1972. Gérard, who was expecting his draft notice any time now, although his beliefs were that the war was wrong, continued to concentrate on finishing his studies and following the family interests in international diplomacy. His relationship with Alicia was passionate in the beginning but they later clashed in fierce arguments. This led him to periods of confusion when Alicia would disappear for days at a time and spent nights in the dormitory of her friends. She was not strange to frequent 'pot' smoking and felt completely free of attachments, without having to give any explanations to anyone about her rebellious nature.

In early 1975, when Gérard barely turned 22, he noticed that Alicia was acting increasingly bizarre, and had discovered she was pregnant. Gérard, a little shocked at first, was moved by the idea of becoming a father, and started making plans for their couple expecting a baby. Soon arguments started, when Alicia considered she had all the rights of a liberated woman, and felt that she was not ready for, nor capable of motherhood. In early April of that year, to top it all, Gérard received his draft notification. He continued to make desperate attempts to convince Alicia to keep the baby and to get married without delay, before he went to Vietnam. Alicia became more detached from Gérard but struck an agreement with him: she would have the baby but not get married.

Since she did not want to remain alone with the baby after Gérard's departure, Alicia started talking about going west, following her friends and returning to California to *her* family. Gérard was in turmoil, devastated at the idea of leaving the future mother alone and not being there for the baby's arrival.

He was torn between his sense of responsibility toward his country and his concern about starting his own family.

Then suddenly, the war ended on April 30, 1975, when Congress voted against increasing funds to supply the South Vietnam offensive support. Gérard was relieved at the idea of having to concentrate only on his family, while Alicia spent more and more time with her friends, occasionally still speaking of her decision to interrupt her pregnancy. But somehow, she lost track of the time running its course, and the baby was determined to live. The mother and the baby were doing great; Alicia looked surprisingly radiant as she gained weight. The extra pounds added to her skinny body were making her look more attractive, but she was getting furious to hear Gérard telling her how well the maternity suited her.

It was maybe the maternal instincts taking over or the peace felt inside her body, but Alicia was more mellow after a few months into her pregnancy. She allowed Gérard to make all the arrangements for the baby's birth, and the expecting mother received the best medical care, while relaxing in the comfort of the apartment provided by him in a residential area of the capital city. They even reached a ceasefire and agreed to work together to give the best chance to the new life about to arrive. However, Alicia pointed out that she was making Gérard a big gift and that she was "sacrificing her freedom", albeit temporarily, to become a mother.

Soon after the baby's birth, a beautiful baby boy they named Patrick Gerald, Alicia began to lose her interest in being a mother. When the baby was six months old and weaned from his mother's nursing, Alicia disappeared, leaving a letter to Gérard, excusing herself for not seeing a future for the three of them together.

Somehow, Gérard was not surprised and from that moment on, threw himself into his new passion of becoming the best possible father for his son. For the years to come, Gérard remained a devoted figure, providing all the love and attention needed for his little boy, and filling the place of two parents. During this time, and under Gérard's and his family's loving attention, Patrick developed more like his father, and a solid bond between the two of them grew deeper each day.

Thus, Gérard found a new and stronger motivation to pursue his career in the diplomatic arena. Due to his extensive knowledge of international law, over the years he became frequently involved in negotiations held within the United Nations. He showed a keen interest in the African, then Serbian camps, and, particularly, in security from any further violence already experienced by the refugees who were mostly women and children. It was a complex and dangerous mission, since he liked to make frequent visits to the most critical areas ravaged by ethnic cleansing.

With time, his presence and ability to quickly assess the situation and find without delay a practical solution, made Gérard well appreciated. His name came up frequently on the list of American representatives who could handle delicate issues. Although quite young, he had shown a keen ability to moderate heated discussions and suggest solutions accepted by the opposite parties, abilities perhaps ingrained in him and passed on from the generations of diplomats in the family.

However, over the years, Gérard managed to maintain a semblance of contact with Alicia, and although she had moved on with her life and her liberal views, she regularly received letters and pictures of Patrick. Gérard kept her abreast of their son's growing up years, from his first steps and baby teeth, to learning how to play ball, ride a bicycle, and what progress he made in school. Alicia soon delayed her reactions to these messages, and by the time Patrick was eight or nine years old, years passed between any bouts of communication were exchanged.

It was very fortunate that Patrick had such a good disposition and was growing up to be a very well-adjusted young boy. All the love and nurturing he needed came from Gérard and his family. Because of this, instead of harboring feelings of rejection by the loss of his mother, Patrick's ties with his father and paternal side of the family developed steadily into a strong and loving bond. When Gérard was called to travel to remote places of the world, Patrick always found under his grandparents' care a natural second home.

-//-

It was a radiant day in this late spring of 1987, and it seemed that Paris had never looked more gorgeous. Avenues and parks displayed their own fashion show with rows of blooming flowers of all colors competing for attention with the unique charm and elegance of Parisians. It was a time when the world was hungry for peace and openness, when Ronald Reagan challenged Mikhail Gorbachev to tear down the Berlin Wall. Pierre Boulez was composing electronic music played by symphonic ensembles, Catherine Deneuve, more beautiful than ever, made a splendid appearance in the "*Agent Double*" film, while Jean-Claude Brialy was starring in "*The Innocents* ".

The talented Zubin Mehta, the Indian conductor, directed orchestras across the planet traveling from his new home, the philharmonic of Florence. He already planned the formation of a series of concerts presenting The Three Tenors, Luciano Pavarotti, Jose Carreras and Placido Domingo.

If one could add a beautiful experience of a cosmopolitan nature to his wish list, he would never forget being in Paris, when the shining sun created a quality of light that was captured by many impressionist painters. From the Jardin de Luxembourg, to the Tuileries, and further up the Champs Élysées, the Gardens of Bagatelle, the forests of Neuilly and Vincennes, and many other avenues and squares in Paris, all radiated colors and designs dispersed by a divine hand. Everyone was filling his souls with all senses, delighting at the view of the colors of Paris, breathing deeply the scent of the blooming linden trees that lined miles of Paris' avenues and boulevards.

On this June day in 1987, around lunch time, on a Friday as a matter of fact, Gérard could not ignore the ever-glorious sight of the Place de la Concorde in front of him, as seen through the shady branches of secular trees from the American Embassy in Paris. For the past few weeks he had been working in the Chancery building where Joe Rodgers was ambassador. Gérard had an office in the next building known as Hôtel Talleyrand, named after Charles Maurice de Talleyrand, bishop and foreign minister under a string of French monarchs from Louis XVI, Napoléon, Louis XVIII, and Louis-Philippe, and who commissioned the beautiful edifice, also contained within the American Embassy grounds.

The baron and banker, James Mayer de Rothschild, later purchased Hôtel Talleyrand and the Hôtel de Pontalba, located close by. Afterward, the two buildings were acquired from the Baron de Rothschild by the United States of America and attached to the Embassy's grounds. These two imposing additions remained privately accessible through the Rue du Faubourg St. Honoré side of the block forming the embassy's compound, while Hôtel de Pontalba was designated as the ambassador's residence.

As a political and cultural attaché, and a member of the American United Nations team, Gérard, now 34, was already shining as a talented young diplomat, with a promising, brilliant future ahead. Besides his busy schedule coordinating the projects developed by the American diplomacy in France, there were significant interconnections with practically all the other American representatives in Europe, including the UN and NATO, in which Gérard continued to remain involved.

During this time, Gérard, in his desire to deepen his understanding of foreign affairs, and thanks to his perfect fluency in French, attended some of the special sections offered at the Institute d'Études Politiques and the École Nationale d'Administration. Here, he frequently met his friend, Jackson McDonald, from Georgetown University where they had both attended the School of Foreign Services in Washington, DC.

They remained in contact over the years, and Jackson, also fluent in French, but also learning Russian, later served as the First Secretary of the Political Affaires in Moscow, before becoming Consul General in Marseilles, France, and Monaco. McDonald filled delicate positions after that as Ambassador of Gambia and Guinea.

Many years had passed since Gérard had become a father and soon after the only parent for Patrick, now 11 years old. Time has passed quickly for Gérard since he assumed this new role, never considering it as an obligation, and completely dedicated to the noble status of parenthood. Gérard, once his studies completed, was fulfilling his diplomatic missions with great passion, encouraged by the steady advancements that made him feel appreciated. He also believed that American interventions abroad could make a positive change in improving other nations' futures.

Patrick adjusted easily to different places, cultures, and languages. His good nature and excitement discovering new ways of living made things not only easier for Gérard's professional obligations, but also revealed in Patrick the heart of an explorer. He shared the same spirit of adventure with his father, as they were experiencing together new places. They felt the same thirst for learning and discovered how diverse the world could be.

They had already built exceptional memories together from going on photo safaris in Zimbabwe, to marveling at the mystery of antique monuments of ancient Greek and Roman empires. More recently, they enjoyed taking short trips into the French countryside, now that they lived in Paris for the last two and a half years. Patrick was enrolled at the International Lycée in Paris, and had decided a few years back he would follow his father's example and become a diplomat.

As Gérard looked out the window at the panorama of the Place de la Concorde, he thought of the telephone call he had the evening before with his parents and Patrick, who, after ending his school year, had gone for a summer vacation at his grandparents' property in Virginia. He had tried to adjust to his temporary "freedom" and quickly reviewed his schedule for the weekend.

Most of his colleagues had gone away early for the weekend to enjoy the endless attractions offered by Paris and its surroundings. He was to attend the ambassador's reception in honor of a military delegation travelling to La Hague for a NATO meeting, but this would not be until 6:00 pm. The day after, Saturday, he was invited to the wedding of his close friend, Lucien Dubois, who had wisely waited until he was 36 years old to tie the knot.

Gérard smiled, remembering their many bachelor jokes. Gérard had fiercely avoided any solid, lengthy relations, while Lucien, who did not hesitate to court any skirt in view, was known as an irresistible philanderer, never hiding his light nature. He met his match when an unexpected stroke of fate caused Lucien to be introduced to Vivianne, 32, and the mother of a six-year-old girl from a previous marriage.

Vivianne was entirely insensitive to Lucien's constant attempts to seduce her, who could not even make her laugh! Soon Lucien was hooked; it might have been her rejection of him that made her more attractive or his stubbornness to face defeat. Regardless, Lucien gained a better understanding of feminine nature in general, and of Vivianne's character in particular. He began to admire this proud woman, who affirmed her independence in everything she did, from raising her daughter alone, to having a very successful career as a journalist for Paris Match Magazine. Not to mention that she was also a very attractive young lady.

And here they were now, the story of many happy endings repeating itself with Lucien and Vivianne. After falling in love and questioning all possibilities for over a year, they were now committing to a new life together, both radiant and full of hope for their future.

"Lucien, is this the guy I knew, swearing he would never get trapped into the boring habits of a domestic life?" Gérard had asked him.

"Well, Gérard, I must say that what you call a *boring life*, I would call a happy life.

"I would definitely recommend it, and you should, above all, find yourself a nice little lady and settle down. Patrick will not stay with you forever, and you know what, Gérard? It is about time, old man."

The wedding would take place in quite elegant settings; now that Lucien was committed, he wanted to offer a grand wedding to his bride at the Interalliée Cercle, considered the most *chic* club in Paris.

Gérard did not know whether it was because everyone had already left for the weekend, or at least for the rest of the day, if they were attending the reception later that day, whether it was the beauty of the day, or the prospect of his good friend's wedding; but whatever it was, it compelled him to call it a day and walk into the City of Light. He thought that it would do him good to continue to the Grand Palais, where an exhibition of the best artwork by Velazquez was being shown.

On an unusual impulse, Gérard told his secretary that all the files were completed and they were ready for the ambassador's signature, and that he would be back in time for the reception. He felt like a little boy as he cut through the magnificent grounds of the Embassy to Avenue Gabriel, where he exited the compound through the gate facing Place de la Concorde.

From there, Gérard went through the gardens of the Champs Élysées, and crossed Place Clémenceau, reaching the Grand Palais in no time at all. It felt good to immerse himself in the sounds of the streets, its crowds, the glorious colors of nature, and the smells of the flowers and shrubs of boxwoods.

Climbing the impressive stairs of the Grand Palais, Gérard entered the museum and slowed down to look around, absorbed by the tranquil mystery of Velazquez' paintings. He admired the many portraits of the nobles from the court of King Filip IV, the portrait of Pope Innocent X, and the more joyful atmosphere present in the "Triumph of Bacchus", better known as "The Drunks". He arrived in front of the last painting made by Velazquez, the painting requested by King Filip IV for the alliance made between Spain and France, sealed by the marriage of Maria Teresa and Louis XIV.

The painting of Infanta Margarita Teresa, one of the highlights of Spanish baroque art, was in front of him, with its delicate, still childish expression of the Infanta. The artful work of light coming from within the painting produced the impression that the future queen of France was stepping out of the frame into a tridimensional space, creating almost an impressionistic effect. After a while, Gérard realized that he was not the only one entranced by the painting.

Sitting on a bench in front of the painting, was another image of another time, almost as a dream creature succeeded to come out from one of the other paintings, lost amongst the other images and not sure of her freedom. From the painting of the Infanta, Gérard now directed his admiration and full attention to this person veiled in her own aura of mystery, but not able to hide an almost unreal beauty.

Gérard noticed her delicate features, her porcelain skin, flowing golden locks, and her beautiful face.

She seemed to be absorbed in her contemplation and oblivious to her surroundings, at ease, but also detached from everything else. Gérard realized in this moment, that he had to know who this endearing creature was.

A few moments later, his contemplation was cut short by a handsome young man who approached the lady of his interest. She gracefully stood up and turned to embrace the newly arrived person. They greeted each other in French and then turned their attention to the painting of the Infanta. As they spoke, Gérard heard her melodious voice say:

"Eric, can you imagine this child bride becoming the queen of the most powerful and sophisticated kingdom of her time in history?"

"Well, do you know that Maria Theresa and Louis the XIV were second cousins, and the Infanta was actually an Archduchess of Austria?"

Isabelle gave her brother a serious look. "Well, how do you know all that?"

Eric looked back at his sister with a mischievous grin, "Louis XIVs father was the brother of Maria Teresa's mother, Elisabeth of France, while her father was the brother of Anne of Austria, Louis XIV's mother.

"You might also want to know that Maria Teresa, later Marie Thérèse Queen of France, was entitled to the throne of Spain as well, until her brother became Charles II of Spain." At this point, Eric sheepishly looked down at a folded brochure he was hiding behind his back. "Actually, I just read it in the catalogue, it is all in here," he said as he handed it to her.

They both burst into a joyous laugh, and Gérard could not help but admire the crystalline tone of her laughter. Doing this, Isabelle took Eric's arm and giggling like two teenagers the two of them left the museum hall and directed their steps toward the exit. Gérard caught a few more words of their conversation.

"Let's have some lunch, I am starving with all this culture," Eric said.

"Sorry, I already had something to eat."

To which Eric answered "We will have dinner at the house, then. And I hope you are coming to the country house for the weekend? It will be splendid weather."

Isabelle's answer fading away, was, "I am afraid I'll stay in town as I am attending a conference…"

Gérard was surprised at how disappointed he felt when the young man approached this delightful creature and how affectionate and in tune with each other they appeared to be. He told himself, "Hey buddy, would you really expect her not to be surrounded by a swarm of suitors?" That thought left him even more puzzled by his reaction, "Anyway, I will find out who she is no matter what," without the slightest idea how or where to start.

-//-

Isabelle woke up Saturday morning happy and refreshed. She'd had a good restful night and was in no hurry to get up as her parents had already left earlier for their summer house in Rambouillet Forest.

Isabelle was thinking of her day ahead, at a conference to attend the same day and at the same place where one of her good friend's wedding was also scheduled practically at the same time. "What are the chances of this to happen?" she was asking to herself. She knew that the conference would be relatively short, only an introduction to the new research program started by her department chief, Dr. Laurent Martin.

Nevertheless, a larger exposé of his achievements and a reward for the best Research Program of the Year given to Institute Pasteur was to follow. The institute was frequently the recipient of prizes owned over many other very competitive programs. As a member of the research team, Isabelle had to be present. It was held on the weekend, so members of the institute could attend along with their spouses, enjoying a reception following the award presentation in one of the most selected places Paris could offer.

Isabelle's dilemma was that the conference was scheduled for two o'clock in the afternoon and the wedding was at four, with the invitees arriving at least 30 minutes earlier to be greeted with champagne and *petits fours* so they could be seated in the hall reserved for the ceremony. She was still trying to figure out how to dress properly for the two events. Her thoughts went to Vivianne and how they had first met a few years back when she came to the children's hospital with her daughter Lucie.

The little girl was barely a toddler and suffered from severe asthma. The institute conducted trials of IGG extracted from the patient's own blood, enriched them in vitro, and then injected back into the patient's blood stream. This treatment was quite successful and Isabelle was in charge of the trials applied in the pediatric ICU.

It was almost no surprise to Isabelle that Lucie responded so well to this kind of treatment, and over the next six month the child had rarer and lighter episodes of bronchospasm, and was considered cured within a year. Isabelle, who was, as usual, elated by the new field of treatments opened by using a patient's own antibodies, became attached to the little girl, while Vivianne in her turn, could not retain her gratitude toward Isabelle. Long after Lucie was discharged from the active treatments and only followed as part of a long-term research program, her mother remained in contact with Isabelle, and in time, they became good friends.

The two young ladies arranged short lunches together; sometimes Isabelle would stop to meet Lucie and her mom in the Luxembourg Gardens, or watch the Guignols together, the open-air puppet theater for children playing in the Tuileries Gardens.

It often happened that Vivianne teased Isabelle about her admirers and reminded her it was time for her to get married and think of her own children. Well, they had the biggest laugh when the most unexpected turn came for Vivianne, now that *she* was the one who had fallen head over heels with Lucien and today was getting married!

Making her usual breakfast, a cup of coffee and a lightly toasted croissant with butter and peach preserve from their garden in Rambouillet, Isabelle called to check on her parents' arrival and reassured them she would be alright by herself for the weekend.

Then, she remembered that, when short on time and ideas of what to wear for an occasion, the best shopping was her own closet. She browsed through her clothes while finishing her coffee, and decided on an emerald sheer dress. It was a very feminine dress she had not yet had the chance to take out of its plastic wrap. She had bought it on a whim the previous season at one of the special sales made by signature stores Rue du Faubourg St. Honoré, where the great "couturiers" had smaller boutiques.

Isabelle liked the simple dress designed in a classical style as it would accommodate any fashion changes, but she most admired the flowing effect of the skirt, ending at the knee level. She was happy she had bought it to have it ready when the occasion presented, as it would save her a lot of running around. With a white silk jacket, matching shoes, and a small purse, she felt confident she could get by for the institute reception and the wedding ceremony later.

The fact that the two events were held at the same location, made it easier for her just to drive her little Morris and park it at the club, where a valet parking was offered. With a beautiful spring day as today, what an ideal time this was for going out! And what an exceptional place to hold these two events: the Interalliée Cercle was possibly the most elegant and refined club in Paris!

Situated on Rue du Faubourg Saint Honoré, the same long street where she purchased the dress, it was a splendid palace and gardens located between the embassies of Britain and Japan, once a property of Henri de Rothschild and offered by him in 1917 to create an alliance between France, England, and the United States, where the officials could meet for private and formal encounters.

The club members' list included some of the most illustrious names of political, military, financial and other social branches, while still open to private members of less public fame and to carefully chosen and quite expensive receptions.

Isabelle went leisurely to her bathroom adjacent to her room and stepped under the shower to shampoo her long blond hair. Dreamily, she remembered one or two occasions when she had visited this spectacular place with its very typical 19th century salons, ballrooms, library, imposing marble staircase, the terraces and tables for high tea and outdoors receptions.

All was completed with magnificent gardens: superbly manicured lawns with waterfalls and reflecting pools, majestic old trees, splendid parterres of flowers, and a private indoor swimming pool. She vaguely remembered that one of the founders of the Cercle was a distant family member, Count Marc de Beaumont, although she was not sure of their exact connection, just that they were of the same family origin. She was aware of another Marc de Beaumont, a general under Napoleon Bonaparte, whose name was engraved, along with other generals' names, on the Arc de Triomphe in the center of the Etoile Square, at the summit of Champs Elysees Avenue.

Around 1: 30 PM, Isabelle was ready to leave for the institute's reception, and checking on her way out with a quick glance in the foyer mirror to see if she was all right, she gave herself a smile of approval. She was not just all right, she looked like an apparition that could take away the breath of anyone.

-//-

Gérard went to the Cercle de Interalliée as promised to Lucien, at three o'clock in the afternoon, as he was also the best man and Lucien was getting more and more nervous and needed a friendly presence to handle the biggest day of his life. Gérard, living in the neighborhood, would have loved to go on foot and enjoy the gorgeous day, but dressed in a gray tuxedo and white tie would have attracted too much attention, and he resolved on taking his car. It was a good decision, for even though Gérard did not pay much attention to his looks, he was even more handsome in this holiday attire. A stunning young man in his prime, he was tall and slender with baby blue eyes, a natural elegance and a charming smile. He was an image of someone very few could resist.

"Ready for your big day, old buddy?" Gérard asked Lucien once he'd arrived on the second floor of the mansion, and entered one of the rooms attached to the ceremonial salon, where the groom was to wait without getting in the way, and definitely not going into the next room, where the bride was getting ready as well.

"I don't know if I am ready for my biggest day, but I feel darn ready for the biggest decision in my life," answered Lucien, who was also very good looking in his white tuxedo as one of the flower ladies tried to pin a red gardenia on his lapel.

"Lucien, quit wiggling! I will prick my finger and stain your white tux with blood and everyone will think you are Dracula or something; it is why no one wanted to marry you until this brave Vivianne took pity on you!" Winking at Gérard she continued, "and the poor fellow doesn't even know how gorgeous she looks next door, otherwise he would die before the wedding."

Lucien, trying to deflect the attention centered on him, said to Gérard, "take note my friend, after me, it is your turn. You can't continue to waste your time any longer without enjoying the family bliss."

Gérard was saved by the wedding coordinator who was coming in to review the sequence of the ceremony with the two of them. After only a few more words of reminder, she, too, got on Gérard's case with a: "Well, after him, we need to start rehearsing for your wedding, next."

To which Gérard answered half laughing, "The stress is not supposed to be on me today, and if you don't need me right now, I think I am going to get some air. Don't you worry, I will be back on time to make sure you get hitched and well tied down." Politely closing the door behind him, he went down the stairs and walked out to relax a little before the ceremony and admire the splendid gardens of the club.

-//-

Isabelle discretely glanced at her bracelet watch and realized that the time was getting tight. It was 15 minutes after three o'clock and the award ceremony was still going on. She had hoped to mingle a little at the reception following the meeting, then go visit Vivianne around three-thirty in her loge, the bride room, as she had promised.

Vivianne had called in the morning to let her know how the short formality of the civil marriage went at the Hôtel de Ville, the City Hall. She seemed happy and under control, but asked Isabelle to come earlier to what she called the actual marriage, the religious wedding blessing at the Cercle Interalliée, since her marriage with Lucie's father had been only a civil one and quickly dissolved shortly after the child was born.

Vivianne, as a journalist and reporter for Paris Match Magazine, had extensive acquaintances in the field of journalism and she was well known and respected by many. Thus, she felt obligated to invite some of her closest colleagues, since they all loved her and were happy to see her finding fulfillment in her personal life. However, Vivianne was also asking the impossible, that they keep it quiet and intimate, knowing that many magazines would mention her marriage as some of their reporters were amongst the invitees. She thought that if she simply invited them and satisfied their curiosity without too much fuss, she would have the upper hand of the extension spread by the news.

Finally, Isabelle was out of the meeting room and making little conversation, slowly approached the salon where small speeches coud be heard, while Champagne and small appetizers were served. The institute reception salon was wide open toward the grand stairwell hall and facing another salon situated across, where the wedding guests were welcomed and served also Champagne and other refreshments.

Shortly after, the wedding guests were to be directed upstairs where the grand hall for the ceremony was set with all the traditional rows of chairs, elevated front stage, and beautiful flower decorations. Downstairs, at the back of the salon reserved for wedding events, a harpist was playing soft music, to the delight of the arriving guests.

Gérard was coming in through the French doors from his walk in the gardens, after crossing the terrace where tables were beautifully dressed with flower centers and candles, ready for the wedding dinner. This would later be served al fresco, when the attendees could enjoy the fresh air and the exceptional settings of the gardens and the fountains. His eyes fell on Isabelle coming out from the conference room and going toward the reception salon reserved by the institute. At her sight, he was transfixed and he recognized her immediately as the lady seen at the museum the day before. He found her even more beautiful in her turquoise dress.

Without realizing, Gérard approached and without thinking that Isabelle would hear him, he said aloud: "You, here?!"

Isabelle was startled and turned around. Looking at him in the eyes and seeing him for the first time, said, "Why, are you following me?"

Gérard was entranced as he gazed into her eyes, the same the color as her dress, and tried to explain, "You were at the Velazquez museum, in front of the Infanta."

To which Isabelle concluded, "So, you *are* following me."

At that point, one of her work colleagues came and taking her by her elbow said, "Come on Isabelle, Doctor Martin wants to share his appreciation with his team."

Shortly after that, Gérard learned that the "other crowd" was a scientific celebration for the Institute Pasteur and the person he was addressing was a young physician herself, part of one of the research teams. And most importantly, he had also learned that her name was Isabelle.

Entering the reception salon that was progressively filling with wedding guests, he relaxed on hearing the soothing music of the harp, and went to speak to some friends and Vivianne's parents. Everyone exchanged pleasantries about the two young people, who, not long ago, were determined to remain single, but today they were to be united in marriage. While Gérard continued socializing, his mind was still troubled by Isabelle.

At a certain moment, one of the stewards of the club, wearing a club uniform and white gloves, approached the harpist and respectfully talked to her in a low voice. The harpist quickly changed her expression and getting up, went to the telephone shown to her in a corner of the salon.

The conversation there was short as well, and the harpist's face now became an image of despair. She went out and finding the wedding coordinator, explained and excused herself after learning her father was at the emergency room of one of the hospitals where he had been taken after suffering of an acute heart attack.

There was nothing to be done; the coordinator had to tell Lucien and Vivianne that they would not have harp music during the ceremony.

-//-

At last, Isabelle found the moment she could leave the Institute reception keeping the best of social appearances, and went upstairs to see Vivianne. With a discrete knock at the door, she made her presence known, but when the door opened practically at the same time, a distraught Vivianne almost fell in her arms.

"Isabelle, the harpist just left, family emergency ... Who is going to play for me, there's the bridal march ... how are we going to do it? I knew something terrible was going to happen, I felt it!" And she went on with her emotions now unbridled.

Isabelle, catching up with the unexpected happenings, was as reassuring and calming as she could be, but Vivianne did not hear any of it. Suddenly, with a look full of hope on her face, Vivianne blurted out pleading in desperation, "Isabelle, you know how to play the harp, you can save my wedding!"

"I only play rarely and never in public anymore, and anyway, I don't know the bridal march," said Isabelle, and taken by surprise, stammered defending herself.

And so, their conversation went on a little longer, but at certain moment they seemed to come to an understanding and the wedding coordinator was called in. Mara, coming out from the groom's room next door after bringing the news to Lucien, was now ready to start inviting the guests to come up the stairs for the beginning of the ceremony.

Lucien was confused and not sure he fully understood the situation, his mind was set only on the moment he would be united with his bride, and seemed to care less about the music or other details. Shortly after that, the harp was brought discretely into the bridal loge and Vivianne and Isabelle convened on a few pieces of music Isabelle could play from memory; the bridal march would be replaced by the Hawaiian Wedding Song as Isabelle had suggested.

Vivianne received the idea with applause: "I just adore that song, a lot more than the traditional march... which is heard at all weddings, anyway."

During this conversation Isabelle, a little nervous, was warming up, playing cords and arpeggios to get familiar with the instrument, a routine necessary for any musician aware that these instruments were the product of artisan work, painstakingly and individually made, giving them a special feel and sound.

Shortly after that, Vivianne was smiling again, although Isabelle was not so sure, while the harp was rolled into the ceremony hall, close to the stage. With a deep breath and a short prayer, Isabelle started playing "The Little Fountain" by Samuel Pratt. The crystalline flow of sound created an atmosphere of complete serenity, and one would never have guessed that Isabelle was not as tranquil as the impression she expressed through her music.

The invitees, who started trickling in to take their seats, were surprised at the sight of the new harp player, and in awe at this angelic image. As she continued to play, Isabelle felt steadily more comfortable in her ability to master the technical difficulty of the compositions played. She even started to enjoy the moment, thrilled that she could be of help to her friend at this very special moment.

-//-

Gérard, going upstairs on his way to the groom's loge, had to walk past the large double doors of the formal salon, when he was attracted, like all the other guests, by the sounds of the music. On the spur of the moment, he decided to enter the salon, cross it, and exit through the door at the end of the stage to reach Lucien's room, so he could closer listen to the harp music.

For the second time that day, more exactly in the same hour, Gérard was again mesmerized at the celestial image and the flow of sounds produced by the same creature who did not miss to surprise and intrigue him. Isabelle was now playing "Ave Maria" by Bach-Gounod, feeling and looking relaxed and happy, completely immersed in her music. She was unaware of the blasting shockwave she created in Gérard, as his whole being was pleading to the universe, "Oh, dear God, have mercy on me."

Now that the things went back under control, the wedding coordinator was happy to direct the ceremony; as planned the groom stepped in accompanied by his best man, Gérard, and the two of them took their places on the right side of the stage. The groom's parents were shown their seats in the front row, and then Vivianne's mom took her seat, whereas nobody ever imagined what was happening in Gérard's heart.

Finally, the audience was awarded with the long-expected moment, when, smiling and exulting with happiness, Vivianne appeared through the main entrance on the arm of her father, who was nearly choked with emotion. The music complemented their emotions and the "Hawaiian Wedding Song" made the bride's entrance truly unique. Behind, trying to imitate her mother's steps, was the most adorable little girl, Lucie, proudly holding the rings. Before entering the room, she had given instructions to some other younger children, a little flower girl and a little boy who was not sure what he was supposed to do besides creating trouble. Lucie, already overwhelmed by emotion, gave a last look behind her to make sure the children were following.

From there on, for most of the attendees, including Gérard and Isabelle, all unfolded like a blur. The bride and the groom took their respective places in front of a very jovial minister who delivered a short but very touching sermon. Next came the ring exchange along with the bride and groom's mutual vows, making all tear a little. Then, following the traditional kiss, the priest introduced to the audience the new Madame and Monsieur Lucien Dubois.

Finally, let free to step down from the stage, the newlywed couple turned to walk down the aisle, almost running away, but they were quickly stopped by the family and guests who wanted to congratulate them. Isabelle began to play a more formal piece of music, "Jesu, Joy of Man's Desiring" by J. S. Bach, but better sensing the emotions of the couple, she ended by gliding her fingers over the strings creating an enchanting combination of glissandi.

The afternoon was getting better and better, finally everyone attending the wedding relaxing and gathering in the lower salon again, after the formal congratulations, and for more Champagne and appetizers. Later, the wedding would continue with a seated dinner on the terrace of the Cercle, meanwhile the photographer ran around taking pictures of the newly married couple, children and family members, using the beautiful settings of the palace and its gardens as a background.

Isabelle, likewise, felt all the stress disappear as soon as she realized that the ceremony was over and she managed to get to the end of her impromptu recital better than expected. Mostly she was happy that Vivianne had enjoyed her wedding as planned. Now she could meet the other guests, and, finally accepting a glass of Champagne offered to her, she walked out into the gardens, admiring the beautiful surroundings.

During this time, the wedding coordinator arriving practically at the end of her obligations, and against all her fears, without problem, was also appreciating the reception like everyone else. However, without thinking too much of it, she made one of the best decisions in her career and suggested changing some of the seating arrangements; she would have Isabelle seated at table of the wedded couple and their family, where the best man was included as well.

It was an idea that came to her mind while she was looking at the bride and groom during the ceremony, and admiring the best man's striking good looks. A little to his right was the beautiful harp player, now quietly waiting to play the last song at the end of the wedding. She was taken by the grace of this delicate image, a cameo profile with an elegant neck, shiny blond hair waves falling gently on her shoulders, and her thin waist with a perfect bosom line. Although a few feet distanced the two from each other, she could picture them perfectly in harmony sitting together. She did not know who they were, only that the best man was single, and the harpist seemed to be by herself as well. Now feeling a little naughty, she decided to play Cupid and slip in a word to get the permission from Vivianne and Lucien and place them together at their table.

The ceremony over with, no one seemed to be in a hurry, and, at this time in June, close to the summer solstice, the days were long in Paris. As sunset approached, the glorious afternoon colors mixed and deepened. The guests enjoyed the spectacular outdoors as they reconnected or simply socialized, slowly moving along the garden paths, sitting on the benches in front of the fountains, or taking more pictures. Mara, the wedding coordinator, letting go of the stress, was moving from group to group, making sure they were well attended to and their glasses were promptly refilled by the perfectly styled servers.

Slowly, the guests started directing their steps back to the large terrace which faced the lawns and ran the full length of the back of this palatial building; lights were lit, in the salons at first, and then outdoors. The music band started playing softly, attracting the guests closer, who found their seats, already anticipating the lavish dinner to come.

Gérard frequently attended impressive receptions due to his position as attaché politic and cultural, but fully appreciated this very special moment and felt privileged to find himself in such rare company and surroundings. Isabelle was even more enchanted by this unique event; she realized how much she needed this relaxing time, so rare in her life, and she started enjoying herself.

She was swiftly surrounded by all the available single man attending the party, something she once more ignored. However, this did not go unnoticed by Gérard, who desperately tried to find the right moment to approach the person of his intense interest. It was not long before the moment presented, when Mara signaled the guests of honor to their designated places.

Isabelle, seldom felt so light of head and at heart, maybe mellowed by the Champagne, maybe by the happy ambience and the relief of finishing her performance after having to play so unexpectedly. She let herself be guided by Mara and realized with surprise only later that she was being directed to the bridal table. And she was even more surprised that she was sitting to the left of "this cocky... good looking... best man, whatever." So far, she had hardy been impressed by his manners and did not know exactly how to react to this situation. She was not sure if she should protest the arrangements or just ignore her table *"voisin"* and continue to enjoy the evening.

-//-

The table of the guests of honor was centrally placed and occupied by the attendees only on one side while the corners faced the other tables and the gardens, framed by the terrace and the elegant turn of the century building behind it. Through French doors, the impeccably trained waiters came and went, getting ready to serve dinner and attend to the guests' desires and needs.

A smaller table was dressed close by for the family and guests' children, and they were already asking for macaroni and cheese, after a little boy came up with the idea, disregarding the gourmet menu offered to them. But kids would always be kids, and in these circumstances, no one could find any wrongdoing.

The bride and groom took their seats, as did their respective parents and other members of the family, at the central table, and Gérard found his place as well at the left side of the groom. He was already sitting when Isabelle was shown her place next to him, who even though pleasantly surprised, was quick to read the name in front of her glasses: Dr. Isabelle Beaumont. He got up, as the wedding coordinator introduced them to each other in French, "*Gérard Forrest, attaché culturel aupres de l'Ambassade des Etats Unis; Mademoiselle, pardon, Docteur Isabelle Beaumont.*"

Gérard caught quickly the slip of the tongue during Mara's introduction with the word *mademoiselle* - Miss. Quite pleased with the last news, he felt that the evening was indeed, getting better and better. Taking Isabelle's hand out of natural courtesy, and bending his head to mimic a *baise main*, as was customary in these occasions, Gérard whispered, "*Alors, vous me suivez?*" (So, are you following me?), bearing the most innocent look and smile he could manage. After doing this, he gallantly pulled the chair out for her and waited until she was seated, then took his own place.

Isabelle, who swiftly understood the irony, was not argumentative in nature and humored him, "No, it is just a simple coincidence."

"As you well know, *Docteur*, there is no such thing as coincidence, not even in the natural science."

"Then what is it?" asked Isabelle, challenging a little.

"I don't know, we'll see. Maybe it's the providence?"

The evening unfolded beautifully; a sumptuous dinner regaled the guests, and the time came for the bride and the groom to open the dance, followed by their parents. Others were called to dance along, including Gérard who invited a delighted Lucie, who could not contain her joy.

113

Isabelle received all the attention one could expect and danced many dances with several of the journalists and reporters. They all thought they would surely impress her with promises of pictures in the most popular magazines, and even possible articles once they learned that she actually had a real profession!

During this time, Gérard was observing and trying not to show too much displeasure at Isabelle's ravaging popularity, and made a few dances with the two mothers of the wedded couple. As the evening was fleeting, everyone was having a wonderful time and hardly noticed the time going by.

The traditional cake was served; a beautiful *piece montée* of three tiers that was light and delicious. Then came the tossing of the bridal bouquet which virtually landed on Isabelle's lap, along with all the exclamations and insinuations expected. Another coincidence or an accurate throw by the bride, no one would ever know!

Finally, Isabelle refused another invitation to dance as she wanted to catch her breath after all the laughing produced by the bouquet she now held close to breathe in all its fragrances. The music started playing a slow dance, "It's now or never" by Elvis Presley, when Gérard seized the opportunity and approached Isabelle.

"This one is easy, no effort required," said Gérard, hoping she would accept the invitation.

Isabelle slowly stood up, continuing to hold the bouquet without paying much attention to him. Lifting her left arm to place it on Gérard's shoulder, they started moving gently in the rhythm of the music.

Then was when the magic happened; their bodies moved naturally in perfect synchronism, fitting flawlessly the contours of their frames, their movements harmonizing as they slowly danced. Gérard's arm held Isabelle with great gentleness, his entire being melting with delight at the touch of her slender and soft body, hoping she would not hear his heart thumping in his chest like an imprisoned eagle. He was also under the spell of new feelings never experienced before, feelings that he could not define but he did not want to restrain either.

Isabelle was, too, letting the sweetness of the moment carry her, when a powerful awareness invaded her that all this was new and wonderful to her. It was the awareness of how much she needed to discover the tenderness of someone who truly cared for her. The events of the day, watching this couple so much in love getting married, had awakened in her a new sense of the possibilities of a true bond and the connection with another being with whom she could experience real happiness.

The dance lasted a long time, many couples enjoying the charm of the moment, and in the end, without much talking, Gérard accompanied Isabelle back to her chair.

Shortly after, Isabelle excused herself, then, deep in her thoughts, she walked inside, then to the main entrance, where she asked for her car to be advanced.

-//-

The Sunday after the wedding, Isabelle slept deeper and longer than usual. Going home after leaving the Cercle, she drove through the beautiful avenues and boulevards aligned with trees and city lights, where many were still walking and enjoying the gorgeous evening. Riding on Rue du Faubourg St. Honoré, she quickly arrived on Place de la Concorde going south on Rue Royale, then going over the Pont de la Place de la Concorde, she reached the bridge going over the Rive Gauche, the left bank of the River Seine.

She could not remain insensitive to the beauty of the architectural marvels seen in her rear mirror that showed la Madeleine at the end of the Rue Royale and beyond Place de la Concorde, and in front of her the Palais Bourbon, site of the National Assembly. The two buildings were designed in neo classical style and mirrored each other across the famous Concorde Square, and were centered symmetrically by the Grand Obelisk. From there, Isabelle was in no time in Boulevard Saint Germain and soon after, home. She tried not to analyze nor understand her feelings, forcing herself to think of it in the morning with a clearer mind.

Waking up in the middle of the morning, she phoned her parents letting them know that she would not drive to Rambouillet for lunch.

"I would have to drive right back after lunch and be ready for the week ahead, and the time is too short," she said. "I will have a quiet day to read and play the harp." This was her favorite past time and she rarely had the time to enjoy it. The following morning, she would return to her usual work routine, and this was exactly what she did for the weeks to come.

The wedding had ended on a festive note and the newlywed couple left a few days later for a long-expected honeymoon on the Adriatic coast of Italy. While everyone else resumed their customary activities, there was one person for whom life was no longer the same.

Gérard's thoughts were constantly brought back to Isabelle sitting at the museum in front of Velazquez's painting, Isabelle playing the harp, Isabelle in his arms slow dancing. He was wondering what had made her leave the reception so suddenly, searching in his mind for anything that could have offended her. He considered himself fortunate enough to know her name and have spent a few special moments together. And, as the days went by, he became even more determined to find a way to see her again.

With this in his mind, as soon as he found out that Lucien and Vivianne were back in town, he contacted his friends.

-//-

"Dr. Beaumont, there is a telephone call for you," her secretary informed, poking her head through the door of the examination room. "You can take it in your office."

"It will be but one minute," Isabelle said, excusing herself to her patient, then stepped out of the room. Picking up the phone, she was pleased to hear Vivianne's voice. "So, you are back, how is married life, how was your honeymoon?" Isabelle showered her friend with questions.

"Just wonderful and Lucien is just perfect," said Vivianne, obviously very much in love. "I was hoping we could get together this Friday. Why don't you come over to my place? Lucien has moved in with me, since my apartment is larger, until we find the right one for all of us. We will have a glass of wine and then have dinner at an Italian restaurant next door."

And upon Isabelle's agreement, Vivianne resumed the conversation reminding her of the address of the apartment.

"See you on Friday, then," was exchanged at both ends, and Isabelle went back to her patients.

-//-

Friday came, and as the days were gently gliding toward July, a warm summer was already anticipated. Isabelle arrived in front of Vivianne's limestone building, a very Haussmann end of 19th century baroque style, like some of the elegant edifices found in Paris. She was excited to talk to Vivianne about their voyage and see the new couple and Lucie. Wearing a yellow summer chiffon dress strewn with light flowery print, she was holding a big bouquet of daisies and sunflowers of the same color as her dress.

Pressing the intercom, she entered the building, then the elevator, and pushing the upper level button, her face brightened with a smile of anticipation. When the door was opened by Vivianne, who gave her a big hug, Isabelle could not help but notice behind her friend, already sitting comfortably in the salon was, who else, but Gérard! He and Lucien were engaged in a friendly conversation, while Lucie came running to Isabelle and practically jumped into her arms, trying to climb and be held like a baby.

Laughs and kisses were exchanged, flowers were taken and safely placed in a vase just before they were dispersed on the floor by little Lucie who was pulling Isabelle to show her room. However, soon the hands of a concerned nanny gently took her away, but not before a few minutes of "serious" and "secret" conversation.

From the foyer, Isabelle entered the salon, relaxed thanks to Lucie's charming welcome. The two gentlemen promptly stood up and salutations were exchanged. Isabelle sat in a beautiful Louis XVI bergere, looking around her and admiring the décor. The apartment was of a classic Parisian style and filled with the light filtering in from the windows framing the French balconies. She was not aware that the same delicate afternoon light was creating a glow in her hair, enhancing the softness of her face. Without any intention, Isabelle seemed a little detached, and she was already wrapped in her own aura created by the light.

At a loss for words in the beginning, Gérard slowly inquired about her work and summer plans, without mentioning anything about her sudden disappearance from the wedding reception. Isabelle directed the conversation toward the Italian Riviera, where their friends vacationed.

Vivianne presented a silver plate with *boudoirs*, lady's fingers, while Lucien proposed a drink, "Wine, cherry, Champagne?"

When Gérard said before Isabelle could answer, "Most of the time she prefers a coup of Champagne," they all look at Gérard in surprise, who raised his shoulders in a comic excuse, making them all laugh.

As they were getting ready to leave for the Italian bistro, Isabelle realized that, with nobody else expected, she had in fact been set up for a blind date.

Chez Ricardo, the Italian bistro, was only a short walk from the Dubois' apartment and they decided to stroll there and enjoy the pleasant end of the afternoon. Their table was reserved in the patio-garden under the canopy of blooming wisteria, while Italian canzonets could be heard in the background. Vivianne and Lucien had chosen this place out of a desire to prolong the ambience of their recent honeymoon, and were obviously very enamored with each other. Stepping into the patio and then going to their table, they sat on one of the two benches, leaving Isabelle and Gérard the bench in front of them.

During dinner, everyone seemed comfortable, enjoying the food, the soft music, and the company. After the reminiscence of the time in Italy, the subject turned to Isabelle's work. Gérard seemed very interested in knowing more about her life.

Isabelle answered modestly in a few words, but with passion, "Presently, we are conducting various studies on the neurophysiology of the brain and the spinal cord, and the research programs are promising; so much can be done to restore the damage done by age or by accidents!"

"So, you are the person I need, I have this vertigo and my head is spinning," Gérard began.

"We have a wonderful new machine using a tomography system, it is like an X-Ray but...", then she stopped short, and being a good sport, she broke into a child-like laugh and said, "I almost fell for you."

To which Gérard's answer was, "And all my hopes would have been fulfilled!" making them all join into joyful laughter.

What Gérard could not express in his words was the way Isabelle looked in that moment; her face was the image of an innocent child, so young and untainted. This image reverberated deep inside him, touching fibers that he was only now discovering the presence.

Isabelle, remembering her brother's words, realized that she could have fun while talking about her work. She also realized how much she enjoyed Gérard's company, and as their evening was slowly approaching to an end, she was engulfed by the same sense she felt when she was dancing with him. This made her think of the reason she ran away that night; all this was so new to her, so soft and again so powerful, and she tried to sort out her reactions.

Not long ago, Isabelle could easily brush off any trouble made by an admirer when she was courted or solicited in the past, as she had done it so many times. But this was so different, and she retreated even more into her world to think, while Gérard felt at a loss. Trying to break the mystery surrounding this mysterious creature, he whispered:

"Isabelle, are you with us still?" asked Gérard, diving the most ultramarine eyes into hers. She was suddenly seized by the charm Gérard was exerting on her, while she realized she was almost at ease with it.

"I am only admiring these two love birds," answered Isabelle, gently deflecting the attention to the happy couple, exulting in tenderness for each other.

"Then, let's not disturb them," said Gérard. "May I ask you what your plans are for this weekend?"

"My parents, my brother and his wife, are going to a concert at Saint Germain Cathedral tomorrow night, and I was counting on tagging along; only I did not make a reservation for myself early enough and now they are all sold out. I think I will take my chances anyway, it plays one of my favorite pieces of music, 'The Requiem' by Giuseppe Verdi."

At once, becoming more animated, Isabelle added, "Do you know that Verdi, who is mostly known as an opera composer, wrote this Oratorio, a liturgical composition, which was played at his Memorial mass, in a way, like Mozart's 'Requiem'? It is my favorite of all, along with Beethoven's 'Missa Solemnis' and Bach's 'Magnificat'."

Gérard was taking notes while he was listening to Isabelle. Then the time came when, after they had listened to more romantic Neapolitan music, they left the restaurant, and in a happy mood started saying their goodbyes. Obviously, Vivianne and Lucien were walking back home, and Gérard offering to accompany Isabelle, she declined as her car was nearby.

Gérard had to be content with simply walking her to her car, and gallantly took his leave after closing her door and watching her pull away. However, already a plan was taking form in his mind.

-//-

Indeed, the following Saturday morning, as soon as the embassy office in service for the weekend was open, Gérard came in. He was happy to see that one of the most pleasant secretaries was at the main desk.

"Maggie, I need your help to get two official tickets to a concert for tonight."

Maggie was fond of Gérard and watched over him with the eyes of a mother. She gave him an amused look and asked, "Going to concerts now? This is a good change for you to get away from those old books of yours! I will get you two of the best diplomatic seats if you will tell me if your date is a pretty one, 'cause I know she is a lucky one," she ended with a wink.

"She is not a date, but she is a very beautiful lady," said Gérard, almost excusing himself.

"Alright, come back in two hours, and good luck anyways. I want all details, and I say ALL details."

At six-thirty that beautiful June evening, Isabelle walked her parents to the door of the Saint Germain Cathedral and after they entered, she went to the box office. Passing in front of it a few moments before, she had already noticed the sign "sold out". Nevertheless, she decided to stick around and try her chance, as it often happened that someone had a spare ticket if a friend or a relative could not make it at the last moment.

Isabelle was wearing a deep blue dress, the color called the "Parisian summer night sky", delicately curving around her feminine figure. She also held a wrap over her arm for later to cover her shoulders. She did not go too far before she noticed Gérard who was making his way toward her, as though he had already seen her.

"I really don't have time for socializing," she quickly thought, but she was pleased to see him. She thought it would feel less awkward in her search for a ticket if she were not alone.

"Good evening Isabelle, I have two tickets, and I wonder if you would join me for the concert tonight?"

"If I would? You are a godsend!" and this time she gave him, for the first time, a peck on both his cheeks with the usual *bisous* French people greeted each other. She suddenly felt happy and so relieved, and taking his arm, she added, "You are full of surprises, *Monsieur!*"

They stepped into the magnificent cathedral, originally an abbey built in the 6th century by one of the sons of Clovis I and a burial site of the Merovingian kings, and later, of René Descartes. What was today the quarter of Saint Germain de Prés and the Latin Quarter, represented the land owned by the abbey in the medieval age. Restored several times over the centuries, Saint Germain Cathedral was one of the first to boast the flying buttresses, and hosted important abbots, like Louis-César de Bourbon, son of Madame de Montespan and Louis XIV.

And tonight, as often in these modern times, there would be a magnificent musical event, thanks to its exceptional acoustic qualities. When walking into the cathedral, one was surrounded by its majestic and powerful beauty, its tranquil arches and massive columns, and its elegant stained glass windows, all imposing respect and reflection.

Advancing toward the front of the church, Isabelle made a discrete sign to her family to reassure them, as they were seated in the middle of the orchestra, a quite suitable place for a concert. Gérard, showing his tickets to the greeters, was deferentially directed to the more official reserved area in front of the orchestra. Isabelle remained quite surprised, but once sitting on the perfectly located and comfortable armchairs, she relaxed and turned her head toward Gérard.

Gérard felt a shudder under her dazzling smile, like a shock wave hitting him without *garde*, stirring his entire being. Somehow, he managed to find his peace, happy to be in Isabelle's company, and enjoy a full evening in her presence.

Suddenly the most incredible harmonious sounds inundated the audience, the first cords of the expansive orchestra lifted everyone's spirit to a higher dimension, making all, including Gérard, experience music like never before. The introduction was made by gentle violins, then there was the cello introduction, followed by the voices announcing the "Requiem", the funeral mass.

Gérard found himself moved and completely immersed in the splendor of the symphonic and vocal sounds, raising his soul with Kyrie Eleison, Misere and Recordare. Then came Ingemisco, the most touching prayer he ever heard in liturgical music carried out by the solo tenor. It continued with the solo voice quartet making a superb dialogue, and Gérard was transported by these powerful moments, as he realized that he could almost grasp some of Isabelle's world, sharing with her this so much beauty.

At the intermission, Isabelle introduced her parents, then Eric and his wife, Danielle, to Gérard. After they promptly thanked Gérard for the unexpected ticket for Isabelle, who by the way just "adored" Verdi's Requiem, the chatting became more animated regarding the musicians' performance. They were getting along so naturally that the call for the end of the *entr'acte* came almost too quickly.

Nevertheless, before regaining their seats, Isabelle's parents invited Gérard for supper after the concert at the nearby Café de Flore. Eric and Danielle declined; they were anxious to go back home after concert, and relieve their babysitter.

Gérard was aware of the customs of Western Europe, particularly French customs, marking the day with specific times designated for meals: *petit dejeuner* or morning breakfast, *dejeuner* or lunch, *gouter* or

125

afternoon snack (mostly reserved for children coming back from school and before doing their extensive homework), and then *diner*, or dinner, and finally supper, usually later than in the US, after going out to the theatre, opera, or concerts.

It was not unusual for restaurants situated close to cultural events, and appreciated by Parisians for their excellent food, stayed open late, sometimes well past midnight, to accommodate the inflamed debates between the artists and their public.

The second part of this magnificent performance continued to the delight of an entranced audience, and ended softly with the choir whispering the *"requiem aeternam"*... when the public needed some time to emerge from the spell of the moment.

Isabelle's parents, Marie-Claire and Thierry Hervé Beaumont, or simply Claire and Thierry, met the young couple at the exit of the cathedral. They were a short walk across Boulevard Saint Germain to Café de Flore. A good crowd from the concert followed inside, and since the Beaumonts were regulars to the place as they lived close by, they were shown a quieter table on the second floor.

Café de Flore, a trendy establishment well known by writers, artists, and tourists, had maintained its fame since the opening in the 1880s, and was named after the statue of Flora, the goddess of the flowers and the spring, who stood watching from across the boulevard.

At first, Gérard maintained a little more formal approach, used to diplomatic manners and French customs, but slowly he relaxed in the warm and friendly presence of Isabelle's parents. He had a hard time to believe sitting with them and learning more about Isabelle and her family.

As all good things, the evening came to an end, and Gérard offered to walk them back to their apartment. They stopped in front of a turn of the century building, a well-maintained limestone construction. Boasting a typical monumental double door entrance leading to an elegant foyer and a large stairwell next to the elevator, an interior garden could also be seen in the back, behind French doors. Gérard bade the Beaumonts' a *"bonne nuit"* in his best manners, and with a light heart watched them disappearing through the entrance door.

Gérard was in the greatest disposition, not because he had just left the person who lately occupied most of his thoughts, but because he had met her parents, learning where they lived, and having obtained her telephone number.

-//-

Isabelle was sitting at her harp looking at Mozart's partition for harp of the Concerto in C for harp, flute, and orchestra. She had studied the part years ago, while at the conservatory and lately she felt the impulse to play it again. She was reviewing with deep concentration the fingering of the first movement of the concerto.

It came back to her easily, although it was a piece of music requiring a good technical level. She remembered what Gérard Devos, her harp teacher, said in finding that many players were like "sewing machines", trying to impress the public with their high speed of execution instead of the musical interpretation. How frustrated he was because they ignored the composer's style. She went on reading the Allegro, lingering a little longer over the Cadenza, one of her favorite segments, where the solo flute and the harp met in beautiful harmonies creating a lacing wave of sound.

The beauty of the music was Isabelle's escape, her way to unwind after intense days at the clinic as it allowed her to clear her mind and help find solutions for complicated cases still occupying her thoughts when she came home from work. While relaxing, something of the atmosphere created by the music suddenly brought back to her the memory of an unexpected event at the office.

Her secretary had come in while she was updating the patients' records between their visits, and told her that there was a patient insisting to see her. She related that "he was presenting his case, of which the doctor was aware of, as 'very serious', but he did not have an appointment because he could not wait until one became available".

Isabelle, who was accustomed to urgent cases and always tried to make time for them, noticed this time a subtle commotion around the nurses' station as she peered from her desk beyond the open door. Isabelle was still half frowning, when she asked Annie to go ahead and bring in the emergency. A few seconds later, Annie, half smiling, introduced Gérard, then, not retaining a wink, closed the door behind her.

For a few seconds Isabelle considered Gérard, hesitating between getting upset and avoiding the mistake of ignoring a true emergency. This gave her the time to notice how seductive he was, with his high stature, feline movements, and an irresistible smile that had obviously already conquered her staff.

"And what that emergency might be?" Isabelle asked trying to keep a professional tone.

"Well, my thoughts are confused, I can't concentrate, and my heart races all the time. Not to mention I find it difficult to sleep at night," Gérard answered, straining hard to look serious.

"I see, and as this condition can be, at times, serious, it is definitely not an emergency", reassured Isabelle, keeping in check her laughter, which was usually easy to surface.

"But I beg your pardon, doctor, I am ... it is very serious and it IS an emergency," Gérard continued under her questioning gaze, "How could I see you otherwise and ask you to go with me to the Bagatelle gardens? The Rose expo will end soon and I would also like to invite you to the 4th of July celebrations."

"Wait a minute, I detect a little confusion here, the Rose expo at the Bagatelle just started and it usually lasts for the summer, and there is still time for the 14th of July!"

"You are right for the first, but wrong for the second; I am talking about the American Independence Day, not about the Bastille Day. We are having a nice celebration tomorrow at the American Embassy, where I work, and you are officially invited."

"Officially? I have not seen any written invitation in my mail lately."

"It is a request of outmost importance that has to be delivered in person, so I personally came to present it without delay."

"Well, thank you and the American Embassy for the kind and urgent invitation, but although it might be a holiday for you, tomorrow is a Thursday and I have to work. I am very sorry!"

129

Recollecting the conversation, Isabelle stopped the harp music, unable to maintain her full attention, while in her mind she was playing rather the events of that strange day. She had agreed to go to the 4th of July celebration after work, and Gérard had no choice but to accept that she wouldn't be there before 6:30 pm. Once she had arrived at the embassy, she presented the guards at the gate her official invitation card, and Gérard showed up miraculously quickly, obviously on the watch for her arrival.

It has been a lovely evening, the festive ambience getting to Isabelle as she was introduced and guided through the beautifully decorated lawns in red, white and blue, with a gigantic buffet, and an engaging music band. Isabelle noticed that quite a few members of the embassy glanced in pleasant surprise at Gérard, as he did not leave her one second out of his reach.

At dusk, everyone was invited to take a seat facing a podium where the Ambassador Joe Rodgers addressed the guest of honor and all the other invitees. However, Gérard went first on stage and thanked the guests for their presence and introduced the ambassador, then regained his place in the front row, where other members of the staff and their spouses welcomed Isabelle.

Isabelle remembered that Gérard let his arm around her waist linger a few moments longer than necessary as he led her to different areas of the celebration, at times pausing to point out some of the buildings and statues of the magnificent compound.

Overall, he behaved as a perfect gentleman, and insisted on accompanying her home to make sure "nothing was going to happen to her" right after the fireworks, aware that it had already been a long day for Isabelle. She also remembered that she'd had a wonderful time and could not say goodnight to Gérard without promising to go with him next Saturday to Bagatelle.

That evening, Gérard took his time to drive back; he remembered watching her as she rapidly but gracefully got out of the car after the usual peck on both cheeks, and disappeared behind the massive doors of her Parisian apartment. He knew he was "in trouble" but also realized that, for once, he did not mind it, he did not mind it at all.

-//-

As convened, Gérard presented himself at Isabelle's place at 10 o'clock in the morning of the next Saturday, feeling like a teenager again and holding a beautiful bouquet of pink roses. This was a holiday weekend for the members of the embassy and this past Friday has been a light work day for him, taking care of scheduling future official visits for the ambassador, although he was not required to be at the office that day. This gave him time to talk to his parents and Patrick in Washington, DC, and listen to his son's jovial voice giving him a full account of his summer activities.

Patrick was not to come back to Paris for another five to six weeks, when his school year would start, and while Gérard missed his son's presence terribly, he almost had the impression that Patrick had a harder time reciprocating his father's feelings. However, Gérard was already trying to figure out how to introduce Isabelle to Patrick and how the two of them would connect. But once again, Gérard realized he was already jumping to conclusions about the relationship.

Arrived at the Beaumont residence, Gérard climbed the stairs two by two instead of taking the elevator to the second floor, and with a racing but singing heart, pressed the doorbell. It was the first time Gérard had been invited to their apartment, although he knew that Isabelle's parents were already gone for the weekend to their summerhouse in Rambouillet. He was there only to take their daughter out for the day, and when a smiling Isabelle opened the door, this image remained engraved in his heart forever.

It was a beautiful summer day and the exposure of the flat allowed the light to flow freely into the double salon. As Isabelle led him from the entrance foyer into the salon, she invited him to wait for her to arrange the flowers in a vase before leaving.

Gérard had the opportunity to take in the striking decor. It was very eclectic, mixing very naturally pieces of artwork, antique artifacts and collectibles, objects that anywhere else would have created an unacceptable collision between periods and styles believed not to fit together. But here, they all spoke the same language, creating a beautiful and harmonious, albeit unusual environment. Isabelle brought in the roses, now prettily displayed in a crystal vase, and sat them on a coffee table.

"Ready to go?" she asked Gérard, swirling around.

Gérard turned to fully look at her and noticed her white summer outfit, skinny white pants and a sheer light top that fell in gentle layers. He had the impression her movements were like pirouettes of a dancer. "Ready," was the only answer he could give.

Coming toward him, Isabelle, in her turn, was seized by his good looks, his athletic body showing well in his light blue polo and khaki slacks, and the intense blue of his eyes.

His hair, although not following the fashion of heavy manes of the late eighties, was long enough to allow dark blond waves to form. She recognized all of sudden that his perfect cheeks, strong jaw line, the fine and perfectly balanced line of his nose, along with sparkling rows of teeth seen through a gentle grin, could let anyone think of him as being a movie star.

During their ride to the Bagatelle Gardens, situated on the south side of Bois de Boulogne, the Boulogne Forest, Isabelle hiding her unexpected trouble, was looking out the window as the Paris magnificent sites went by, trying to sort out the nature of her emotions, pondering if she wanted them to invade her peace.

Gérard was very much at ease finding his way around the city of Paris and its surroundings. He followed the left bank of the Seine River, crossed the bridge at the Place de la Concorde to the right bank, then, in a straight shot went to the Avenue des Champs Elysees.

Reaching the top of the famous avenue, he turned skillfully into the usually busy roundabout of the Place de l'Étoile, and continued along the splendid Avenue Foch to Bois de Boulogne. While driving, Gérard was very much aware of Isabelle's presence, and attributed her silence to her reserved manners and the beauty of the streets they were driving. He was happy just to have her sitting next to him, sharing this ride, privileged to be in a place that most people only dreamed about. But, here they were already, on Avenue de Longchamp arriving at the southwest entrance of the Bagatelle Gardens.

They took a long stroll through elegant alleys running alongside elaborate parterres loaded with fragrant roses, irises, and peonies of all colors, admiring arbors holding climbing wisterias and jasmine.

They appreciated the statuaries and fountains, the water lilies on the reflecting ponds, feeling almost lightheaded at the intoxicating perfumed combinations of the flowers and symmetry of shrubs that created intricate geometries of the French parterres.

For a moment, they stopped in front of the Château de Bagatelle, the "little nothing", an extravagant "joke" resulting from a bet between Marie-Antoinette and the Count d'Artois, her brother-in-law. Marie-Antoinette challenged him that he would not be able to build it in three months, but he won the bet and finished it in 64 days!

Other visitors who crossed their path often turned their admiration from the decor to this handsome couple, who seemed to fit so well with their surroundings. While looking around, Isabelle and Gérard exchanged impressions, getting to know each other, and Gérard noticed how well they were getting along. Finally, arriving in front of the Restaurant des Jardin, Gérard inquired if she would like to have lunch.

"I am not hungry quite yet, maybe something to drink?", Isabelle answered.

The place was so inviting, and Gérard looked at the tables under the canopies of flowers, and guided her closer, eyeing for a waiter.

"Good, because it is my whisky time," he said and winked when he received a shocked stare from Isabelle. But secretly, she started to greatly appreciate his sense of humor.

They were directed to one of the tables under a beautiful canopy of scented roses and sipped their drinks; for her a diabolo, Perrier water and cassis syrup, and for him a similar beverage with menthe instead of cassis. They exchange impressions regarding the endless varieties of flowers and the new roses that had been presented in international competitions that year with surprising names.

"I would like to take you for lunch to another place, not far from here." When Isabelle asked where that place was, he answered, "It is my secret place, on my secret island."

"You have a secret place on a secret island, here?"

"There is an island in the lake of the Parc de Boulogne, while Bagatelle is another attraction of the area."

"I know the lake, Papa took me on a rowboat ride when I was little, but I did not know it had an island. *Vous êtes encore plain de surprises, Monsieur!* You are again full of surprises, Mister!"

"I would love to show it to you, and there is also a good restaurant called the 'Chalet des Îles'."

"Now I think I am getting curious and hungry," said Isabelle finishing her diabolo and standing up.

After a short drive, out of Bagatelle Gardens but remaining inside Boulogne Forest, Gérard arrived on the shore of the lake. Shortly after they were taken across to the restaurant by the motorboat of the Chalet des Îles, The Chalet of the Islands. Isabelle looked at the place with delight. It was built in cozy Swiss chalet style with tables close to the water, where they were greeted with a glass of Champagne.

"Do you think we can sit by the water?" Isabelle asked politely. "I don't like the smell of tobacco if someone around smokes."

"Absolutely, I don't smoke either, and the view is even more beautiful close to the water."

They were invited to a table close to the lake, and as they sipped their glasses of Champagne, Gérard examined the menu, amused by the English translation of its French counterpart, while Isabelle admired the place and its surroundings. The waiter had mentioned that the chalet's original construction was done for Napoléon's wife, Joséphine, in the late 1800s. He also mentioned that at nightfall, there would be music and fireworks at dark. With regret Isabelle declined for it would be too long of a stretch until the evening, as it was now only just past 2 pm.

"This is a surprise for me, I never knew about the isle and its chalet and I have lived in Paris practically all my life," said Isabelle.

"Don't be too hard on yourself. I told you, it is a secret and very few people, including Parisians, have discovered this place. The inhabitants are too eager leaving Paris and going south for holidays, while the tourists just rush through to see the high points, then, they run out of time."

"And how many people have you brought here … I mean, to how many people have you showed your 'secret island'?" asked Isabelle, this time switching to English.

"Well, I did bring here my parents and my son, Patrick, a few years ago, but I was brought here for the first time by our ambassador, Joe Rodgers. He knows how to get away to quiet places without having to leave Paris, for obvious reasons. And the food is first class." Eager to know more about her he said, "I noticed your English was excellent when we were at the 4th of July party, and you have practically no French accent. Where did you learn how to speak English so well?"

"It might be a long story and I don't intend to bore you."

To which Gérard interrupted, "Please tell me, I have all the time in the world."

"Alright, but only if you would tell me more about your son," she concluded. And when he nodded in agreement, Isabelle continued, "When I was quite young, seven or eight years old, my mother became very ill, and after long debate and hesitancy, my parents agreed to send me to spend some time with my favorite aunt in Geneva, Switzerland. She was my father's oldest sister and a widow, and probably the only one in the family to be wealthy after marrying a Swiss banker.

"My aunt had a great personality but was childless, and considered me almost like her own child. In Geneva, she enrolled me in the best international school, insisting I take the section that was taught in English, stating that English was the language of the future. I think this was another thing she has been right about.

"She was convinced that this was the perfect age to learn a foreign language without effort, and I got a little exposure to Italian as well; I've always been fascinated by Italians and their art and culture.

"When I was 10 years old, my mother recovered from her depression, and later I learned that she'd had a miscarriage. At the same time she had lost a trial to recover property and money that had belonged to her parents, blocked on the other side of the iron curtain., It was a long drawn out battle and after losing it all, she panicked about the future. But slowly she returned to herself, being the well-balanced person I know - the center of our family."

"And how about your aunt, how is she now?" Gérard almost immediately regretted his question seeing the sad expression on her face.

"Aunt Chantal? She passed away a few years ago. Although in her early 70s, she was still skiing in Cran sur Sierre in the Alps. On one of her daily walks she was run over by a car that lost control on an icy patch of snow." After a while she said, "Now it's your turn to tell me more about yourself and your son."

Without realizing it, the two of them enjoyed learning more about each other, as they slowly savored the delicious food served. They started with a terrine au canard, duck terrine, served on a bed of greens. They also ordered the chef's recommendation of a sole farcie aux coquilles St. Jacques, flounder staffed with clams, and returned to Perrier after the glass of Champagne.

"My son, Patrick, is 11 and right now on summer vacation in Washington, DC, with my parents. He will be back mid-August with my parents and we will have a little time together before he starts the school in September."

She asked a few more questions about Patrick, his mother, and his interests in life, and Gérard was happy to volunteer with more information. Isabelle was touched to discover this tender side of Gérard's life, learning about the strong bond he had with his son and his absolute dedication to raising him alone. She asked one more question regarding his vacation this summer, and Gérard informed her that he rarely took any, reserving his absences when traveling to faraway places for UN missions.

"I have a few days here and there with holidays and slow seasons in Paris. How about you, any vacation coming up?"

"I took some time off this year, exceptionally. I learned that I work better if I don't burn out completely, like I almost did sometimes in the past. It was hard for me to realize I don't have to be at the institute all the time and they can function very well without me... So, this year I will go to Tuscany and tour some places staying in Florence and Lucca, then I will take small trips from there to Sienna, Pistoia, and maybe some other cities. I might take some painting lessons or Italian cuisine classes, depending on how I feel. I decided that this year I would not pressure myself as much as usual."

Calmly and naturally, they kept exchanging bits of information, and while knowing each other better, they relaxed and realized how much they enjoyed this time together. The beauty of the place and the splendid weather created a perfect decorum to make these moments special. Their closeness and attraction grew naturally and imperceptibly. They ventured to share more personal thoughts and memories, preferences and reasons for their choices in life.

When Gérard asked Isabelle why she decided to choose science after growing up learning music she said, "I remember very well the moment I made that decision. I always was attracted by science, medicine and medical research, in particular, but it seemed out of reach when I was still very young. One day at the conservatory, when several of my colleagues gathered with our teachers after a rehearsal in the auditorium, one of our mentors brought up the importance of protecting our hands.

"He was insisting how easily one could lose the ability to perform, how fragile a musical career was, regardless of all the efforts one could make to avoid accidents. It is an ephemeral condition for any performing artist, and all the talent in the world can decline if they do not stay at the top of their form, continuously practicing and sacrificing all for the musical profession. And your career can depend on the sudden shutting of a door crushing your hand!"

Isabelle paused, looking far away, lost in her thoughts. Gérard waited patiently for her to continue.

"I already knew that medical science can be of a greater contribution to humanity when it comes to saving lives or finding cures for diseases, or at least make certain conditions tolerable.

"I grew up learning how hard my relatives had been hurt during the war and long after that. They practically lost everything, not just their security, which made me realize that having medical expertise could also help one stay alive in any circumstances.

In addition, at that rehearsal I understood that although music was part of my life, part of me, in extreme circumstances I had very little chance of surviving by entertaining people, and I always could play for my own satisfaction. As a result, I made the conversion to medicine. I am very satisfied with this change, but it is not true that I can play anytime I want," she ended with a laugh.

"It has sometimes been years since I've had time to practice, and I can say that it has been very hard on me."

"I have not seen, or rather have not heard any problem with your playing," Gérard replied with eagerness, sincerely reassuring her.

They ended their lunch talking until the middle of the afternoon, not unusual for places where people come to enjoy the outdoors. Gérard proposed a walk on the island and Isabelle said she would be thrilled to discover a little more about his secret island. At one point, helping her to get closer to a large cider deploying his magnificent branches in the middle of a clearing, Gérard took her hand to lead her closer and she let it be, surprised by how natural all this felt.

They walked hand in hand for a while, the gorgeous day casting a mixture of bright rays through the shadows of the majestic trees. A swan floated graciously by, barely cutting the mirror of the lake, and later, a mother duck coaxing her playful ducklings to the water, brought smiles to their faces.

Gérard was aware of the quiet enchantment setting in and did not want to break the spell, but an urgent thought was invading his mind for a while, and finally he dared ask, "Is there any special man in your life at the present time?" and quickly he apologized, "I am overstepping my boundaries, I am afraid?"

"I thought that you might want to know by now, and no, there is not any special man occupying my heart presently." After a few moments passed she shyly added, "How about yourself, any woman waiting for you in some port?"

"Of course not," he was quick to reply, and reading in her eyes a profound apprehension, he added turning her gently to face her, holding both her shoulders as if they were the most precious objects. "I wouldn't be here with you right now if there was, and there is no other place I would want to be."

The two of them were looking tenderly at each other, lost in the new feelings storming inside them. Gérard was surprised by the candor of her reactions, all preparing him to expect the self-assured, very much in charge, professional woman he'd seen so far. And now, he realized how fragile, how vulnerable she was, and his heart opened even more in the desire to protect her, to make sure no harm would ever be done to this gentle creature.

He expressed his feelings simply by looking at her, and noticed how transparent the porcelain of her skin appeared in this light, how her eyes took a deeper shade of green under the long lashes, and how sweet and inviting her lips were smiling. Isabelle almost surrendered to his charm, his incredibly azure eyes, and how unaware he seemed to be of his seduction. Would she fall for it?

Before she could realize it, she felt his kiss. It was a tender and soft kiss at first, both taken by surprise by the amazing chemistry that broke their last conventional barriers. Lost in each other, holding and kissing, they discovered the wonder of the most magical attraction they had ever felt before.

Later in their lives, every time they thought of this first date, this first kiss, they remembered it as though finding the other having traveled across galaxies and life times, to finally be reunited in this very unique moment.

-//-

The magic moments continued as the beautiful light and colors changed, celebrating the unaltered beauty of the island, or was it their newly discovered connection? Walking in no hurry through the paths naturally winding between trees and shrubs, lost in their own world, they were unveiling sensations and saving the images of a story they had started creating together.

Was it this wonder taking them both by the unexpected impression of reading into each other's soul? With their spirits now lifted by this undeniable surprise of discovering the person they had always longed for, having given up hope of finding it in this lifetime, they now felt so complete, and all became so simple and so sublime.

Isabelle and Gérard realized at a certain time that the shadows were getting longer and quietly the sun had changed the colors of the horizon to spectacular shades of pink and red, then purple and indigo, and finally the light blue turning on darker hues with the approaching evening. None of them wanted this day to end, they wanted to retain the spell cast by their emerging feelings for each other, the joy and certainty of discovering their other half.

However, they made their way back to the boat, then to their car, and slowly through the July traffic in Paris; a blessed time for tourists and residents, when half of the population went on holiday in July, and the other half left the city in August, giving this new couple in love the leisure to admire and enjoy the unrivalled spectacle. Gérard was driving mostly with his left hand and holding Isabelle's hand with the right. When they arrived in front of her place, Isabelle, after exchanging a few more kisses of infinite sweetness, made Gérard understand that she would say her goodnight there.

He kindly took his leave promising he would call her every day, in fact as soon as he arrived at his apartment. And he kept his promise, and the two of them went to sleep wishing the other sweet dreams. Isabelle was more lightheaded than she had ever felt before and her voice on the phone must have sounded like a happy child lulled by a bedtime fairytale. They knew that they would be together again soon and that their dreams would, indeed, be sweet.

-//-

The morning came sending timid sunny rays through the closed drapes, making Isabelle aware of her surroundings, as she slowly stretched and realized that she felt happy and relaxed. She had slept a sound, restful sleep that she'd not had in a long time. She remembered the previous day with details of each moment with Gérard, and it made her feel elated and very apprehensive at the same time. Suddenly she remembered she was to join her parents in Rambouillet for lunch, then come back home in the afternoon and prepare for her work week the following morning.

Consulting the clock, she panicked seeing it was already 9 o'clock, leaving her little time to get ready and make it to the RER station on time for Rambouillet. She would not drive her car, as her father would fetch her at the train station in Rambouillet. Making her way to take a shower, she felt a pang of hunger and she quickly decided to make a *chocolat au lait*, milk chocolate, and munch a croissant in a hurry.

She managed to have her breakfast and get dressed in a black and white striped summer dress, matching white handbag, white lace wrist-length gloves, a white straw hat, and sunglasses. Grabbing her keys, she was about to rush out the door, when the intercom stopped her with a chime. She was surprised and pleased to hear Gérard's voice.

"The florist would not deliver on Sunday," he claimed as an excuse.

To which her answer was, "I will be down in a minute, I am late."

Arriving in front of the building, Isabelle saw Gérard at the entrance holding a beautiful bouquet of yellow daffodils. Isabelle explained that she was on her way to Gare Montparnasse, the train station, to see her parents. Seeing Gérard holding the flowers, her face became illuminated like the face of a happy child. After a few more explanations, Isabelle had the chance to thank Gérard for the flowers and he asked her to seal it with a kiss, which she gladly complied.

"Why don't I give you a ride to Rambouillet, and then you don't have to change metro and risk being late? I have a telephone in my car and you can call your dad not to come to the train station."

"And you can give the flowers to maman so they won't get wilted," said Isabelle, all of a sudden delighted by the turn of the situation.

This said, they were on their way, however, Gérard, although happy for the change of the events, was planning to give Isabelle only a ride to her parents' summerhouse. They were so happy to be together again and enjoying the nice weather! The traffic exiting Paris was light and they easily gained its southwest outskirts, the surroundings of Paris called Île de France, French Island. He was once again taken by the beauty and elegance of the places they were going through. Soon they reached the hilly sides of the countryside, and then Rambouillet Forest, some 60 kilometers, or 38 miles, southwest of Paris. From there, they entered the beautiful town, leaving Nationale 10 and, and, as Isabelle suggested, taking a short cut through Rue de Eveuses they avoided the train station, soon reaching the Beaumont cottage.

Hidden by the dense foliage of flowers and shrubs behind a five foot, old stone wall, they reached the house through rough iron gates, and parked under the canopy formed by a pergola on a gravel cleared space, next to a silver Renault 30.

The pergola was laden with hanging wisteria that even extended to some trees close by. Irises, roses, peonies, and lilac trees infused the air with competing fragrances, some climbing roses making a vertical decor on the old stones of the house. Gérard, already immersed in the charm of the place, stopped in the middle of the alley, when he saw the front door opening and the jovial face of Thierry Beaumont showing up.

"What a pleasant surprise! Please come on in, Claire is making her final touches to lunch."

When Gérard explained that he was not staying for lunch but had only brought their daughter to them, he insisted. "Nonsense, I will have a man around to talk to. Eric and his family are on vacation at La Baule, on the Atlantic coast, and this way we can let mother and daughter have their little chat. Plus, I would love to show you the Rambouillet Castle. Do you know it is one of the summer residences for the French president? We could go visit its gardens, as the president is not there this weekend."

Thierry placed his arm around Gérard's shoulder and gently led him inside.

The tantalizing smell of lamb roast made Gérard drop his last resistance and he was suddenly feeling at ease as he rarely had before.

Lunch was exquisite and simple by French standards for a Sunday meal. It was, composed of lamb roast garnished with Brussels sprouts and baked small new potatoes, valley greens salad and *fromage* plateau, and completed with a tart of fresh berries for dessert. Claire was complimented for her culinary talents, as they were getting along beautifully conversing in French, a natural habit for the Beaumonts, but perfectly mastered by Gérard.

Later, after coffee, and nursing a round amber glass of aged Cognac, Thierry sat in the small library with Gérard telling him a little more about the town of Rambouillet and its quite prestigious history.

"Do you know that there is an American monument in this town?" he asked and continued enthusiastically when Gérard shook his head. "Seven American soldiers died here in August 1944 when they were caught in an ambush. The monument displays an American eagle and the names of the soldiers are etched below an inscription of the tragic event. We can stop by on our way to the castle, it will be a lovely stroll in the beautiful park, and it will do us good," suggested Isabelle's father touching a little swell under his shirt with allusion to his satisfied belly.

Without delay, they left for a tour of the town and the park, Isabelle and her mom relaxing with their cup of coffee after tiding up the dining room and the kitchen after lunch. A little current of understanding went between Isabelle and her mother that Thierry had felt a natural impulse to check Gérard out. As they went out the door, Claire watched them with an amused grin as she continued sipping from her cup.

During lunch, Isabelle learned that her parents would not mind staying at the summer house a few more days and avoid being back in Paris the following weekend, since 14th of July, Bastille Day, fell on the Sunday. After so many years enjoying the Parisian festivities, they were looking forward to a quieter celebration. From one thing to another, Isabelle agreed that it was wiser and easier for everyone if she went back to Paris the way she came, taking advantage of her new chauffeur.

Things were settled and she would return to Paris without delay, as soon as Gérard was back with her father from their little visit to town. She had a very busy few days before the holiday weekend and Gérard had also expressed his anticipation of a heavy workload after his long weekend.

Once Gérard was back with Isabelle's father, the young couple took their leave. Little was exchanged between them of what was said during their time apart; Isabelle and her mother, and Gérard and her dad.

-//-

After their return to Paris, Gérard and Isabelle talked on the phone often, mostly in the evenings, spending hours getting to better know each other or just exchanging impressions of daily events. Gérard, although preparing papers for the next UN and other international sessions and presentations for the ambassador's future conferences, learned that some of the diplomatic corps were invited for special festivities held in Versailles the following Sunday. He quickly arranged to add Isabelle to the guest list, hoping she would agree to accompany him.

Gérard was aware that this would be a significant step forward in their personal relationship, becoming visible also within the social circles they were frequenting. He called Lucien and asked him what his thoughts were about it, and after giving a little more detail the facetious Lucien was pressing for, Gérard received an animated encouragement.

"This is the best news I've heard since my marriage, Gérard! It was about time you met someone, and you could not find anyone better than Isabelle. You two look fantastic together and she is a great lady on all accounts. The only thing I don't understand *mon vieux*, old man, is what on earth she finds in *you*?" he continued with a friendly laughter.

The whole country was on holiday for at least three days until the following Tuesday, including Gérard and Isabelle. The members of the American Embassy invited to attend the festivities in Versailles, were staying for two or three nights at the Versailles Trianon Palace Hotel, a Waldorf Astoria hotel.

Gérard's room had already been booked for two nights, the Saturday and Sunday to follow. Isabelle was added to the guest list and promised a room in the same hotel. The Waldorf Astoria Hotel, located in the former Trianon palaces, a small addition to Versailles, was located on the right side of the Versailles gardens with easy access and views to the Versailles Palace.

Saturday, the 13th of July, was a day of gathering, in which they were free to explore, followed by a reception in the afternoon at the Versailles Palace in front of the gardens at the opening of the Royale Court.

On Sunday, the 14th, there was a more official reception, followed by a show of laser lights, music and water jets, and finally, fireworks.

The guests could enjoy the spectacle from comfortable bleachers placed in front of the immense panorama of the gardens and fountains. The schedule allowed plenty of time for visiting and exploring the famous palace and its grounds, and the weather forecast announced pleasant summer temperatures to the joy of everyone attending the outdoor celebrations.

Towards the end of the week everybody displayed a festive mood, the ones left to work on the offices or the clinics, not having had yet the big summer vacation, were looking forward to a break and getting ready to have a good time on the French National Day.

By Thursday, people would exchange their plans for the weekend and on Friday many took an additional day off, with only the minimum functioning staff to be found in the offices. Isabelle and Gérard also found themselves with a lighter workload than usual, a welcome breath after the marathon of the first four days of the week.

At Gérard's suggestion to meet for dinner at the Italian restaurant with Lucien and Vivianne, they were all eager to get together. Gérard was subconsciously attracted by the place he had previously had dinner with Isabelle, albeit thanks to his dear friends. He needed also to give Isabelle the last details of the Versailles trip they were to take the day after. As planned, Friday night a joyous company was gathered at Chez Ricardo for an early celebration of the holiday weekend ahead.

-//-

The trip to Versailles was a blur of spectacular receptions in one of the most sophisticated sites in the world. The final show overlooking the esplanade of the royal parks beyond the palace, had been an explosion of mighty geysers from the fountains who spewed water in all directions and configurations mixed with laser lights and music, and lastly, crowned by the final fireworks.

All attendees, overwhelmed by the vastness and artistry of the spectacles, were happy to regain their hotel room or their home for a more relaxing day to follow. So were Isabelle and Gérard, elated to spend time together and be transported to a world of wonder.

The other members of the American committee had naturally included Isabelle as Gérard's "new friend" and looked at them tenderly, happy to see Gérard in feminine company. On Monday, the new couple lingered a little longer in the gardens of the superb hotel before going back to Paris. Isabelle called her parents from the hotel and took her time to describe the show of the last evening, but she also let them know that she would not have the time to stop by Rambouillet, on her way back to Paris.

The following days, the two young people seemed to float on a charming mood, trying to retain the magic they had felt during their trip. Before her summer trip to Tuscany Isabelle had to complete a few papers in addition to her two clinic days per week seeing patients included in the clinical trials.

Gérard, with the approach of her departure, grew more unsettled. He already thought of finding a way to see again Isabelle one more time before her vacation, and, if at all possible, in a quieter and more intimate setting this time.

Gérard kept busy enough at the embassy, although the summer schedule was less grueling, with many of the staff members already away on vacation, the workload remained steady. This was in a way good for him during the daytime, but the evenings when he was not on the phone with Isabelle, and at night, he could no longer find his peace. Her image and flashes of the moments they had spent together recently, occupied his mind constantly.

He had wanted to spend even more time together since the weekend in Versailles, and days without her became harder for him; he felt that now his life had not much sense being alone, and for the first time longed for a family.

With his son away on vacation, although staying in touch with frequent phone calls, Gérard was alone in Paris, the most attractive place to be in summer when single. He had lost all interest in attending any of the myriad of open air concerts, art displays, and acting events announced in the weekly Paris Guide and held in practically every square, park or church.

Gérard thought of taking Isabelle on a trip out of Paris that was not too far or too long, so she would not get scared and refuse. He perused through lists of sites he had visited in the past either with his son or during embassy functions. Many were close to Paris and charged with unique historical attractions in the most charming settings. He finally decided for Château de Chantilly, Chantilly Castle.

However, inviting Isabelle for a private getaway weekend meant bringing their relations to a different level of intimacy. He could not help but think of holding Isabelle in his arms and showing his love for her. Because he admitted to himself that it was, indeed, love what he felt for her.

Reflecting on the time he had shared with Isabelle and the feelings that grew like the fast waters of a cascade invading every thought, every fiber of his being, these feelings were true feelings of love. He knew that he was very attracted by her beauty and sitting next to her became harder for him to control his impulse to wrap her in his arms.

And he became even more fascinated by the complexity and mystery of what he considered as the ideal of femininity, as he had never been as close to anyone before. Gérard was, without realizing, ready to dive head over heels into a new and complete passion; his only desire was to surrender to this deep and ravaging flame. He was the rare kind of person to which love meant absolute commitment and gave himself entirely.

Gérard chose Chantilly Castel because he remembered spending some time there with his son on this huge property less than 20 miles from Paris. The castle, restored by Henry d'Orleans, Duke d'Aumale and son of the last king of France, Louis Philippe, in the late 1800s, was donated in 1886 to the Institute de France and offered many attractions. In the past, Gérard had visited with Patrick the "Écuries Royales" (the Royal Stables) located on the domain of the Castle, which were the largest horse training and racing facilities in France.

Gérard remembered how much Patrick had enjoyed horse riding along with a visit to the buildings and training corrals; the old tradition of breeding and training here was done in one of the most prestigious academies in Europe. The Royal Stables were part of the massive buildings of the domain entrance, not far from Auberge du Jeu de Paume, a splendid five-star hotel with its famous restaurant, La table du

153

Connétable, a Jardin d'Hiver, the winter conservatory, its private pool and a spa, ready to satisfy the most exigent of the jet setters visiting the place.

There were also other beautiful buildings besides the extraordinary château, which contained a superb art collection, Condé Museum. One could find in the different corners of the large formal gardens Le Hameau restaurant, a Chinese garden, an English garden, and a romantic pavilion, La Maison de Sylvie.

Having in mind the prospective weekend trip to Chantilly, Gérard took all his courage and called Isabelle the next Thursday and invited her to dinner intending to discuss the details of the last weekend before Isabelle's departure for Italy. While Gérard felt more attracted by Isabelle every day and did not fight any longer his feelings for her, Isabelle was shying away by the hasty progression taken by their relationship.

Realizing the novelty and the intensity of the attraction she felt for Gérard, part of her wanted to find refuge in her demanding work before her vacation, while needing to keep a little more distance sorting out the nature of the last encounters with Gérard.

Isabelle was counting on the few weeks ahead of her in Italy, and hoped the distance and the time away would allow her to bring more clarity regarding her own feelings before they made any further attachment. So, when Gérard called at her office and invited her to dinner, her response was, "I don't think the Dubois are in town to dine with us at Chez Ricardo; the last I heard was that they went for a short trip to Spain and are basking on the Costa del Sol at Torremolinos."

"Lucky them", said Gérard, "obviously they are still on honeymoon."

"Well, some people have to work!", replied Isabelle, "I have tons of things to wrap up before my voyage to Italy in two weeks. All I can do is lunch somewhere close to my office."

This quickly settled the matter, and on Thursday they were seated at a café across from her medical building, both ordering quiche and salad, water and espresso for her, and only water for him.

The conversation came naturally and friendly. Gérard knew how to make her relax and after complimenting her on how well she looked, he even made her laugh a few times. For some reason, Gérard looked into her eyes, lowered his voice and said, "You must have countless admirers. I wonder how you are still single ... there must be someone you see in secret." It was a statement and a question at the same time, and he paused in expectation.

Isabelle suddenly became alive, as something struck a chord, a little bit like the time they had first met and he gave her the impression of being a supremely self-assured male, sure of his abilities to seduce whomever he wished.

Without raising her voice, but her chin slightly lifted and her posture straightened, she answered, "You must think, like many men who enjoying a certain social and financial privileges, that this gives you the upper hand when it comes to impressing any woman with your interest. And that, of course, the 'lucky lady' should melt under your attentions."

"I am so sorry," for one rare occasion Gérard was stammering, "It came out all wrong, let's forget the whole thing. I want you to know though, that I never act like that, I do not try to impress anyone. I respect all women, I respect you Isabelle!" He almost wanted to shout, "I love you" but he said instead, "I only wanted to know if your heart is free."

"It is good for you to know that my heart is free, I am, and I feel free. But I am not available. I am not looking for, and I do not desire a relationship at this time."

Those words fell like an axe breaking the spell. Gérard realized that his plans, his desire to see a life with Isabelle from now on was all an illusion that had just dissipated.

After a few moments of silence, Isabelle said with great softness in her voice, looking at him almost tenderly, "Gérard, I don't have room in my life for a relationship at this time, I am so sorry." Then grabbing her purse ready to leave she said, "I think we should take some time without seeing each other." As she left, she suddenly came around the table and gave him a little peck on the cheek.

With a few steps, she was gone and Gérard followed her with a sadness in his eyes he could not hide. He stood there a little longer having difficulty absorbing her last words and straining to recover. He whispered to himself and almost laughed, "I have to cancel the reservation for Chantilly." Then he got up and went to his office determined to finish his week at work and quit making a fool of himself.

-//-

It was the day after, early on Friday afternoon, when Maggie was helping Gérard with a fundraising event supporting UNICEF to be held on the following Saturday. Gérard was the main representative of the

US embassy as the *attaché culturel* for the events held in France, but also in Europe for humanitarian functions, and with many of the other diplomatic corps members on vacation, his plate was full.

Initially, the event was planned to take place at the Royaumont Abbey in an idyllic location 30 kilometers north of Paris, but it was finally decided they would use the embassy grounds instead at the request of some celebrities who were performing and preferred to stay in town. It was one of the summer balls most sought after by the philanthropic organizations and other charitable personalities.

Maggie, entering Gérard's office, was excited to tell him the latest information regarding the performances that would be offered on the Saturday evening. "We will have Alain Delon reading a poem, Serge Reggiani singing, followed by Mireille Mathieu and Dalida. Maybe we will get George Brassens, I don't have an answer yet, but your friend, Isabelle Beaumont, agreed to play a couple of classical pieces on the harp."

And in the same breath Maggie added, "She tried to refuse, she doesn't have a way to transport the harp, as her parents took the larger car with them on vacation, but I told her we will take care of it and we will send a big van to bring it over."

Gérard stopped in his tracks, puzzled and confused.

Maggie giggled and said, "I wanted to surprise you, but I know your friend will be a hit."

He almost wanted to say she was not his friend, or not anymore, but decided it was better to let it all rest, as things were already as hectic as they could be.

The entire Friday afternoon, Gérard was busy with the last touches to his introduction of the main sponsors for the reception the next day. He also prepared a list of thank you letters to be addressed to the contributors who could not attend the ball. Work kept him busy from thinking and he did not want to even imagine how he would act in Isabelle's presence at the reception. He was thankful to God he would be busy until then and would remain throughout the entire evening! Maggie and other embassy employees continued to come and go with questions or new information.

Maggie, usually quiet and efficient, remained animated every time she had more news to share, "Régine Crespin will sing an aria from Carmen, Michel Aumont, societaire of the Comédie Française, will play a part from Cyrano de Bergerac," she announced.

The artistic animator asked to confer with Gérard about the weather forecast, announcing that rain was a strong possibility for Saturday night. He was concerned the rain might arrive earlier in the afternoon and wanted to make sure that the artists would perform inside. He left reassured by Gérard that the gardens would be used only for the early part of the reception during cocktails and aperitifs, while the official salons would host the main events.

In one of the salons was erected a stage facing a suite of several salons where elegant tables would be set with buffets offering a variety of delicious selections of food made by the best chefs in town.

-//-

Isabelle spent a good part of Saturday morning tuning and rehearsing for the evening reception at the American Embassy. When Maggie called the day before, she had surprised herself by agreeing to play, again with almost no notice. She had already had some friendly contact with Maggie; just recently they had exchanged a few phone calls regarding the reservations for the French Independence Day.

As it was a question of helping children of the Third World it was hard to turn down, at least she did not have the heart to say no, and they only required two or three pieces of popular music to make everyone happy. Early in the afternoon a van from the embassy came, loading the harp with great attention. She also agreed with La Crespin, the famous soprano, to accompany her when she will sing Ave Maria by Bach-Gounod.

Later that afternoon, Isabelle on a green cocktail satin dress, left her apartment deep in thought about the music she would play. She was not aware how beautiful she looked, nor how the dress enhanced the color of her eyes, and made her fair complexion glow. She pinned the sides of her hair up, leaving a few locks fall down her back and shoulders. Her profile appeared lovelier than ever, her figures reminding of a river fairy, all elegance and grace.

Isabelle went to the place where her little Morris was parked and drove to Avenue Gabriel, where a pass allowed her to enter the embassy grounds. She was quite nervous and tried to quiet her heart by repeating to herself that playing just a few notes was a small contribution to the event, while real artists would be there for the major performance of the evening.

Once back stage, she used the time left to tune the harp and warm up. Isabelle was surprised to find that some of the artists were already there, and they were at least as nervous as she was. Maggie was nice enough to welcome all of them, mentioning that Gérard Forrest was busy at the front of the reception where the guests were to arrive.

As soon as Régine Crespin came in, she went straight to Isabelle for a proper introduction, since they had only exchanged a short conversation over the phone. They rehearsed together a few bars of the music and soon, the two of them smiled and felt more relaxed as they just enjoyed playing together, pleased that all was going so smoothly.

During this time, the other performing artists arrived and engaged in conversation, since most of them already knew each other. Alain D., confident in his dazzling looks, was intrigued by Isabelle, the eternal Don Juan in him wondering how he was not aware of such a beauty in town. He asked to be introduced to her and was received with polite reserve, something that excited his interest even more.

The reception went as expected; after cocktails and speeches the guests were eventually seated at their tables, letting the artists entertain them. It was a smashing success, with talented artists offering a heartfelt contribution to the Children of the World.

Isabelle and Régine played Ave Maria and everyone in the room was moved. Isabelle began to relax and challenged herself for the second number by playing a neck breaking, high virtuosity harp solo music from "Lucia de Lammermoor" by Donizetti. Although she wondered at the impulse for this difficult choice and tried to concentrate on her playing, she appeared to the others as serene and impressed the audience with her agility and the light touch of her technique.

Although pulled in all directions by the obligations of his position as the main diplomatic attaché of the evening, Gérard felt his heart stir when he saw Isabelle amongst the attendants. When she was performing, he felt he could fall in love with her there and then, if he was not already under her spell. They exchanged only a nod of acknowledgement from afar, without any chance of getting closer. Gérard noticed, however, the interest Alain D. showed, without trying to hide it, toward Isabelle the entire evening.

Without letting his feelings be noticed, Gérard continued making sure that everything was going well and everyone was attended perfectly. He effortlessly changed languages during conversations with his guests of various nations, while he discretely supervised his staff, all this keeping him stay busy going through the evening without any flow.

As planned, it all seemed to unfold flawlessly, at least until now.

-//-

As soon as the cocktails were over and the guests entered the embassy's salons for the reception, the heavy clouds hanging over the city began to unload. At first, there were only a few splashes here and there, and then the rain started falling heavier and heavier. Soon the outdoor staff was scrambling to bring tables and chairs inside from the lawn, and the valet service was running around closing car windows that some guests had left open. Gérard hurried discretely to ensure that all possible was done to prevent the rain from ruining the evening.

Sure enough, after the performances had ended, and everyone was getting comfortable, enjoying the conversation, the food, and the good Champagne, thunder could be heard getting louder and more frequent. However, the guests showed little concern, and carried on for a while longer.

As though there was not enough to deal with, Gérard was informed that a newly arrived young male secretary from the visa office had gotten carried away and, in a drunken state, had started making some inappropriate advances to a guest's wife. He even made some insulting racial slurs about her husband, the guest being a member from the delegation of Ghana, one of the recipients of the evening's proceedings.

Luckily, no other attendee noticed the incident and the young secretary was removed from the room, a serious reprimand to follow along with his permanent return to the US. Gérard apologized profusely to the Ghanaian delegate who reassured him that he'd had to deal in the past with a similar situation amongst his own staff.

This gave Gérard no time to relax, when the guests started to show more concerned about the storm. Initially, the embassy staff tried to keep the guests there, hopeful that the squall would pass quickly, but the lightening and deafening thunder was making the windows shake and chandeliers rattle, raising concerns that this might be a tempest of huge proportions.

Cars were pulled up at the front entrance under the little protection provided by the awning of the *porte cochère*. Umbrellas were held overhead but rendered useless in the wind. Soon it was impossible to move the cars because of the raising amount of water flooding the parking. The valet service was completely overwhelmed but tried their best running all directions.

With great help from every member of the embassy staff present, all guests finally found a way of transportation, swore that they'd had a fantastic time and the rain would only make it more memorable!

Isabelle had to accept the idea of having her harp brought back to her home next week, as she was in no rush. Nevertheless, when she tried to have her car advanced to leave as well, the water was already too high in that part of the parking lot and the car could not be started.

However, she was reassured that the car would be pushed to higher ground and taken to a garage when possible. She did not want to add to the chaos her hosts were already dealing with, and when Gérard came to apologize and offered to accompany her with one of the embassy's bigger cars, she had no choice but to accept.

The caterers managed to leave with their vans, offering transport to their crewmembers, while the embassy staff was allocated a safe place to stay if needed. When it was finally time for Isabelle to leave, she made a dash for the door of the car Gérard was holding open for her against the furious wind.

Gérard, who knew that the route to Isabelle's apartment should not take more than 15-20 minutes in normal circumstances, gave all his attention to driving there safely as the rain was blinding the view. It was after 10 o'clock at night, and because of the storm, there were few cars on the road. Gérard kept quiet during the ride, all eyes on the road.

The downpour seemed to get stronger by the minute, with no sign of the wind easing, still coming down in harsh gusts. Isabelle realized how tired Gérard must be with all the work and responsibility weighing heavily on his shoulders. She said something to this effect and thanked him for the extra effort he was making to drive her home.

Gérard dismissed any impression of having done anything out of the ordinary. He fought, however, the impulse of saying something about Alain D.'s gallant behavior; he knew he had no right to ask any questions, particularly after their last conversation, when Isabelle made clear that she did not wish any form of attachment. It was easy to understand that men would continue to be attracted by such a beautiful woman for many years to come.

Going across the Place de la Concorde and reaching the quays and the bridge going over to the left bank of the River Seine, they were stopped by a police barrage at the traffic lights flickering to red. One of the officers told them that the waters of the river had risen quickly and the quays were covert by the flush flooding strong currents.

The two riverbanks were from now closed to traffic for the public safety. Gérard went out to talk with the police and to ask for an alternate route, but came back defeated and to realize that his car was taking water and soon the engine stalled as well. He tried to restart his car several times, when the gendarmes came to assist him.

"The waters are rising quickly and we need to move your car out of the way," they said, then started pushing the car a little higher up on the road.

The gendarmes, additional National Guard troupers, readily helped the Parisian police in the event of any disaster, and after moving the car, they called a tow truck for Gérard.

Now, with his evening attire drenched through, Gérard was unable to stop a few bouts of shiver. After a while, the two of them were relieved to see the truck coming. The driver hooked up Gérard's car, but he decided he could not cross the bridge either, and after a short debate, the truck driver offered to drop them off at Gérard's place, just north of the embassy, on Rue du Fg. Saint Honoré.

Gérard and Isabelle squeezed into the front cabin, next to the driver; the two of them were soaked, shivering but thankful for the ride. Isabelle accepted Gérard's offer of accommodation, after he explained that his son's room could serve as a guest room.

"I don't care at this point, I only want some dry place and dry clothes," she managed to say.

In order to make room for them in the driver's cabin, Gérard, caught in the middle, had to bring his arm around Isabelle's shoulders. As they found their bodies tight against each other's, they started warming from this unexpected and exquisite embrace. Soon he felt her tension releasing, as she was leaning comfortably against his shoulder.

They stayed quiet the remainder of the ride in a delightful and unexpected truce. Gérard was transported back to his dreams again, not trying to fight them, but taking in the sweetness of the moment. Isabelle was surprised by the powerful seduction this man continued to have over her, and she was too weary at the end of this frightful day, at least for now, did not want to disrupt this unexpected peaceful moment.

-//-

"There we go," the driver announced, making them both startle, "is this your building?"

Gérard looked through sheets of rain abating against the windshield and could barely recognize it, but he lowered his head in acknowledgement. They dashed for the building door, taking in more rain, while the tow truck quickly disappeared, after showering them with angry water spray from its enormous wheels. Finally, after Gérard activated the entrance code, he gently guided Isabelle through the elegant entrance hall to the elevator, and pressed the button for the third floor.

The building, like the streets, was strangely quiet, only the thunder could still be heard, menacing intermittently. They entered Gérard's flat and Isabelle discovered where he lived for the first time. Taking in the spacious living room, she noticed the sober elegance of the place, with deep leather couches, an extension of the living room doubling the space with an office and library. The wood paneling and bookshelves were laid with books, artifacts from Africa and other parts of the world, and a few pictures of Patrick and Gérard's family.

As she looked around, Gérard hurried to make his bedroom ready for Isabelle against all her protests, and now was in his bathroom pulling out a large bathrobe for her and looking for what else she might need. He gently directed her to the master bedroom and then showed her the attached bathroom.

He told her to get out of her wet clothes and take a warm shower, while he would do the same in Patrick's bathroom, and then he would make hot tea before they both caught their death from the cold. Isabelle was eager at the idea of a long, hot shower and a dry and cozy bathrobe, like the one Gérard had left on the bench next to the bathtub.

Gérard, after taking pajamas and a dry change from his wardrobe, went to the opposite side of the apartment to Patrick's bedroom and ensuite bathroom. He was already sighing with anticipation of his shower, when he noticed that he had not brought his toothbrush from his bathroom.

"Isabelle, I am so sorry, I need you to hand me my toothbrush, if it is possible," said Gérard knocking at the door.

"So sorry, but I already used it," was the answer as Isabelle appeared still wearing her pretty dress that was now half unzipped, still wet and stuck to her body. "And I can't get off my dress, the zipper is stuck."

Gérard entered and covered the few steps separating them to help her; but it must have been the fatigue of this long and trying day, the insane situation at seeing Isabelle so incredibly beautiful, now, that the dress was revealing more of her slender figure and her long blond hair was dripping in ringlets, that he staggered. Isabelle opened her arms in a reflex to support him, and suddenly they were holding each other, unable to let go.

They held on to the other gently at first, then tighter as they started probing and discovering each other's body with their hands, sliding over and around each other. They started kissing passionately and soon hungry hands were reaching to undo the other's clothes. The shower was running, the steam calling, and they spontaneously entered the shower. Laughing like children, they let out all the joy they felt, the small pleasure of sponges filled with bubbles to wash each other.

Isabelle dropped all her resistance and showed so much pleasure and relief in doing so. She was spellbound by his ravaging looks, his hair now freed from conventional combing and falling in gentle waves, his impossible smile and the most seductive azure eyes she had ever seen. And with the warmth of the water their bodies relaxed, the nervous tension fell away, and they continued splashing and laughing, kissing and embracing, discovering each other's body and loving it.

They eventually came out of the shower and dried off, happily covering up with comfortable dry robes, and they naturally went to the large bed and jumped on it to roll around and kiss again. It seemed they would never get enough of the pleasure of tasting and discovering each other, marveling at the beauty of the other one's young body, and the joy finding more attraction, more desire with each moment, with each caress.

They shared the wonder of finding each other again, as if after the longest separation across ages and galactic distances. Somewhere their minds realized that this was a reunion long expected, a gift the universe gave them in allowing them to find their way back together.

They gave themselves to the other with the utmost natural longing, melting their bodies into each other in wonder. They made love, and then they held tight to the other, and made love again. Out came whispers of the most loving words, and slowly they drifted into a blissful sleep where their whole beings were just smiles. The delight continued into their dreams; their bodies were spent and tranquil, but their souls in the depth of the serenity found, continued to unveil moments from a forgotten paradise.

Images of simple, innocent moments of childhood appeared in their dreams, and the profound happiness of unscathed images. Through their child eyes, they watched in awe lights shimmering on a beautiful beach at sunset, the blue sky filtering through tall trees. There were sounds of a music that awakened the soul and their young lives resonated to its deep harmonies, or a gentle touch from a loved hand swiping away a stray strand of hair. The two of them had similar dreams, carried by the enjoyment of having each other, holding the other through their reverie.

At some time in the early hours of the morning, Isabelle woke up and became aware of this new place. She looked at Gérard sleeping, her eyes filled with love as her gaze caressed his attractive features, the perfect design of his face, and his large shoulders and one arm extended in a generous gesture of protection over the small of her back. Looking at him, she knew she was safe and fell asleep again, so deeply this time that she did not hear him later getting up.

Much later, when the city was waking up under a gloriously bright sun in its attempt to wipe away the damage done by the storm, the same sun filtered through the Venetian blinds and reached Isabelle's eyelashes. Gérard already went out to find an open *boulangerie* and buy croissants, reassured to learn from people gathering in the streets that the waters had started to recede as fast as they rose. He checked on his car parked in the building's garage and was relieved to see the concrete floors all dry and the cars protected from the havoc left outdoors by the storm. Coming back up, he made coffee, and then cautiously entered the bedroom to check on Isabelle.

She started stretching voluptuously like a cat, and when she saw him, she murmured, "I want to stay in bed all day." She patted the bed with her hand, inviting Gérard to come closer.

He paused only for a few seconds before joining her, trying to fix in his memory how adorable she was. His embraces and his kisses, their kisses, became passionate, hungry, demanding, liberating them from any worries they'd ever had before, from any memory of pain that might have left them with a wounded heart. The joy they shared was complete because of the trust they felt in each other; an entirely new experience for them both.

Along with this liberating joy came an enormous craving for affection, and only much later they relaxed, satisfied and their fever quenched. Gérard thought that he would never want to stop caressing and feeling under his lips the velvety silk of her diaphanous skin, while Isabelle realized that she would always melt under his kisses, and would never resist the stir of sensuality he incited in her.

As she had said earlier, they spent most of the day in bed, had croissants and coffee, with butter and jelly. However, reality crept up on them so insidiously and they soon had to think of their work for the next day and that eventually Isabelle would have to leave and go home. Gérard had already called the embassy that morning to make sure nothing major had happened. He learned that a few staff members had similar bad experiences, getting water in their cars, but overall, everyone was fine. However, the office would be open on Monday only for emergencies.

By the time Isabelle made it home, having to wear the same dress, now dry even if not closing perfectly, it was getting late and Gérard had to leave shortly after bringing her all the way up to her apartment. They both knew that demanding problems would need their attention for the days to come. However, Gérard was thrilled that Isabelle agreed to go with him the following weekend to Chantilly, the way he had planned it all along. Only the thought of their trip together gave Gérard the strength to remove himself from her, and he drove back home in the night, all smiles, whistling all the way.

-//-

The days of the following week went by fast with busy working days, while the evenings and the nights advanced slowly, the two lovers missing each other immensely. At lunch break on Monday, Gérard returned to his office with a purple bouquet of peonies and handed them to Maggie.

When she looked at him in surprise, he came around her desk and hugged her saying: "This is to thank you for all the hard work you did this week and this weekend." In his mind, he was mainly grateful for her having invited Isabelle to play at the reception, which set in motion all the happy events that followed. While at the florist, Gérard had first chosen the most gorgeous dozen red roses to be delivered to Isabelle's place, then ordered another dozen for every evening until they were together again.

When Isabelle arrived at her apartment building late that afternoon, the concierge came out of her loge and gave her the bouquet of flowers. Isabelle went up to her flat smelling the roses and reading the small note that said, "Four more days until I hold you in my arms again." She was happy that he could not see her blushing, moved and secretly very pleased to discover what a romantic Gérard appeared to be. After that, every evening she found the concierge coming out handing her another dozen red roses, with a note saying: "three more days", then "two more days" then on Thursday evening, "tomorrow, my love".

Eventually Friday came and Gérard was at Isabelle's doorstep early in the afternoon. The ride to Chantilly was easy and pleasant, this time of the year Paris having the summer respite from its inhabitants leaving for vacation.

Their weekend, as planned and dreamed by Gérard even before Isabelle could fully presume the depth of his feelings, even less her own emotions, became a revelation beyond their wildest dreams. They shared enchanted moments, heightened by the superb and tranquil surroundings, that helped them realize how well suited they were, how much they had in common, and how naturally they understood each other.

From moments of passion, to long strolls in the park, visits to the stables, pavilions or the castle's library, a profound and strong bond was growing. It was like a parenthesis in life without disruption and worry, when one wishes to stop the time, with images they both wanted to forever mark their memory.

There was only one thing they avoided talking about—Isabelle's imminent departure for Tuscany at the end of the following week—as neither of them wished to break the spell of these special moments. Therefore, they continued to wander around the splendid castle and its surroundings, lost in their own world and unaware of the admiration they provoked in the people that crossed their path, pleasantly surprised at the sight of this attractive young couple.

Sunday came fast, much too fast, and although Isabelle and Gérard lingered most of the day at the *auberge*, they eventually had to get on the road and head back to Paris and to their regular obligations. Only then, Gérard found the courage and opened up a discussion about her vacation. He told her how much he would miss her and how lost he would feel without her.

Isabelle answered very sincerely that she would miss him too, but it was probably for the best. Trying to analyze her own feelings, she admitted to herself that it was *definitely* for the best; she needed this temporary time of reflection before she panicked again and ran away from Gérard. So much had happened in such a short period of time, and she wanted to give herself the chance to make sure they had the same feelings when far from each other, as the proof that this was the *real* thing.

Their drive back was a mixture of sweet sensations from the closeness they now shared, and sadness at having to part again. Gérard had to resign himself to the facts and wait for Isabelle's return. They might still have one more night together before she left, but he knew that this would make their separation even harder. And in the middle of August, Patrick was coming back from the United States accompanied by his parents, and as they planned before Patrick left for vacation, Gérard would spend a few days with him and his parents.

This was also the last two weeks of Patrick's free time before starting school again in September. He wanted to have a great father–son time together, realizing how much he missed his son, now even more torn between how to reconcile the time and the attention toward the two persons he cared for the most in the world.

-//-

The last few days before Isabelle's departure were intense, with last touches of papers to be published by Dr. Martin containing the latest studies they had been working on and for which the institute obtained a research grant. Reviewing the articles before Dr. Martin's final approval, Isabelle remembered that the same work was the subject of the award celebrated the day Vivianne and Lucien got married, the same day she and Gérard met.

She could not resist from taking a few instants to wonder of how much had happened since that fateful day. She had to struggle not to get distracted by the fleeting images of the last two weekends that had seemed to change her life. Was her life changed forever? She was the kind of person that never did anything lightly, moreover when it involved her heart, her relationships, and her future.

Before leaving town, Isabelle managed to have lunch with Vivianne with whom she had become increasingly attached. And she needed a friend, with her parents away on vacation at La Baule, joining Eric and his family. Besides, there was nothing like the advice from a young friend.

When Vivianne learned Isabelle and Gérard had fallen in love and gone away on a weekend together, somehow Vivianne was not terribly surprised. In fact, she was ecstatic for them, and became all fired up, asking one question after another. How did it happen, were they going to Italy together, etc.?

"This is exactly why I am going by myself. I need time to think; am I making a big mistake, are things going too fast?" an anxious Isabelle answered and questioned at the same time.

"Of course, only you can answer those questions, but I can tell you that Lucien and I noticed how well the two of you looked together; we made some remarks long ago about how wonderful it would be if you were to become a couple. Lucien has known Gérard for a long time and thinks the world of him. He knows he is a perfect father raising his son by himself, and he does not know of any particular woman hanging around.

"He is definitely not the type running the bars and collecting those "eye-catching dolls". And for a man as attractive as him and in a city like Paris, where men are tempted all day long with the best looking models or celebrities on the rise, this is not a little thing to consider."

Isabelle did not say anything, sipping her Orangina and reflecting on Vivianne's words.

After a while, Vivianne added, "And you know, Isabelle, to be very honest with you, it was not long ago I was thinking the same way. I was satisfied with my life, my daughter and my career, and I did not need any complications.

"After meeting Lucien, I realized that all can be very different, and many people go through life without having the chance to meet 'the other half' like I did, like perhaps you are now... So, why don't you go on your trip and take your sweet time to think about it?" Vivianne ended with a lower voice, and padded Isabelle's hand in understanding.

After her conversation with Vivianne, Isabelle felt much better and was able to go through her days at work. Nevertheless, overwhelmed by the fatigue and lassitude accumulated, she started looking forward to her vacation.

At last, the time came for Isabelle to leave. She boarded her airplane after a long kiss with Gérard, who insisted on taking her to the airport. In the rush of the airport formalities, Isabelle missed seeing the sadness in Gérard's face, as he watched her disappear into the gangway as though losing her forever.

-//-

After a short flight, she arrived at her first destination, Peretolo Airport, where she rented a car, and 30 minutes later, she reached Florence, Italy. For the time she would spend in Florence, Isabelle chose to stay at the Villa Jacopone, a family-run residence, built on a hilltop looking over Florence.

Isabelle had already enjoyed staying there in the past, while on vacation with her parents. Having to deal with the hustle of the traveling, luggage handling, and riding the rental car to the villa, all seemed helping Isabelle to keep her mind away from Gérard.

Once in view of the Tuscan villa, its beautiful gardens, the pool and the terraces overlooking the old city of Florence, Isabelle sighed with relief, unwinding at last. She found her comfortable room, done in a rustic Italian country style, with an adjacent spacious and well-garnished bathroom, and a good-sized terrace offering breathtaking views of Florence.

It did not take her long to unpack, and feeling the pangs of hunger at the delicious flavors coming from the villa's onsite restaurant, she went downstairs.

 The property owners were a middle-aged couple who had a passion for growing a large garden filled with fragrant herbs and a large variety of vegetables for the restaurant preparations for which the place had a great reputation. They were also offering a personal selection of wines from the close by vineyards.

Isabelle called Gérard from the beautiful villa's reception lounge. She reassured him her trip had been uneventful, and she was pleased as well when he encouraged her to enjoy her trip and the well-deserved rest. Gérard did not want to spoil her vacation by telling her how much he already missed her and how much at a loss he felt.

While waiting for lunch to be served to the guests, Isabelle strolled randomly through the alleys of the villa's garden. Lunch was served on the lower terrace under a canopy of vines; the atmosphere was friendly and the food exceptional with a variety of greens and pasta, tomatoes and mozzarella, olives and pesto, all from local farmers or from the villa's grounds.

Then, the August sun becoming a little warmer even in the shade, Isabelle decided that a good start of her vacation with a relaxing little nap was in order. At first, she waited for the fatigue, the good meal, and the glass of red Tuscan wine to take effect, but soon she was breathing slowly and fell deeply asleep.

When she woke up, caressed gently by the breeze entering the room and moving the French door curtains, the sun bathed everything in its setting glow and Isabelle felt like floating along with everything in the room. Moving her arm, she tried to reach for Gérard and share with him the magic of the moment, when it occurred to her that he was not there and she realized how much she missed him.

Isabelle spent the evening hours admiring the beautiful Renaissance city from afar in the quiet of the gardens, breathing the strong summer air and listening to the crickets' songs. The following day she decided to take her rental Fiat and spend a day visiting Florence.

This time, she planned to stay away from the summer crowds of the old city, and after the usual visit to the Cathedral, she followed the long walk to the Piazza Della Signoria, cut across the inner court of the Uffizi Gallery, and took her time on the Ponte Vecchio, admiring some of the small shops filled with attractions. In San Lorenzo, she stopped for a snack at a trattoria and then retraced her footsteps to the Santa Croce Basilica, taking a few minutes to contemplate the burial sites of Michelangelo, Galileo, and Rossini.

Isabelle returned to the villa happy to refresh by the pool after a long walking day, and enjoyed another gourmet dinner along with a glass of Chianti.

The day after was to be another full day, as she was to drive south to Siena. However, before she went to bed she called her parents and Gérard to describe her fascinating day. While the Beaumonts were happy with Isabelle's account of her vacation, Gérard was not so sure if her enthusiasm was a sign she was already forgetting him.

-//-

The day after, Isabelle discussed her plans over breakfast with Emilio and Veronica, the owners of the Villa Jacopone. They advised her against going to Siena on a Sunday during the peak of the tourist season.

"The place will be packed, and the driving or parking a nightmare. It is better to wait another day, and anyways, you are on vacation, there is no reason to hurry."

Isabelle recognized that she would prefer staying at the villa, quickly changed her plans and attire, and went to the pool with a book. She was fascinated with the Medici family and had purchased a new book about them at the Uffizi Gallery. The day went by peacefully, Isabelle taking advantage of the beautiful grounds of the villa, the superb vista over Florence and beyond, of the green Tuscan hills.

Veronica was happy to show Isabelle the gardens, the rows of ripened tomatoes on the vine, the fresh greens and red bell peppers, broccoli, cauliflowers, and string beans. They stopped to pick herbs for the menu of the day, fragrant thyme, rosemary, Italian parsley with huge leaves, tarragon, and several types of menthe. They passed a few beehives on their way to the orchard where some peaches were ready for the table, and apples showed their rosy cheeks from the tree branches. Picking also a few grapes of a deep red color and muscatel from some vines lining a low stone wall, their baskets became heavy with treasures ready for the dinner table.

Later that afternoon, many of the guests returned from their explorations and gathered on the outdoor terraces, happy to relax and taste a few well-chosen selections from the local wineries. Sipping their wine and sitting comfortably on lounge chairs, they admired the sun setting over Florence.

Some exchanged their impressions of the places they had visited that day, while others limited their conversation to the bouquet of the wine, with the exception of an aging man who gazed with admiration in Isabelle's direction. He managed to get closer when appetizers were served, and introduced himself a bit less casually than the others.

"Allow me to introduce myself," he spoke a little ceremoniously, "I am Giuseppe d'Aruzzi", and extending his arm, he bowed slightly.

Isabelle kept a polite distance, as she had already assessed the man, someone in his sixties but trying to appear younger, with a flashing smile and a dandy attitude. However, she had no choice but to listen to the pompous exposé of Signore d'Aruzzi, that he was somehow related with the Montalbano, one of the most important Chianti wine producing families in Italy.

Signore d'Aruzzi was on his way from their wineries south of Pistoia, to Colle di Val d'Elsa near San Gimignano, situated south of Florence. He described the competition his family had continued for centuries with Frescobaldi family, the most prevalent Florentine merchant of Chianti wine production in the area. He mentioned that he was anxious to arrive in San Gimignano before the Frescobaldis snatched the coveted property.

Shortly after, Isabelle got up and mingled with other guests, before she found a place away from Signore d'Aruzzi. However, a few days of holiday and Tuscan sun had given her a relaxed, tanned glow, and in her white lace summer dress she looked more beautiful than ever. It was no wonder that many of the guests were entranced by her grace and beauty. D'Aruzzi, a couple of glasses of strong Tuscan red wine already down, became more and more animated and declared to an older couple near him, "Here is Botticelli's Primavera, sitting amongst us!"

This remark made the man next to him laugh and say in return, "She did not have to come from far; she only had to step out of the Uffizi Gallery and climb the hill!"

"The owners of the villa told us that she even plays the harp," his wife added. "I asked myself who she was but she's very secretive," she whispered with a little gossipy smile on her face.

"*Un angelo!*" Signore d'Aruzzi burst out, "*ti dico io, e' un angelo,*" (an angel, I am telling you, she is an angel).

When dinner was announced, Isabelle pretended she had an urgent phone call, and returned from her room a few minutes later so she could choose her place at a table away from the nosy creatures. Later, back in her room, she made the real phone calls as she had every night, calling her parents and Gérard. She described the gardens of the villa and how much she loved the regional cuisine. At the end, with a laugh, she briefly mentioned Signore d'Aruzzi, mostly out of the annoyance she felt about this kind of character.

Then she checked the stations on the radio clock in her room and found a nice Sunday evening summer concert broadcast by the BBC to listen to. She relaxed with a book on the balcony, intending to get up early for her trip to Siena.

Slowly, the voices and laughter of the villa's guests faded away into the night, and the only remaining sounds were Albinoni's concerto, the crickets and occasional call of the peacocks. Isabelle put down her book, taken in by the beauty of the place, of the moment, and once more, the powerful feeling of dearly missing Gérard.

-//

That Monday was not to be, again, the day Isabelle went to Siena. During the night, clouds and winds came over the Tuscan capital and in the early hours of the morning a heavy and steady rain drenched the hills and valleys. Rain was forecast for the most part of the day, but the locals were pleased with the downpour; "good showers in summer time, means ripe grapes at harvest time" they said.

Thus, she resigned herself to the situation, deciding it was better to stay off the roads during the rain and treat herself to a spa day, reading, and resting. She would also use this time to write the pretty postcards she had bought in Florence.

In the afternoon, she called Gérard earlier than usual, telling him about the rain and the restful day. "I am getting lazy, and I could get used to it," she laughed.

"You are only getting the rest your body was trying to tell you it's needed for a long time," was his answer.

"Oh well, I only wish you were here, I miss you," she let out.

He promptly told her how much he missed her too. "Perhaps next time," he added with a whisper.

The day after the rain, Isabelle finally made it to Siena, travelling south about 65 kilometers on the superstrada. She went to the Duomo, a massive Roman basilica from the 12th century, admiring the frescoes by Ghirlandaio and Pinturicchio in the sacristy, artists that also contributed to the Florence cathedral. In the Baptistry, she admired some of Donatello's sculptures.

After the Duomo, Isabelle made a stop in front of the Capitoline wolf statue, the she-wolf that was suckling Romulus and Remus, the legendary twin brothers who established the eternal city of Rome. The statue was saved by one of Remus' sons after his father was killed by Romulus, and brought it to an old Etruscan settlement where he founded Siena.

Isabelle walked the old streets of Siena to the Palazzo Publico, and then spent a little time at the Pinacoteca admiring some of the many Italian early Renaissance painters. However, she was happy that the Palio di Siena, the traditional horse race held since medieval times, was not scheduled until the 16 of August. She had heard about it, described as a brutal and dangerous race. Isabelle, who was a very passionate defender of animal rights, disliked this kind of competitions or similar circus, which she considered driven by barbaric human instincts.

The day was beautiful and a brilliant sun was shining, and after meandering through town all morning, Isabelle decided to stop in the Piazza del Campo, at the center of Siena. She found a place in the shade at an outdoor restaurant, where she could relax. The young waiter made suggestions of some Tuscan specialties on the menu, and Isabelle ordered *fagioli col formaggio*, a hearty and simple peasant dish of beans and cheese, cooked in a wood fire oven.

She found the food delicious, but remained indifferent at the waiter, who tried to flirt with her like a typical Italian male. He also recommended a traditional Tuscan chestnut cake made by locals, which turned out to be very tasty.

After a good lunch and with the heat of the middle of the afternoon getting uncomfortable, Isabelle was ready to drive back to the villa. She planned short visits to Florence for the Wednesday and Thursday to come, and then she would leave on Friday, going north to Pistoia before reaching Lucca. However, although there were summer crowds invading the space everywhere, she had never felt so lonely.

-//-

For the first days after Isabelle's departure, Gérard gathered all his strength to give his attention to his work. It was hard as the workload had become lighter in August; a few tourists came in having lost their passports, and others applied for US visas, but there was nothing really pertaining to his department. That left him plenty of free moments to feel his loneliness since Isabelle's departure. After work, it was even worse for he had lost any taste for the usual Parisian attractions in the squares, theatres, concert halls and museums.

Everywhere he turned, in every corner of Paris, everything displayed a happy atmosphere of vacation. People were speaking various languages, there were fewer cars except for the tour buses, and attractive posters announced outdoor events or visits to historic places. All seemed happy, couples tenderly holding hands, enjoying the free times together.

Maggie noticed how miserable Gérard looked and soon found the reason of it from some of the other staff members, aware that Gérard's "friend" had had transportation problems in the night of the big storm.

They had little to go on and intended no ill, but the two new interns Gérard was training were convinced that there was something going on between Gérard and Isabelle.

Everyone in the office hoped Gérard would soon have something else in his life besides his work and his son. This only reinforced Maggie's own suspicions, and while she initially watched Gérard in amusement, she soon felt sorry for her favorite attaché.

As Gérard's feelings toward Isabelle were maturing and decisions were becoming clearer in his mind, Maggie and the two interns started plotting, and quickly came up with a plan: Gérard should take a vacation and he was not needed at the embassy, at least not until the ambassador's return from his own vacation at the end of August.

And so, early on Tuesday afternoon, Maggie entered Gérard's office and asked, "Do you have a minute?"

Gérard invited her to come in and sit down, somehow happy for the interruption.

Maggie launched straight into her plan, telling him that everyone thought he needed to take some time off and suggested he went on a holiday. When he refused categorically, she became more enflamed and tried the heavy ammunition: "You don't understand, we don't need you here!"

"That hurts," he said.

She mellowed instantly at his shocked expression and her tone became motherly as she suggested it was time for him to go to Italy and find his friend; it would do him a lot of good to remember that he was still young and this was the time to enjoy himself and that it had been too long since he had thought of his own happiness. She continued a little longer, coaxing him gently while Gérard listened.

"It's settled then," she concluded, "go home now, pack, and tomorrow you can take a flight or drive to wherever Isabelle is. Florence, is it? Beautiful, so romantic, go and surprise her!"

While it was all quite simple in their eyes, Gérard was initially uncertain. Reflecting to what was said, he got up and started arranging his papers. Then, his assistants appearing as if by magic, they reviewed the schedule and their tasks during Gérard's absence. Suddenly, Gérard was seized by a frenzy of impatient joy, now realizing it was after all possible to join Isabelle. And he did just what Maggie said; went home and packed, after stopping by the mechanic servicing the embassy's cars, who checked over his 1986 red convertible Eldorado Biarritz Cadillac.

As he arrived at home, he heard the phone ringing and ran to catch it. He was happy not to miss Isabelle's call and to learn she would be still in Florence for the next two days; however, he did not want to tell her he was coming to Florence, although he felt reassured by the tone in her voice telling him how much she wished they were together.

When he finished packing and made himself a plate of food out of the bag full of treats Maggie had shoved in his arms when he left the office, he started studying the route to Florence from the package gathered for him by his assistants. He learned that there were over 300 miles to Florence from Paris, which would take him about 12 hours to drive. He consulted his watch; it was only 6 o'clock in the afternoon, he was all fired up and he knew he would not be able to sleep.

As everything was ready, he decided on a whim to get on the road immediately and take advantage of the three or four hours of daylight left. He would go to Lyon taking the A6 Highway, and then try to push to Chambéry in the French Alps where, he would spend a few hours of rest during the night. With a little luck, he would have good weather going through the Alps early the next morning and reach Turin.

From there, it would be easier to avoid the busy E70 to Parma and Bologna and take the southern route to Genoa, then the coast route to Massa, where he would turn east on the A11 to Florence.

"Piece of cake," he thought, and arranged his duffel bag in the trunk, leaving Paris with a light heart!

-//-

Getting out of Paris at this time of the day and in the middle of the week was a breeze. He made good time also up to Lyon, speeding most of the time on the highway, and against his habits, Gérard decided that he would use his diplomatic service card if needed. Obviously, the good fairies were with him, and after Lyon, the traffic became very light, as it was now late at night. He kept driving through the mountains toward Chambéry, and it was after midnight that he started looking for an inn that was still open.

He drove through Chambéry and it was not until Les Marches, a little place before Sainte-Hélène du Lac, that Gérard spotted an open *auberge* with some vacationers entering the place singing merrily after a well-showered dinner. He was tired, and stretching his legs, went into the building following the young couples.

He tried his luck at the desk with the receptionist, a young and pretty girl, pleading that it would be safer for him to get some rest before continuing the drive and that "If you could find me a room to rest in for a few hours, you will save a soul from falling asleep at the wheel and killing himself."

The young receptionist quickly fell for Gérard's charm and became very impressed when he produced his diplomatic passport to fill out the registration form. She could not hide her admiration at how well he spoke French and she was flattered by Gérard's polished manners. Finally, she was completely seduced when, following Gérard to retrieve his duffel bag, she saw his car, after which she eagerly let him know that the inn served a lavish petit dejeuner in the morning.

It was nearly one o'clock in the morning when Gérard settled into a very comfortable room decorated in Savoyard chalet style, and succumbing to the fatigue and emotions of this long day, fell asleep immediately.

Although Gérard was planning on getting up at six in the morning and be on the road shortly after, the quiet place gave him a longer respite, and when he opened his eyes and looked at his watch, it was already past eight o'clock! He jumped out of bed, took a quick shower and changed into clean clothes, before going down to the dining room.

It was a beautiful morning and he felt rested after his deep sleep. As he took a long breath of the crisp mountain air, he joined the other guests on the terrace facing the beautiful mountains and lingered a little longer to appreciate the gourmet breakfast. He felt invigorated by the rest and the fresh air, and thought that a good meal would help him continue to drive without stopping until his final destination.

Back on the road, Gérard looked around for a gas station and felt relieved when he finally found one, not an easy task cruising the mountainous roads. When the road was winding and hugged the steep sides of the mountains, he kept his attention on his driving.

But, once he left the Alps mountains behind him and approached Turin, the road turned onto the A6, and he picked up speed.

It seemed that the other auto motorists at the wheel of Ferrari models of the Turin industry showed no concern for the speed limits and drove along at full roaring engines.

This way he reached Alessandria in no time where he turned on to A7, headed south, and by the end of the morning, he was in Genova. After a short stop to refuel and stretch his legs, he was on the coastal A17, and admired the spectacular vistas, while thrilled with anticipation as he drew closer to Florence.

-//-

It was around four o'clock on Wednesday that Isabelle came back from a day spent wandering the old streets of Florence. After parking her car in one of the back alleys of Via Pro Consolo, she stopped at the house of Dante Alighieri, then at the Bargello, a former prison and home of the chief of the police at one time, and considered now as second only to the Uffizi Museum, hosting some of the finest Renaissance sculptures, including those of Michelangelo and Donatello.

Back in her car, she drove across the Ponte Vecchio and stopped at Palazzo Pitti on the other side of the River Arno at the main residence of the Medici family. However, she preferred to stay mostly outdoors and spent less time in the gallery, enjoying the unique light of the Italian summer sky. She went through the large terrace into the Boboli Gardens, the palazzo's splendid gardens, admiring artfully designed boxed shrubs, statues, and fountains.

Back at the Villa Jacopone, she took a cool shower and changed into a lilac colored crocheted lace dress. Before going downstairs, she laid down closing her eyes for a good 30 minutes, preferring to stay away from some of the too friendly guests. In her heart, she had recognized the unbearable evidence that it did not make any more sense for her to be alone on vacation in this idyllic place. Finally leaving her room in no hurry, she slowly climbed down the two flights of stairs, suddenly overcome by an overwhelming desire to be with Gérard.

At the bottom of the stairs, walking toward the terrace, she casually glanced over at the main entrance and thought she was dreaming. For turning around from the reception desk with a large grin on his face ... was Gérard! She stopped only for a very short instant, as her heart skipped a beat, before running towards him and the two of them found the other in a tight embrace. They could not find the words and kept laughing, until she began crying with unrestrained joy, thinking that this must be the happiest surprise of her life.

Leaving the main entrance hall, they sought out a quieter place to be alone and found themselves on the deserted terrace. Gérard, still holding her waist, leaned his head back to look at her, then lifted her off the floor, turning her round and round, feeling the happiest he had ever been.

He began to say words that were dear to his heart, kept inside, now evading freely: "Isabelle, you have to give me a date, we need to fix a date..."

"What are you saying ... a date?"

"Yes, a date, we have to get married, we can't ever be apart again, I can't, I will die!"

"You mean, you want us to get married?" still quite confused Isabelle repeated, "Is this a proposal?"

With a little childish gesture, Gérard dropped on one knee and said, "The ring has to wait until tomorrow, we can go to Florence and you will choose one, but I need your answer now."

A soft "yes" was the only word she could get out. She looked tenderly at him and pulling him up to her, she said, "Come here, silly," and they fell into each other's arms, sealing their love forever with a passionate kiss.

The two of them were ecstatic with joy, crying and kissing, laughing and kissing again, and a little crowd started forming around them. Emilio and Veronica, the villa's owners, came out to see what the commotion was about and announced that this called for a celebration. Champagne appeared readily and was offered to all around. Then, with the glasses filled, hugs and warm congratulations followed from all the guests.

When things calmed down, Isabelle started to realize Gérard must be tired and hungry after racing over to Italy. She started apologizing and grabbed his luggage left by the reception, showed him her room and invited him to have a shower before dinner. He took a shower, all right, but coming out from the bathroom all refreshed, they found themselves quieting another hunger, the too long retained desire for each other.

Their bodies found again a perfect sensual harmony, the calm and peace came, and they fell asleep in each other's arms. It was the beginning of a superb evening in the Tuscan summer when Isabelle and Gérard finally descended arm in arm to their dinner table. Veronica and Emilio had set it apart, with a gorgeous bouquet decorating it, and the two of them enjoyed a supper that would forever be encrypted in their memory.

As Gérard had said, the day after his arrival in Tuscany he insisted going into Florence, and like happy children, they browsed the expensive shops of the Ponte Vecchio. He pressed to go for broke, but this time Isabelle would not hear any of it, and she found the perfect ring: an iris shaped diamond ring, which was rapidly adjusted to her small finger. Gérard placed it on her finger and they left, now officially engaged!

Isabelle and Gérard were, indeed, happier than they ever had been, living the dream that any couple in love should experience, the magic pause that suspended everything else but love. Time that would fuel them and fill them with the energy would certainly be needed later, when trials and hardships would inevitably test them later in life.

They spent that day wandering the old streets of Florence with no particular plan, just happy to be together. It was the same for the following days, when, after dropping Isabelle's rental car back to the airport, they drove north in Gérard's beautiful open red car, taking their time to visit Prato, and stay for a day in Pistoia. They admired the ancient Thermes of Montecatini, before arriving at their final destination in Lucca, some 85 kilometers, or 50 miles, northwest of Florence.

The three days spent in Lucca were filled with the excitement of discovery. These were times devoid of worries and filled with the anticipation of endless attractions. They stayed at Palazzo Rocchi across from San Michele Cathedral in the center of the city and were happy to obtain the upper floor suite, enjoying the rooftop terrace that offered 360 degrees view of the old city.

Roberto, the manager, made sure their smallest wishes were attended to; he even came to the terrace to point out the monuments, some which dated back to the Etruscans, some from the Roman era when Julius Caesar came to Lucca, and the more recent ages, when Napoléon's sister Élisa Bonaparte and another

Duchess of Lucca, Maria Luisa of Spain, had their residence there.

One day they strolled along Lucca's famous wall, the best preserved ramparts in Italy. The four-kilometer-long wall was topped with grass and trees, allowing bicycles and pedestrians to use the promenade.

One evening they walked to the nearby church of St. Giovanni to attend a Puccini concert. Puccini, a native of Lucca, was celebrated each summer from March to September with special programs, and many opera productions were held in an open-air theater in Torre del Lago, a few kilometers from Lucca. Their final visit was to the sublime Villa Torrigiani to complete their time in Lucca.

These special days created an everlasting connection between the two of them, Isabelle and Gérard discovering each other's inclinations and preferences. They strengthened this special bond connecting two beings recognizing to belong to each other. With every day, with every moment that passed, they had the certitude that they could not live without the other in their life. Every place they were visiting opened up a conversation for the future; at first, they tried to envision it, then they started planning their life together. Every discussion was a reason for happiness, received with joy and laughter.

They had to return to Paris in a few more days but for now they enjoyed their time together so much that their glowing happiness attracted the attention of other people. Patrick's return date was also getting closer, and they talked for hours about him and how the three of them would see their life from now on. Isabelle did not hide how intimidated and anxious she felt about becoming a "good mom for a teenage boy".

She asked if there was a likelihood they would be competing for Gérard's love and attention?

Gérard gave her all the reassurance that his heart could contain all this new affection, just adding another person to love. Like a mother is able to love each one of her children equally, and the love for a new baby would not take away anything from the others, the same, their lives would only be enriched with their love for each other.

Gérard and Isabelle also considered their respective careers. Their work and personal accomplishments were important to them, and they were aware how much effort and time went into them. Kind and considerate, they were able to embrace each other's own satisfaction, and find solutions, reflecting on the various options and possibilities. They also knew that in the future they would encounter obstacles and they would have to make sacrifices, but they were committed to make the effort to preserve their happiness and life together.

However, when the conversation became too intense, Gérard sensed it was time to gently turn the conversation around and be practical: they would need to get married soon as they could no longer bear to live apart and that meant finding a new apartment for the three of them.

Another particularity started taking shape the more time they spent together; they bounced back and forth from French to English during their conversations, freely using the language that came first to them and best expressed their thoughts. Their communication became another connection pertaining to them only, their secret weapon when they needed to keep the conversation to themselves.

In Italy, they interacted with the locals in Italian, but when alone, they used either French or English, whichever felt more natural, although Isabelle expressed herself more in French and Gérard in English. Without knowing it, they were creating another unique bond that would remain with them for their entire life.

-//-

The months following their return to Paris went by in a blur. There were so many details to take care of, and so many directions to focus their attention. Many concerns were swept away after Isabelle met Patrick. They were shy in the beginning as they tried to get to know each other, but with time, they felt so much more at ease, and soon they enjoyed being together. Isabelle, like Patrick, was of an affectionate nature, and as an attachment began, they felt more reassured that they would get along in the future just fine. Isabelle tried not to interfere in the time Gérard needed with his son. Patrick in return, started regarding her as the ideal woman that could bring happiness to his father. He was also secretly considering how great it would be having a feminine presence in the house, like the mother he had never known.

Then, there were the wedding preparations to consider, after telling parents, relatives, work relations and friends of their plans. Vivianne and Lucien were ecstatic to hear of their two friends' engagement.

"We must be contagious, we passed you the bug of marriage!" they laughed, promising that Lucien would be the best man and Vivianne the bridesmaid. They even threw a little party at their apartment to discuss future preparations. Isabelle tried to oppose the idea of a big wedding, however she had to make the concession for something in between: a very simple and intimate ceremony with only family members and a few friends at Saint Julien le Pauvre, the old Roman church across from Notre Dame de Paris. Then a nice reception in the embassy gardens, offered "without any right of refusal" by the ambassador himself.

Finally, and after a lengthy debate, all was settled, and after the wedding, Isabelle and Gérard would spend their honeymoon in Venice.

Meanwhile Gérard found a larger apartment on the ground floor of the same building he lived in. It unexpectedly came up for sale and while it was a little pricy, it had high ceilings, large rooms and two marble fireplaces, the kitchen had been completely redone recently, and opened to a private courtyard through double French doors from the salon and the master bedroom.

It was a great choice and an easy moving situation for Gérard and Patrick, leaving them more time to see to Isabelle's arrangements. In addition, the library-den could accommodate both Gérard's and Isabelle's desks so they each had their own work space. Patrick was thrilled with his bedroom a little apart in a wing of the apartment. As a teenage boy, he was fond of his own private place. With the living situation organized, Gérard was relieved and content to concentrate on other duties. Once the sale had been completed and the papers signed, the three of them enjoyed arranging and decorating their future home.

Isabelle's parents, along with her brother, Eric, and his family, had already met with Gérard's parents when they brought Patrick back from vacation. They were all taken a little by surprise by the unexpected engagement, but after meeting Isabelle and her family, the Forrests could not have been more gracious, and fell completely under Isabelle's charms. Gérard's parents were happy for their son, and quickly became close to his future wife's family.

The date for the wedding was set for spring of the following year. It was the earliest they could manage, but even this seemed too far away for the two lovers. However, Gérard came up again with a compromise— he was a diplomat after all—to have their civil marriage secretly during the fall. It was at the 1st Arrondissement city hall, the district falling under the main city hall in Paris, at the impressive Mairie de Paris, a spectacular architectural structure where they signed their marriage contract. Thus, they conformed to conventional traditions becoming an official couple and satisfied any parental reservations when going away together.

After the civil marriage, Laura and Thierry Beaumont surprised all of them, with an intimate reception at their country house in Rambouillet. This included Gérard's parents who came back from Rome, where Jim Forrest was American Ambassador to Italy, rendering much easier the trip to Paris for this special occasion.

Gérard and Isabelle had decided she would only move into the new apartment after their religious ceremony. At that time, Gérard had not yet found a new home for them, and they did not want to spoil their initial plans, something very much appreciated by their parents who were still old fashioned. However, they snuck away at times for a weekend or a night together. They even managed a week vacation to see the Loire castles, taking Patrick with them. It was the first time the three of them had gone on a trip together and it helped them become a closer family unit.

When the new apartment was acquired, a home inspector revised everything, and repairs and modern changes were made to utility installations. Small renovations were ordered such as softer coats of paint on the walls and crown moldings, or new varnish on the doors and windows. Most of the work was done by a young team of decorators, enthusiastic to exercise their talents on such a beautiful sample of classical Parisian architecture.

Then, they selected the furniture and heirlooms from their respective family sides to bring into their new home and passionately roamed the antique stores, the flea markets, and went to some auctions at Hôtel Drouot for anything else they needed. Each find was received with exclamations of victory when a new bedroom set, rug, or piece of furniture was brought in and found its ideal placement.

This entire process enhanced their expectations and excitement for the life they were preparing together. This was also the place they would live in the years to come, and would hold an everlasting meaning to them as marking the beginning of their marriage.

Gérard's work obligations required him to leave Paris on a few occasions as his negotiation skills were highly prized by the UN, EU, and UNICEF. Most of the time, the visits were short and held in Brussels or Geneva, made easier by reaching them with a quick flight or using the high-speed train, the TGV.

On one occasion, Gérard's presence was needed for a week in Angola, for the talks regarding the resolution of the Angolan civil war. During every absence, the decision was made, at Isabelle's insistence, that she would stay with Patrick. This made things not only easier for all of them, but soon Isabelle and Patrick became "best buddies".

Busy with their lives, Isabelle and Gérard endured the months until the following May, when their wedding date was scheduled. They made the best of it enjoying every moment together and planning their future. These few months until the wedding seemed at times to go by slowly, at other times their demanding schedule made them seem to fly past.

Eventually this very special day arrived, and, as expected, they had a fairytale wedding. It was not the biggest, nor the most pompous wedding, but it was the most magical. Lucie was asked again to be the rings bearer and was beside herself with joy, while Eric's children and Patrick had their own designated parts to play as well. Patrick, now 12 years old, was best man with Lucien, and Marielle, now six, was the flower girl, while Benjamin, four years old, trailed along behind. However, Benjamin could not contain his delight when Isabelle invited him to dance later and held him in her arms. He told her "a secret" at the end of their dance, whispering in her ear, "This is our wedding, right?"

-//-

The new Forrest family moved into their home and settled down to enjoy family life. They all tried their best to harmonize and to become comfortable with their routine. When Gérard visited places where wars were still raging, Isabelle often feared for his safety. Isabelle had a very difficult time adjusting, waiting and worrying until he came back to her and Patrick. Something that became evident to Isabelle from the beginning of their relationship was her interest in the world problems Gérard dealt with.

Questioning him incessantly, she wanted to learn more about the areas he traveled to, their geographical, political, or social particularities and what kind of assistance people needed.

In a short time, ideas formed in her mind, and when she had a clearer plan, she approached Gérard. "Is there anything I can do to help when you visit the refugee camps?" she asked. "I am sure there are medical teams assisting these unfortunate people, especially the women and children and I really want to get more involved. I like what you do Gérard, it is magnificent!"

Gérard, taken by surprise, but recalling the appalling condition of the camps, tried to dissuade her with strong reasons and examples. However, Isabelle had already her own store of information and contacts with Docteurs sans Frontières (Doctors without Borders), and pleaded her cause. "Gérard, there are camps that are quite safe, although in dire need of medical care. And we could be there together; you can watch over me!"

After talking over this possibility, they came up with a compromise: Isabelle would go on short missions without needing to quit her work at the institute, and if there were any problems, she would immediately come back home.

As a result, Isabelle received the vaccinations for her travel requirements to Africa at the Institute Pasteur where she worked. She needed proper protection not only against tropical diseases, but also prevention related to the harsh conditions of the camps where she would stay where malaria, dysentery, or even scabies were ravaging the refugees.

She learned how to prevent dehydration when water was scarce or poorly sanitized, and the use of limited supplies of medication and disinfectants, when sterile conditions were practically inexistent, but vital.

Well into their first year of marriage, the young married couple participated in several missions. Some were of short duration and when they offered more decent life conditions, it permitted them even to have Patrick join them. Patrick was always very eager to visit and learn about children less privileged than him. These experiences made him even more appreciative of having a far better life. He was constantly offering to help in any capacity and asked to spend all his vacations on missions with the two he now considered both as his parents.

It was one of the most thrilling times in their life, when they felt that their work was giving them purpose and satisfaction. Sometimes these trips raised serious safety questions, when unexpected dangers threatened everyone. There was also the occasional ambush by the guerilla soldiers in raided areas, supposedly clear of danger, at times exposing the camp members, but equally UN members and Doctors without Borders, to their cruelty.

The mass immunizations and grueling work schedule of Doctors without Borders, and having to catch up with her program at the institute when she came back, appeared to be far too strenuous for Isabelle's delicate nature.

When she contracted Salmonella gastroenteritis, Isabelle took leave from the institute and was forced to rest, placed in isolation in order to be adequately treated and to regain her strength. Needless to say, Gérard was concerned, considering himself responsible for letting Isabelle come to Africa in the first place.

A couple of years into their marriage, Gérard received assignments for conferences in Geneva, where he began to stay more often than usual. As his time there increased, they started looking into alternative solutions. Isabelle, who during her recovery, had thought about future professional directions, became attracted by the idea of going to Montreux, Switzerland, to follow new researches and technologies testing brain function.

She was interested in using emerging computerized systems that could be useful in correcting or treating human conditions. This French-speaking region of Switzerland was in the canton of Vaud on the north side of Lake Geneva and at the foot of the Alps, and offered an ideal living and working situation for a family.

Isabelle already had in mind some far-reaching concepts regarding the understanding, treatment, and use of the brain's capabilities, and thought that this new institution, the Blue Brain project, would be the perfect place for her future scientific orientation.

Patrick, who was now going on 15 years of age, was growing and developing beautifully within his loving and supportive family. The spitting image of his father, he was open to Helvetic education, and particularly excited to learn more about the financial aspects of business transactions that would eventually help him in his future career of international relations.

When Gérard discussed Isabelle's research ideas she always became very animated and, although a little shy about him finding her too optimistic or "futuristic", she would answer, "This might sound like science fiction, but given the electronic circuits miniaturized in the future, this should not be completely rejected.

"You see," she would continue, "we could use small devices planted under the skin of the skull and stimulate areas of the brain that have stopped functioning as a result of a stroke, blindness, loss of hearing, etc. The areas that became hyperactive during a seizure activity could be restored as well, and that particular function would return to normal. Imagine if we used microchips to activate the deficient area directly, instead of ingesting potentially toxic chemicals.

"And we have not even started talking about extending the use of miniaturized electronics to restore the motor function of the limbs. We could stimulate the damaged brain cortex controlling the movements of the body, or even the diaphragm or other respiratory muscles. We could get rid of paralysis and people could walk and breathe on their own again!"

"That would be great if they could use those chips to stimulate the areas of pleasure," Gérard said winking at her, and smiled, as she shot him back an inquisitor look.

Thus, after lengthy fervent discussion, the Forrest family started consolidating the idea of a new direction their life was taking, and the final decision was made, they were moving to Switzerland.

BOOK FIVE

There had been a big storm over the Gulf of Mexico, a monster larger than Texas had formed in the warm Caribbean waters, sweeping devastation on its track. From the northern basin above Venezuela, touching the Antilles, hurricane Enriche raged over Espanola and Cuba, American Keys and over Miami in south Florida, churned for a while in the Gulf of Mexico to regain strength and then shot straight up to Louisiana. Its strong winds and rain soaked and battered the entire Emerald Coast of Florida, the beaches of Alabama and Mississippi as well.

Now, that the storm was over, everywhere the locals who had stayed to endure it, came out to evaluate the damages done to their proprieties and to the community. They were better prepared for the changes brought about by the climate alterations of the last few decades, as they were expecting to handle a few strong storms every year. Old structures were long gone, replaced by better and safer new buildings that had benefited from the advanced technologies and new materials imposed by the new building codes. This allowed some visionary architects to design handsome avant-garde structures that were environmentally friendly, economical, and used clean and natural energy to operate them.

Thus, more buildings appeared everywhere, even on the coastlines, to accommodate the planet's expanding population. However, there were trees and damaged roads, and many areas of beach erosion. All kinds of shops that opened during the high season and were made of less durable materials had been destroyed and tossed around in the sand. Some small boats had also been thrown around, but somehow nature returned to normal and a glorious sunshine cast bright rays over the sea and the land once more.

After reaching the beach walk overlooking the shoreline all the way to the emerald waters of the ocean, Gérard was resting on a bench. Leaning his chin on his cane, he was deep in thought enjoying the view he loved so much, and trying to fill his lungs with the vigorous air of the large sea. The strong ocean air was good for his breathing and just what he needed to bring renewed life to his lungs damaged by bullet wounds received in Liberia so many years ago.

Now, at 93, he was frail and needed the assistance of his cane, a small oxygen tank when going somewhere of a higher altitude, and he was usually provided with oxygen when traveling by plane. Otherwise, he was healthy and his mind remained as sharp as always. Staring at the sea, his azure eyes seemed to reflect the same color as the water, but in his mind, it was a pair of deep green eyes he remembered and still missed so much.

Francesca, a beautiful young lady, walked over to him and put her arms around his shoulders and gently kissed his cheek. She had the same striking emerald eyes as his, but the body shape that reminded Gérard of someone else.

"Ready to go back, Grandpa?" she asked.

"Why don't you come sit here for a little while?" asked Gérard, patting the bench next to him.

"Alright, Pa Gérard," she said, knowing she could not refuse anything to her grandfather she adored. She loved coming to see him every occasion she had, simply sitting without having to talk or listening to stories of a long and exciting life, from which she always found inspiration. She also loved to come to this corner of the world where life retained the sweetness of the southern living with a pleasant pace and a climate calming and restoring visitors and locals.

During her visits, Francesca was recharged with great energy and enthusiasm, and every stay became a chance to share with her grandfather her ideas and plans for the future. They had this incredible understanding of each other, this complicity that brought across generations so much love and happiness in their hearts.

Nevertheless, this time Francesca was visiting her grandfather for a very important reason; she was to have her wedding at her grandfather's estate on the sound by the water's edge. She could not think of a more romantic and more beautiful place that remained so dear to her since she was a little girl. This was the place where she had spent so many vacations, and where family continued to gather for special events and holidays.

As Gérard enjoyed Francesca's company, memories flooded his heart, and he realized how much she was the reason he had been able to go on with his life after Isabelle's death. He had even accepted this temporary separation from Isabelle to make new choices in his life that had taken him in unexpected directions.

After all, he recognized that he could find satisfaction, if not complete happiness, and new interests to fulfill his life through his family and his work. He thought that his life was worth living and had been kind to him; he had met the love of his life and they'd had an exceptional relationship before Isabelle was taken away from him. However, he felt deprived not having her with him, of not being able to share this earthly existence with her, and their time together still seemed too short.

-//-

Even after Marina left Gérard by himself a few months after her mother's death, she remained worried about him. She had been able to help him for a while, but she had her husband Gunter, her three-year-old Benjamin, and an international career to concentrate on as well. She made every effort to remain in touch with her father in between her visits, and she pleaded ardently with his friends to check on Gérard, as much and as frequently as they all possibly could.

Gérard promised to better take care of himself and honor Isabelle's desire for him to continue to enjoy life and be happy again. But when Marina was away, he slowly sank back into despair, losing interest in everything. He avoided even his closest friends, who after a while, most of them quit calling or coming to offer support or just a simple presence. The property, house pets, bills, and the home and business management were frequently neglected, as Gérard felt even more discouraged and detached from everything.

Vivianne and Lucien Dubois, good friends of Gérard and Isabelle, and very much responsible of them meeting in Paris, had followed their beautiful romance and marriage, and had remained in contact with the couple for all the years, regardless of the distances. Lucie, Vivianne's daughter, had become a lifelong friend of Marina's, even though she was 11 years older.

The Parisian couple was devastated by the tragic news of Isabelle's passing and came to Florida for the funeral and stayed in close contact with Gérard afterwards. Lucien and Vivianne provided as much support and compassion as they possibly could in such terrible circumstances. Promises of visiting were exchanged, although in the end Gérard did not return the invitation.

However, on the first-year anniversary of Isabelle's death, Vivianne and Lucien showed a great deal of devotion by coming to Florida. They prolonged their visit after the children and Eric and his family left, keeping Gérard afloat with activities around the property. They even managed to take him away for a few short trips in the area. For a while, Gérard remained under the good influence of their presence, but when they left, with the time and erosion of their cheerful presence, he fell into despair again.

This continued for about two years, with little improvement when family members came to stay and check on him. Then, Marina announced that she was expecting another child, and a new effervescence became the focal point of the family. Although Marina and Gunter had hoped to have more children, it had been more than five years since they had had Benjamin.

The arrival of a new member of the family became the center of everyone's attention, and when a baby girl was announced, Gérard became as involved as Gunter and little Benjamin in making sure Marina had good care and the attention she needed during her pregnancy. There were a few minor problems this time, nothing very serious, just accumulated fatigue during a few concerts away from their home base, New York. Nevertheless, Gérard was so concerned, they all thought that this was actually a good way of keeping his mind away from his usually depressing thoughts.

209

From that time on, Gérard concentrated on the well-being of his daughter and the baby that was to come. Providentially, everything took an incredible turn when the baby was born. Gérard made arrangements to keep things under control at home in Florida, then he flew to New York where he decided to stay for a while.

When the time for the baby's delivery came, he too went to the private clinic in Manhattan, and paced nervously in the waiting room. He felt it was not right to only let the father of the baby in the room with his daughter! He was tortured not knowing what was going on, and the anxiety tightened his chest with the memories and fear of another agonizing wait in a hospital.

Finally, Gunter came out from the delivery room with a radiant smile on his face, announcing, "We have a beautiful baby girl, her name is Francesca!" He invited Gérard into the room where Marina was beaming with relief and happiness, and where the medical staff was busy fussing over the baby.

The little Francesca was soon found perfectly healthy and passed all the attentive checks and tests of the doctor and the nurses, and finally handed back to her mother. It was a very powerful and happy event that finally came into their lives, and they let themselves become immersed in the curative catharsis of those sweet moments.

Little Benjamin and Gunter's parents, Johann and Lauren von Stadolf, came in as well, and they all marveled over the little baby, admiring her beautiful and delicate features. They all laughed when everyone tried to appropriate one of the baby's resemblances, fighting over whom she looked more alike.

Johann von Stadolf made them all roared with laughter when he declared, "There is no contest, Francesca is my mirrored image!"

Most of all, the real miracle happened when Gérard finally held the tiny baby in his arms. He was filled with wonder and love, holding the fragile creature in his gentle embrace, and, looking at the new baby, started to discover many traits of his recently lost love. Without him realizing it, this was good for him as it was the beginning of the healing and of a desire to dedicate his life to someone who would need his help. For the first time in a long while, this thought inspired him and he felt positive about the future.

This brought back many other memories of the time Isabelle gave him the gift of another little delicate baby girl, their unique child, Marina. They chose a private clinic in Locarno, Switzerland, close to Lake Maggiore, as the place to bring little Marina into the world and the baby's arrival gave their marriage a newer and stronger meaning.

Then, Gérard admired this miracle of life and discovered just how much this new little person, with just a little suckling noise, forever stole his heart. He followed her, as she became this beautiful small image of her mother, amused by the feminine ways that came so naturally to little girls, so charming and disarming, that no one teaches them. He could never resist her sweet smiles and the way she knew how to wrap her arms around his neck giving kisses and tell him he was the best dad in the whole world. In fact, she gave him the surname "the best". "The best, the smartest, the plus awesome" were her favorite nicknames for him, and she had, as her father reciprocated in turn, a real adoration for him.

He remembered how Marina changed with each new stage of her life; he felt that it had only been yesterday when he took her to kindergarten when Isabelle could not free herself from her professional obligations, but phoned him many times and kept on giving him instructions and worrying how Marina would adapt alone her first day of school. And how relieved they were, when later on, the two of them managed to be there at the end of her short school day, and when they saw a smiling pretty face coming out serene and content, without even knowing that she already had seduced everyone in her class.

Then Marina enrolled in international schools, her parents being aware this was a great privilege as it would open many opportunities, for they travelled and worked in different countries. For her, school was uneventful, studying came easy to her and she loved to learn, making her the darling of the teachers.

Musical inclination was another natural disposition of this well-balanced and happy child, raised in a loving and caring family. From her mother's grandparents, she inherited an early inclination for arts, further facilitated by exposure to most of Europe's famous artistic sites that she visited with her parents when Gérard was sent to different diplomatic missions.

Marina was always eager to absorb the local cultural traditions but she was also keen on history and regional politics; she loved the fascinating conversations she sometimes heard at the dinner table or receptions given by her parents. Marina was very attached to Patrick, her stepbrother and 16 years her senior. Despite their age gap, they were very close, and they both grew strong and loving ties they cherished forever. Patrick watched over his little sister like an eagle, while Marina followed him everywhere, constantly asking questions. She relied on Patrick her entire life, his strong and balanced personality and his sense of humor often came to her rescue when she needed a friend.

Because her parents lived for extended periods abroad, she met many different people, and thanks to her musical ear, she found it easy to learn foreign languages. This helped her later in her musical career as well as being able to communicate in English, French, and Spanish, with a good knowledge of Italian and German. Marina's knowledge of several foreign languages gave her free access to interact practically everywhere she travelled.

When Marina's musical talents became evident to all, and from a general introduction received with piano lessons, she slowly followed her interest to a more formal musical education, wishing to become an opera singer. Her parents watched proudly as their little daughter evolved and blossomed like a rose, ultimately leading Marina to become this very talented, rising new star of the lyrical arts. She never ceased to surprise and impress her parents with her stage presence and natural command of her performances. Her parents were more involved in the cultural events than sports events and accompanied their daughter on after-school activities, but this was compensated by the fact that Gérard's diplomatic positions took them to live in cities such as Paris, Madrid, Geneva, and Rome. Even short stays in Berlin allowed them to attend prestigious art events or musical festivals.

In Gérard's opinion, his cherished little girl had become an adult too quickly, and now had her own growing family, concerns and responsibilities. This realization came in the middle of all this commotion, and Gérard decided that time went by too fast and he no longer wanted to miss any of the important moments in the lives of his loved ones.

-//-

They were in Italy, Gérard taking his wife and daughter to Venice for a holiday. This was a very special place for Gérard and Isabelle as they had spent their honeymoon here, and they loved to return and let the magic of this fairytale place envelop them.

Gérard and Isabelle were celebrating their twenty-third anniversary of marriage with a young daughter of 19. Their daughter, Marina, was a stunning beauty unaware of the effect she stirred around her. In fact, this dazzling trio made quite an impression on everyone they passed as they admired the alleys, bridges and beautiful palazzos. Vendors on the streets, locals and tourists, diners in the restaurants and patrons of art galleries, all stopped for an instant to admire this serene family and wondered who they were.

Marina had inherited her mother's willowy elegant stature and the delicate features of her face. Her eyes though were of the same intense azure of her father's and from him she had also inherited his expressions when she was concentrating or reflective. Her parents had lived in the US since she turned 15, and at 17, she started attending the Julliard School of Performing Arts in New York, while her parents divided their time between their Manhattan apartment and the family estate in Washington, DC.

Her father assumed a position of representative of the US at the United Nations, but he was often in Europe to attend international UN conferences. Marina loved to accompany him and spend time in the countries that with time and many visits became so familiar to her.

Now enjoying their vacation in Venice, the three of them went to attend an outdoor concert in the enchanting décor of the inner courtyard of the Doge's Palace. Musici Venetti were playing Vivaldi, the air was pleasant with a light breeze, and an elegant crowd was held under the charm of this unique atmosphere created by the music.

There was another family trio in the audience enjoying the night. Originally from Vienna, The von Stadolfs had arrived a little earlier to the old palace, and their 26-year-old son, Gunter, was absently scanning the guests entering the place, as they slowly looked for their seats. He became intrigued by an exceptional looking family, and particularly by the ravaging beauty of the two women, the slightly older one a Nordic blond, and the younger one, with luxurious deep brown-red hair.

For the entire duration of the concert, Gunter could not take his eyes from this stunning, tall and graceful young beauty that appeared to be the daughter of the couple. He knew from the first glance that he desperately desired to know who the young lady was.

At the end of the concert, the Stadolfs' exited the magnificent courtyard of the palace after the Forrests', and Gunter was a little distressed staying behind a long line of people who were taking their time to leave. He was the only son of this aristocratic Austrian family, and his father could afford to follow his passions and be an art collector. However, he was also very good at his job and his extreme sense of assessing the artistic value of a large variety of paintings and art objects had made him quite wealthy.

Gunter's grandparents had lost almost everything under the German occupation during World War II, and Johann Stadolf's extensive education and knowledge of Austro-Hungarian art and history permitted him to become, over the years, an authority in the art dealing business, which enabled him to restore most of the family assets.

Gunter was also interested in art, but his exposure to the rich musical life in Vienna, along with Salzburg and many other smaller places that hosted the highest level of musical concerts and festivals helped him develop early in life a true interest in music. Gunter was especially fascinated by the effect made when an entire orchestra and its multiple instruments played together. He was intrigued to find out the secret of how they could play in an ensemble while they kept their individuality. In fact, he was especially attracted by the director's role, who, with just a few gestures could spark a sea of sounds.

Gunter had worked hard for years to learn about musical styles and composers, and the technical particularities of instruments, and became a very talented pianist himself. But his greatest enjoyment was the thrill of conducting the whole orchestra and getting the musicians to play on his commend and follow his style. Gunter had an exceptional musical memory, talent, and passion for music, which made him be regarded as one of best conductors of the younger generation.

Marina was unaware of the strong impression she made on Gunter during the concert they both, in separated way, attended. She and her parents continued to enjoy the gorgeous surroundings, and take full advantage of the many exciting events they wanted to attend when they were in Venice. This way they visited Santa Maria delle Salute and Saint Giorgio Maggiore, after stopping as usual at the grand San Marco Basilica, a few steps away from their hotel, Il Palazzo Bauer. They took gondola rides and listened to the gondoliers' serenades; they went out during the daytime further afield to the islands of Murano and Burano, and even ventured to Lido Beach.

Since he had seen Marina at the concert, Gunter had continuously searched for her face everywhere he turned. His parents had noticed how distracted he was and absent he appeared during their conversations. At long last, Gunter felt a jolt of delight when this time, attending one of the belcanto evenings at the Fenice Theatre, he recognized her in one of the boxes with her parents. He was not in the least aware that Marina was there for her own musical interests, and that the arias from Rossini, Verdi, Puccini, and Mozart presented were the ones Marina had already included in her repertoire.

Fenice was a small but famous opera house, and its baroque architecture suited the music concerts that were often played there. The intimate size of the theater permitted Gunter to get closer to Marina, and he had the impression that she was quite knowledgeable about what she was listening to, as she was taken by her favorite pieces of music.

Gunter could only admire Marina from far away, since he did not have any opportunity to approach her and even less to engage in a conversation. Unexpectedly, his hopes were rewarded when, the same evening and after the concert, the two families were sitting not far from each other at the outdoor tables of the Café Florian, the famous café on the San Marco Piazza.

It was an enchanting after dinnertime in this unique decorum, and a small orchestra was playing a combination of popular Italian canzoni and pop arrangements of opera and symphonic music.

It was so romantic that Marina understood why Venice was such a favorite place for her parents, who were still very much in love. Gunter had fallen under the spell of this atmosphere and was stirred by feelings he had never experienced before.

For many it was vacation time, and as the gentleness of the music relaxed people's actions, there was frequently interaction between the guests, facilitated by the conductor who took suggestions from the attendance for what piece music was to be played next. Giorgio was one of the dearest servers of the café and knew the Forrests from their previous visits as regular customers for staying in a most convenient close by hotel. He stopped in his tracks to chat with them, and Gunter could appreciate that they were conversing fluently in Italian. He was even more intrigued, since he did not see them as Italians. Then, he became more confused when he heard them speaking in French, not knowing that the Forrests spoke spontaneously in French as a family.

When the "The Blue Danube Waltz" by Johann Strauss Jr. ended, director Antonio Lombardi turned to the audience for the next musical request someone might like to hear. "The Barcarolle' from the 'The Tales of Hoffmann'," Marina asked, thinking of the aria sung by Giulietta accompanied by the solo harp, the story happening in Venice; she had loved this aria since she was a little girl, when her mother would play and sing it for her.

"Tristan song for Iseult," shouted Gunter at the same time, thinking of the romantic love song by Richard Wagner, art he was studying as a young director accepted to perform at Bayreuth festival.

Their responses made in unison triggered spontaneous laughter and made them look at each other, Marina noticing the young man for the first time. Some spectators were now caught in the action, so was director Lombardi, who said in English with a melodic accent, "Well, what is it going to be, the soprano, or the tenor?" making a game of words, for the two parts requested were respectively written for a soprano and for a tenor.

Gunter answered gallantly, "Ladies first, of course," to which Lombardi returned, "That's better," and started playing the Barcarolle for the pleasure of a spellbound audience.

When the music ended, the orchestra took a break, and Gunter and his parents came close to Marina's parents table. Gunter wished to apologize but let his father introduce them first. While Gérard and Marina were quite fluent in German, Isabelle had more limited knowledge of this language, and all were relieved to hear this nice gentlemen, looking rather like the Kaiser, but addressing them in English.

"Please allow us to introduce ourselves and accept my son's apologies. I am Johann von Stadolf, this is my wife Lauren, and here is our son Gunter."

At this point, Gérard got up and with an elegant gesture said, "No apologies necessary, we truly enjoyed your son's enthusiasm, and please join us at our table."

"Gladly," was the response from Herr von Stadolf, "only if you would accept us to offer a bottle of champagne for our intrusion."

At this, Gérard introduced at his turn his family, and hands were shaken across the table in all directions.

Without any particular forethought, Gunter found himself sitting next to Marina, and now that he had learned her name, for once he was at a loss for words. He was even more intimidated by her beauty seen up close. He was sure he had never seen such a perfect complexion and such pure blue eyes, but when she politely smiled as she greeted his parents, she was absolutely dazzling, and Gunter knew from that very moment that he would forever be at the mercy of her will.

Gérard was sitting between his wife and his daughter, Gunter was next to Marina, Gérard was across from Herr von Stadolf, while Lauren found a place next to Isabelle. The two mothers engaged in a courteous conversation, while the fathers exchanged information about their own activities.

"I am with the Foreign Affairs, now in Washington DC, but I've been in diplomatic missions mostly in Europe. It is fortunate, because we love Europe, and my wife is originally from Paris. We also would like to spend more time in our family property, in the panhandle of Florida. As a matter of fact, we are looking to be there full time as my wife has opened a new medical practice following a new research study. I plan to continue working on my assignments, since I work mostly contracts, and I can live anywhere I want. Is it not a luxury, to work and to be where you love to be?"

The two of them laughed at the idea of working for pleasure, but Johann admitted, "I am the one who has the best job; I am an art collector, and my only heartache is when I fail to acquire a coveted piece."

Finally, Gunter managed to speak to Marina and said, "I am sorry I stepped on your request."

"Oh, you did not do anything wrong, and I am sorry you did not get to listen to the music of your choice," answered Marina without realizing how bewitched Gunter was by her voice, her smile, and her entire persona.

"Do you go often to musical presentations?"

"They are my favorite," was the answer. "My parents love this place, and so do I."

"I came another time with my parents too, but I was only a young boy at that time." Suddenly Gunter felt very comfortable in her presence and started telling her how much he liked being an orchestra conductor, and that he was in fact taking a break between weeks of preparations to appear in Bayreuth for a full presentation of Tristan and Iseult, at the Wagner festival. He told her how important this was for him after years and years of hard work, and how excited but scared he felt.

After a while, Gunter realized that he had lost track of the time, his parents chatting amiably with Marina's parents, until now his father saying something to him:

"Gunter, would you offer this glass of champagne to this lovely young lady?' and handed him two flutes of champagne, one for each of them. Gunter handed one glass to Marina, a little too ceremoniously perhaps, to which she smiled saying, "In the States I am not allowed to drink until I am 21, but we are in Europe and I am permitted a glass of champagne for special occasions, and since champagne is my favorite, I think I have my parents' approval."

"But even in Europe you must be 18 to drink," said Gunter, who was afraid that his fears were real, since she looked like a little girl when seen so close.

"I am 19!" quickly shot back Marina, wanting to be taken seriously as a grownup with an important air about herself.

Gunter could not repress a big laughter, to which Marina joined in with the most crystalline thrilling laugh. The two pairs of parents became aware of them and stopped short their conversations, quite surprised by how well their children were getting along.

"Are you going to attend other concerts in Venice?" Gunter asked. "I guess you like Vivaldi," he said thinking of the evening he first saw her in the Doge's Palace Courtyard.

"Oh, I love Vivaldi, it is so romantic!"

Romantic? thought Gunter, quick to judge Marina's musical knowledge and decided to probe her, as she probably did not know that Vivaldi was from the classical period. "His wife must have been very lucky with all the nice music he wrote for her," said Gunter, who could not refrain from making a little joke.

At this moment, Marina gave him a serious look and said, "Vivaldi was a priest his entire life, he never married!" Then sensing the irony, she got a little offended and added, "Is this a test?"

"I am so sorry, I did not mean to upset you, it was just a stupid joke on my part. Please forgive me."

Marina seeing a sincere distress in his deep blue eyes, relaxed and said gently, "That's alright, my parents humor me all the time, I am used to it."

When it came time to part and say their goodnights, the families learnt they would see each other at the ball of the season held in the 17th century Palazzo Labia, for which they had both made arrangements.

Each family was delighted to meet such nice, distinguished people. But the most elated was Gunter, after learning that their hotel, the Centurion Palace, was so close to the Forrests' and he would get to see Marina again. But he also realized that, even though he had mostly talked about himself, he did not learn much about her, just that, praise God, she was 19!

BOOK SIX

"Bonjour, mon amour," (good morning, my love) I said looking at Gérard who was still sleepy, but slowly moving, sensing the morning sun flooding the garden. Birds were already competing in beautiful duos for a while, making him aware of the world awakening outside. I greeted him as usual, when morning arrived. I kissed, oh so gently, his eyelashes and his cheeks, and caressed his forehead, lifting a few strands of hair from his face. He was still so handsome after all the years of sorrow and trials! This was one of the special moments when I liked so much to be with him and welcome him to a new terrestrial day.

"Je t'aime mon chéri," (I love you, my darling) I whispered when he opened his eyes, and I tried one more time to see myself in them. He was in no hurry; he looked around thinking of a reason to get up.

I was sometimes present with him, present in his dreams. At first, he hurt even more when waking up from them, but with time, he learned how to see them as a way for us to be together. In a sense, we discovered how love remained present and strong across time and dimensions.

I was learning that my short time spent as an embodied person on Earth was only a minuscule part of my existence. As it is true for all of us, it was another experience during which I was to grow and to learn how to accomplish my destiny, and if I were lucky, to reunite with my soul mate for a terrestrial experience. Coming back for successive lives served to resolve some unfinished matters, define new facets of our personality, or expand new possibilities.

It also helped us uncover character traits and talents of another person and contribute to their progression. It gives us the chance to take a different look at our relationships we established in the past that we enjoyed or hated, and according to very diverse social, cultural, and historical situations, we could allow a completely new story to unfold in the next passage on Earth.

I was learning so much, and again, so much more remained to be learned and discovered. For in the beginning, I was still bound by this sense of security and desire to remain connected to my last terrestrial life. Getting to know my recent new dimension, I had instantly the recognition though, that this was a place where we would all come back to someday, to rest or recharge and prepare for the next life; I knew instantly that this was the real place, that this was Home. And, as an ultimate gift one receives upon arrival Home, I could transition and be on Earth at will, close to anyone I wished, but in an immaterial world, in a different dimension that defined the same planet.

I was light, pure energy myself, perfectly content, and free of all worries, above any pain. All was pure joy, love, knowledge, and beauty. I knew that I had become again my own self, I retained all my sensations and emotions, had back all the memories of people, places, and situations, but did not feel any of the sorrow. Yes, I remembered everything from my past lives, as I understood why each of them was essential for the evolution of my soul, and everything made perfect sense.

Each person I had known at one time or another had a place that fit into the design of my destinies of each of my earthly experiences, while a divine hand was helping my spirit to grow, watching with loving attention over me. Yet, I was still to understand what was the reason for this last past life I had gone through so fast, searching for the sense of it as I looked to complete a full circle.

I quickly discovered, reviewing the string of my consecutive lives, that I had done my best in trying to reach a higher stage of understanding, and that made me feel at peace. I was more loving and tolerant, I had made more effort at developing my talents and assisting others.

I was cognizant that others were in fact us and how essential it was to touch someone else's life, how important it was to make a difference. And at the same time, how imperative it is to be happy. Not just to obtain personal satisfaction, or to fulfill an egotistic desire to possess or dominate, but to experience this essential quality in everything we do and how we relate with others - love.

It became so clear that those loving moments we share are the real moments that count. The supreme revelation is that love is the essence of all universal laws of the visible and invisible worlds.

It was also easy to see that I could share moments with Gérard anytime I desired to. I could be there with him, look at him, feel his emotions, his love. What an awesome gift!

I also learned why it was so hard for humans to accept the loss of a loved one, why they felt torn to pieces and dismembered. They lost the contact, they could not see us, or at most feel only a faint presence, and they so missed us, "the departed". At least, some of them knew that this was only a temporary state, but for them it was still such a little consolation.

-//-

Finally, Gérard decided to leave his soft cocoon, and face the day. He felt the urge to go around the house the way he used to when Isabelle and he were together. So many years had passed and he did not really feel that much had changed, at least not since Francesca was born and he had regained a new purpose in life, when he returned home to make sure the house was well taken care of, and that his life kept at least an appearance of decency.

There was also this secret desire not to disappoint Isabelle, if that could be in some way possible. Gérard opened the French doors and stepped onto the terrace facing the sound, taking in the splendid day at the end of summer. He wanted to remember this place and the great pleasure this house had always given to him, as a longtime and tested friend, faithfully waiting for him.

He understood that after Francesca's wedding, he would be leaving this home for a more modest place; he was getting old, and he had started feeling his 93 years of age, and this was too big of a house to look after by himself. He knew that the time had come when he needed some assistance and had to let other people take care of the more trivial facts of life for him, as he did not want to burden any of his family with his care.

He had already visited a few places and made some arrangements to move to an adult living facility, they call it, and give up his dear independence of living alone.

The pool sparkled in the sun, the flowers were bright, and all was a shimmer of natural delight. How much he wanted to tell Isabelle how young he was still feeling inside when so much beauty surrounded him.

He remembered the taste of the pressed oranges she made for him, and got busy making a full glass of orange juice right away, then lifting the glass in her memory, he drunk it in one go.

Then in a spontaneous impulse, he went to the pool and entered in the water. He felt like jumping and splashing, but his body moved so much slower since his injuries. The water caressed him and he enjoyed this element so much, as it surrounded him and held him.

Suddenly, he remembered a time, so long ago, when he was holding Isabelle in his arms in the same pool, and, so gently, they were floating and dancing together in the water, when time did not exist, where their space was the whole universe, and their love the only law. And for a moment, oh, such a real and special moment, Gérard was back in time with his dear Isabelle. "Oh, my love, where are you?"

I was again floating so gently in his arms, holding him like I did so many years ago, so many times. I was embracing him and we were turning, and laughing, and nothing else was in the whole world but the two of us, our happiness, and our love. "Mon amour, je suis la, et j'y serai toujours, rien ne peut jamais nous séparer," (My love, I am here, and I will always be, nothing can ever separate us).

-//-

Getting out of the water, Gérard felt invigorated, and suddenly realized that he had a busy day ahead of him. He stayed involved in the wedding preparations, offering his contribution in his limited way, but his help appeared to be very valuable with his presence coordinating things, while the others were so far. He had to sign agreements with the retirement home, and meet with the real estate agent for the house to be set on the market, and start sorting through the property where things would have to go.

Gérard was aware that his estate had grown immensely in value over the years thanks to its magnificent location, architecture, and gardens, in a place where a simple studio by the beach was worth a fortune.

He had realized years ago that, although Marina and her family enjoyed coming regularly to spend vacation time here and the grandchildren had their life memories linked with Pa Gérard's house on the sound, this was too much of enterprise for them to manage from a distance.

It was good for Gérard to remain occupied, and he knew that, but he was pushing away the moments when he needed to start selecting among the rooms filled with precious souvenirs and other valuable objects to be passed on to the family or donated to charities. And this time was coming, and Gérard understood that his property would sell quickly, having already had some offers recently, when the house was not even officially on the market.

He took, however, his time to walk around the grounds, admiring the beauty of the gardens, the well grown oak trees, willows, and fig trees, that mixed with dazzling colored bushes and competed with the exuberance of the rose beds. And while he leisurely wandered the alleys, letting his body warm in the sun, Gérard was invaded again by memories of happy days lived in this place. There were not only memories but feelings, true sensations that reminded him so vividly of voices and laughter, the time of the year, and even the smell in the air.

Back came the images of the exact green shade of Isabelle's eyes, the delicate glow of her complexion, the sweetness of her skin under his soft caress when he was touching her neck or shoulder. And with the souvenirs came also the pain; suddenly he felt the pain of his old wounds, the tightness in his chest, and the hurt of his heart. He realized that nothing had changed, and that his grief was still the same, he had only learned how to bury it deeper inside, how to live with it.

Gérard found his way back to the house, walking slowly, almost shuffling, fighting hard to remain focused on his plans for the future, and he smiled when he remembered that he needed to be at his best for Francesca's wedding.

-//-

I enjoy so much my time in the Sanctuary where animals of all kind come and go. Their stay is brief even by the eternity-timeless consideration. They all come frightened, wounded, and abused, but they quickly regain their beautiful appearance and strength, and shortly after, they leave more alive than ever. I started to wonder if it really was with my help that they were recovering, or just being in this place was all they needed.

I was not foolish enough to believe I was the one healing them; I knew that a divine grace was embracing them upon their terrestrial demise, and I quickly understood that they would be made whole and happy whether I was there or not.

And this was all that I needed, attending and admiring for my own satisfaction, to see my beloved creatures returning to their original condition, perfect and complete.

The Sanctuary was getting increasingly larger as I was gaining understanding of what and how I could build my own place in Heaven. Trees, plants, and flowers of all kinds and colors the imagination of a terrestrial cannot conceive, were displayed around meadows, hills, lakes, and valleys. Some arrangements were in park-like configurations, with fountains and reflecting pools, where statues and vases took different colors as a concert could be heard in a sound and light show.

Birds sang and showed their amazing feathers, fish came gracefully close to the water's edge, rabbits and deer walked freely, while cheetahs and lions stood quietly watching them. And I was able to communicate with them without any difficulty, as they were looking so kindly into my eyes telling me their stories.

In time, I saw people coming; at first, a few children that looked lost and neglected, but I found out that nice little homes were there for them and ready to offer shelter upon their arrival. Once here, any sign of suffering vanished and they had a short stay to recover and be reunited with their loved ones. But what an immense joy it was to hold them in my arms and surround them with all my love, feeling that all the love that the universe could contain was pouring through me.

Then, the older people arrived, and I held them too, against my chest as I did with the children, as though they all were my babies, my loved ones. They stopped in my Sanctuary also for a short stay, but what a gift it was to see them renew themselves. Flourishing in my arms, they became young and full of energy again, reuniting with the relatives waiting for them.

More people and more creatures of all sorts continued to come, and I felt a renewed adoration for my profession as a doctor, as a helper in God's miracles, *giving me the privilege to assist Him in this noble occupation.*

I also discovered other ways, I call miraculous, of the eternal life orderliness: I could be at any desired time somewhere else, to learn, or visit. All I discovered was enchanting magnificence and harmony. When I wanted to visit my parents, I could be there and spend some animated moments debating the human condition as we did while on Earth, or just cuddle close by and be again the child I used to be when I was little, experiencing again those blessed moments. I watched my parents as they continued to grow, learn, and create, discovering new ways of artistic and cultural expression.

One by one came back to me the memories of other lives, and I could immerse myself in those realities, see the people that were important for me at that time, and understand why. I had a different thrill of meeting them, emotions that are never possible to express in words, but it was an instant recollection of unique situations. With some of the persons, I encountered special connections that lasted several lives, and being again in their presence was a new experience, expanding my understanding and knowledge to a much vaster dimension of the role they played during these special times spent together.

It was a new discovery that served a great purpose for me to re-live different lives or moments; so much to comprehend and to resolve in one life after another! On other occasions, I almost played with the pleasure of going back to re-experience moments I cherished. This way I had a more profound sense of the moment and replayed, or re-lived, the grand moments of my marriage, the birth of my daughter, or more simple ones like a dinner together, or a stroll on the beach with Gérard.

I could go back and be again the little Isabelle learning how to walk, to swim, to play the harp. I had birthdays, and auditions, times of reflection about my career and understanding my choice for science, with the strong desire to serve, to mend, and being attracted by the mystery of the human body and its functions. I appreciated the importance of the music and art that played in my life to satisfy my need of all that was beautiful.

Music became my secret world where I could go in my imagination to find peace and joy, the cherished place I reached when I needed serenity. Now I could continue to listen and practice music as well; I could play instantly an infinity of melodies with the greatest facility and virtuosity, or I could join other musicians and play together in small or huge formations. What a sublime experience it was to hear those choirs and orchestras performing together and be part of them!

To the musical experience, one could add other visual once, and myself I could dance along with my harp. What an extraordinary feeling this was, being able to float weightlessly in the air in all directions, swirl with the birds and continue to play, while my musical notes and my movements in the space became lights of all colors and shapes I had never encountered before! It was all splendor, with new feelings to experience, while words could not describe the intense happiness that flooded my being.

These sensations were even more profound when I played for my little patients and shared their emotions and joy, and had them join in a divine, renewed harmony.

There were moments when, walking through an alley, I could hear a plant or a flower calling, and on turning to look in their direction, I would receive a splendid arrangement of flowers never seen before, diffusing the most pleasing fragrance. When inquiring about it, I readily heard a voice telling me, "You gave me water when I was hot and thirsty, you talked to me and told me how pretty I was."

Other times, I received visitors to my Sanctuary that were beautiful cats I did not recognize and they definitely did not need my help; when I questioned what I could do for them, they answered most of the time with a simple "thank you". They took pleasure in coming often and stayed a little while, keeping the newly arrived company.

I heard a few of them say, "She gave us food and told us that she loved us, that we were beautiful when we were scruffy and starving. She did not feel like she did much giving us a little food and milk, but she was keeping us alive one more day, slowly adding a few more years to an existence that could have been so miserable otherwise. She offered us a place we knew we could always go when we were hungry, a place where we felt safe."

It was such a great gift to review the acts of our lives that were of real value, to know that they could never really go away, that they never died. What a splendid gift to me, to all of us. I went again on vacation with Gérard and Marina, we lived our Christmases, Marina's first day of school, her dance lessons; we went on our walks, exchanged ideas as in the past, while feeling this incommensurable, eternal love.

Another divine gift was that all the bad things and situations I ever suffered, I could instantly reverse and transform into good ones, with the outcome I could fashion upon my desire. I also had the ability to fulfill wishes and yearnings, and live situations I never could during my stay on Earth.

I was smiling remembering the latest scientific theories talking about the same person living in different dimensions and having an infinity of destinies based on different choices made for the same circumstance.

It is true; there are an infinity of choices, but there is only one of myself, choosing to live only one eternity, in one dimension at a time.

-//

My new existence in Heaven, the place I was now calling Home, was not about discovering how this place was made and functions, but a slow recognition of something I already knew or I rediscovered longing after it. I started remembering this place, my Real Home, feeling happier and happier if that could be possible, being back where I was coming from and where I belonged.

The instant appearance of an imaginary desire or place was easier for me to grasp, since I knew and I had the constant demonstration that all that existed in our mind could also be a reality in another dimension. Multiple dimensions, as an infinity of different universes, were not only a reality but they could also coexist together, and my present condition permitted me to easily go from one realm to another.

I am still emerging from this long sleep I call "my terrestrial life", shaking off this mind numbness from seeing fully my new, real life. But the sensations found here were so much stronger, more powerful, and beautiful, that they helped my being to recognize them, to get engulfed into the magnificence of colors, forms, and designs of my Home.

However, I tried to understand why there were so many different levels or universes, and this came to me easier and easier, since the answers were quicker to form. I only had to listen to them in my soul, for there was no need for words; the knowledge was "pouring" into me as I wanted to grasp that concept.

Sometimes there were other superior, "wise", men or women who appeared when I wanted someone to explain something to me, as I used to during my conversations on Earth. Other times I invoked God as my Creator to guide me, and the answers flooded back to me right away and the most wonderful feeling ever experienced embraced my whole soul instantly.

This way has been revealed to me that there are, along with the different dimensions, also different levels of our soul evolution; our spiritual growth progresses from the heavy and dark material existence I could see in my recent universe, to others, where the beings inhabiting those universes could access any of them by simply appearing.

I realized, also, that I could experience these different places that would manifest as I inquired about them; some seemed more familiar but others remained far more difficult to comprehend. I understood that on Earth I had no ability to leave behind that reality, although some more advanced beings could come occasionally, manifesting at will even in the limited universe I had recently left.

The most profound and beautiful answers came to me when I "talked" with God and asked him the reason I had had this past earthly experience. I instantly understood that there was only one God, the same one who created the universe I had just known and left. He also created all the infinitely rich and complex universes, all part of the same Creation. But the response He gave me was as simple as one word to unify all of them. And this word, this reason for me to go to Earth and come back in such a dramatic way, was LOVE.

As I had almost revolted at having my earthly life cut short, considering there was no good reason for that, God showed me that LOVE unifies all the worlds, all the souls at any different realm of manifestation. God allowed all His creatures, simple or superior, to experience His infinite love and to see that love is truly infinite. He also made me realize that, even after leaving my earthly physical existence, nothing had changed about my love for Gérard.

If I chose to linger a little longer around that level and the place where he was still present, there was no rush in the eternal time for me to go to other places. This was an infinitely sweet present, offering me to love from any place I wanted to be, that the earthly death could not take away my love to another soul, regardless of where we were.

I also realized that "talking with God" was possible at any time. When I inquired how this was possible, He gave me another simple answer: "I am always here. I am always here for you and for everyone, for I am omnipresent. Just ask, because I gave to all of you the free will, another gift to my beloved creatures to show them my respect and love."

BOOK SEVEN

Francesca arrived into this world bringing great joy to her family, and most importantly, new directions for the future in Gérard's life. As he multiplied his trips to New York, Gérard valued immensely his visits to Marina and her little family. While in Washington, DC, likewise, Gérard enjoyed spending more extended time with his son, Patrick, his wife, and their growing children. He became more involved in their lives, closer to their interests and occupations, participating actively in their usual activities; in one word, he was living his life through their eyes, and taking great pleasure in it.

This situation, after the first few years after Isabelle's death, brought him back to daily reality, and if he did not find consolation in his loss, being with his young family prevented him from sinking into the emptiness left by her disappearance, giving him a reason to go on.

He was very proud of his children's successes and accomplishments, and deeply satisfied to see them happy in their marriages. Marina continued to be recognized internationally in her career, always busy between her performances and her two children. Often she had the chance to sing in productions her husband, Gunter, was directing, and this situation kept them together most of their trips away from home. It was also fortunate that they had such a great professional connection, keeping alive the admiration and attraction they had for each other over the years.

Patrick was another reason for enormous satisfaction, assuming a governmental position for foreign affairs.

Now living in the familial mansion his father grew up in, he watched also for a while over his grandparents, who lived a long and well filled life, passing away quietly and in peace. His wife, Bridgett, and their two teenage boys, kept him busy and satisfied; Bridgett, an international lawyer for civil rights, took a consulting position while the boys, Eduard and Oliver, were still very young. It was only now, when they reached 15 and 17 years of age, that Bridgett felt at ease going back full time to her consulting firm.

Patrick, too, had to travel to New York occasionally, being assigned to similar missions Gérard had been in the past at the UN, but his work would require at times representing the US abroad as well. Patrick took the habit to ask Gérard's opinion in many of the matters he was involved in, inciting lengthy debates, the way they did it when Patrick was much younger.

It was during one of these evening conversations when Patrick suggested to his father that "it was time for him to get back on the saddle", and that his father "was wasting his talents when the world was in turmoil in many places".

Over the years, Gérard maintained cordial relations with many of the colleagues he had worked with in various places of the world; however, after his wife's death he kept away and detached from his previously busy social life. But now, things had changed, and slowly he agreed to accompany his son to some informal meetings and renew ties with former coworkers.

One of the friends he had met as a young student in Paris was Jackson McDonald, who was now back in Washington, DC, with an impressive résumé of his successful career. The two of them enjoyed immensely seeing each other again, and from now on, they remained close their entire lives.

It did not take too long for Gérard to distinguish himself with his knowledge and abilities to present outstanding solutions to many of the top issues in the international arena. He stayed at the Forrest mansion in a private area dedicated to him, and having the pleasant advantage to come and go at his will, but he also could enjoy his son's family when they all desired to be together.

With time, Gérard joined more frequently luncheons and dinners with his friends, and was increasingly asked to attend meetings and reunions between the Secretary of State office with the delegates to the UN and other foreign missions, in a consultant capacity. Although many times Patrick and he participated in the same sessions, Gérard belonged to separate committees and presentations as well, and was in no time "back in the saddle" again as Patrick had fervently expressed.

The post Darfur war situation was on many discussion agendas when serious ethnic tensions arose again against the Darfur Peace Agreement signed in 2011. Darfur, a southern region of Sudan, was the size of a country like France, and suffered from the genocide when ethnic cleansing was carried out against the non-Arab population. The Arab Apartheid intensified their campaign, instigating land disputes between the non-Arab semi-nomadic livestock herders and the more sedentary agricultural tribes.

More than 20 years of fighting between the Arab-dominated government and the Darfur Liberation Front resulted in several hundreds of thousand civilians killed and millions becoming refugees. Over the years, disputes escalated and, with recent reemergence of frequent attacks, there was disregard to the immunity of peacekeeping operations trying to improve the inhumane conditions of the refugee camps.

The crises were frequent and this situation reached a climax after September 2012, when the violence worsened. Human Rights First discovered that 90 percent of the arms used in the conflicts in Sudan were imported from China. Then, the Geneva Convention was violated by the Russians dispersing military equipment and weaponry to guerilla factions carried by Russian airplanes disguised as UN planes, with arm sales reaching a value of over 21 million dollars.

Agencies of the United Nations were informed and summits held periodically in New York, Brussels, and Paris. During these assemblies, witnesses came to raise the attention to the Darfur events. Decisions were needed, with urgent intervention and humanitarian aid provided for the population, and sanctions against the perpetrators. Things were not simple, since a direct intervention of peacekeeping armed forces was not always permitted by the national authorities, and local protection was not reliable for the civilians and the UN commissions during humanitarian functions.

In the midst of these intense international events, Gérard's experience was increasingly needed and appreciated, and without realizing it, Gérard felt more alive and excited than he had been in a longtime. He became more involved and enthusiastic, at ease dealing with situations he was familiar with after an entire life of practice. Above all, he had a purpose and his life was making sense again.

Things evolved quickly, and after traveling to Europe for a UN summit in Paris, Gérard was sent to Khartoum as part of a small committee, and from there, to some refugee camps for inspection. Reports to the UN were that over 4.7 million Darfuris still relied on humanitarian aid. Gérard was part of this international team, and he could not help but remember other times when he visited rescue camps in Isabelle's company. In a way, he was curious to see the changes, hoping for progress in the conditions of these places.

In addition to the refugees, there were 1.8 million internally displaced persons (IDP) from Sudan, some living in shantytowns in the greater Khartoum area, Somalia, and Chad, but also Cairo, Beirut, and Damascus.

Gérard's next trip was to Cairo, Egypt, where a large makeshift camp had been set up for several years in the city's surroundings. After visiting the camp and seeing and learning firsthand about the primitive and repulsive conditions people endured, the UN team tried to work with the local authorities. Several Sudanese women shyly came to him, and he was shocked by their accounts; families had been split up on their departure, men away from their wives and children.

For the women coming to the camp in Egypt was the beginning of another ordeal. Local men, often leaving their wives and children or simply ignoring the low forbidding polygamy, looked for young, single women in the camp to make them their concubines. In the camp, women did not have a way of making a living, they did not know the fate of their husbands after many years of separation, there was no school for their children, and many Christian women were forced to convert to Islam. They felt trapped in despicable living conditions with little sanitation or running water, with sewage flowing through the middle of the narrow alleys between the cardboard shacks.

The children born there were not provided with birth certificates, and an application to return to their village could not even be filed. Most of them had completely lost contact with their families and some were forced to divorce their legal spouse. Despite all of this, they were eager to find work, to learn, and dreamed of going back to their home and family left behind.

Gérard threw himself into the enormous task of finding all the possible solutions to improve the refugees' conditions and coordinate a future return to Sudan. It was an immense undertaking, involving negotiation between different countries and international agencies. Nevertheless, here was where Gérard presented at his best. His stay in Cairo lasted longer than expected and he finally returned home with major changes set in motion and with the promise that he would keep a close watch on the progress made regarding a variety of programs already started.

After Cairo, came visits to other camps followed by heated debates about the conditions found, and efforts to connect the local institutions with the interventions made by international aid. This way, Gérard visited Djabal in Eastern Sudan, then, he went to Dossey, Zalingei and Hassa Hissa.

All the camps were the image of desolation and despair; people had built shabby inhabitations from dry grass and mud, and survived on rations close to starvation level. In some of the camps the suicide rate was higher than ever, in other camps, some refugees tried to survive doing small jobs outside of the camp, but they needed the protection of armored vehicles of the UN or the African Union patrol.

No one felt safe leaving the camp even for a short time and distance, since women were raped and men attacked and robbed by bands of militia. There were frequent reports of raids breaching the camps' borders, making people feel even more insecure and exposed to potential aggression. In some camps, alcohol and drugs were rampant.

During one of the conferences in Paris, Gérard heard horrendous stories of desperate Sudanese men from Zamzam camp, in Libya. They worked in horrific conditions in gold mines for many years in order to buy their passage to Europe. Some arrived in England, then crossed the 50 km (31 mile) Channel on foot to France, dodging high-speed trains in the dark. Surprisingly, they still found the courage to say that their life in Europe was good!

-//-

Arrived inside the Krystal Pyramid of Light, gently floating in the beautiful silvery energy surrounding me, and being part of it as well, I met Raphael. I was already aware that he was the Healing Archangel, loving medicine and helping doctors and healers.

Suddenly I realized that he could answer many of my questions and explain the mysteries I had tried so long and hard to penetrate during my earthly journey. And instantly, I realized also that all feelings were enhanced many, many thousands of times, and I was now able to sense other feelings and sensations I had never experienced before. As questions were forming in my mind, an enormous thrill of joy was enveloping me, as answers and understanding were poured into my soul.

Although few words were ever exchanged, they could have been reduced to something like this:

"Before humans came to Earth, they had already chosen the theme of their life and their mission, for it is about defining who they are, and their choices during this journey depend on their free will. One accomplishes their lifetime mission, grows or declines, according to how one decides to live it."

"On Earth, you know one form of existence in your biological body and your mind. Even this body, particularly the brain, has the ability to evolve, gain more knowledge and understanding of the whole existence, because man has a consciousness, a sense of self.

"However, your view of the world, what you are aware of, is limited to a few sensory organs that give information about your surroundings, but this is only a very narrow view of reality, a very partial perception of what there is, even at your physical level. Moreover, in many instances, this perception is erroneous. But man has tremendous potential to expand his abilities, as he uses less than 10 percent of his brain, which means 90 percent of reality is not utilized because he is not even aware of it."

"How important is this life on Earth?" I asked, and added, "there are beliefs that this is all there is, and all ends with our bodily demise, while others think that all this is an illusion, all a figment of our imagination to which one should not give much importance."

"It is true that this life is a transition during a much longer journey," Raphael answered. "Coming to your *planet is like coming to a school, quite an elementary school, that is, where one has to learn how to elevate one's self. And although this is just an episode, a passage through, it is not an illusion! This is very real, and it is important," he emphasized.*

"The truth is that doing this, going over and over again through these transforming episodes called life times, all beings, all souls, will ultimately unite their consciousness with the universal consciousness, and attain the highest level of evolution. Human beings are part of this magnificent design."

"What do you think about religion?" I asked after a while.

"There are numerous ancient spiritual teachings in all human cultures. They have been and continue to be used by many different religions across the world, all pretending to be the only right one and owning the whole truth. Unfortunately, many religions are institutions made by men who have an immense ego, who often try to scare, enslave, and dictate to others what to believe and how to comport themselves.

"This has often nothing to do with faith, which is a very personal relationship with God, the divine creator and force of the universe. God is loving, God is good and understanding. He listens and forgives. He does not ask for any sacrifices, nor for money or any other form of retribution. He can make a whole universe at His will, He is above petty material form of recognition that are often used with the intention to buy His forgiveness or seek future advantages.

"The extreme digression of the soul is when it commits crimes in the name of God. We see it when someone claims to hold the absolute truth and forces others to

adhere to it. Unfortunately, we observe this happening repeatedly, attaining unspeakable foolishness.

"Cult leaders and radical extremists have deviated others even further from their own beliefs; their exercise of absolute power over ill-informed people, in their irrational desire to satisfy an enormous ego, they bring themselves and their followers into darkness. This is their own darkness, created from ignorance and presently spreading across the world, bringing senseless suffering and destruction."

After a little while, Raphael continued, "Another frequent habit humans have, is the desire to be right. This desire, this "need" for righteousness they proclaim in front of people is just another form of overpowering others, and it is generated, again, by their own ego. In reality, it is a way to prevent exposing their own serious flaws.

"The 'righteous' ones are often very vocal, critical, and intolerant; they cannot be further from the teachings they refer to as they take into their own hands the right to judge everyone else.

"And we can easily see from here that the ones they put to judgment are far better than the conceited 'educator'.

"You ask why God tolerates crimes and injustice? Again, God does not punish, does not seek revenge. Men do, and because He granted them free will, what one sees is only what one person does to another. Men hate, destroy, and dishonor, and God often sends His angels to protect in times and in situations that one could cannot even fathom of what could have been without His intervention.

"As I said when we first met, one should beware of its actions, the energy produced by a person's behavior *comes back, enhanced a thousand-fold, and one gets what he released into the universe. Those close to us also suffer the consequences of our actions, from our children, to our parents, and close relatives. It is not advisable to stay close or to worship evil people, and sadly there are many of them and they bring bad things around, sooner or later.*

"Something that can be done to tip the balance in favor of improvement on Earth, is to understand that humans can create their own hell and paradise here, on their own planet. Here you will find what has been described in all cultures, religions, and all through history as the men interpretation and description of Heaven and Hell.

"Alas, few recognize that the Earth was given to them as a jewel, as a divine gift to enjoy, but also to respect, protect and love. This place was, and can be again, the Eden men describe, mirroring the eternal Paradise."

-//-

Milu Elba Lopes was settling in her hotel in Manhattan close to the United Nations building, preparing to attend one of its sessions. It was one of many and she had long quit keeping count of them. She was at the San Carlos where she liked to stay most of the time, but Renwick and The William were as convenient, although she would not mind a room at the nearby Waldorf Astoria, on Park Avenue.

Flying straight from Rio, Brazil, where she was from, Milu was happy to have the whole afternoon to herself and get ready for the UN conference the day after. It was a crisp winter day in mid-February, and the sun shone timidly in a clear sky. She decided to take a walk on Park Avenue towards the Rockefeller Center and check out the ice skating rink, which was always a lot of fun for her, coming from the hot summer of Rio.

Milu was part of the Brazilian delegation to the Humanitarian Rescue Intervention Committee, and participated not only in the UN assembles, but accompanied the actual interventions in places affected by natural disasters or civil wars. Divorced twice and now in her early fifties, she remained an attractive and voluptuous woman, self-assured not only in her feminine charms she liked to play occasionally, but her professional abilities as well.

A former nurse by education, Milu had succeeded with time and had proven herself as a single woman after each of her divorces. She had also acquired a strong knowledge of the international law and the mechanisms of humanitarian campaigns for medical and emergency relief missions, but also regarding various fundraising proceedings. She loved to travel and felt free and at ease in third world places, in conditions she had experienced herself as a child raised in the hillside slums of Rio.

Since she was very young, Milu knew that she wanted desperately to get out of poverty. Determined to get an education, she sometimes accompanied her mother when she was cleaning a few rich houses and benefitted from occasional financial help from some philanthropic hearts. Her mother, a very young single woman raising a couple of small children alone, was blessed with good looks that helped her in obtaining some unexpected "entrees" in wealthy families. When she was barely a teenager, Milu mastered the art of seduction, and it was no surprise that she obtained the favors of an older man.

This way, Milu had met Rosario, a widower, who agreed to marry her, even though his children were close to her age. Milu had not kidded herself; she did not love Rosario, but he was her ticket out of misery and she promised to be a good and a grateful wife.

Although she lived now in the upper-class society, she was barely accepted within it; considered a nouveau rich and frequently branded a "gold digger". However, she decided to continue her education and gain more security in life, while helping her mother and her little brother. Soon becoming a mother, Milu tried her best to properly take care of her child.

Against all good intentions and after being married for about 10 years, Milu, an ardent and sensual woman in her prime, fell in love with a young doctor, and they began a very passionate and public affair. She was convinced that her lover would leave his wife and children, and marry her.

To her surprise, the doctor did not leave his family, and she learned that he had many other extramarital flings. To top it all, her husband, pressured by his children and having lost his interest in pleasing too young of a wife, divorced her. After the shock, Milu recovered her senses enough to ask for a large compensation, but her stepchildren had taken the precaution of gathering an indisputable amount of evidence against her. She fought as best she could, with demands for her son if not grounds for herself, and ended up obtaining a modest settlement, representing nevertheless a decent stability compared to her life before marriage.

More broken hearted from the rejection from her lover than her divorce, Milu became more resolute not to trust anyone, particularly men. She decided she would be the one in charge from now on, and aware of men's weaknesses, she could use this skill to her benefit. Like a "Carmen" of the new era, she had long, curly jet-black hair, a curvy body, and deep dark eyes.

She continued to be focused at work, but daring and challenging when away. When she discovered the possibility of going abroad on medical missions of rescue, she first went as a nurse to get away from the humiliation after her affair with the doctor, then taking a liking on the adventure of it.

Milu continued to have adventures and many 'liaisons' or just temporary passions with a number of team members, but with total disregard for any serious relationship. She was on a quest for revenge on all men and reaffirmation of her power over them after her double failure, being equally rejected by her husband and her lover.

This continued for six or seven years until she had a boyfriend that appeared very different from the others. He was a sweet and considerate man, and a soft-spoken dreamer who came along for some missions to build wells for isolated African villages. She was attracted by his blue eyes and his fair hair. Dieter was from Munich, a musician and writer, but engaged in saving the planet and making people's lives better.

They were proof that opposites attract, and after living together for a couple of years, they decided to marry. But this came to an end after only a few years; their union not surviving the frequent separations during programs sending them apart, and Milu's temptations of other loves. After her second divorce, Milu decided that she was not cut out for marital life and enjoyed her independence too much.

Milu liked coming back to New York, and here she was today. After walking a while and stopping to admire some of the window decorations of sumptuous fashion boutiques and jewelry stores, she started feeling the jetlag setting in and decided to return to her hotel. What the heck, it was cocktail time anyway, and she was ready for one.

After changing into a red dress that revealed her feminine curves, she applied a blistery carmine lipstick and redefined the liner of her black eyes. Then she went down to the hotel bar for a drink. She was quite a looker, when confident, she entered strait into the bar lounge.

Andres, the barman, knew Milu from her previous visits and smiled at her as she approached. Milu slowed down a little near the entrance, for she had spotted sitting alone at the bar one of the most handsome men she had ever seen. And it occurred to her that she had seen him before, but where?

-//-

Gérard was in New York City on one of his regular trips to the UN and staying, as usual, with Marina and her family, and doubly enjoying his visit. His longtime friend, Lucien Dubois, was in New York and the two of them were meeting at San Carlos for dinner and for the pleasure to catch up with the latest news. Gérard appreciated the convenience of Marina's apartment, close enough to the United Nations UN Headquarters compound, and joining Lucien at San Carlos was also a convenient location for the two of them. Gérard arrived a little earlier before their 6:00 pm appointment and chose to wait for Lucien at the hotel bar, as they would decide later if they would go somewhere close by for dinner or they would try the hotel's restaurant.

Gérard was testing his Kyr Royal, a French cocktail made of Champagne and crème de cassis, (blackcurrant syrup), when he heard a close by voice addressing him. He turned around, but he did not see anyone safe for the lady adjusting her bar stool next to him, and repeating, "I know we've met before but I can't remember exactly where, can you help me find out where?"

The voice was deep and sensuous, with a pronounced Latino accent, and the lady was indeed talking to him. Staring at him intensely, she waited for him to speak, wondering if he was a little dense considering how long it took him to respond.

"That is quite possible, but *you* may want to help me remember," Gérard answered, recovering from the surprise, and his perfect manners quickly reacting thanks to lifelong practice. Still, he feverously searched through his mind who she was and where they have met, if indeed she was not mistaken.

"Then let's see," undisturbed the lady shot back, "perhaps a Martini might help us in the meantime."

"But of course, please barman, lady's desires are my orders."

"Milu, Milu Elba Lopes, is the name. And Andres knows how I like my Martini. Andres, don't forget, give it 50 shakes to do it properly." After which, she turned back to Gérard, "Now that this is settled, tell me what you do in life, what you do in New York, what is your name?"

Trying to slow her down and feeling almost invaded by the questions, Gérard answered, "Indeed, this seems to be my interview! But, I am not looking for a job. Are you a private investigator?"

Milu was all charm, and with her best smile looked at him innocently, "I told you my name, did I not?" All the while Milu was smitten inside by this man's striking looks from the moment he turned around to face her, so she was not ready to give up, she needed to learn this man's name, and she silently made the bet he will not resist her charms.

Keeping a straight and polite face, Gérard felt uneasy, still trying to figure out what kind of situation she was creating. She was polished and nice looking, but obviously also alone at a bar approaching a stranger and very at ease with this. Then again, she might be just friendly, and he was the only person there, yet, why did her dress and her behavior scream that she was there to seduce him?

He was not wrong, she *was* there to seduce, but what he did not comprehend, is that this time she had a very precise prey in mind, and *he* became the center of her attention. Gérard decided to play it low and get away from the lady.

"I am sorry, I am expecting to meet with someone shortly, so I will not take up any of your time any longer."

"I see, your wife perhaps?" Milu pressed on.

Without knowing, this abruptly brought back a dear image into Gérard's mind, and his expression saddened imperceptibly. "Oh no, it is a friend visiting, I have not seen him in a while."

Reassured Milu added, "You are staying at the hotel I suppose, me too."

"No, I am not, just meeting my friend. Although I am in town for a conference at the United Nations."

"That's it," she almost screamed, "this is where I've seen you before; I am a member of the Brazilian representatives and here for a session tomorrow morning regarding a rescue mission for the children in Sudan. I mean one of the camps in Darfur."

At this point, Gérard felt relieved and was glad to find common grounds of conversation, "I am Gérard Forrest, with the American delegation to the UN for foreign affairs," he said and extended his hand to shake hers, giving the conversation a more professional direction.

Milu was glad to learn his name and his position in an activity that was fortunately creating a situation for them to be together sometimes in the future, hopefully tomorrow, when he gave her the confirmation she was looking for: "I will attend the same session tomorrow morning, it is why I came to town."

"San Carlos is a very good hotel with a great location for the UN meetings, is yours far away?"

"I stay at my daughter's place usually, and no, it is not far from here, on Park Avenue," Gérard answered.

The conversation took a friendly turn, with all the attempts Milu made to impress him in every way. When finally Lucien showed up, the conversation had lasted only a few minutes, when he found them exchanging animated impressions of the agency's activities. Lucien was a little surprised though, and after Gérard made the usual introductions, the two of them took their leave, as Gérard said, "I might see you at the meeting tomorrow." To which Milu gave him the assurance that he definitely would.

Lucien could not help but tease Gérard as soon as they were out of the hotel and on their way to dinner. "Oh my, Gérard, I am glad to see that you are back on the dating game, and what a hot one that is."

Gérard jumped to defend himself and make sure there was no mistake made once or ever, but how much Lucien really believed, remained hard to tell.

-//-

The next morning was another clear winter day in the Big Apple, but at seven in the morning the air was so cold that made the children's cheeks pink when they went to school. Marina was already awoken and entered Benjamin's room first, to watch her son a few moments before waking him up with a kiss. Benjamin was a lovely boy, going on nine years of age.

Reflective and responsible, he was quiet but very affectionate with his family, never giving his parents any reason to worry. When he was a little child and his parents had to go on a trip for their contract performances, he was deeply affected, but he took it like a big boy and did not let his sadness show.

Later, when Francesca arrived, he took care of his younger sister, always comforting and offering his protection. Waking, Benjamin smiled at his mother and they took the usual two minutes of tenderness they always shared, before getting out of his bed.

Marina caressed his front and told him how much she loved him, and after a "bonjour Maman", Benjamin wrapped his arms around her neck and whispered in her ear that he loved her, too. There was never rush or panic during this little ritual the family established for the school mornings, things went better and faster this way, as they rarely were late.

Marina spoke in French to her children, often amused by their cute pronunciation and the childish words they made up, looking at her in surprise when she did not understand. Was she not telling them lots of strange words *they* were supposed to understand?

Benjamin started to play the piano at around five years of age. In the beginning, he was climbing up next to his father on the piano bench, when he was rehearsing for recitals or opera performances, or when Gunter was working on the partitions he had to direct. Benjamin listened in deep concentration, entranced by the music.

His father started giving him piano lessons at his request, but the two parents were wise enough not to push him and let him take his own pace playing and listening to the music. Soon, Benjamin dedicated so much time to lessons or just tagging along with them in the music room his parents had to come up with a schedule and reserve time for play outdoors as well. They wanted to introduce their children to many aspects and activities they might like in life, as they wanted them to be sure to make the right choice for later.

However, Benjamin was already happy with his music, and if he were not going somewhere where music was played, he would create his own world of sounds. Thus, by now it was established that Benjamin wanted to be a musician, a pianist and a composer for that matter, and Gunter was giving him regular lessons in both areas, at home after his homework was finished. Plans were to enroll Benjamin in private classes with other teachers, and who knows, maybe later he would follow in his mother's steps and attend Julliard's. But for now, their son was happy to hurry back home after school, finish his schoolwork, and then begin his music lessons.

Marina waited a little longer before going to Francesca's room, stopping by the kitchen and supervising the nanny making the children's breakfast. There, she was happy to see her father already up, and they sat at the kitchen table looking out the window as the darkness dissipated and light filtered through the branches of the trees lining the avenue, still barren fault of the green of the leaves. They tenderly exchanged the usual kisses on the cheeks, then, daughter and father had their coffee together.

Marina was approaching her mid-30s and kept the most splendid looks; Gérard's heart was filled with love and pride as he watched her move about in a fluffy robe without any makeup, her flawless complexion still rosy with sleep. "Good Lord, how much she looks like her mother," he thought, his heart melting with bittersweet feelings!

Marina looked at her father thinking of Francesca, who was now three and a half years old and started going to the PreK School. It was her belief that her little Francesca brought her father back from the depths of despair after losing his wife.

Marina was happy to see how handsome her father remained, although he was now in his late 60s. Any spectator would have been touched to see this tête-à-tête between father and daughter as they looked at each other with the same emerald blue eyes.

"Marina, you don't have to get dressed, I can drop Benjamin at school this morning by 8:30 am, then Francesca at 9:00 am at her PreK. I want to get to the headquarters around 9: 30 am and get ready a few papers for the 10 o'clock meeting."

He really enjoyed taking the little ones to school, and Francesca was very excited her Pa Gérard was in town for a special event at her school later that day: a group of actors were coming to perform a play for the children. She obtained from him to promise, using her sweetest hugs and kisses, that he would come. "Like she needed to even ask, but I will take the kisses any time," thought Gérard.

Marina continued her morning rounds, stepped into Francesca's room, and all started again, kisses, "*Bonjour Maman, je t'aime.*" They decided on an outfit for the cold day; a light green and gray pair of wool tights, and a light green wool dress. Of course, it had to go with assorted gloves, scarf, and a hat covering her little ears.

Marina looked at her children with so much love as they had breakfast, and this was filling her heart with everything she wanted. She had a very loving husband, her dear children and her family. Her career was fulfilling her highest expectations, but she was always seized by the desire to share this with her mother, now departed for over five years.

In these moments, and they were frequent, she knew not to allow the sorrow to invade her again, thinking that her mother would not want her to be sad, but to live her life the best she could and appreciate all the blessings she could be thankful for. This was, and remained for always, her way to honor her mother's memory.

The nanny, back in the kitchen, looked at the family sitting at the breakfast table, and admired the gentle way they interacted, so different to the morning dramas in other places she had worked.

"Marina, you, your father, and Francesca have the same blue eyes," Bernadette said in French. She was a middle-aged woman from Normandy and was chosen to help the children practice their mother's native tongue, and because the two parents believed this would be good if they were raised bilingual.

They also believed that classical music enhanced their abstract thinking and the connections of the cortex, as Marina's mother had said when she was expecting Benjamin. Practicing regularly at home, the two young parents found this a natural and easy way to expose their children to classical music.

"Only Benjamin has dark green eyes, and his father's are blue!" Bernadette continued.

"Benjamin has his grandmother's eyes," Marina and Gérard answered almost at the same time.

"I have Isabelle's eyes," Benjamin said caught up with his mouth full of brioche.

It was a rare and strong affirmation, and a good thing, as the sadness of the memory was washed away by his hilarious interjection, making them all laugh.

-//-

After dropping off Francesca, with one more kiss and the promise that he would be there for the four o'clock play, Gérard walked briskly to the UN headquarters. He needed a good 15 to 20 minutes to reach the Turtle Bay area, and the cold wind forced him to keep up a good speed. He arrived at the 48th Street entrance reserved for the UN members and strolled quickly through the gardens between the main structures of this place considered an 'extraterritorial' campus, as on international land within New York City.

Gérard passed the iconic sculptures, including the 'Knotted Gun' by Colt Python showing a revolver with its barrel tied in a knot. He could not see the line of flagpoles where the 193 flags of the state members, plus the flag of the UN, all aligned in English alphabetical order, facing east, which could be seen only from Franklin D. Roosevelt Drive or the East River.

He directed his steps to the General Assembly and the Council Chambers, the long horizontal structure along with the 39-story Secretariat Tower. This main complex was completed in 1952 from the plans designed by Le Corbusier, the visionary French architect. The UN headquarters were then moved to New York City from Geneva, Switzerland, and served as a multinational organization promoting international cooperation.

Gérard alternated his presence between the American division for the Office of Political Affairs and Humanitarian Affairs. This morning he was expected in the Security Council Chamber in the Assembly Hall. The participation of different representatives of the peacekeeping divisions was often expected at the request of the Secretary-General Ban Ki-moon of South Korea, who had followed Kofi Annan of Ghana since 2007.

A few representatives of UNICEF, the World Health Organization, and Red Cross, were also anticipated to attend. Entering the hall, he admired the two murals made by the French artist Fernand Leger, and the stained glasses by Marc Chagall. There was also a tapestry from a design by Pablo Picasso.

Passing through the hall, Gérard entered one of the many meeting chambers, where seats with Wi-Fi connections, individual lamps and headphones for translations were present. He would not need the help of translation service since the working sessions were held in English and French, and he was fluent in both languages, while the six official languages during the general assemblies included also Arabic, Chinese, Russian and Spanish.

After an exposé made by the Security Council for the prevention of genocide in South Sudan, smaller groups would confer, Gérard participating in the special division of Political Affairs. He opened his iPad to a folder filled with material to review for the later part of the morning and started perusing through the reports.

He had almost finished scrolling through his iPad and was making a few personal footnotes, when he heard a voice behind him.

"Oh, hello, Mr. Gérard Forrest, we were obviously meant to meet again."

Gérard, broke his attention from his screen, turned slightly and encountered a smiling woman who was now standing at his row level. He recognized the lady from the San Carlos bar, but she had transformed a little, and in a good way: her hair was tight up in a bun, and she was wearing a professional dark blue pantsuit. However, her face was made up with an expert use of cosmetics, although an elegant pair of eyeglasses dimmed any intended ostentation.

Gérard answered back in a casual way with a "Good morning, how are you?" and returned his attention to the report shown on the screen.

Milu insisted a little longer, "We might be sitting in a same commission after this meeting; I am with the Humanitarian assistance for Darfur." When Gérard said he would be part of a different one, she added with a mischievous look, "We might get together for cocktails afterwards, is your friend still in town?"

"I promised my granddaughter to be at her school play today, and I will have to run as soon as we end our session. Sorry."

Milu left nonchalantly with a, "Well, we will be running into each other probably," to which Gérard got up half way and politely nodded. He thought for a fraction of a second that she might be into him, but then he dismissed it and went back to his work. Milu, however, thought that they would surely be seeing a lot of each other, and that she would put to use all her feminine ammunition until this "irresistibly, devastatingly, awesomely handsome man was hers. "He will be hooked soon enough," she thought, or was she the one?

-//-

Life continued unchanged for a while. Gérard participated in periodic meetings, becoming increasingly involved in decisions regarding areas of the world United States representatives shared with United Nations actions. Now rarely going back to Florida, he was happy that he had arranged for the property to be run by a couple of Ecuadorian emigrants staying in the gate pavilion. His children visited every time they had a break; the grandchildren enjoying as much as their parents the family summer house. Gérard would accompany them for family holidays, continuing the family traditions started by his parents, and when he could not come, he remained periodically informed by Patrick or Marina about the condition of the estate.

On a few occasions, Gérard ran into Milu during some joint sections of the committees, even exchanging impressions or having casual lunches at the cafeteria. When summer time came and the sessions went on a temporary leave, Gérard could, one more time, spend an extended stretch of time in Florida during the children's summer vacation.

The grandfather, Pa Gérard, along with the parents and grandchildren, had a formidable time together going to the magnificent beaches, taking boat rides on the sound at sunset and admiring the fireworks on the 4th of July.

They went scuba diving, board surfing, or just lay on the beach or by the pool with a book. They grilled meals on the outdoor kitchen or roasted marshmallows on the beach, and they often feasted on the delicious Ecuadorian meals Juanita prepared.

They shared again these blessed summer times, when children filled their souls with lasting and enchanted moments, carefree and devoid of any concerns or stress, saving treasured images that would resurface when confidence was needed later in life. The peacefulness of these moments strengthened the belief and the trust in a future full of possibilities. They stored all these precious times deep inside their hearts, where they would tap into when they needed new energy and reassurance.

It was a pleasure to see Patrick and Bridgett, and their two boys, Eduard and Oliver, getting along so well with Marina's family. Their conversations were always animated because of their contrasting professional orientations, but they used the time together to learn a little more about each other. Patrick and Bridgett would keep the two artists abreast of the world political realities, while Marina and Gunter were glad to reassure them that there was "still beauty and talent in this world they were defending".

Marina's children always looked forward to spending vacation time with Patrick's boys. They followed their older cousins who were more advanced in swimming and boating, and constantly asked them questions. When the whole family dined at one of the local seafood restaurants or just walked along the marinas, they offered to other passersby quite a sight: their beautiful tan enhancing the young and older family members' beauty, with their magnetic emerald eyes.

During the last week in Florida, Gérard was going through some projects for the seasons to follow with his friend, the housekeeper Paolo, when he received a message about an emergency situation developing in Africa. He cut short the last few days of his vacation, and leaving his children and grandchildren until the end of their vacation, he reached the UN headquarters.

Things were deteriorating again rapidly in a temporarily displaced family camp in Darfur. Negotiations between the Sudan government and the rebels were getting tense, and a delegation of the UN was desirable for a positive outcome. There were also reports of malaria and dysentery ravaging the refugees. Since Gérard had already visited Hassa Hissa camp and was somewhat knowledgeable with that particular situation, he was, after a detailed briefing, shipped to the area without delay.

-//-

He had barely stepped out of the Jeep and exchanged summary greetings with the camp's scarce administration, when Gérard was surrounded by children and members of the camp of all ages. He was appalled by their condition, their thin bodies near starvation and wearing ragged clothes and no shoes, reminded him of the times when the country was in full blown civil war.

They all looked with hope to the UN delegation, and expressed more than ever their fear for their security.

Shortly after, Gérard and the small team accompanying him toured the camp and made an inventory of their immediate needs; not much had improved since his last visit and had obviously been left to fall apart. However, a tent with a medical team was already in place and the most acute patients were treated and once stabilized and hydrated, were shipped to a larger medical center close by. Gérard could not hide his surprise when Milu came out from the tent, and with a big smile, she reminded him that she was a trained nurse. Gérard let Milu give him a big hug, as if they were longtime friends.

A routine developed momentarily in the camp between the members of the UN team and the medical annex. With long, exhausting days in the unbearable heat and with basic food, sanitation, and limited privacy, the UN team was nevertheless provided with relatively privileged living conditions. Gérard discovered though, as from his previous missions, how appreciative the camp members were and followed him around everywhere.

Gérard had always admired their resilience, their courage, and appreciation of even very little improvements without any complaints. They were inventive and resourceful, using any material or supplies available, stirring the rescue team's great admiration. And they always offered their participation for all the projects started; small school classes were organized, buildings with showers and separate latrines appeared, supplied by well water that was powered by the newest, most efficient solar panels.

Some of the well-water was soon directed through simple ditches to vegetable gardens scattered throughout the camp and provided a much needed resource of fresh produce. Once the refugees had been treated for their ailments, the entire camp population was vaccinated, and malaria prevention medication was distributed.

Small groups also started attending classes about the prevention of sexually transmitted diseases and birth control education. Young mothers and expecting mothers had their health checked and were trained about baby food using supplies provided by the Red Cross and other humanitarian organizations. Efforts were made to obtain severely needed supplies of clean water and septic tanks, commodities rare even in the areas not affected by war.

Milu was familiar with the dreadful conditions she had lived in during her childhood, and she displayed admirable skills of readapting to the harsh environment and showed great kindness to her patients. Team members were reunited in the evening for a meal under makeshift tables protected by rudimentary awnings, which became their only distraction of the day. This gave the team also the occasion to exchange information, review their daily schedule, and connect.

Milu managed to sit next to Gérard every time she could, and in time, a friendship was established. Milu behaved in a much more professional and amicable manner, and Gérard started appreciating the devotion she had for her work.

Once the situation in Hassa Hissa camp had relatively stabilized, Gérard made a few short trips to Khartoum, the capital of Sudan.

It was a delicate task not of a lesser importance in order to facilitate the proper distribution of the material shipped under the UN and Red Cross, and to make sure it arrived at its designated locations. It was also intended to avoid the bribery of local officials as much as possible that could easily compromise the security of the supplies.

From there, Gérard visited other places of displaced families, scattered over a large area. He remembered that, until the referendum of 2011 when the south separated from the north part of the country, Sudan was the largest African and Arabic country. Still, both bore the vestiges of civil war, and the memory of genocide was still fresh in the minds of many tribal villagers in the south. In spite of this tragic recent past, north and south shared the same ancient origins in the Old Nubian language, the oldest recorded Nilo-Saharan language.

When in Khartoum, Gérard chose to stay at the Kanon Hotel, as did many of the other members of the UN committees. A vibrant metropolis of five million inhabitants, the city of Khartoum has an exceptional geographic advantage thanks to its location situated at the confluence of the White Nile coming from the south, and the Blue Nile joining from the west, which formed an aquatic letter Y centering in the city. Running through the town, the Nile River offers superb scenery of the three split areas of the town facing each other across the river.

Kanon Hotel was close to the airport and had air conditioning that was well appreciated in this climate where the temperature practically never dropped below 100 F. Although the plumbing was not always perfect, and both the water and power not always functioned, the staff was friendly and the rooms clean.

There was also a good European breakfast served and conference rooms were available. Other members of Hassa Hissa and other camps frequently reunited here for meetings so they could stay in touch about the situation in other parts of Sudan, and although the country now had separate North and South governments, they remained linked through common projects and interests.

The short stay in the northern capital was also a long-expected chance to exchange news with families and keep up with the latest events in the world. On occasions, Gérard joined his colleagues at the restaurant or at the bar lounge for more relaxed gatherings, exchanging impressions and appreciating the comfort of the civilized world.

Milu was part of these briefings, and after living most of the time in scrubs at the infirmary of the camp, she was happy to change into civilian clothes again. Here she felt like a woman again, eager to regain the attention of her male counterparts. If complimented, she would not hide her pleasure and say with a laugh, "I don't mind compliments, and if this is harassment, then harass me!"

Indeed, Milu was attractive, liked to create a more relaxed atmosphere by adopting a flirty attitude with her many friends, and soon she extended her ways of subtle teasing toward Gérard as well. They were all short of complaining after coming back from living difficult experiences, like children in a spring break, unwinding and happy to exchange innocent jokes.

-//-

I met again with Raphael; I went to the Krystal Pyramid of Light, which I also called the Pyramid of Knowledge.

"I am happy to be with you again, my child," he greeted me.

"This time I need clarification. Raphael, what do you mean by universe and universes?" I asked.

"I see, you're always looking for precision, always seeking explicit details," he chuckled.

"Well, it gets confusing, this mountain of information you try to make me absorb," I excused myself.

"Because it is so simple, Isabelle, think," he said and waited a little longer before gently leading me to look at the pyramid, and beyond its invisible walls made of bright light.

It was then when I realized we were moving! We were flying across universes, at times changing directions, or simply slowing down and floating in the middle of worlds totally unbeknownst to me.

"This is what you see, Isabelle, or very little of it. The universe, by your definition is the one you just left and contains the type of existence you knew during your terrestrial life. Some humans have learned that there are other universes, parallel or intertwined, that are accessible to them only in their imagination. And now you are able to conceive them as we have just traversed some of them."

I nodded in agreement, and he continued, "The eternal reality, though, is that there is only one Universe, the way there is only one Reality. This Universe, spiritual and physical one, includes all that you call universes and dimensions, and it is all that is Creation. This

Universe contains every level of evolution of the soul, with some of its beings able to transcend and freely reach different levels of it, while others, have some limitations to overcome."

Indeed, all became clear to me. "So, it is as simple as that," I almost laughed.

"Do not worry much, Isabelle, it is the same with everyone that first comes here. And it is normal, they enclosed themselves creating their own limits, and 'walled' in their single universe."

"My Universe, our Universe, is only one, yours and all the other universes or dimensions of creation. This is the **first mystery**."

Raphael allowed me to ponder at leisure what I just heard, so I enjoyed the clarity of this simple explanation for a while. Then, sensing that I was ready for more, he continued, "The truth is that no one dies and nothing is ever lost. This is the **second mystery**.

Every invention, every piece of art ever created, even every thought or great idea, they all are stored forever in the Universe. Once an image is sent into the Universe, it also becomes energy. So, every person's thoughts, creativity, emotions, all that defines that person, is ever lasting; it is why one never really dies."

"You mean, it is like all the connections contained in somebody's brain are stored like in a super-sophisticated microchip and stowed in the Universe?" I asked.

"I see the researcher in you coming back!" he chuckled. The smile on his face did not fade when he added, "Considering that one would insert that microchip of yours into a robot, it would contain some information and memory, but that artificial creature or even this *artificial intelligence, would not be able to feel, create, have empathy or fall in love.*

"The mind holds the particular experience of that individual, its personality, sense of humor, wisdom, and discernment, experiences, attraction and displeasure. It is the expression of that individual that can make a joke, even get angry, or be self-deprecating. It lacks what it makes you that unique and very special being. It is why the soul is a conscious mind, immaterial but a powerful energy, a part of the creation. It is why, Beethoven, or Michelangelo, a parent, or yourself, never dies."

After a while, contemplating this truth that spoke of the eternal soul, our destiny seemed so much more uplifting, and this truth came to me as though I had known it all along.

I heard Raphael continue, "Before going any further, it is important to mention that what we think, and the words we form, are very important because they are part of our conscious mind and charged with their own energy. They make one vibrate at the level and quality of those words, thoughts, and actions, which will resonate with similar energies present in the universe.

"This way, you will attract and surround yourself with events, persons, and situations at the same level of that particular energy. It is what some call it the "law of attraction", Karma, or simply, that you harvest what you sow. Your life is the product of your thoughts. The result is that you make your life in a given existence based on your own choices and decisions. It is as simple as that."

*After a pause, Raphael continued, "You were and still are so interested in healing, so here is the **third mystery** that can help you: all the knowledge, all the means are already there, one only needs to tap into the* infinite energy of the universe. This energy, generated by sub-atomical particles, something humans call quantum energy and activated by the law of entanglement, but infinitely more powerful and ever-present, can restore, regenerate, change shape and color, rejuvenate and purify at your will.

"In one word, it can bring back someone's health or image to its ideal and divine condition. All organs, functions, cells, and minute particles can be rearranged, and re-energized once one learns how to attract and trust this divine, universal, and everlasting energy. And this can be done instantaneously across galaxies and regardless of their universal definition.

"The same goes for knowledge; the answers are all there. On Earth, many already solved this third mystery; they understood the truth that knowledge and its energy are omnipresent and infinite, and have tried to use it and spread this truth on Earth. Nicolas Tesla, Leonardo Da Vinci, Albert Einstein and others, brought to humanity ideas that could advance progress and make life on Earth much easier and more pleasant.

"Tesla spent his entire life trying to offer everyone access to free, clean, and unlimited energy, but like many others too much ahead of his time, he was rejected.

"And because the essence of what makes one to be self—the thoughts, feelings, creativity, actions, desires, and talents—this essence remains present eternally in the form of energy. This energy is and belongs to the whole universe. This is what some religions describe as the immortal soul, and some beliefs claim that one never dies, the connections resting with the ones left behind - love being the feeling connecting us all, across physical and ethereal existence.

*"The truth of the **fourth mystery** we will share for now, comes from what we described as the soul; the energy containing everything that defines a being, its conscious mind. And you, as a scientist, considered at one time that you could contain in a capsule the computerized brain's complete records, that could travel anywhere in the universe, defying space and time, since it was freed from its biological limitations.*

"Why not understand, that likewise, the soul is eternal, can travel everywhere across space, time, universes or dimensions. This is how some describe, the soul, the vessel across dimensions, making one cross all "universes", transcending any biological form of existence, while love is its universal language.

*"The **fifth mystery** is that there are beings originating from other corners of the universe, or from other "universes", that evolved to the level that they can traverse from one material appearance to another. And some entities can transcend from a material manifestation to pure energy, pure spirit, because they belong to the same Universe that comprises all."*

Raphael gave me a little more time to absorb this idea of wholeness, of inclusion of the infinite aspects of reality, all contained in the same Universe. Then, he continued, "While most people of the Earth cannot see them, many become aware of their presence. These light spirits, these divine entities are everywhere, and they are here to help elevate and make your lives better.

"Know that they can do this easily; humans have only to appeal to them, to freely express their desire to invite them in their lives, and exercise at any time, their freewill. God gave humankind this incommensurable spiritual gift, this immense power to call upon their help and guidance, and end the struggle during the time one devotes on Earth.

"Time after time, messengers have been sent; they came to bring help and understanding, but most of them have not been recognized. Humans failed to distinguish friend from foe, God's sons from the false prophets."

Lowering my head, I whispered, *"And instead we rejected them, humiliated them, and even crucified them. One can see every day and in many places adoring crowds celebrate one charming antichrist after another. We are incapable of distinguishing the good from the bad, and we wonder why we continue to make ourselves unhappy."*

After a long pause, Raphael ended our encounter with an encouraging promise. *"When one prays, does anything for the wellbeing of mankind, or sends into the Universe his wishes of love and goodwill to all, a vast amount of divine energy is released and surrounds the Earth. Bringing all together, the universal consciousness creates this energy that heals and restores, bringing peace and prosperity. Any act of love and forgiveness reverses the hurt and misery, replacing it with happiness. This can lead men closer to the original design; Earth becoming Eden again."*

-//-

The "Lost Boys of Sudan" were another painful phenomenon resulting from the civil war. Children suddenly became orphans when villages were attacked and their parents captured or killed, as they were tending the cattle far from the village and had time to hide in the dense African brush.

Malnourished, at the mercy of wild animals or other attackers, facing starvation, dehydration and diseases, they slowly organized into small, then larger groups, led by the oldest teens to find survival from village to village. Many died or were captured by soldiers, some were taken by the rebels and brain washed, forced to become child soldiers.

These children started a long journey to Ethiopia and Kenya, two of Sudan's bordering countries. In the beginning, they hid in the bushes during the day and traveled at night, owning only the clothes on their backs. Barefoot and famished, they ranged between five and 10 years old.

Eventually the groups expanded, becoming an exodus of biblical proportions and extending their journey over years and thousands of miles on foot. Amongst the ones lucky to survive, some arrived at refugee camps and were saved by the United Nations High Commission of Refugees, others by the International Rescue Committee (IRC), World Relief, Catholic charities, or other organizations.

UNICEF intervened even when they were accepted in refugee camps, making sure that the rescued children received proper nutrition and schooling. A smaller but more fortunate number of them were adopted by families in Canada and the USA. However, a large group of children, even after finding refuge in Ethiopia, were later chased out at gunpoint over the Gilo River, forced to restart their exodus, this time finding refuge in Kakuma Camp in Kenya.

Some of them stayed there for over 10 years before feeling safe enough to go back to their country. And there were also the older boys who were educated in the US, who came back to "pay ahead" and help improve the living conditions in their own villages.

Akim Mogo, Koor Ajik and Taban Nhial were now 18, 19 and 21 years of age, respectively, after a group of rebels captured them 12 years earlier, when they were making their way to Kenya to join the other orphaned children. Rugs barely covering their bodies, digging for roots as the only means of survival, they were frightened and lost, not having slept in a bed or having a roof over their head for almost a year. They did not see the rebels approaching, closing in on the village and getting ready to attack.

At first, the rebels told them that they were fighting along with the Liberation Front against the oppressive northern troupes. They gave them food and some basic clothing and the children thought they were saved and showed them gratitude. Soon after, though, it appeared that they were one of the rogue bands, pillaging the villages, killing men and raping girls and women, while declaring the Islamic faith as the only one tolerated.

Akim, Koor and Taban were handed over to the group of other captive children, converted to Islam, and trained to become children soldiers. The brain washing process was aggressive and brutal; slowly the children lost any sense of kinship or cultural traditions, while showing no pity became considered bravery. They were sometimes when children under 10 years of age were included in genocide. When the war ended and the insurgent groups dismantled, scattered rebels continued acting as gangs of savages, going into hiding at first, then intensifying their attacks and becoming increasingly ruthless.

The minds of children fighters, now reaching young adult age, were imprinted with such a cruel and violent way of living it had become for them the only known life possible. Left on their own, some relied on surviving by attacking and robbing isolated homes at the edge of villages, like the older rebels. They attacked refugees who left the camps for water or firewood, biting and raping frequently. But for the rogue bandits, the most prized charges were against the humanitarian convoys bringing supplies to remote areas.

The three young men, like hungry lions, were tracking a line of five UN trucks, loaded with what seemed to be precious goods coming toward Hassa Hissa camp. They kept hidden, and were planning an assault as they had done successfully other times, although they were resigned to get close to a camp only when in dire need. They would strike once the trucks entered the camp, and when men, women and children gathered around the trucks and the guards were less alert. So, they did, taking advantage of the surprise effect; they entered the open gates, and created even more chaos in the middle of the general noise, shooting up in the air.

They were bold and ready to kill one or two of the truck drivers if any were still in the cabin, then dash through the crowd out of the camp stealing two of the loaded trucks before the guards could get hold of them.

The refugees froze instantly, traumatized by bad memories and fearing again those atrocious moments, until a few coming out of their stupor, started reacting. Many prevented the guards from seeing what was happening, assess the attackers' intentions and intervene. Akim, Koor and Taban pushed their way to the closest trucks. Unfortunately, the drivers were still inside the cabins, and they would have to kill them or render them powerless.

Akim and Koor went for the first cabin, while Taban, the oldest and the toughest of the three, opened the door of the second truck stopped only a few feet from the last in line, the cabins of the two tracks almost facing each other. They harshly pulled out the drivers, hitting them on their heads with the butts of their AK-45 rifles, and dropping them on the ground, against some of the onlookers, who fell as well. Then, they jumped inside the cabin and restarted the engines.

However, Taban would not take any risks, and with a close shot to the head, splashed the driver's brains around. This time, the horrified refugees were fleeing, creating a terrible stampede, some taking protection behind any object in their way, creating even more confusion and blocking the passage of the guards.

Taban was the first to put the truck in gear, and after backing up a few yards, moved forward charging through the crowd, while shooting widely and opening a way out through the crowd. Akim and Koor followed him, their advance slowing as the wounded or dead increased blocking the way, for the refugees were unarmed and the guards dared not shoot for fear of hurting the civilians in the crossfire.

Gérard was back in the camp from Khartoum, as were all the other UN members, and they were alerted from the first moments of the skirmish. Gérard came out from his tent where they were holding a meeting, and quickly assessed the situation. His instinct was right, he shouted at the top of his lungs to let the robbers go, they were after the provisions not the women.

Once they were gone, the camp would be at least momentarily, safe until military reinforcements arrived. Soon after the two trucks made their way out of the camp and the medical teams started to assess and treat the wounded, Gérard went back inside the tent and used a satellite phone to reach the command center of the UN peacekeeping forces. They usually were available in the regions where the convoys were dispatched, and Gérard obtained the connection with the closest one.

They would rush and be at the camp in a few hours, meanwhile they would look out for the bandits disguised behind two regular UN trucks.

Back at the campgrounds, Gérard was informed that, besides the truck driver killed, there were two other victims; a young mother and her toddler. There were five or six wounded; two with blows to the head and one to the abdomen, but one of them had a serious injury to the legs, when a truck ran over him. Secretly, Gérard thought that it could have been worse and even more victims, and called again the troupe of peacekeepers, notifying them that they would need medical transport to a trauma center along with military protection to remain in place from now on.

Gérard and his team, the medical personnel and the camp workers, spent the remainder of the day reorganizing life inside the campsite. Reinforcements were placed at the gates until the armed forces of the Green Berets arrived. They reassured the refugees, attended the wounded and isolated the dead getting them ready for transfer outside the camp.

Once the Blue Berets arrived and met with the camp personnel in charge, they assessed the damage and waited for orders for further intervention. Other camps and settlements were on alert, even though the attackers seemed to have vanished; nevertheless, they had the means to attack again.

Towards the evening, when everyone was exhausted and nervously drained, Gérard had a conference call with UN and peacekeeping headquarters.

The orders were for the military to take over the camp and defend it for an undetermined period of time. The medical team accompanying the wounded was long gone and on the way to the capital. The camp doctor,

Milu, and the driver, followed by a UN truck, left with a few soldiers dispatched for their protection just in case of another attack, although the thieves seemed to be long gone by now, gaining distance from the busy roads. Only a few nurses and aids remained at camp infirmary providing the usual basic care to the refugees.

After emptying the UN trucks from their supplies, Gérard and his team received orders to return to Khartoum and wait for new instructions there. When Gérard tried to protest leaving the camp, he was told that the camp would be safer under the peacekeepers' military protection, and that anyone else would create even more liability; besides, their quarters were needed to lodge the military troupes.

At the crack of the dawn, the other two remaining trucks emptied, were loaded with the UN team members and a few summary records stashed in plastic containers, some food supplies and cases of bottled water. They would be on the road for the next two days, shaken by the insecurity of the last events still possible so many years after the peace agreement. Looking back, some were expressing their gratitude, glad to still be alive when they had such little protection during their stay in Hassa Hissa. At least for a while now, the refugees were protected, and the injured ones were almost a day ahead of them.

Back in Kanon Hotel in Khartoum, they were almost haggard with fatigue from the two and a half days on the dirt roads, finding a little sleep when giving some rest to the drivers, and without being able to shave or shower. As soon as they arrived, they all darted to their rooms to take a long shower, making the hotel hot water supply almost run out. Then they gathered in the lobby lounge, waiting to go together to the restaurant for a warm meal.

There, they were met by members of the medical team, who, after having promptly handed their patients to the University Medical Center, were waiting for their new assignments. They'd had the time to clean up and rest for over a day now, and learning that the Humanitarian Affairs team had arrived, they gathered at the lobby to celebrate their safe arrival.

Milu, almost recovered from the intense emotions and fatigue that followed the camp attack, was rested and at her best in a blue dress with red flowers, her hair done in long tight curls that fell down her back, and masterfully applied make up. They were all hugging, giving pecks on the cheeks and taps on the back, while cocktails were ordered. Without even realizing, Gérard had a straight up double whisky shoved in his hand, receiving and giving hugs around. Milu appeared before long close to him, and her embraces were a little longer and a little tighter than the others. Happy voices were raised when the maître d' announced that their table was ready, and finally their growling bellies received some food, slowing down the alcohol reaching their already stressed brains.

It was a joyous and friendly dinner, although some got a little carried away with too many glasses of wine "for hydration", but "what the heck, no one is driving tonight" was heard. Gérard, trying to keep a hold on his drinking, let himself enjoy the party, but since he was not used to alcohol his head was spinning a little. He thought that it might be the fatigue doing tricks on him. After the dinner was finally over and everyone was full and satisfied, the party moved to the bar lounge, and with everyone now mellow, they had their last nightcaps before hitting the pillows in real beds.

Gérard had a phone call from the administration enquiring of their safe return, which helped clear his head. He also had a good conversation with Patrick and reassured his family back in New York that he was well and safe, and coming back to the States shortly. It was fortunate that only Patrick was really aware of the dangers he had been through recently, learning this through his international affaires' channels. He promised to give only generic information to the other family members, as they had taken the habit of doing in the past; Patrick will keep it simple, like other routine phone calls when Gérard was far away.

Coming back to the lounge, Gérard realized that he had been gone for quite a while since everyone had already left; almost everyone, for Milu was still there, languorously relaxing in a club chair. When Gérard saw her, he started excusing himself, stating that it has been a very long day, in fact, a long week, and he was glad to follow the example of the others and return to his room.

Milu answered that she understood, and added how lonely she was feeling, and how scared. Hearing this, and looking at Milu and how soft her eyes had become under a little mist of sadness, he sat next to her and took her hand to reassure her that now all would be all right and she was out of danger.

She leaned close to him and gently put her head against his chest, and Gérard wrapped his arms around her to console her like a child. All this felt so sweet, and feelings came to him that he almost forgotten, making him realize how much he craved some tenderness, and how lonely he has been for so long. She raised her head toward him, and gave him a tender kiss on the cheek, then, their lips found their way together and they started kissing passionately, almost in desperation.

Gérard was surrendering to his emotions brought about by the fatigue of the last days, and Milu to a ravaging passion that was growing inside her for this attractive man. For the first time in her life she really felt that she could drop her guard with the only man that made her feel weak, letting go of her control, and finally abandoning herself to fully enjoy her emotions.

Gérard would have had a hard time recollecting how he was then gently guided toward the elevator and arrived in Milu's room. He was sure that they shared a passionate night making love and slept until the late hours of the following day. They had room service, and Gérard becoming more aware of reality, was in great need of checking on the other members of his team and headquarters for new orders. Above all, he absolutely needed to see where he was heading to with this new relationship.

Finally in his room, after Milu slumbered in a deep sleep, he found two messages: one making recommendations for breakfast choices, the other just arrived, from the central office. Calling back at once, he learned that arrangements were made for him to join the team in Monrovia, Liberia, for the next morning. The other members of his team would be reassigned later, and, lucky them, after getting some R & R in a resort in Haifa, Israel.

-//-

Over a long shower, Gérard became lost in thought about the events of the last days. So much had happened! The request to go without delay to Liberia and his presence needed at the American Embassy in Monrovia, not at one of the UN committees, made him think that the matter was rather of a diplomatic nature. No email, faxed documents, nor telephone details were offered, and that seemed to be a sensible situation developing, and that he might be the suitable person to handle it. Still, he searched in his mind for a possible answer but he could not find one. Well, he would have to wait and see when he arrived there.

Meanwhile, he was facing a more serious reality, his involvement with Milu. It had all happened too fast, and he'd felt he let himself go with the temptation of the moment. He did not like to take any relations lightly, not even when he was young and foolish, as he had long since learned his lesson with Alice!

Milu was a lovely lady, it was a given, as was the fact that she knew how to seduce a man and how to bring him to heights of ecstasy. Then, why did he feel so empty and sad? The two of them were free and lonely, and they had just gone through life threatening events. They had found consolation in each other's arms and there was nothing wrong with that. Then, where was this feeling of desperation coming from? Because this is what ravaged him deep inside, making him feel lonelier and more desolate than ever.

In the middle of this inner tempest, Gérard was invaded by this overwhelming craving to touch and to hold this other person, gone forever with the devastating truth that he never would again. Brought to his knees, sobbing desperately for a long time, he let the water run over him. He missed Isabelle so! And he realized that no one could ever fill the place she had left in his heart.

-//-

Gérard spent the few hours of the evening scheduling his early flight in the morning and writing to Milu. He felt that it was fortunate he had been called to another location to gently put some distance and time between the two of them. He searched for a while to find the right words, explaining he admired her as a woman, but it would be in their best interests to keep their relations professional, that they were grown people and had lost their control in stressful circumstances, etc., etc.

Early the next morning Gérard took a taxicab to the airport, and during his flight to Monrovia, he refreshed on his new destination demographics. He already knew that Liberia was the first republic in Africa, situated on the west coast of the continent and about the size of Tennessee. It was bordered by Sierra Leone, Guinea and Cote d'Ivoire. Monrovia was the capital and had a population of over a million, was established in 1822 and named after the American president, James Monroe, who encouraged the freed black slaves to go back to Africa and gain emancipation under the American Colonization Society.

Eventually the new country developed rubber plantations, cargo shipping along the African coast, and a mining industry. The two civil wars between 1990 and 2003, put a halt on the economy, with many homeless children on the streets of the capital, but also increasing armed robbery and rape, with drug dealers and pickpockets on the rise. Monrovia was once a place known for its friendly people, beaches and beautiful resorts, but was now considered unsafe.

The UN banned the export of diamonds in 2001 in order to stop the diamonds-for-weapons traffic during the civil war and the "blood diamonds" that led to child slavery. However, the diamond trade resumed in 2007, supposedly under the supervision of an international program, preventing the rough diamond trade from financing any further armed conflict.

To make the situation even grimmer, life expectancy averaged 39 years for males and 42 for females, and Liberia went through the worst epidemic of EBOLA Viral Hemorrhagic fever that started in 2010 and killed over four thousand people. Although the World Health Organization declared that Liberia had the disease under control in September 2015, caution was recommended and the Doctors Without Borders remained in place.

When Gérard finally made it to Monrovia, then presented to the American Embassy for his mysterious meeting, he was quickly received by a pleasant secretary, who, after offering some iced tea, informed him that a room was reserved for him at Mamba Point Hotel, a safe nearby hotel, and then went to inform the staff about his arrival.

Soon after, the meeting room door opened, and one of his former colleges during a diplomatic mission in Geneva, Malcolm Thomas, rushed in to give Gérard a strong handshake with a big tap on the back. Gérard noticed at the first glance that Malcolm was tired and that intense stress marked his expression. They exchanged the usual initial greetings, then, they went swiftly to the core of their meeting.

"Gérard, my son Reginald, Regis, is in trouble. He is a very good person, but I think he got in a situation he did not anticipate. He joined a Greenpeace organization a few years ago, and with finances coming from the Linda and Bill Gates Foundation, he organized a team going around isolated areas in Africa digging wells to be further activated with a solar panel system.

"This practice is not uncommon and has been made available in many areas of the Third World. The equipment to dig in dry and mountainous terrain is expensive and it is difficult to reach those areas, but once in place, the population is assured to have for a while clean and constant water supply.

"Now, in the middle of October, in Liberia, the rainy season will end soon and the drought will begin again, depleting the limited water reserves. In anticipation, Regis moved into a region in the center of the country with the equipment to dig as soon as the rain stops, and to have at least a couple of wells ready for the dry season. He was assured that the UNMIL, United Nation Mission in Liberia, would make that region safe, but in the Bong Range close to Bong Town, are gold and diamond mines, controlled by ruthless owners.

"They seized this unexpected opportunity and requested having the wells dug for their mines, instead of the wells needed by poorer and desolated population. Jamil Bulhami has a stronghold in the area and there are rumors of him exploiting children for his diamond mines. He seems to be protected by corrupt government employees, who are powerless to fight his huge company, and he benefits from extended ramifications with all kind of worldwide cartels.

"Well, Jamil 'kidnapped' my son, and although he is not officially asking for a ransom, he made it clear that Regis will not be let go before he provides his mines with the wells and the solar system operating them.

"As you can imagine, Regis refuses adamantly, making the whole situation very tense and very dangerous; these monsters try to put to their private use the foreign humanitarian aid intended to help the population, and, in the same way they've acted through the civil war atrocities, they think that nothing can stop them."

Gérard absorbed the brief description, and wondered what was expected from him.

Malcolm continued his explanation with increased passion, "As you can imagine, armed troupes cannot be sent, at least as long as we could endanger Regis' life, since there is still no formal demand for a ransom, and the equipment will be forcefully taken and lost anyways. The American government will never offer money in exchange of a prisoner or any one detained against his own will."

Letting this sink in, he continued, "We will need a person in place, and I cannot be this person even though I am ready to leave on the spot, but I have been warned against it because my ties with the person detained, giving Jamil an even stronger negotiation power having the father and the son in his custody."

Finally, the words were dropped, "We need you, Gérard. I need you to go and use all your talents of the great negotiator you are and get Jamil to let my son go. I need you to save my son, I beg you Gérard!" Malcolm pleaded with a look of desperation on his face.

Gérard stayed silent for a while, then, as from nowhere, a sensation of peace and clarity came over him, and his decision was made. He was filled with the desire to help his friend, of making a difference in this world as Regis had tried to do so courageously. He felt strongly to at least try to stop the bad with something good, something positive, like Regis and the people dedicating their lives, their energy, and their resources to think of someone else's good.

His answer was rewarded with the image of relief and gratitude he read on his friend's face, and at once they got busy studying the plan of their intervention. There would be very limited back up once they left the base in Gbamga, where he would be flown by helicopter, by far the best and fastest means of traveling reserved to the UN personnel.

There, a four-wheel-drive jeep would take him through the ragged terrain and flooded roads to meet Jamil at his main base close to Bong mine. They studied the satellite map and GPS tracks, the only way they would stay in touch. Limited supplies, a driver, and two armed marines would accompany him from Gbamga to Bong Town, then he would be on his own besides the driver as no armed individuals were allowed near Jamil's place.

The last hours of the afternoon were spent preparing for the trip. Gérard would leave at dawn, carried by a helicopter as they were frequently used to transport diplomatic members to and from the airport, this time going straight from the embassy's grounds to Gbamga. Gérard would carry his diplomatic passport for whatever use that might be in those lands far from civilization. He requested as much information as he could gather about Jamil and his whereabouts, his family, hobbies, his connections, and his weaknesses. After a short restful night at Mamba Point Hotel, he received the heartfelt wishes from his friend Malcolm Thomas, and stepped into a Sikorsky HH-60 Pave Hawk, and in no time, they were in the air.

As soon as they left the coast, there was a heavy downpour and the warm, humid air made it hard to distinguish the landmarks in the curtains of rain and fog. It was fortunate that they were flying a US Force version of the Pave Hawk, a modified version of the army model with high capabilities for all weather conditions, and perfectly adapted for rescues, search, and retrieval of special forces or for humanitarian missions.

They were equipped with night detection and advanced communication operations, and although the helicopter was of a medium sized lift, its four-blade main and tail rotors could accommodate two pilots, a flight engineer, and a spacious cabin for eight. If needed, it could be modified into a special room for a gunman, a medical litter and medical personnel. During the flight, Gérard pondered over this delicate and dangerous situation. He learned that Jamil had lost several of his sons in reckless associations; two in military guerilla attacks, and another one involved in drug dealing, had overdosed and died. There was only one son left, the youngest, that Jamil tried to keep close and was grooming to succeed him in his mine exploitation.

It was said that Kumar wanted to get away from his father and had frequent arguments with him. It was not clear what his position was in all this, but somehow, Gérard kept this detail in mind. The flight lasted less than two hours, Gérard using the isolation provided by the muffled rotors sound and the grey mist outside, mulling over the conditions to be expected at their destination.

There was a brief stop at a military base used by UN forces near Gbamga where Gérard met his companions and transferred into a jeep, with the helicopter pilots' wishes for a safe and prompt return.

They arranged for a tentative meeting at the same place the day after, considering that all would go as planned. Here started a long and rocky trip on muddy roads, and soon the jeep was climbing on the hillside, lost in the tropical forest. They had five hours before the nightfall, and another 80 kilometers to cover.

There were four of them all together: in addition to Gérard were two marines and the driver. They planned to go to Bong Town and the mining site nearby early that evening. The marines were heavily armed and superbly trained, but they would have to take cover in the jungle away from the mine. From there, the only ammunition they would carry past Bong would be the driver's machete just in case they need to cut their way through the bushes, and a hunting rifle they expected to be taken away once arrived at Jamil's camp.

They left the hills and the tropical forest as they approached Bong area; the day remained dark with heavy, low clouds, and relying on the GPS maps, they decided to go straight through the clearances shown by the satellite map and avoid the town all together. They could gain some time if the terrain was not too soggy from the rain, for there was no road, just trails visible during the dry season.

Everyone was watching the road tensely, holding tight while the driver tried to avoid the countless holes and puddles of water. They stopped only one time, briefly, to stretch their legs and have a snack, just a few kilometers from the mine site. They reviewed the strategic points of their plan, and when in view of the camp, they lay low and the marines disappeared into a patch of tropical forest, leaving Gérard and the driver on their own.

-//-

The Bulhami settlement sat on a small, man-made clearance at the foot of a hill facing the diamond mine, the back of it not far from a thick forest. Although the rain fell hard at times, the production at the mine was in full throttle with the anticipated dry season, when the limited water supply would considerably slow down the washing and sorting part of the mining process. Jamil Bulhami, a known "control freak", was busy over his head pressuring the guards and foremen at the mine. There was a considerable number of young children working here, some under 10 years old, against all interdictions of international and Liberian organizations.

Jamil was also sleep deprived after keeping an open eye on his prisoner, but he was excited with anticipation at the imminent arrival of an American representative who would help take care of the problem at hand. He knew that Greenpeace organizations, although supported by the UN and other humanitarian groups, did not have military forces to defend them in dangerous locations. The members of the various humanitarian programs, notoriously pacific and idealistic individuals, did not carry guns and did not start a project until the main committees gave them the green light.

Regis had entered this isolated area, stopping in a cluster of villages a few miles apart from each other, where the geo ground satellite images had shown a good source of underground aquifers, a solid guarantee for successful well diggings. Regis, invited for a hospitality dinner by the mine owner in the region, went unarmed and without apprehension, with the intent to calm any potential tension created by their presence in the region and to reassure him he would not interfere with local businesses.

However, he went alone, instructing other members of his team, three men operating the drilling machinery and a woman taking care of the camp electronics, using satellite connections for their phone and internet, that they should inform their main office only if he did not return after 24 hours.

It had now been 72 hours since Regis went to Bulhami camp, and Doris had already contacted not only the Greenpeace main office, but also the American Embassy, who swiftly put in place a plan to bring all of them back to Monrovia, then home if a repatriation to the US was needed. Doris was informed that a team of UN forces working in agreement with the Security Committee was already on the way to the camp.

The UN forces would protect them and assist on evaluating the situation regarding Regis Thomas as well. But the situation had taken a different turn with Regis detention, now the American Embassy added Gérard Forrest into play, with the intention of increasing the chances of peacefully resolving the problem.

Regis was sitting in a secluded area of the compound in a wing connected to the main building. His overheated, dark room had the door and the only window shutters locked from the outside. An iron bed and a simple mattress was covered only with a few sheets because of the intense heat. There was a water jug and a small basin on a table, and a wooden door led to a "toilet" accommodation, a simple cemented area with a hole in the center. The "guest" kept the door closed at all times to avoid the stench.

That morning, and the previous one, Regis was visited by Kumar, after Bulhami left for the mine and the servant/guard brought in some old rice from the evening meal. The two young men had acknowledged each other during the first evening Regis came to visit, and exchanged a casual dialogue. Kumar, however, was burning with the desire to find someone from the outside world and open up to him. He almost disregarded any trouble he was getting into and confided to Regis that he did not approve of his father's dealings and ways of running his business. He told him that he wanted to get away and have a different life of his own choosing.

Kumar wanted to learn more about the free world, truly democratic countries and find his own path in life. This morning, Kumar came again and told Regis that his mother, a young and naive Polish girl, had met his father in Europe and was dazzled by his manners and display of generosity and wealth as a gold and diamond mine owner. They stared dating, Jamil promising her a fairytale life, and she fell for it. She ignored the fact that Jamil, once he returned to Liberia, repudiated his two other wives. As expected, this attracted the hate of his older sons, but Jamil continued to command them as usual.

Soon after, Sonja gave Jamil a son, Kumar, and in her ignorance, continued to enjoy a lavish life, which was to last only briefly. Soon enough, Sonja realized that she was isolated and under the complete control of her husband, who did not hide his drinking habits any longer, was regularly spending the nights with women of bad reputation, and often showed his quick temper. She was also concerned, and rightfully so, about contracting one of the sexually transmitted diseases ravaging the continent.

When she invoked a visit to her country to see her family, Jamil refused harshly. Shortly after, Sonja planned to escape and take her son with her. She became more subdued and stayed for a while in Monrovia at their beautiful home in town. However, she was under constant surveillance by the house guards who reported to Jamil every movement and contact she had. Kumar was five by then and very attached to his mother, listening to the stories about her far away country, the snow and Christmas trees, and that she would take him there one day, and they would visit the beautiful streets, monuments, and churches.

In the late 90s when life became more dangerous in the capital, Jamil asked Sonja to come back to Bong Town for her safety. Sonja panicked and decided that now was the time for her to escape with her son, and return to her country. When she asked her chauffeur for a ride, then a stop at the airport, she was rapidly brought back to the villa. When Jamil came home, a strong argument ignited, and in his rage, Jamil beat, and then shot Sonja dead.

The little Kumar heard all that happened and he swore to avenge his mother and get away as far as possible from his father. Now, almost 20 years old, and feeling like a stranger in this place, he wanted more than ever to flee, and secretly decided to help, already admiring Regis' directions and aspirations in life.

-//-

Jamil Bulhami was finishing his dinner and was looking forward to sitting in his recliner with a glass of his best XO Napoleon Martell cognac, when his house guard informed him that, as expected, a car was advancing on the main alley. Jamil put on his most cordial face when he showed himself at the door to receive his two guests. Gérard offered excuses for being muddy and drenched as he stepped in.

The host invited Gérard into the living room, but showed the kitchen to the driver, Steven. Gérard made a sign to Steven that this was fine for now, and entered the main room alone where he was introduced to Kumar.

During the short time Jamil was giving orders for dinner to be served to his guests, Gérard had the time to quickly assess his surroundings and have a closer look at Kumar. He was surprised by the lighter shade of his skin and his almost blue eyes, and most impressed by his polished way of speaking English. He also noticed that his demeanor was friendlier, although he could sense reserve and sadness in his eyes, and he thought what a fine young man he seemed and how out of place he appeared.

Back in the lounge room, Jamil invited his guest through a large archway to the dining area where they sat at the table as food was brought in from the kitchen. To be polite, Gérard accepted some vegetables and rice, but he let his host know that he was a vegetarian and he would only have bottled water to drink. Gérard had taken for a long time the habit not to drink any alcohol when he was conducting business. He definitely did not trust that drinks would not be tampered with in this particular situation. Jamil appeared as an exaggerated host, pushing his congeniality a little too much, and this observation made Gérard remain on his guards even more.

With no further introduction, Gérard asked to see Regis Thomas, to which Bulhami answered that he would see him in due time. There was a short reply from Gérard, who looked his host straight in his eyes and answered that no further discussion would take place before he was sure Mr. Thomas was well.

"All right, all right," Jamil said, lacing his voice with honey, "I assure you he is doing great, but I want to know first if your representatives are willing to satisfy my demands."

"I assure you that my offer will plainly satisfy you, Mr. Bulhami," was all that Gérard offered, with a cold voice and a look showing no fear and complete determination.

Bulhami took a few seconds to consider his guest, but the two of them and in different ways, knew that if harm came to Gérard, retaliation would be fast and deadly, and thus, Bulhami would get nothing. Jamil also suspected that not too far from there must be some back up, for the American Embassy would not send one of their own without assuring protection. He might have taken a bigger bite than he could chew, after all. Leaving the room to ask a servant to get Mr. Thomas, gave him time to think that he needed to be careful and listen to what the US representative had to offer before making any rash decision.

When Regis entered the room and Gérard met him, there was a short exchange of questions as to his condition, and Gérard was reassured that Regis was in good health and no obvious harm had been done to him. Following this succinct but important assessment, Gérard felt a great deal of relief, although he tried to show little of it. Regis opened the discussions, giving a short summary of the situation, without letting Bulhami take over, and relived that he had an ally in the room, or maybe two, over his capturer.

"I was doing a humanitarian work for Greenpeace organization, offering to dig wells and then have them operating via solar panels with all material very generously provided by private American citizens, when I was captured. The valuable equipment, vital for the living conditions improvement of hundreds of underserved villagers, was about to be taken away for the use and to profit the private interests of a wealthy individual. "

Turning toward Bulhami, with clear accusatory intent, he added, "and I have been given the clear warning that if I refused to comply, I would be detained indefinitely, the material would be forcefully brought to the mine, without guarantee that human lives would be spared in the process. Once all trace of the camp and of ourselves disappeared, no one would know what really happened in this godforsaken corner of the world. In short, Mr. Bulhami planned to take our equipment and get rid of us one way or the other, his best interests being that no one ever be found."

Regis looked without intimidation into Bulhami's until his statement of events was finished. Bulhami, trying to distend the seriousness of the accusations, wore a patronizing smile as if all this were a child's imagination and not to be taken too seriously.

"I invited Mr. Thomas and I treated him as my guest! I only made the mistake to show him too much interest in the digging material. It is true that it is new for these remote areas and would tremendously help with our mining productivity."

"You mean that Mr. Thomas can leave your home anytime he wishes, even at this instant?" Gérard interrupted at once.

"Well, I tried to convince Mr. Thomas to bring some of the material here at the mine for me to try, and then decide if it is worth to actually..."

"And if he refuses, since this is not the scope of his presence in this country?" Gérard pressed on.

"As any business man, I tried to convince him that this is another way to help my country. I employ hundreds of people and help them and their families that otherwise would starve to death." Then gradually losing his temper, he blared out, "And I do not tolerate people telling me what I can and I cannot do!"

There was a moment when all could have gone to hell and everyone could show its immovable position.

Here is when Gérard responded with a calm voice that caught everyone's attention, "Of course, Mr. Bulhami, we understand your interests and your determination. We all understand and by this I mean the United States Foreign Service of the American Embassy, The United Nations Committee for African Development of Agriculture and Economy, that assists humanitarian organizations such as Greenpeace interventions, the UN Security Committee, and myself, as representative of all these entities."

Reading a faint panic in Bulhami's eyes at this long list of authorities, particularly the mention of The Security Committee, Gérard did not give his opponent any chance to recover. "Because we are informed that you are a strong negotiator and because you like to see a good conclusion to a transaction, in the name of all the offices I represent, I make you this offer; but I have to emphasize that this is the only offer I am going to present to you."

As his voice became stronger and more decisive, he spoke, "There is no money involved once or ever, and the United States never bends under any kind of pressure to pay off any ransom or extortion, as it is well known that the US stands behind the safety of each and every one of its citizens.

"In addition, there is no digging material that will be handed over, as this belongs to the charities that offered this equipment for a very specific mission. However, there are several universities in the US that are willing to grant a full scholarship to your son for the duration of studies required to obtain a diploma in Business and Administration or Agricultural Development.

"Your country has based its education model on American universities and we would like to facilitate further exchange between our countries. After the completion of his degrees and his return to Liberia, your son could help the recovery of the economy in many directions and bring the necessary knowhow to the benefit not only to himself, but also his fellow countrymen. The only thing you have to do is to allow Mr. Thomas to get in the car with me and my driver, and leave. No one will be hurt, everybody gains, particularly you, since your son can benefit from the best education and insure a future for his entire life."

Bulhami, a shrewd businessman, considered the facts, and rapidly weighed the points presented to him; he realized that if harm was done to the visitors, quick retaliation was to be expected, and he had to let them go, at least for now. He was surprised though by the offer, and suddenly he realized that if Kumar became somebody important in the government, and enough strings he could pull to make sure of that, he might even become a minister of one of the state departments one day, and from there, he could obtain every favor he wanted. His enterprises could thrive and the sky would be the limit. As greed started taking hold of him, in an impulse, the way he usually did business, Jamil turned toward Gérard and said extending his arm to shake hands, "We have a deal! "

Gérard did not want to show his joy, but he reacted as if pleased by Bulhami's agreement.

Bulhami then continued, "It is too late into the night now, you will have to wait for the morning as the roads are not visible in this rain."

They did not have any choice but to accept the offer, however, they refused the drinks Jamil poured while he was talking. Gérard and Regis rightly pretended that they were already too tired to drink. Their host raised toward them his glass of cognac and, having finally the chance to enjoy it, gulped it down in one go.

Regis returned to his room, which this time was not locked, but had a hard time falling asleep, excited by the recent events. He was very impressed from the start by Gérard's offer. "What a great idea; I am so happy for Kumar and for bringing all things to a positive outcome."

In its his turn, Kumar was still shocked by this unexpected opportunity; the dream for his future plans in life had been answered. Nevertheless, knowing Jamil, he decided to keep a close lookout from now on and prepared for a watch during the night.

Before settling temporarily for the night in the same room with Steven, Gérard thought with a little grin in his face, "There is no university in America offering a scholarship to Kumar as far as I know, but I will personally pay for his education if needed."

-//-

"Psst, Regis..." with a gentle but firm shake of Regis' shoulder, Kumar was trying to wake up his new friend.

"What is it?" Regis rapidly answered, sitting up, all alert.

"We need to wake up your friends and leave right now, I don't trust my father." Kumar explained that this might be their only chance before his father changed his mind and becomes irrational, as had happened in the past. Then he told Regis that after they left, his father felt once more like drinking, and not having anyone else, he called his two goons and got completely wasted, and all of them had fallen into a deep torpor. "The only guard left is the old groundkeeper, but he is deaf as a rock, although he does not want to admit it as he's scared he'll be kicked out and has no place to go. Since Jamil does not pay attention to his servants, the old man has managed to get away with it so far"

While Regis was pulling on his pants and stashed his few belongings quickly in his travel bag, Kumar woke up Gérard and Steve, and they were ready to go in no time. Quietly they made their way to the Jeep and with the lights off, they started advancing cautiously out of the property, the engine in idle.

Until the edge of the rain forest, it was difficult to make progress, and Kumar's knowledge of the landscape was of a major help, as they gained distance between the Bulhami settlement and the mine. Back on the road, they approached the place where they had left the two marines. On their way to meet them, Gérard had notified them of their return using his satellite phone, and the marines were already advancing in their direction.

The marines also informed him that a small detachment of peacekeepers was already at the Greenpeace camp to insure their security, and that they would stay there until the operation was completed, preventing any further attempt to steal the equipment. However, there were already changes made; Doris, the only woman in the camp, would leave and return to Monrovia, and Regis would join his father, then they would be assigned to safer places to work.

After a mere 20 minutes of advancing carefully to the edge of the jungle, the marines signaled their presence; they had made good time, thanks to their great training and the short cuts shown by Kumar. Then, all squeezing inside the jeep and pushing through potholes and muddy roads, Gérard continued to receive more information, the marines having kept in touch with the embassy all along.

They took the direction of the well digging camp, now only 10-15 minutes away. There, the helicopter that had flown them to Gbamga would meet them and fly them to Monrovia so they did not have to take the long drive back through the jungle. The chopper would need about 45 minutes to fly from the Gbamga base in a good day, but at night with the dense rain and the canopy of the rainforest, flying on instruments could be precarious.

At the Greenpeace camp, it would embark with Regis, Doris, Gérard, and Kumar, bringing them back to the capital, whereas the marines would stay with the peacekeeper troupe until a new team replaced the three men operating the drills.

Then, the marines and the jeep driver would return bringing the older team back, while the Green Berets would stay for the duration of the well digging and installation of solar panels, deterring anyone's desire to interfere with the peaceful mission.

With great relief, they finally arrived at the drilling camp. There, they now had the two marines and a small detachment of soldiers, trained and armed to defend them in case of trouble, Regis was back, and they had even collected a friendly ally, Kumar. With the Sikorsky HH-60 on the way, Gérard met Doris, and against all her protests, she was asked "to get her stuff ready" for the ride back to Monrovia.

It was still peach dark around the camp, but the installation had battery-operated lights, and after they became quickly acquainted with each other, they waited quietly in case the villagers started wondering what was happening.

In less than 30 minutes, a faint rumbling pierced the night as the rotors' sound became clearer, and finally they signaled to the Paver Hawk the safest place to land. Goodbyes were exchanged and wishes of happy endings, then the four passengers were on board, ready to close the doors. At that precise moment, Doris let out a scream when she saw a small stray dog she had been feeding appear from nowhere. Gérard stopped her with a gentle squeeze of reassurance, and got out of the helicopter to pick up the dog. He took him in his arms and rushed back to the waiting chopper. With one arm holding the mutt and the right the door handle, Gérard placed one foot on the helicopter floor, when he felt his chest exploding and all went black.

-//-

Suddenly, all hell broke loose in the well-digging camp. The well-trained marines and Blue Berets took up a defensive position around the eight civilians and the camp. Four were still on the ground including the camp team and the driver Steve, while the other four were already in the chopper getting ready for takeoff.

Inside the helicopter, at the loud orders given by the captain to Regis and Kumar, Gérard was pulled inside while the chopper remained on the ground. The gunner of the S HH-60, sent a flare in the direction of the suspected shot, and oriented a powerful searchlight into that direction, with the intention to expose the attackers and to blind their target vision as well.

On the ground, the military swiftly did the same, inverting the few floodlights available, and with arms at the ready, looked for the attackers through their night goggles. However, no sounds or shadows could be seen, perhaps one of the marines caught a glimpse of a faint bush shaking in the direction of the hills, but nothing else. After a while, they concluded that it must have been an isolated sniper, looking for a sneaky revenge, a cowardly attack of someone defeated and trying to do harm, even though he could not take on the entire camp dwellers all by himself.

Nevertheless, the military personnel kept watch, while there was a more urgent situation to deal with: Gérard lying unconscious on the chopper's floor and severely wounded.

There was neither a doctor, nor a medic present, but one of the Blue Berets' team, a robust youth from Montana, had some training in first aid and he was actively assessing Gérard's condition.

Doris came forward too, and let the others know that she had been a practicing veterinarian until recently, when she joined Greenpeace.

Gérard, still unresponsive, was taking shallow breaths that became further apart and a rattle gurgled in his airways. He was not wearing a Kevlar vest for protection, and the light shirt donned for hot weather was drenched with bright red blood, extending from his mid to lower right chest area, and a puddle started accumulating on the floor. Using the emergency kit, Doris listened to his chest with high concentration using all her experience she'd had with domestic pets, and occasionally with horses. There was definitely a penetrating wound caused by a bullet with a delayed exploding effect, creating more damage than the initial impact.

Doris could not obtain any breathing sound from the mid-right lung all the way down to the waist, while she felt a swelling growing above the liver area, probably from the blood accumulating there. She was dealing with a nasty hemothorax, the lower half of the right lung deflating like a pierced balloon losing air, and blood rushing into the thoracic cavity, eating rapidly all the space available. It would soon fill most of the right lung, which would no longer have the capacity to provide the oxygenation needed to the organs, but also the volume of the blood accumulating would compress the remainder of the functional upper right lung, then the left lung, and another vital organ, the heart.

Pushing downward, the pressure would compromise the diaphragm, the principal respiratory muscle, from allowing the air to actively enter the body. There was hope that the trachea was not penetrated and at least for now, not filled with blood, shutting down any possible spontaneous respiration. Nevertheless, with so much lung tissue loss, the air reaching the alveoli, the tiny respiratory units insuring the oxygen exchange with the blood vessels, there was not sufficient freshly oxygenated blood reaching all the organs.

There was an urgent need to supply the brain and the heart with oxygen before irreversible damage set in. The blood hemorrhaging into the lung and leaving the blood vessels would also soon create a dramatic fall in blood pressure, pressure necessary to reach and maintain the proper body functions, otherwise precipitating a renal and other organ failure, and ultimately leading the body to shut down.

Doris and Brian, the Montana soldier, exchanged information quickly and briefly; Brian started an IV with a large gauge opening wide the D5-½ NS line in the hope of maintaining the liquid volume and the arterial pressure, while Doris, short of finding an intubation equipment in the emergency kit of the Paver Hawk, applied an oxygen mask over Gérard's face and started "bagging", pushing air forcefully in with a high oxygen concentration into his collapsing lungs. Once the IV line started, Brian patched the right lung wound, preventing more blood loss.

Tension was high, and realizing that they had a critical patient, the only hope was to stabilize Gérard's condition the best they could until they reached a hospital. The pilot and the copilot were ready to take off when they considered the conditions safe from another attack.

Soon they were in the air, and the American Hospital in Monrovia was expecting them with an emergency team at ready. During the flight, Doris and Brian communicated with the trauma unit doctor on call who inquired repeatedly about the patient's condition and gave them directions, which, although under constricted conditions, gave a great deal of encouragement the two improvised doctors.

The captain pushed the two engines hoping to get to the hospital in less than two hours if granted straight flight permission, and asked if the hospital would give ground clearance for landing a larger helicopter. Reassured that the hospital would accommodate evacuations and arrivals from military bases of the central and west Africa, he just focused on the flight as the night lifted and a timid glow grew through the clouds.

The flight engineer kept busy communicating with the American Embassy, UN Security and humanitarian agencies, and the peacekeeper detachment for the camp security they had just left.

There would be a speedy investigation into Mr. Bulhami's whereabouts at the time of the attack to see if there was any evidence of his direct involvement in attacking and wounding an American diplomat and UN representative. There would also be a report from Regis Thomas of his detention, and the Liberian government would have to show good faith and order an inspection of his mines using underage children.

Thanks to the corruption of government employees and the influence Bulhami possessed, this would not last forever, but it was about all they could do against Jamil. He would not get his well equipment, would see his production decline drastically without the exploitation of cheap labor, the authorities would be on his back for a while, and most of all, he felt betrayed by his own son!

During these dramatic moments, there were many people concerned about Gérard. Regis and Kumar felt powerless and almost guilty for their new friend's condition, everyone in the HH-60, at the well digging camp, at the American Embassy, even his friends remaining in Khartoum, and the others at home were all worried and they all prayed.

-//

"Oh God, I feel so good! All the fatigue is gone, the atrocious pain in my chest and the terrible, suffocating need for air, are all gone. I feel so good!" I was relieved from the pressure, weightless, floating. I let myself enjoy this new, delightful sensation for as long as I could. I did not want to know where I was, nor what had happened. Just be, filled with indescribable happiness.

The joy was expanding as feelings of peace, reassurance, hope, and embracing, incommensurable love were added. I felt cradled by the long forgotten, heavenly state of infinite love!

I recognized instantly where I was and ready to leave all behind with eager anticipation of an eternity of total bliss. I realized I was back Home! At last!

The surroundings became clearer as I moved toward a bright, intense light, soon immersed in more light; not blinding but pure and a vibrating, living entity. And here He was, welcoming me, not a face, but His Holiness, the Holy of the Hollies, splendor and grace, the Light.

Slowly, a face emerged from the light, advancing toward me, smiling, and beautiful. Isabelle! I screamed her name, I cried out the word, but there was no sound, no need for it. Reunited again, understanding one another was simple and complete. Complete was also the pure joy, the recognition of the pain and the longing I had gone through was now over. Forever.

Isabelle, without the use of words, gave me the assurance that, yes, love is eternal and carried along with us wherever we go, and yes, there is a place called Heaven, our Eternal Home. Isabelle took my hand and walked me a little further to show me all that reminded me of Heaven. Being together made us complete again, as we have never been since we were separated, and I received infinite power from it, I was energized, regaining a state of supreme contentment.

We sat for a long time by a garden lake, beauty which can't be described in human words, and simply connecting. Isabelle infused my being with knowledge: that she was always with us when we wanted her presence close and her love continued to grow for all of us. Images came also about her Sanctuary and the fulfilled time she had been spending in Heaven.

Above all, she wanted me and all of us to know that she was happy, and her desire was for all of us to be happy. She insisted on how important it was for us to enjoy our time on Earth and to carry on feelings of happiness for her, happiness for each other, happiness for ourselves. She added that she was now more alive than ever before. At one point, Isabelle made me see and sense the reason she left Earth, and as it made her then understand, all made sense to me as well. She would not have had a life worth living any longer if she had stayed, and I finally accepted that she would not have deserved such suffering.

My heart was also talking to her, telling her how much I missed her, that my love for her had no limits, and that now we would be, finally, together forever and ever. I told her that I could not live without her.

This is when Isabelle came to a halt, the reflective pause I remember so well she used to make. "Gérard, you cannot stay here, we can't be together, yet. You have to go back; it is not your time to leave your life on Earth."

Suddenly, this was beyond my understanding, beyond my acceptance, and I rebelled. This glimpse of happiness was suddenly too short lived, too cruel to be taken away so quickly.

Nonetheless, Isabelle with a sweet expression I never knew even existed, explained, "Gérard, you will have to go back to Earth to complete your destiny, to fulfill the work you started. Otherwise, you will have to go back no matter what, and start all over again.

"There are people who need you Gérard, our children and our grandchildren need you too, you cannot abandon them. I am not there in person like you are, and you can do so much more for all of them."

I was ready to scream and to fight, as I had no desire of leaving Isabelle now that I had found her again, when I was so close to her and we were so happy. With infinite patience and gentleness, Isabelle continued to explain that I had to go back. She wanted to let me know, to show me what was there for me when I was called back Home. It was the image, the reality of what to expect and hope for when leaving Earth. It was the reassurance that there was nothing to fear as love and loved ones were not lost, and that they were all waiting to be reunited with us again.

"This is a gift to you, Gérard, to let you know that I am here and love you, to show you where we will be when the time will come, to help you carry on until then."

A moment later, I felt a "swoosh" ...through my body and I could at once feel I was back, and with it, a crushing pain ravaged my entire being, as I desperately gasped for air.

"He is back, we have a pulse, and he is breathing on his own", Gérard heard, blinded by a crude halogen light attached to the ceiling, stretched on a gurney, tubes in his veins and two in his right lung. "Now that he is coming around, we need to give him a light sedation, the pain will be unbearable and he needs to regain his strength," he heard voices of the medical professionals.

As the sedation started to take effect, the pain lessened and I fell asleep peacefully. I dreamed of Isabelle, a dream as vivid as the reality I had just experienced. She was with me, lovingly watching over me. I could feel her caress on my forehead as the cool water of a river. Along with her lovable, endearing presence, came her message that I would be alright, that all will be just fine.

"N'ai pas peur, mon amour, je serai toujours la quand tu as besoin. Tu n'as qu' appeler mon nom et je serai la. Do not be afraid, my love, I will always be there when you need me. Just call my name and I will be here."

BOOK EIGHT

Marina was sitting at the kitchen table early that morning with a cup of strong coffee in front of her; she would need it for she had a long list to go through for Francesca's wedding. Still in New York waiting for Gunter's arrival from the Bayreuth Festival where he was conducting Wagner's "Tannhauser", Marina had her plate full making sure that the wedding dress would be ready for her to bring it to Florida. Francesca, now 27, had expressed her desire, with the intensity and passion she did everything else in life, that she wanted to wear her grandmother's wedding dress.

Marina, retaining her parents' good genes and stunning looks at 57, was just about of the age when her mother died, and managed to find the dress at the family estate in Florida, where her father kept some precious mementos from the past.

It was during a recent visit made to visit her father, when Francesca, who wanted to come along, announced to him that she was getting married to Cameron. She added that she wished to have the ceremony in Florida, and she would love, "please, please", to wear Isabelle's wedding dress if possible!

As expected, Gérard, who could not refuse anything to Francesca, agreed to all of the above, and Marina and Francesca returned to New York with the dress. There was no real need for an alteration to be made, the mother and the daughter marveling at the elegance and finesse of the lacy dress, a beauty created by Givenchy in the late 80's. They found a specialized haute couture cleaning place to bring back all the freshness of the dress, and with all the reassurance that there was no damage done to it, the mother and daughter left it there, still nervous until they saw it again with their own eyes.

Marina could not stop reminiscing about the past years of her life, hardly believing that her little Francesca was grown up enough to start her own family now. Benjamin had pursued his childhood inclination and become a successful pianist and composer. Too involved in his passion for music, he did not have a busy social life besides the contact with his audience. Only recently, after meeting Charlotte, a writer freelancing for various websites who specialized in classical music in order to make a living while writing novels, Benjamin became engaged at the age of 32.

Marina had already reduced her traveling and public appearances, holding only a few recitals a year when accompanying her husband. She dedicated most of her time to her family and to giving singing lessons during the summer festivals in Chicago and New York. She kept some of her devoted students coming periodically to New York to improve their performance and when needed to brush up before public performances.

Marina smiled remembering a touching detail when Francesca was only a little over 18 months old; Marina was pushing the baby stroller home with a few errands after their usual promenade in Central Park. They were getting ready to enter the building, when Francesca with a big smile illuminating her entire face, lifted her arms as if to be picked up.

At first, Marina thought that Francesca was smiling at the concierge standing by the door, but looking in that direction, she noticed her father, who, stepping out of a taxicab, was walking toward them.

"Papa!" Marina called pleasantly surprised. It was at that precise moment that they heard a soft but distinct cooing of "Pa...Pa..." as Francesca made a funny smacking noise with her lips.

Marina looking at the baby, pointed in Gérard's direction and said, "Papa Gérard", to which Francesca repeated with a serious baby expression, "Pa Jei... a... ad." Gérard, dropping his suitcase in the middle of the sidewalk, almost with tears in his eyes, took the baby in his arms, and from then on, he became the beloved "Pa Gérard" for the adoring Francesca, as for all the other grandchildren who adopted his new name.

That was just one of the many heart-warming memories that came to mind as Marina prepared for her daughter's wedding. Emotions brought about by the anticipation of future events mixed with the memories of her own wedding, the thrill of the preparations and choosing from so many tempting offers.

Perhaps, all this was meant to ease the transition from the caring arms of a mother seeing her child step out into her own path of life alone, with the trials and worries of her own. It might help let go of her baby, after they shared a few more special and last private times together.

Marina felt that it was only a little while ago that she and her mother, Isabelle, were overwhelmed with excitement as she prepared for her own marriage to Gunter, and here she was, 35 years later, preparing her daughter's wedding! Where did the time fly? Without realizing it, she started day dreaming, remembering these enchanted episodes of her life, considering them as treasures that enriched one's soul, always there to reclaim and enjoy as often as desired.

Gunter and Marina had decided to have their wedding in Vienna, Austria, the place where the Von Stadolf family originated. During their engagement, Gunter made a point of showing Marina the monuments and the best cultural places in the Waltz Capital, but also the rich history of Salzburg and other charming corners of the Austrian countryside.

During the later years in their life, the musical career brought them often back to Vienna, Salzburg or Bayreuth, and they became quite familiarized with the places of the beginning of their lasting romance.

Marina began thinking of her wedding day, vividly remembering every small detail; the Von Stadolf and the Forrests having retained the Strauss Pavilion in Stadpark, a royal pavilion built in superb baroque style, where concerts and dancers from the Opera House were offered to the public on special occasions.

They held the ceremony in one of the larger chapels of the St. Stephen Cathedral, and a horse pulled carriage made the trip along the Ringstrasse to Stadpark. It was a splendid September day, when foliage was already turning all shades from yellow to deep burgundy, the park was still resplendent with famous flower arrangements, offering a superb outdoor backdrop for the wedding reception.

A group of musicians from the Vienna Orchestra came to play at the reception, to honor Gunter who had directed them during past concerts, adding another unforgettable memory to Marina's and Gunter's wedding. They all danced the evening away, swirling through the Viennese waltzes, as during the imperial times.

Their honeymoon started in Vienna, with a river cruise taking them to the best sites of the Danube coastal vineyards, after which they transitioned back against the current, reaching the Rhine valley. They let the river gently carry them through Bavaria and Westphalia visiting enchanted castles. From Neuschwanstein Castle, built by Ludwig II of Bavaria and inspiring Walt Disney as the place for Sleeping Beauty, they continued taking a day to visit Ludwig's second castle built in Linderhof, tucked away in the mountains.

They dreamed in these places of the Nibelungen mythology, which had given inspiration to Richard Wagner for his tetralogy. "The Ring of Nibelungen", a monumental artwork written by Wagner in four operas, was part of music highly admired by Gunter, who, as an orchestra director, had and would continue to direct these operas. They visited Oberammergau and Hohenschwanstein, Pfaltzgrafenstein and Koblenz Fortress, and many other places and castles, making their journey as romantic a honeymoon as could be dreamed of.

-//-

With all the confidence and promising expectations a young person could hold for the future, Francesca was also making preparations for her new life. It was also a time for reflection and her thoughts brought her back to instants that had marked her life. She reflected on what had been the significant turning points in her life that had taken her in new directions over the years. She smiled to herself, remembering the incident when it all started, when Gérard was in New York, a few years after the attack in Liberia.

Gérard had recovered from most of the damage caused by the wounds to his chest, and insisted on returning to his previous activities dedicated to international affairs. He was more than ever committed to bringing his contribution of freedom and peace in the world. Although Francesca was then about seven years old, she could see her dear Pa Gérard was more relaxed, more at peace with himself in life, and the whole family relaxed and enjoyed frequent extended vacations in Florida. They all observed a tranquil serenity in Gérard's attitude and they felt happy to see that he must have come to accept Isabelle's passing.

Francesca having finished her homework, asked Pa Gérard if they could go to the park and walk together. She wanted to be out in nature, for there had been a few days of constant misty rain and spring was having a hard time arriving. The rain had stopped, but the day was still grey, and she knew that her grandfather would find a way to cheer her up.

Indeed, they had had a good time; she rode a pony, fed the ducks on the lake, and they finished with a nice afternoon "gouter" at the pastry in the corner with hot chocolate and vanilla puffs. Francesca was so content, she wanted to jump and skip all the way back home.

Not far from there, a commotion began on the street, somewhere behind them. A van was making strange whistling sounds and some screams joined the racket. They noticed a barking along with the other noise and now, all bystanders had turned to see a van marked Animal Protection chasing a frightened little dog. Somewhere, his innocent instincts were telling him that nothing good could happen from the "protection" offered by this car and the people running after him. He needed to find a place to escape; he had no bad intentions, only love to give and find somewhere to go. He only wanted to live, that's it, but it seemed that in this crowded world there was no more place for someone little like him.

In desperation and completely out of breath, with no strength to fight any longer and finally giving up, he landed at the feet of a little girl. Right away, the little girl bent down to him, wrapped her arms around his little neck, and he felt protected. With his entire body still trembling and his heart racing out of control, the men chasing finally caught up with him as the little girl held him with all her might in a tight and protective embrace.

The three burly, angry agents started shouting questions to Gérard, "Is this dog yours? Why doesn't he have a collar and an ID? Why don't you keep him on a leash? This is dangerous, a citizen should respect the rules."

And they kept on going with their reprimands. As usual, Gérard, although profusely apologizing, found the right answers, paid a hefty fine, and managed to slowly calm the conundrum around him. Some of the bystanders expressed aloud their discontent at him letting his dog run wild and being so poorly kept.

All this time, Gérard showed, to Francesca's surprise, no intention to argue or explain, only the desire to save the dog and to get him away from there. It was only when the crowd had dissipated and he felt that the small little creature was out of danger, Gérard dropped to his knees, held the dog in his arms and looked at Francesca.

"Francesca, this dog came to you to be saved. Do you want him?" When the little girl, crying and overwhelmed with emotion, nodded her head vigorously, he added with a kind and soft voice, "Then you will have to take him home, give him a good bath, food, water, and a lot of love, because from now on, he is yours for his entire life."

Gérard, holding the little terrier mixed with other hard to name breeds, entered the first general store; there, he bought a carrier bag large enough to contain the dog, plenty of best dog food and treats, a flea repellant, tear free baby shampoo, a nice collar and leash, and a plush dog bed. Francesca was now in heaven with happiness and "could not wait to give a bath to Scotty, give him milk and food, and take him to her room and set up his bed, and..."

When Scotty found Francesca and entered into her life, he was not in his prime. He already had a few white whiskers around his nose and his beard. The veterinarian gave him a thorough examination and started his immunizations, saying Scotty was around seven years of age. However, from that moment on, Scotty became not only Francesca's best friend for over 10 years of happy dog life, but most of all, he revealed in her the love for animals and her desire to rescue those who were in danger.

-//

It was not difficult for Scotty to gain everyone's love; he immediately demonstrated an ability to learn and be on his best behavior and did not need to attend an obedience school to understand how to ask when he needed to go out, when it was time to eat and how to walk on a leash. There were a few oversights, though, when it came to begging for some extra treats.

He was affectionate and he played the funniest tricks, greeting the members of his new family with unconditional and unlimited love. He soon became the center of attention, all competing to hold or play with him, and there was never a shortage of volunteers to take him for a walk.

Although Benjamin had an immense affection for the dog and wanted him close by all the time, Scotty was Francesca's shadow, following her everywhere. Sleeping at first in his bed at the foot of hers, soon he inched his sweet charms to climbing into her bed, and slept nuzzled against her back, and if possible, on her pillow, stuck against her neck. When Marina and Gunter came into her room to bade her a good night or to wake her up in the morning, they found Francesca and Scotty the picture of perfect contentment, sleeping in heavenly peace.

Without knowing and above all intentions, Scotty brought into the children's life not only affection and filled the place of a pet-play companion, but he taught and opened to these city children the door of realizing the importance animals occupy in our life. Scotty showed not only love and loyalty, but also how we could live in harmony with the other creatures, what they really were and how much they had to give, when about to be brutally discarded by a society that considers them as vermin and a nuisance.

Francesca, in discovering her love for Scotty, also discovered and deepened her love of all animals, and from that point in life she chose to dedicate her career to taking care of as many as she could. At first, she did not know how, but soon she heard the others mentioning a word that sounded like "veterinarian" or something like that—hard to pronounce—but she decided that this is what she would do when she got older. Thus, the Von Stadolf family did not have to worry about what kind of education their children would have in the future; their inclinations showed through very early in their lives, and indeed, they would follow and succeed in the directions they had chosen.

-//-

Growing up and going through the delicate and subtle changes a little girl goes through during teenage years, Francesca developed beautifully into a happy young lady, having already found a strong purpose in life. Learning from the large amount of information the wide web could offer, she became aware of the large scale of abuse humans inflicted on other species. She went through periods of great turmoil ranging from shock, horror, disgust and revolt at the practice of the mass production of meat and dairy, but also against the senseless urban development taking over other creatures' territories so inconsiderately, with many species becoming endangered or extinct.

With the positive disposition of her character, she used this strong flux of energy to find solutions to this planet-wide problem. She discovered that many organizations and societies had started years before an immense movement of spreading the awareness against the corporates and companies related to the food or construction industry. These companies often used methods and policies based only on profit which destroyed the environment and manipulated our own genetic and biological integrity, and at times allowed practices that were in truth sadistic toward animals.

Francesca forced herself to view documentaries about slaughterhouses, in order to understand the most hellish places on Earth that men had created. Soon after, she became a vegan and educated her entire family, putting all her passion into it to get them all to become vegetarian. She did not relent until she converted all of them. Except for Gérard, who was already a vegetarian, all the others realized how much better they felt, how much more energetic and healthy, and most of all, how happy they felt not eating anything that had ever taken breath.

She joined many animal and environmental protection societies, and continued this through her entire life. After her veterinarian degree, she completed her education spending various periods of time with older vet groups in different areas of the country learning more about treating and healing pets, farm animals, and wildlife as well. Then, she extended her interest to tropical animals, and went to Africa to offer her services to several national parks and reservations, which were increasingly growing in areas where the superb species used to be hunted close to complete extermination.

Francesca, in choosing this way of living, was making her own contribution to saving the planet, and dedicated her life to protecting animals, by actively providing treatments to them wherever she could. This is how she met Cameron.

Hunter Cameron Ascott started working a few years earlier for Botswana's Elephants Without Borders project, at the African Kavango Zambezi Transfrontier Project, also known as the KASA TFCA Conservation area.

The KASA TFCA project extended over a large territory in central, and from east to west, side of Africa, including Angola and Zambia to the north, Zimbabwe to the east, and Namibia and Botswana to the south side.

Botswana became the first country to stop trophy hunting and in the early 21st century, its president obtained and educated the population on how they could make a gainful occupation and at the same time save their national treasures, by inviting the Picture Safaris to their country.

It appeared that the huge momentum initiated by the young generations determined to make a change and insure their future natural life, had a huge impact on public opinion and the rich trophy hunters became the major donor conservationists. Instead of taking lives and exposing them in hideous stuffed displays in sinister parts of their mansions, they saved lives and covered walls with pictures and filled rooms with holograms of the animals they saved, shown in their natural environment and living a happy life, raising their descendants and multiplying!

Francesca was working for a while in Serengeti, a large animal reservation in Tanzania, as part of teams studying the large lion population. Serengeti, one of the Seven Natural Wonders of Africa, contained the largest mammal migration territory in the world. She was in Ngoro Ngoro Conservation Center, from where a great wildebeest migration began from early January until March, during the calving season, when the rainy season brought plenty of grassy pastures. Each year this circular migratory phenomenon would cover approximately 500 miles from Ngoro Ngoro southeast side of Serengeti going north to the Maasai Mara National Reserve in southwestern Kenya, when game will move through, counting gazelles, zebras, and other grazing wildebeest.

The lions lived within the trail protected by the project, and Francesca's team was following this well-balanced ecosystem created between the prides living in their natural environment and the moving game. Because this place was one of the first to bring back the lion numbers from a few dozens to several thousands, it had also been the inspiration of Disney's

"The Lion King". Elegant photo safaris were organized starting close to this conservation center, which also offered separate luxury resort accommodations and wealthy visitors did not hesitate to pay in good conscience for a good cause.

Francesca was happy to see that the world was changing and the trend established several decades before, was rapidly growing and bringing a new era, when people showed respect and love towards nature. The privileged members of society were competing now to offer financial support to the ones providing help and solutions to maintain the population of creatures that not long ago were decimated without any consideration.

As a descendent of a long lineage of beautiful and talented women, Francesca continued naturally and effortlessly the tradition; she was admired everywhere she went for her stunning looks and her knowledge acquired as a veterinarian. For her team members, she was their star, although Francesca always referred to the older and more experienced scientists working with her, all the while demonstrating a nature that was easy to get along with everyone.

Team members became used to hearing her trills of laughter when she was caring for all kinds of patients, for she had a genuine talent of communicating with them, making her little and large friends relax and trust her, and often play with her, to her ecstatic joy.

Francesca considered her work as a great privilege, never complaining and finding immense satisfaction in taking care of animals, always marveling at their beauty and adaptability. She was happy to see those that had been injured return to good condition, at times playing mommy to orphaned baby lions, gazelles, or even rhinos, taking them to her own bungalow where they learned how to grow together like one same family.

One day, a National Geographic team filming in the Serengeti National park, arrived in Ngoro Ngoro following a group of people on a safari that were tracing the journey of the wild life. They met Francesca and her team as well, and recorded their progress and their observations of the lion prides distribution within migratory tracks. Very impressed with Francesca's professional command, they swiftly proposed her to join their filming itinerary further south in Kavango Zambezi Conservation Area. Francesca had heard about the famous multinational efforts of wildlife preservation, but had not had the opportunity to visit it yet, and had a difficult time resisting the temptation of this exceptional prospect.

As wildlife started moving north for the annual migration away from Ngoro Ngoro, and with the residents of the conservation center all stable, Francesca made all the necessary preparations for a long trip across a large part of the African savanna with the help of fellow team members. She made sure she had her own recording material that would be easy to store on her cyber mailbox via satellite. So, a small convoy of five jeeps equipped with GPS and loaded with technical material, tents, food and water, and extra batteries for the electrical powered engines, left at dawn for the adventure, including the most excited member, Francesca.

They first went south with a short detour to a reservation on Lake Malawi, then, shifting southwest to Tanzania, they boarded the cars on the ferry crossing Lake Tanganyika. It was not possible to stop overnight at all of the 36 national parks belonging to this extended conservation trail, but they planned their trip making stops in a different one at the end of each day.

Continuing south to Zimbabwe and west on Lake Kariba, after visiting the rich fauna of the area, and the restored fish and aquatic life, they went further west. Reaching the Zambezi River, they stopped for a while at the Victoria Falls, bordering Zambia to the north and Zimbabwe to the south. They were already a good two weeks into their adventure, when they finally travelled further south to Botswana, arriving at Chobe National Park.

Although the travel was tiring at times, Francesca savored every minute of this very unique experience, thrilled by the variety of the natural beauty encountered and witnessing a large density of wild animals adjusting to live in surprising harmony.

She had one more place she could not wait to visit, and this was the Elephants Without Borders center.

-//-

Hunter Cameron Ascott had already worked at the Elephants Without Borders center for a few years and he now considered this African place his home. The center was dedicated to maintaining a large migratory elephant area safe from poachers, giving him all the satisfaction and excitement in life he had always dreamed of. Cameron, raised in Austin, Texas, of a family of university professors, was inclined towards studies and was expected to choose an academic professional orientation in the future. Cameron went often with his parents and his older sister to their vacation cabin on Lake Travis, north of Austin on one of the chain of lakes made by the Colorado River.

Cameron always loved seeing the deer up close roaming freely in the middle of these small towns along Lake Travis, grazing on the sidewalks and crossing the shaded alleys. Cars and pedestrians became accustomed to them, people and deer finding a natural way of tolerating and living with each other. No one complained at having to go slowly, and because the deer and their "Bambys" were well fed, there were no complaints of them picking from the flower beds.

After graduating from high school, Cameron went to one of the many colleges in his hometown, and obtained a degree in science and biology, with an interest in marine biology, of anything else. During his internship off the coast of North Carolina, he came in contact with an older couple working on the same offshore ship, and learned about the Elephant Project. The Elephants Without Borders center was started with a fund created a few decades before by Paul and Jody Allen, the Microsoft philanthropists, who donated millions of dollars to start and maintain the project.

At the time when it all started, in the early 1990s, elephants were killed by trophy hunters or by poachers by hundreds each week, and the Angolan elephant population slimmed from 200,000 to a few hundred during the long civil war of the 90s and their disappearance was imminent. Along with the hunt for meat and ivory trade, the elephants were deprived of the migratory trail they had used for thousands of years.

Farming was initiated without considering their paths and often blocking their tracks, and when elephants crossed their fields it gave the rural population even more excuses to exterminate them as well. The project was intended to study and trace their migration lines, and then work to find solutions to respect and protect those trails while helping the farmers to coexist with the wildlife in the territory. And this was working now; elephant populations returned to larger families, poaching became a fact of the past, and many wondered how this was even possible not so long ago.

Cameron, who always was a conservationist at heart and who hated any form of hurting an animal, was often teased because of his name; it was a joke that made him change from using his first name Hunter, to using his middle name, Cameron, on a regular basis.

One day, as Cameron was returning from his usual visit to the animal infirmary where sick or injured elephants were cared for, he lost track of time, and he felt a little embarrassed to receive his visitors without having had time to take a shower to refresh. The visitors made good time and Cameron was informed that the Jeeps had already unloaded the 10 visitors who were in the reception lounge having an icy cold tea. Coming through the door, he noticed the back of a feminine silhouette, removing her hat and shaking off a cascade of blond waves.

"They must have brought some 'ritzy princess' along," he thought, not used to seeing such refinement in this remote place.

When the customary salutations and introductions followed, Cameron was taken by surprise to discover that the "princess" was a young veterinarian researcher from another African project. But the most intimidating thing for him was coming face to face with a beauty that seemed stepping out of a dream.

-//-

The visit to the center was a source of wonder and enthusiasm for the National Geographic team, and the handful of safari guests, as it was for Francesca. At the dinner to follow, the conversation flowed easily between the guests and the hosts, everyone enjoying the exchange of information. Cameron listened to every word Francesca said and every touching story about her own work at the Serengeti center. A spontaneous current of understanding became established between the two of them as they found many common interests in their professions and in life in general.

At a certain point of their conversation, Cameron expressed his concern about 'Pumpkin', the last addition to an elephant family lead by an older matriarch, Lantern. He was born later than they had hoped, and Pumpkin had started the migration north too young for the thousand-mile journey, during which time he could become easy pray for lions, cheetahs, crocodiles, and even for hyenas. He had left tugging along with his mother who had the vital charge of leading the family made up of over 50 young and adult elephants, but Pumpkin would need to keep up with her brisk pace and depend on her for milk.

Before leaving, they placed a tracking collar to follow their progress during the migration, and they hoped to see him back safe and grown in 10 to 11 months. During the conversation, they both came up with the idea that Francesca could look for Pumpkin once arriving in the Serengeti, where they were expected at the end of their travel north. They would match their GPS tracking system and stay in touch with their findings. All this became suddenly very exciting, and Cameron was thrilled to remain in contact with Francesca.

A few months later, after Francesca's return to her work at the center in Serengeti, she had good news for Cameron: the Lantern family was approaching Ngoro Ngoro, a good thing because the reservation offered suitable protection and plenty of water and foliage, along with the rescue center to care for animals in need.

Francesca went ahead with two other members of the center and two of the guards charged with the tracking. The GPS collar averted very helpful in identifying the elephants, and they found they were on a direct path straight to the center, perhaps thanks to the acute sense of smell of the matriarch in detecting the presence of water.

While keeping a safe distance in order not to disturb this already exhausted family, they could evaluate the condition of their members. Pumpkin was with them, barely able to follow at the tail of the herd, and it was a miracle he has not been snatched by a predator yet. His left hind leg, however, was hardly touching the ground, and the limping was slowing his walk even more.

Closely observing Pumpkin, Francesca continued feeding Cameron with information through her videophone since she spotted Pumpkin, and reassured him that they would protect the elephants from now on until they reached the reservation. It seemed to take a long time before they could relax watching the elephants closing in on the large pond of water at the reservation, when, after entering the water, they started splashing and playing happily. Slowly, the little Pumpkin caught up with his mother, and as she had already had the chance to drink water to her heart's content, she started showering her son with the water sucked with her trunk.

While the elephant family started relaxing on the shady banks of the pond, they were delivered a treat in honor of their arrival: a full truckload of huge juicy watermelons and papayas was dropped on the opposite side of the pond from where they were resting, in an effort to avoid scaring the exhausted elephant family.

It is then that the members of the refuge had the chance to film a more hilarious scene; it seemed as though there was a communion between elephants and humans in sharing love and happiness, enjoying the simple pleasures of life and a delicious meal after a hard journey. They could almost say that the elephants were thanking them for this reception and they relished in the succulent fruits like children in a candy store. Even Pumpkin managed to arrive at the other side of the pond and it looked like he was discovering the use his trunk for the first time, but this made him even more adorable and more touching in his resolve to live.

Cameron followed all these events thanks to the transmission of the recorded images. They all, elephants and humans alike, had the best time of their lives. The Lantern family would linger a little longer, probably a couple of more weeks, on the grounds of the reserve, getting stronger for their journey back south, to Botswana's Chobe Park. Nevertheless, there was an urgent need for the team to assess Pumpkin's left rear leg.

The day after their arrival, the elephants were given the time to recover from the intense fatigue of the trip and general nutritional deprivation. The great intelligence and experience of the matriarch seemed to allow the rescue team closer, since they had tried to make their presence as friendly as possible. Another load of bananas and more watermelons the day after enabled the team to approach the elephants closer, and soon, some of the guards and Francesca had teased them with branches of large leaves and even with offerings of bananas.

Because Pumpkin was often on the edge of the group having a hard time keeping up with all the action, at a certain point Francesca offered him a peeled banana. Pumpkin was not sure how he was supposed to hold it, and at that moment, Francesca just brought it right up to his mouth. And bingo, the baby elephant was soon under the charm, and considered Francesca a surrogate mother.

After a few more similar times together, and when Pumpkin would hobble on his own toward Francesca looking for a good treat, they finally got a look at Pumpkin's foot. Even Lantern, close by, showed trust when Francesca and the senior veterinarian of the center managed to lift and look at Pumpkin's foot. Pumpkin let them hold it and they saw the reason for the limping: a big and sharp stone had lodged deep in the baby elephant's shoe, and the more he was stepping on the sole of the foot, the deeper it was penetrating.

They removed from their instrument box a strong clamp, and pulled the stone from the baby elephant's foot without need for anesthesia. Then, they applied an antiseptic and gently lowered his foot to the ground. Baby Pumpkin tried shyly to put pressure on his foot, probing at first, and quickly realizing he was not hurting anymore, straightened his back and lowered his weight on his legs.

The mother stayed close and stroked the little one with her trunk. As if she knew that her baby had been cured, she turned toward the two wildlife doctors, and made soft sounds reaching with her trunk toward them. It was as if she was trying to draw them close to her, wanting to hug them!

The Ngoro Ngoro rescue center team found out later that the recordings of this touching encounter became a sensation around the world, another proof of the gentle communication one could establish with animals. As a result, more donations poured into rescue centers in Africa. This was followed by phone calls by another National Geographic team, who asked Francesca to continue this experience following the Lantern family back south, and offered her to join the team during the return journey.

Again, Francesca received encouragements from the other members of the center, and she went along into one of the most extraordinary times of her life. At the end of the journey, Pumpkin was a pretty boy of 10 months, and Cameron, the most loving conservationist, was waiting impatiently to see them all, especially Francesca.

The couple was soon in love and continued to share amazing times together at the elephant center, where Francesca remained for a while. The following New Year's Eve, Cameron proposed and the two of them became engaged.

They did not have many projects for the future, and Cameron responded to an offer to join the team of the Yellowstone National Park-Yukon Canada Park Project. This gave the two lovers another adventure to look forward to, this time closer to home. Francesca would, without any doubt, find a situation as a veterinarian at one of the rescue centers. They learned that this project was an immense undertaking between the United States and Canada, creating a wildlife migratory corridor called the "Kid Creek Corridor".

It was a 2000-mile corridor extending from the Yellowstone area to the Yukon. This natural trail extends from the Rocky Mountains in Yellowstone in the US, to a series of national parks in Canada, from Glacier Waterton, to Banff National Park, Wilderness, the Peel Watershed National Parks, and all the way up, near to the Arctic Circle.

Nevertheless, before leaping into a new adventure, they were looking forward to their marriage soon to be celebrated in Florida, at Pa Gérard's estate.

-//-

I was making my regular tour of the Sanctuary, one of the activities I liked doing the most. As many other times, there was not much to mend today, just to welcome a few newcomers and talk and play with a few squirrels, one rabbit, and a giant 200-year-old turtle.

I continued for a while my walk followed by a small army of cats, dogs, and birds, jumping in front and behind me, all singing and talking at the same time, some remaining behind for a play with friends calling along the way. This little routine usually gave me the time to reflect and absorb more of the teachings received in Heaven. But today, I felt the impulse to visit with Raphael again, although I did not have any particular question to ask.

With no surprise to me, the thought only took me to the Krystal Pyramid of Light, and soon I heard Raphael's gentle voice greeting me.

"Ah, here you are Isabelle. I am pleased to see you." Then after a while he opened the conversation, "Do you know why there is evil in your world?"

It was a subject I had not considered since I came to Heaven, thinking that I had left all malevolent spirits behind on Earth but I tried to come up with an answer. "I think it is the opposite of God, the negative forces men choose from, the wicked tendency that exists in all of us and allows us to make the choice between good and bad, the freewill God gave us," I tried.

"That's right. In some of your religious teachings, Satan is described as a real being. He was created by God, Who named him Lucifer, which means 'the star of the morning'. God gave him beauty, wisdom, and intelligence far above the other angels, and he was described in your Scriptures as one of the three archangels. God placed him to dwell eternally in the throne room of Heaven in His very presence. But Lucifer, as you already know, wanted more, and he wanted to be above all and possess all the powers his Father held."

"And he was chased from Paradise, and he became the hateful being in Hell, tempting humans to join him with all the worldly sins," I added.

"Yes, all this could be the general image of Satan," Raphael continued. "But do you know that Lucifer himself is tired of the bad things going on Earth? That the atrocities and the evil deeds perpetrated by men are far worse than what he ever imagined?"

Waiting for the shock I felt to subside, Raphael continued, "Lucifer is tired and longs to come back Home to his Creator; he is done, he does not want any more of the Hell he created. But men keep him prisoner of his own creation, and the vicious and horrid acts of mankind prevent him from seeing Hell destroyed and forever disappear, and finally be able to return to God."

A few more words resonated in my mind as Raphael was already disappearing from the sight.

"Lucifer repented a long time ago, he is not as bad as humans, and he craves for love and peace for the entire creation of God. He wants to be with his father again and forever."

-//-

Gérard was satisfied with the wedding preparations and all he could manage to take care of for the day, and went to the dock and sat by the boathouse, relaxing and waiting for the sun to set. It was this special time he always enjoyed, and coming to the dock became a ritual a long time ago, when him and Isabelle slowed down at the end of the day, delighted by the magical display of the setting sun.

In a way, he felt strong and energetic, but he knew better; his 93 years would remind him of the time that had passed and of his old wounds, and he was getting tired much faster. He thought that he was not the only one who had changed; there was so much he had seen in the 30 years since Isabelle had left this world.

Indeed, the world had changed tremendously, and contrary to the older generations used to the nostalgia of the past, Gérard admitted that this time the changes were for the best.

Over the years, Gérard kept in contact with Isabelle's side of the family in France, and made arrangements for the Forrest side, making sure they all had fair security for the future. Eric Beaumont, Isabelle's brother, was getting along in age too and was now 90.

Eric continued to manage and enjoy the Rambouillet property and the Boulevard Saint Germain apartment his parents had left behind, spending time there with his children and grandchildren.

Marina, as a child, and later her children, met occasionally in Paris with her mother's family, and the cousins and grand cousins retained strong ties, visiting across the two sides of the ocean and exchanging cultural experiences.

Gérard and Isabelle's apartment in Rue du Fg. St. Honoré, remained a place where Marina and the other Forrest side of the family occupied during their stay in Europe, although Gunter also had his property in Vienna left by the Von Stadolfs. However, it became a habit for all of them to offer the use of those comfortable places to the other members of the family when needed.

It had been also quite a long time since Gérard had transferred the Park Avenue apartment left by his parents to him, to Marina and Gunter, while the house in Washington, DC, went to Patrick and his family. He continued to stay at these places every time he visited or worked in New York or DC, and they were all welcome to the vast property in Florida.

Now, Gérard was happy that he had completed his last step of his succession: after Francesca's wedding at the Florida mansion, the property would close and the sale be completed, after a careful selection had been made from the offers proposed by different buyers. The proceeds would be used to purchase a large piece of land on the Yellowstone-Yukon Conservation Corridor, where Francesca would have her own sanctuary and tend to the animals passing through the area in need of medical care. The mansion itself had been bought by the Florida State and would be transformed into a place for stately receptions and discreet foreign dignitary visits, while the grounds would become a public park; it all waited only for the final signature after the wedding.

Progress had been made rapidly not only in the technology in this age of the mid 2040s, but most importantly in people's mentality, and in a good way. As expected, scientific advances could be seen in every aspect of everyday living routines at a level never dreamed of before but in science fiction movies, even those surpassed a long time ago. Practically all homes were equipped with an "intelligent center" that controlled their functions and made adjustments that responded to close or distant verbal or digital wireless commands.

This way, the comfort and energy savings were automatically adjusted. The fossil fuels used as source of energy were replaced decades ago by solar or waste processing energy.

Urban or countryside transportation had also been resolved entirely by providing citizens free vehicles that were computer operated and used solar electrical batteries or hydrogen generated power. Most of them transformed a small quantity of water into hydrogen for power, and oxygen was released into the atmosphere. When a person needed to go somewhere, a vehicle close by could be used, or a car or van was ordered to come to the desired address, as many were available at various sites in the community. Then, the small or large capacity vehicles were left for other people to use, no one needing to own, maintain or insure one, while no one remained isolated.

Long distance transportations were ensured by silent low or highflying crafts, where hydrogen was often used. Without creating any pollution and the ozone layers completely restored many years before, this offered clean air to breathe to all, while considerably slowing down the warming of the planet. The cost of this kind of energy used for transportation or utilitarian functions became a fraction of what had been used for centuries and the planet resources were spared. Senior citizens, students, or a variety of social categories needing assistance did not pay and were issued a pin or a bracelet giving them temporary or permanent access not only to individual vehicles, but also to larger forms of mass transportation, medical care, and other social services.

Communication was also made easy and attractive: a hologram system followed one around the house replacing the former telephone communication, and people could, at will, replace the audio reception of their fancy ear devices to directly see each other. They could have conference calls, or attend classes or meetings live, using long distance holographic imaging participation, which were instantaneous and free.

Thus, the college education became not only very affordable, but people could improve their education at any time and from any place, classes containing an unlimited number of students, since they were transmitted worldwide.

People became more educated and consequently, more responsible concerning the sustainability of the planet resources. Without lows imposing measures of limiting the overpopulation of the planet, couples wishing to become parents, considered more carefully bringing children in the world only when they could offer them a decent quality of life. It was no longer about just having children, but when a baby was welcomed into a family, providing every possible need. From a nice and clean place to live, with plenty of clothes and food, along with a loving environment, all was guaranteed for the children's education and medical care. All efforts were made to ensure that every child could become a happy and well-adjusted member of the society.

Moreover, techniques acquired from open and peaceful communication and interventions from extraterrestrial collaboration were applied increasingly. The use of magnetic waves and anti-gravitational energy became infinitely more efficient and replaced the use of limited fossil energy.

Thus, the planet was operating using renewable, clean, unlimited, and free energy, and planet Earth's natural beauty and future were respected and cherished, and now under the attentive control of interplanetary committees created between Earth's inhabitants and other, more advanced extraterrestrial civilizations. New jobs were created to replace the older technologies and to maintain the good function of the new ones.

The entire planetary population became an inclusive society, where people of all races, cultures, religions or ethnicity were equal. However, the particularities of regional traditions, art, culture, and languages were embraced, respected and promoted, creating a kaleidoscope of rich existential variety of immense value. People happiness became the number one wealth and social denominator of countries when assessing national progress, all nations exchanging and learning from each other the most technically and spiritually valuable or advanced ideas.

Enormous and revolutionary changes took place regarding the way we humans treated animal species, now considered as co-inhabitants of this planet and sharing similar rights to occupy it as well. Through enormous information and efforts made to expose the barbarian and atrocious practice of mass meat and dairy production, all this became a horrible nightmare of the past, people becoming either vegetarian or considerably limiting meat consumption, making the demand so low, that traditional farming came back with the technology helping with easy ways of producing crops and feed the local population.

Gérard thought of Francesca and Cameron, and their magnificent work dedicated to wildlife conservation, as part of the changes occurred these last generations. He was proud of his children and grandchildren being part of the new directions the younger generations were taking the world, providing a friendlier and more respectful attitude toward the planet and all its creatures, ultimately benefiting all.

As Gérard mused over his life, the sky was blazing for him a night show with incendiary reds on the horizon with colors Van Gogh would have loved to steal and throw into his paintings. As Gérard continued his reverie, he thought with satisfaction that there was now peace in the world, lasting peace for the generations to come. He thought about his friends including lifetime ones like Lucien and Vivianne Dubois. Even Milu had remained a good friend for many years.

After his injury in Liberia, he was transferred to the American Hospital in Monrovia, and once stabilized, to the American Hospital in Paris. Treated for complications with pneumonia from the wounds to his lungs, they feared a contamination by Ebola in the hospital in Monrovia.

However, it was just the usual complication of dirty blasting wounds, and again Gérard recovered and his condition enabled him to go back to the US, arriving finally in New York. Admitted to Mount Sinai Hospital and resting in the hospital building located in

Manhattan on Madison Avenue, he was regularly visited by Marina and her family who lived nearby.

Gérard went into relapses, but with an excellent medical team and great respiratory rehabilitation, he eventually recovered. During his stay in New York, Milu came to see him too, and she provided encouragements mixed with strong coaxing for his therapies, which helped to shorten his recovery time.

Once his condition stabilized, Gérard went into a semiretired period when he spent most of his time in his home in Florida. He kept in touch with Milu and learned that she continued her work at the UN, and she even bought an apartment in New York, where she started spending most of her time. She loved this vibrant city, the human interactions, and the endless choices of activities. During the years to follow, Gérard and Milu met occasionally for a drink when she introduced him to her latest boyfriend.

As the colors of the evening sky continued turning from light pink, then to purple and violet, Gérard's thoughts drifted, and he remembered some very significant events that followed a few years after his injury. Regis Thomas married Doris, and at the insistence of his father, he went back into a political career. His father had the strong intention to keep his only son away from dangerous places, while Regis excelled in bringing new ideas into the political arena.

After traveling the world for a while, he acquired a deeper understanding of relations between populations of very different cultural backgrounds. The new generations liked him and started seeing him as the representative of their aspirations for a more peaceful world and for more justice in society.

This way and against traditional expectations, at 39 years of age, Reginald Jefferson Thomas was elected as the youngest and 47th President of the United States of America. To Gérard's great surprise, the presidential cabinet immediately contacted him, and Regis who was preparing for the takeover in January 2029, came to the telephone and asked him to be his Secretary of State.

Regis had already recruited Kumar Bulhami, who became one of the house personal secretaries, but had a much harder time convincing Gérard to accept this difficult and prestigious position. It took Regis' father, Malcolm, to call one more time upon his friend, and father and son to personally travel to Florida, reminding Gérard about the way he had negotiated Regis' release, in order for Gérard to finally accept the offer.

Time showed that the choices were right, for it was a team blessed by the heavens in a country ready for progressive changes, with a president who listened to the younger generations' aspirations and had the true determination to transform them into reality. During his two four-year terms, more social democratic justice was introduced, advanced technology applied in all aspects of society, including medicine, education and economy, largely introduced to the masses and exported around the world.

America was living an era of great renaissance, a rebirth of the original principles uniting all strata of society into this profound restorative movement, bringing the country to unprecedented levels of prosperity.

During that time, Gérard traveled across the world into the most sensitive political situations, and intense negotiations took place. He organized alliances intended to eradicate extremist movements, negotiated fair economical exchanges within political agreements, and slowly, there was detente in international relations. The time was right, when in the Middle East the tension eased up and peaceful discussions came to a happy end. At last, the treaty for the foundation of an independent Palestinian state was signed with Israel, and the entire region was ready for peace, and with it, the Middle East discovered the joy of friendly relationships.

Somewhere in his mind, Gérard smiled with satisfaction that his relentless struggle to help establish peace in the world had achieved the results so long expected. He was pleased he had not given up once he made the decision to dedicate the years left in his life to contribute to making the world a better place to live. However, Gérard felt a little embarrassed and overwhelmed when he recollected the time when, a few years later and because of the peace agreement between the Arabic world and Israel, he was granted the Nobel Prize for Peace.

-//-

I have met Raphael a few more times, always with more questions and I always felt attracted to see him in the Krystal Pyramid of Light. The complete love, peace, and understanding I already felt since I returned home, were enhanced by many folds when I was there and in his presence. I also had the impression that my questions received a clarity that penetrated my being instantly. My searing desire for knowledge found the fresh water of the fountain of enlightenment, and I immersed in it with immeasurable joy.

This time I entered with the sense that I would not see Raphael for a while, although I knew that I remained welcome to call upon him any time. I announced my questions without need for an introduction, and this time, it was received as though he was waiting for me to come to their formulation.

"Who is God?" and to his bemused look, I kept on justifying my question. "I know He is the creator of all that is, the divine spirit behind life and everything that exists. I understood that He is omnipresent and the supreme Power and Knowledge, and that He created us all. I learned that He sent His messengers, His Sons, as the embodiment of Him on Earth for us to better grasp His will, getting at our level to allow us to reach Him."

Feeling that I had to stop somewhere, I search into his kind eyes for an answer, and I, again, discovered his endless patience.

"Finally, Isabelle, you came to the ultimate question for the **Ultimate Truth**: Who Is God...? As you said, He is everything you already mentioned, and more. He is the supreme power, the light and the energy that makes all function. He is the absolute knowledge and the spirit of all that breathes life, everywhere and anytime. He is the beginning and the end of all there is.

"God has been called by many names, but He is the same and the only one, and many terrestrials have understood that. However, even now believers in various parts of the world continue to celebrate Him as the manifestation of many gods and goddesses, which in fact represent His spirit present in an infinity of forms. And God understands that.

"Others pretend that they are God, as everyone else is God, albeit, none of them are able to create a planet, a universe, not even themselves. And, God understands that too.

"This is because all these people hold some truth, but they try to understand God through a very limited image. Many tried to envision God, to give Him a face. An old scripture talks about God asking not to make Him an idol. Not because He is not the One to venerate, and He is, in truth, everything that can be seen and unseen, but because God does not ask anything for His own glory.

"Recognizing that God is everything, makes it easy to understand that His Spirit is present in every being, simple or evolved, in every plant, in every stone, mountain, or river. He is the energy of the sun, the stars, and the galaxies. This is what you could call oneness.

"God made you, and He is the essence of who you are, of your 'soul'. And He is in everyone as much as He is everywhere. Your final destiny is to raise yourself to become one with this divine essence present in you, across life times and choices you make here on Earth, or other places of the Universe. The absolute, the foremost destiny, of yours and of all beings, is to achieve again the pure divine essence given to all by God from the beginning, and to return, becoming one with Him again. Only then, we can claim that we are God.

"Returning and becoming one with the source is the ultimate, the fundamental concept, when we are all one God, and its name is LOVE."

-//-

It had been one of the most beautiful mid-June days in northwest Florida, with a perfect clear sky morning and a fresh breeze. For one more time the Forrest, Von Stadolf, and Beaumont family members reunited for Francesca and Cameron's wedding. Francesca and Cameron would have been content with a very simple wedding, just being together was the greatest happiness for them, and, as for any young people, it was all they wanted.

Having their wedding ceremony at the Florida mansion had already fulfilled their highest wishes. However, their wedding matched the magic of these special moments, when couples of the same family had been blessed with in the past, not in the grandeur and the expense, but for the beauty and the love present at every moment.

In the small chapel by the sea, the groom was, as expected, nervous and on the brim of fainting, Francesca was magnificent in Isabelle's wedding dress, and no one could have imagined a more beautiful bride. They were all invaded by a profound emotion. Marina, the mother of the bride, Gunter the father, with his chest tight under the pressure of giving his daughter away, and all the audience made of family and close friends, arrived from all over the world.

Gérard felt almost dizzy, his head turning when the image of Francesca wearing the same dress as Isabelle, brought back memories of their wedding day, with the same powerful reality, the same intensity of feelings he had kept alive over so many years. He could almost have said Isabelle was there, with him, with all of them.

The reception was an enchantment, with tables set under the old oak trees, beautifully decorated with white and pink bouquets made of seasonal fragrant flowers, white gardenias, jasmine, and lilies, along with light pink plumerias. They spent unforgettable times with the joy of seeing the new couple starting their life together; there was also good food, music and dance, jokes and children playing late into the day. They slowed down only at sunset, relaxing and building new happy memories.

After the wedding, the new Ascott couple left for their honeymoon. They chose to go to Alaska on a three-week cruise, for a change from the African heat, and to discover new places. After that, they were very excited to go to the Rockies and find the perfect land for Francesca's sanctuary, somewhere close to Cameron's place of work at one of the Conservation centers along the Yellowstone-Yukon Corridor.

-//-

The Florida estate sale was finalized, the closing signed and sealed, and the money transferred to the Ascott couple's account. When coming back from their honeymoon trip and looking for a suitable property for their future projects, their wishes were fulfilled when they found the perfect place close to the National Elk Refuge in Wyoming.

Following U.S. Route 89 and 191 south from Yellowstone and Grand Teton National Parks, they approached the famous Jackson Hole by following the Snake River. There, tucked between the river and the Hoback Mountains, they found a gently sloping 200-acre piece of land extending from the clear river waters to the foot of the mountain. This was a great passage of wildlife where massive bull elks, moose, but also black bear, cougar, mountain goat, and bighorn sheep, could be frequently seen.

Gérard was to spend one last night at the mansion, finishing a few more small details of his transfer to the assisted living residence nearby where he would be staying from now on. A car was coming in the morning to take him to his new residence, while the administration from the County would take possession of the property.

He went for one more walk in the gardens and stopped by the dock, to say his goodbyes to the sunset. He was calm and happy, and sat on the bench facing the sound. He thought about his family, wondering if he had done well by them.

He felt at peace, thinking that, if he had not perfectly succeeded, at least he had tried his best. Then, thinking of Isabelle, he hoped that she would have been satisfied with what he had accomplished; the world was a better place now than when they were young. He understood why she wanted him to come back and continue his mission.

Gently, he went back to the house and as the night came, he went to bed. Before falling asleep, he said a mental goodnight to Isabelle, and then he dreamed of her. He returned to that moment when he had seen her so clearly in heaven, showing him her new place, holding him by his hand. But this time it was not for him to leave anymore, now it was the time for them to stay together forever.

When the two ladies from the Senior Center came to take him, they found he had passed away, with the most serene smile on his still beautiful face. The family came for the last time to this place in Florida, and they took him and laid him in the ground next to Isabelle's tomb, at the top of the shady hill, facing the Gulf of Mexico.

Gérard and Isabelle were walking and holding their arms around each other's waist, as young and beautiful as the day they first met. Their love fused their souls in the most divine happiness, now delighting in eternal bliss. At last, they were reunited and rediscovering each other, after a longing they had thought was far too painful. Radiant with joy, they were here together, in their new life to last forever, in their Heaven, their Heaven Rediscovered.

END

EPILOGUE

In reality, Chi-Chi lived only a few days. After a beautiful spring day spent on the back porch being reconnected with her parents, I found her on the ground, dying.

What happened? It is still a mystery. She could not fly well yet and she was only hopping from one low branch to another; did she try to go higher and fall and injure herself even more?

I took her and comforted her with a little water and food, and with many words of love. I wrapped her in a soft cloth and cradled her like a baby, holding her on my chest for a long time. She moved once in a while and I started, one more time, to hope she would recover again. Then, she gently opened her wings, and resting her head against my heart, she took a last breath.

We buried her the day after, under the sadness of a rainy day. Placed in a small box layered with spring flowers, we made her a little grave next to Purr-Purr, and covered it with branches of fresh rosemary and jasmine.

I questioned again the sense of living and dying, the whole purpose of appearing in someone's life and disappearing shortly after touching it so deeply? And it became clear to me that the love I felt for Chi-Chi, this little baby mocking bird, would forever remain in my heart, giving me, during her short existence, the inspiration to write this story, another story of eternal love.

Made in the USA
Lexington, KY
28 May 2017